**DO NOT REMOVE
CARDS FROM POCKET**

by the same author
FURTHER ADVENTURES

LONG PIG

JON STEPHEN FINK

JONATHAN CAPE
LONDON

First published 1995

1 3 5 7 9 10 8 6 4 2

© Jon Stephen Fink 1995

Jon Stephen Fink has asserted his right
under the Copyright, Designs and Patents Act 1988
to be identified as the author of this work

First published in the United Kingdom in 1995 by Jonathan Cape
Random House, 20 Vauxhall Bridge Road, London SW1V 2SA

Random House Australia (Pty) Limited
20 Alfred Street, Milsons Point, Sydney,
New South Wales 2061, Australia

Random House New Zealand Limited
18 Poland Road, Glenfield,
Auckland 10, New Zealand

Random House Africa (Pty) Limited
PO Box 337, Bergvlei, 2012 South Africa

Random House UK Limited Reg. No. 954009

A CIP catalogue record for this book
is available from the British Library

Papers used by Random House UK Limited are natural,
recyclable products made from wood grown in sustainable forests.
The manufacturing processes conform to the environmental
regulations of the country of origin.

ISBN 0–224–04081–2

Typeset by Deltatype Limited, Ellesmere Port, Cheshire
Printed and bound in Great Britain by
Mackays of Chatham PLC

To
Michelle, the VC, at least

and to
Alison, the DSO

When you are negotiating to buy or sell something, a car or a house perhaps, and you are left alone to discuss an offer, either move to a different area or, better still, use a previously prepared and rehearsed conversation. Remember — a bug which the victim is aware of or suspects is likely to threaten only the eavesdropper.

John Wingfield, *Bugging, A Complete Survey of Electronic Surveillance Today*

Yet the evidence for God is so clear and certain that the Psalmist could exclaim that only 'The fool hath said in his heart, There is no God!'

Henry M. Morris and Martin E. Clark, *The Bible Has the Answer*

The pig keeper must learn to observe normal and abnormal behaviour in pigs.

Neville Beynon, *Pigs, A Guide to Management*

Contents

One

SO THROUGH THE EYES LOVE ATTAINS THE HEART

1   The Invisible Hand, Part 1

THE first pang I felt for Alex Berry came with the same shudder of discovery that shot through me forty-odd years before, when I fell in love with Senator Joseph McCarthy. Minus Joe McCarthy's rampaging opportunism and extravagant suspicion, one vital drive that Alex shared with the anti-communist Witchfinder General was the surging if-only readiness of a freshly hatched utopian. Seated among the House Un-American Activities Committee, McCarthy's spuddy shape and reptile squint absorbed the glamour of institutional power – from the national government, the national press, the national mood – and the sight of such a man filling the bill as a fundamental American made him irresistible to a young historian beginning to sniff the musk of his own arrival.

On my way to the Senate hearing rooms from my hotel each morning I could walk past bookstore window displays of my premiere in the best-seller lists, *The Last Days of President Lincoln*, and wonder how it was that I could be as entranced by the smug vindictive showboating of Tailgunner Joe as by the judicious temperance and colossal humanity of Old Father Abe. This is a riddle I still can't answer. Now, with eyes weakened from so much close work, set behind trifocals, I was watching Alex, eavesdropping on him, entranced by the serious-faced up-and-comer who seemed to be about the age I'd been back in that vanished red menaced world, at the beginning of my twin careers.

Then, conformity was praised as loyalty to our heritage, or to a very special rendition of it, and dissent was denounced as a foreign perversion cooked up personally by Stalin in his Kremlin basement. Then we waltz thirty-eight times around the sun and, look, Alex Berry sits at a computer terminal that lets him infotrawl the world from a shopfront in an arcade a few sandy paces away from a Southern California beach. The Global Video Café is one of a mushrooming number of wired-up keyed-in logged-on bistros strung out along an electronic communication circuit whose glowing nodes lay in

3

sidestreets as nearby as Culver City and as distant as Managua, Seoul, Berlin, Taipei, Helsinki, Riyadh . . .

No place for the eye to rest, no gap in the scenery. A steady feed of pictures carouseled across the video monitors stacked in a bank five high by four wide, a churning supply of ghetto street scenes, camel caravans, neon boulevards, souks, rock concerts, exercise classes, rebel soldiers, the carnival backdrop to my view of Alex and his sometime associate Chick Uchiyama. Both of them with strong dark hair, Chick's genuinely black and threadlike, falling into his eyes, and Alex's the brown of old oiled wood, wavy, piled back anxiously from his forehead. They leaned together over the keyboard, Chick working the keys, Alex ducking his head toward him to read the screen or poke in with an instruction over the room noise. Other keyboards were softly clacking, peripherals chirping, games squawking and pinging at every other table.

One monitor on the video wall played a live transmission from the fisheye of a roving surveillance camera crawling automatically along a rail slung under the ceiling. The wide-angle relayed a dioramic picture of creatures separately at play in their electronic habitat, students, ex-students, children of a borderless country. In spite of being the oldest man there I fit in comfortably, at home with the hardware as well as the simmering atmosphere, the fervent air of a changing era that Alex, at a glance, brought to life for me.

I didn't follow him in, I'd already planted myself at a table on official business, in the unofficial service of Assemblyman (as he was then) Bobby Dyson. The Global Video Café was a bijou business owned by Reverend Jim Tickell, or more accurately, by Worldview Life Ministry which he founded and which gratefully in turn employed him as its director at a salary of one dollar per annum, plus unlimited expenses.

Bobby had acquired information (not from me; from a source inside Worldview) which strongly suggested that contributions of stock, furs, vintage cars, rare coins, stamps and art raised by JT for named relief projects were routinely diverted into the expanding tele-communications branch of the ministry. Since the Reverend's parent operation was based in Bobby's state assembly district Bobby was working to end his third term, and roll into his run to be the Democrats' candidate for governor, by exploding the fraud and wading in on behalf of the victims to give JT a public spanking.

4

Behavior or interests unbecoming to a popular Christian evangelist, if I could discover any, would make Bobby's job easier and it was regular gossip around Venice Beach that the Global Video Café suffered from a very quick turnover of waitresses.

With no *droit de seigneur* going on behind the sandwich counter as I sat waiting, I listened to Alex read Chick a rejection letter from the executive assistant of Dinu Cristescu, one of the city's most noticeable émigré businessmen. When he got to the dry impersonal end of it and collected Chick's mild accepting shrug Alex said, 'No, uh-uh. That's not *it*, nothing's *it* until I hear him say it to me himself. At least I'd be there with him and I could kick into selling mode.'

Chick didn't take his eyes off the incoming mail scrolling on the screen. 'Sell it to somebody else. This guy can't see it.'

'He *hasn't* seen it. It's this Miss Weiss. I'm going to squat in his office until he lets me pitch him my business plan.'

'And calls security.'

'Look, why did he come to this country? Because it's better for him here than it was in Romania. So I just have to make him realize how much better it can be here if he invests in *this*,' tapping his thumb on the manila folder on the table between them, selling it to Chick.

Over his shoulder on the live-action screen the roving camera picked up the school emblem on the folder's cover, and I saw the crested helmet of USC's Trojan mascot. Such is fate. He stole my heart, Alex Berry the entrepreneur with a mission, and the mission was to incorporate Dinu Cristescu into his history. If Only I Can Pitch Him My Business Plan.

Alex was never going to know how he opened a gate into a new existence for me, into his. The electronic surveillance devices which can take a hidden (or even absent) observer into the unlit crannies of a person's life have become miracles of miniaturization in the thirty years I've had access to them. Today (the spring of 1991) I can attach a lens one quarter-inch in diameter to the end of a fiber-optic filament, plant it in the corner of the ceiling with a matchbox transmitter lost under the roof and, sitting in my van down the street, I can read the expressions on the faces of everybody in a room thirty feet deep. With the current generation of laser bugs I have recorded the voices in an office four hundred yards away. This development is a present-day artefact of *homo sapiens*' engineering genius: the laser dot senses and transmits down its beam the vibrations on the window pane being made by conversation inside, a feat which plain astounds me.

There's a metaphysical poetry in the nomenclature – *lost transmitter, infinity transmitter, nightscope*, all evocative attractions for me although some of my meatiest gleaning has been done with the simplest equipment. An audio bug in a lamp can work off of a battery all day and then when the light is switched on at night it runs off of the mains electricity which also recharges the battery. Means of camouflage are rich and various. With twenty safe minutes in a virgin room I've wired video cameras into overhead lights, I've seeded contact mikes behind wall brackets and headboards, I've planted bugs in paperweights and executoys, I've finicked microphones into shirt collar buttons. More than once I've had the luck and the time to get into a building under construction and that opened up a dramatic vista of possibilities for concealment. My paraphernalia blended into the fabric of the structure disguised as a rivet head, a bolt in a beam, a bathroom fixture, a thermostat, the faceplate on a lightswitch, the lightswitch itself. If I'm on the move, as I was at the Global Video Café, I rely on a directional mike that I wear as a wristwatch. It pipes its signal into my hearing-aid, practical and necessary, alas.

The real power of this technology, its emotional power, lies in the way it extends the reach of my senses, sight and hearing and less definable sensations, re-evoked by the faultless memory of my tape recorders. Equipment in locations spread out across the city, homes, businesses, cars, and my listening posts, stationary and mobile, my pastiche of ubiquity.

My primary source of material is this harvest of objective facts – who said what to whom, who was present, so on and so forth, the loose weave of meaningful specifics which I can compare and collate with diaries, letters, hearsay, to work up the probable truth. A single fact can be like a single frame of film, a static image taken from a scene in motion and the next one a twenty-fourth of a second later; the missing time between them, connecting those stopped fractions into lifelike movement, is a participatory trick of the mind, it bridges the gaps, fills in what ought to be there. Even the evasions, distortions of memory, falsifications, denials and contradictions throw light on deeper motives – and there's the useful work of an historian, there are the hard bright bones of history.

To the unconcealed dismay of my colleagues, both at USC and out among the movable symposium of American historians, my approach to the gaps in what is finally knowable – unexpressed thoughts, withered motives, incomplete documents, unintelligible or uncompleted sentences – is to bridge them with empathy instead of an academically recognized reductive bias. There is the jump and then the fall into another life. I feel this sometimes when I'm writing, I feel myself pass into transparency to let the other life in and I realize I'm writing in that other's voice. The irritable carping turned raucous only once, and then only as a sharp blow-off of steam from a faction of untenured Foucaultistas when on my sixty-fourth birthday USC wreathed me with the honor of Professor Emeritus. I'm not in harmony with cloistered minds, teacher or student, I feel more warmth for the people in my books.

Before I wrote one word about him I felt that kind of warmth for Bobby Dyson, the same trembling wave that went through me when I ran across Alex. Both of them born with a biting instinct for the times. In 1964 the Free Speech movement at Berkeley awoke the natural crusader in Bobby so I wasn't surprised to see him in 1968 on the network evening news as a spokesman for the National Mobilization Committee, attacking the Pentagon lie of the domino theory and, in white shirt, black tie, corduroy jacket and hair like licks of flame from the burning bush, doing his polite best to convince America that 'the war in South-east Asia' (that touch of Orwell!) was being fought, ' . . . for the stockholders of Dow Chemical and General Electric, and your friendly neighborhood Republican or Democrat.'

Bobby had no fellow feeling for the Weather Underground or other apocalyptic outlaws bringing the war back home, and in Chicago he split with the brethren of the NMC whose only ambition for civil disobedience in that hostage city was to 'Tie it up and bust it up' (Rennie Davies). Bobby hoped for something beyond chaos, a patriotic assertion of the right to question and oppose decisions made in his name and to debate government policies free from police intimidation. His political conscience used to reach out beyond himself.

He believed in the fairer, less competitive, more spiritual world that social convulsions would set free. These were the birth throes of the Age of Aquarius – Yippies nominating a pig for president, the sit-in at the Hilton Hotel, the snake-dance through police lines, Allen Ginsberg incanting *Howl* ('Moloch the stunned government . . .'), and shouting from the fringe of the stampede while platoons of Mayor Daley's blue-helmeted centurions chopped through the trapped and retreating crowd with riot batons, 'They have gassed the cross of Christ!'

Twenty years later our country was a rumbling turbulence of opportunity for neighborhood Republicans and Democrats, for young entrepreneurs who understood the (re)public out there: the stimulant in their bloodstream is the promise of new products, buying is a breakthrough and on the other side at least one item on life's agenda is secure – they'll never have to look for another shampoo, deodorant or moisturizer, this is the one they'll use from now on to preserve the childlike lustre of their hair, the dry confidence of their armpits, the creamy softness of their skin.

In this place today personalities drain into the slick uncomplicated solidity of property and shine out again luridly tinted by the charisma of ownership, the pride of acquisition, the steaming potence of display. They see their faces minted on the dials of instrument-panels, etched into mobile phones, watch-crystals, crouched fenders and snouty hoods, on the appliances in every room, in the view from every window, and then while they're staring absently at their cold reflections a tremor grips them. It's the hint of coming disintegration, the verge of loss. In the Los Angeles that I knew at the end of the 1980s the steady state of consumers wasn't very different from frantic teenage romance, where they pick a new haircut and are sure that's serious evidence of an imaginative life, where they mistake emotional intensity for personal depth and mental confusion for rebellious spontaneity.

This is where they all groan in, the gorgeous sows, the blocky hogs, all straight legs and sleek haunches, heads up and sniffing the air for traces of heat, dying to breed more spenders just like them. I walk through the shopping malls sometimes and take in every variation of the human scenery, every voice, every face, as if the futile outpouring of individual joys and sorrows were rolling toward me in slow motion. I listen to business calls going back and forth on car phones, desperate ultimatums, I receive their lamentations, I catch a burst of romantic whispering on the back stairs of an empty building, and I imagine the voices are trying to find me during their secret fits of despair and relief.

'Al-ex!' That nasal squeal punched a hole in my hearing. 'Let me give you a kiss, Lexie!'

Dry daylight crashed straight down from the broad sky, the hard flat glare of it bounced off the pink brick walls, up off the bleached concrete sidewalks, light that fell and rose in sheets, in slabs, with sharp edges that cut right angles in the air. Heat drifted like a fog over the long black parking lot where it slanted off rows of windshields and splashed chaotically onto scorching bumpers and grilles. Between the curling paper bark of the hissing eucalyptus trees and the four lanes of downtown traffic coupling and uncoupling at the twitchy intersection, the same heat throbbed down in wide, slow pulses on the sunken rectangle of the rose garden, it sweated fragrance out of those plump burgundy and vanilla blooms, trapped it there a few inches above each bush. Springtime in Los Angeles, on the campus of the University of Southern California.

A change surfaced in the human population, it increased by one hormone-rampant adult male, defiant and audacious, red muscles tensed and ready to slam the old bulls in the ribcage, push them off their choice patches and humiliate them in front of their harems. Two weeks after I followed him out of the Global Video Café I made sure that I was there to see him pick up his Master of Business Administration degree, to stand back and gangway for the man and his moment.

He felt his grandmom's tiny papery hands reach up, clamp onto his head, jerk his neck down, tilt his face forward and hold it rigid while she aimed a loose damp kiss someplace between his mouth and nose. His very next breath dragged in the misty aroma of her apartment, a heavy perfume of crushed gardenias and chicken fat that shimmered up from her lips like heatwaves. When Alex smelled it he was one limp puppy all right, landing gear down, hanging by the scruff from the firm jaws of a sensual, secret nostalgia. I passed by so close to her that I could smell the salty-sour odor of her spit coming off the tips of her fingers as she smeared her coral lip-print into a comet-shaped smudge, frozen in mid-arc on its orbit toward Alex's ear.

'Gotta go.' Alex straightened up out of her hug. He was ready to be gone, off on his heel clicking way to the Emerald City, passing his diploma over to his father's care. 'This can go with the rest of my stuff, okay?' A passport to be stamped at the border of his old life, Alex's life at home.

His parents, Meyer and Ellen, had never felt excluded from the thrust of Alex's choices, which seemed conventional but imaginative, independent but never delinquent, never reckless. Their only child benefited from his background, valued the precedent, the achieved comfort and safety, followed his family's lead in a style which reminded them of Ellen's immigrant grand-father. Self-contained, avid for experience, Alex was as fearless today as he was as a three-year-old, pumping his trike magnificently down the sidewalk. And they would always see him brake decisively at the corner, turn his little red tricycle around and pedal home, making it clear that this was his decision. They knew him as a boy of stubborn attachments. The story of 'Skipper' had become a piece of Berry family folk-lore; Alex dragged around his favorite stuffed animal, a toy dog, until it was just an earless severed head. Even that cranky, tiny-tot fixation had the look of something more idealized in him, something like loyalty.

'You aren't coming with us, doll?' his grandmom asked him, Alex's hand folded in hers.

Meyer stepped in saying, 'Alex's still got a few things to move over to his apartment.' A considerate, deliberate reminder to his son that there was one more carload of his belongings waiting in numbered and inventoried boxes to be cleared out of the parental hallway.

'I'll get it done today.'

'I know, Lex,' any hint of irritation smilingly eased away, 'it's not a problem yet.' The needle that was skewering Meyer right then was the same one that he wriggled on when Alex was five and straddling the seat of his first two-wheeler, training wheels and the wrench that removed them in Daddy's grown-up hands. 'This is going to be your year, Alex.'

The MBA was a stage and marker in his life story that Alex knew also marked the limit of his family's understanding of his actual motives. Of course he agreed with them that anything less than concrete achievement in the world outside the walls of the family home, out there in the unforgiving population of strangers, amounts to living nowhere but in his imagination. But it was what Alex imagined for himself that lifted him bravely beyond the usual expectations.

Where Meyer's and Ellen's ambitions for him were confined to shelter, family life and financial insulation stretching into retirement,

Alex's estimate of the possible was less narrow and more dangerous. If uncertainty was the harshest demand on the faith he had in his talent, then discipline and optimism were the secret rituals that kept doubt at bay. Success on the scale that he was going to arrange for himself would be more significant, more individual, than a paid-up pension plan.

'What's the next move?' Meyer let it sound like a little question.

'Get out in the economy,' Alex said. 'You know. Can't wait.'

'You should talk to Korngold again. Tell him you thought everything over, and now. . . You don't have to work there forever.'

'I don't want to be an assistant production manager in a cut-price toy factory, Dad. That's just not how I see myself.'

'A start's a start.'

'It doesn't feel like it to me.'

'Feels.' Meyer shook his head, as if he had never heard the word before. High-running feelings, he worried, would only cloud Alex's judgment. What's going to happen when he gets knocked back, what will he find out if he fails? How would he 'see himself' after *that* crushing experience?

'You hate all of this attention, don't you!' Ellen was naughtily sticking Alex in the ribs now. '*Don't* you!' He was a baby on the rug for her and didn't she know it. She kissed him twice, deep in his cheek, and wrapped both her arms around his back, as if this was some tactic to make her boy holler uncle before he skidded out of her life for good. Releasing him, blessing him with a laugh she said, 'Just thank God you're not going into the movie business.'

Ellen's bracing antidote to unsupported optimism was to remind Alex of the uglier, likelier possibilities waiting for him in the New Stone Age. She was free of illusions about Los Angeles, had established her place in the city and wasn't repelled by its crude hierarchy. Brutal behavior, some of which she met on the receiving end, was on display to Ellen every day. Selling real estate to local and global princelings gave her an unobstructed view of the bullying parade of money and muscle, of fashion without style, that created and supported so many service industries, hers included. In the condominiums she showed, in the shark-shaped cars her clients pushed around town, and in all the amassing and consolidating she clearly saw the effects of the absence of this money-making drive – invisibility. One of her past clients, she reminded Alex, had her arrange the purchase of his two million dollar beach house in January and in June she was arranging its sale.

'I heard from his wife a week ago, Alex,' Ellen was saying. 'You want to know what Ben Tattin is doing now?'

'More than anything.'

'He's a greeter in Las Vegas. A glorified doorman. He stands inside the front door of the MGM Grand and says hello to the guests when they walk in with their suitcases.'

'I know what a greeter does, Mom.'

Fables like this one, based somehow on truth, came across to Alex not as protective concern but as a nagging lack of confidence. And his mother's worry was elastic enough to cover every other major area of Alex's existence. Since high school he had heavily edited any report about who he was seeing or not seeing, how far in any direction he'd gone with any of the women he might have mentioned over breakfast. His mother (and inevitably *her* mother), knew the names, the neighborhoods and sometimes even, remotely, the parents of girlfriends who'd be part of his conversation for a number of weeks or months, but on the reasons for any break-up Alex would be closed.

'Lexie, tell me something,' his small grandmom nudged him, 'you're celebrating tonight with that Rhonda?'

'I haven't seen her for a while. Busy-busy.'

'Her picture looked so beautiful,' she remembered. 'You don't go with her anymore?'

'We went out for Mexican food about three weeks ago,' he said. 'That's all.'

She cupped his hand, got the message. 'Why don't you call her up and say you're sorry. We liked the sound of Rhonda.'

Alex pulled his hand back, let it drop into his jacket pocket. 'We aren't going to vote on it, okay?'

Ellen remembered, 'Her mother works in the Sepulveda branch of our office. Wasn't Rhonda pre-law?' Meaning, here was somebody he shouldn't have passed up, here's a lapse into bad judgment.

Alex, though, remained sure that romantic rewards, and all the rest, would come as consequences of his stardom in business. The earthly and mysterious components of permanent success were all in motion, converging out there, waiting for him to catch up. For the last two years he had accounted his time in semesters. The antfarm of producer-consumer society was stripped down for him to expose its widget factories, distribution networks and part-owned subsidiaries, the graphable dynamics of boom and bust, fluctuations in supply and anticipation of demand. He sharpened his talent to respond with business plans for projected enterprises, feasibility studies, market research, hothouse speculations about the next most likely opportunity in products or services, classroom bull sessions aimed at poking toe-holds in the crumbling upward slope of commercial competition.

Now Alex, fit and lean, was turned loose to stalk the buttercup meadows of production and consumption in the most fertile market in the world. He was a new creature, hungry and horny, a would-be exploiter of niches still hidden in the Galapagos of free enterprise, vacant adaptive zones unknown until a flash of insight lights them up and lifts them out of the background. The spiraling twinge he felt in his gut, the change under his skin, was the knowledge that any picture formed in the vapors of his imagination could be made, through his own effort, into an object as substantial and marketable as a brick.

Way beyond that he carried around the idea that he'd been born with the creative power to father a new species of product as elegant and unavoidable as a paper clip, as simple and functional as a stack of Dixie cups, as necessary and efficient as a roll of toilet paper. He was going to conceive a brand name that would go on to earn sentimental presence in the public mind, throughout whole lifetimes of customers, an original line that was going to become generic like Hoover, Kleenex, Xerox and Band-Aid.

Alex would sire the Odo-bag.

'Gilbert's waiting over in the parking lot. Really, gotta go.' Alex decided he was in some sort of hurry. He started away walking backwards, and shouted to the whole departing bunch, 'Call me!' and when he straightened out again he picked up speed, coolly breezing through the loose clumps of postgrads, boyfriends in slick suits, girlfriends in party dresses, he slipped so easily around them, the way clear water flows around rocks in a stream-bed.

2   His Little Black Box

DESTROY All Monsters was the Saturday Creature Feature blaring reveille when Alex tumbled into the living-room, massaging the crumbs out of the crusty rims of his eyes. The TV volume was cranked up loud enough to make their downstairs neighbors think that some panicked undomesticated animal was cornered in the boys' apartment, burrowing for safety into the furniture. A pretty fair caricature of Alex's roommate Gilbert Sherman, a friend since glee club in junior high school. Compact, red-haired, Gil ushered around the same friendly paunch he was born with. Open-faced and deeply unworried, you could count on his fizzing gonadal wit to turn a newsy chat about air pollution density and summer smog alerts into a cue for a gag about blind dates and Braille condoms.

Gilbert had been Alex's Virgil in the dark wood of their teenage, but he was a missionary spirit with a much more ironic attitude to carefree depravity, taboo and wanton hedonism. Alone in the Berry family duplex in the middle of a shapeless weekend afternoon, Gilbert and Alex decided to salvage the day by inventing a brand-new mixed drink. After many hours of taste-testing and quality control the cocktail that they brought into the world was a subtle aromatic blend of only two ingredients, seven parts vodka and one part prune juice, called a Plop and served in a martini glass with a whole prune bobbing under the liquid brown surface. At midnight Alex and Gilbert, falling down drunk, were still toasting each other and trying to prove that it was physically possible to gargle with peanut butter.

Half consciously, Alex leaned right in front of the screen to find the volume control and tweak the rough edge off the sound.

'C'mon, Alex, *move*,' Gilbert snapped at him from the sofa, his cranky protest squeaking upwards into frantic emergency. 'It's Godzilla's big fight with Ghidorah the Space Monster.' This reptile violence triggered a hiccuping squeal from Gilbert, his signature laugh, which had the warmth of a couple of empty tin cans clattering down a flight of metal steps.

Alex still wasn't completely awake. 'Can I turn it down now?'

'A little.'

'Half.'

'Don't, Alex. A quarter,' Gil negotiated. 'I can't hear their cries of horror and sudden death.'

Alex didn't try to dislodge Gilbert from the grip he was held in by this movie, eyes pouchy, jaw brainlessly slack, arms limp, his thick copper hair scraped up into a topknot, Samurai style, with a chopstick skewered through the middle for decoration. He even thought that it could be medically risky to pull Gil out of it before the next commercial, so he sat down on the sofa with him, their twin kimonos flagging open, Alex thinking this must be how tired housewives feel on a Saturday morning.

While Gilbert watched the rubber suits of Monsterland gang up on the three-headed puppet from outer space, Alex sat fidgeting with three teabag-sized pouches, one of them linen, one rice paper and one stainless steel mesh. They made a shushing noise when he shuffled them between his hands.

'Do those do anything else?' Gilbert inquired without taking his eyes off the TV. 'Let me see one.' Alex handed him the metal mesh pouch. Gil felt the smooth beads inside it. 'I just like . . . holding it,' rubbing the bag between his thumb and forefinger, giving Alex a cracked, moronic, child-molester grin.

'They'll make me my first million.'

'It's cool to loaf with. Like those Greek worry beads. You could sell these things for loafing. Say they come from Armenia. Armenian Worry Bags.'

'Odo-bags,' Alex said. 'That's not what they're for.'

'Right.'

'You're not really interested in this, are you.'

Gilbert pointed at the TV screen. 'Ghidorah's going to get creamed. Watch this.' For the *coup de grace* Baby Godzilla burped out a halo of radioactive fire that choked the last hiss out of the gold lamé flying snake. 'Sayo*nara*!' He tossed the Odo-bag back to Alex. 'Where'd you get the idea from?'

Every one of Alex's business plans came from the same source, one source that was many sources. Through both years of grad school he bought up – for twenty, forty and in a rare case one hundred dollars – product prototypes, feasibility studies and partnership agreements from fellow Trojans, contracts that he made sure were fair, legal and binding. He kept all of those plans incubating in a black file box under his bed, a cache as aphrodisiac as a loverboy's address book, as devotional as a hope chest.

His little black box was the resource that Alex talked up whenever Gilbert talked up his own enterprising sex life. The substitute of work for romance worried Gil who pushed the theory to its bleak conclusion and warned his pal of the humiliating and obvious signs of regular self-abuse. Whatever the remote consequences might be, schemes busted or booming, a palace in Bel-Air or a nursing home in the Valley, they weren't any part of the point. Unless Alex got serious about the shallow opportunities bouncing around campus he'd be a sad old man before he was out of his twenties.

Whenever they slid into this argument Alex's defense was that the problem had been the same one since he started college. It was the category of female he attracted. The Gails and Rhondas and Deborahs in their cute sweater and skirt combinations, the single braid of 24 carat gold around her neck or decorating her wrist, her straightened teeth, her exercise class, her foregone, concluded adult life, padded out in everything except original accomplishment. He attracted young women who had no doubts about their motives or questions about the larger world, who had armor-plated confidence in the acceptability of their ambitions. Gail Levitsky, interior decorator wannabe, wanted an unaffordable off-campus life with him, gilt plaster lamps and plastic wrapped suede sofa thrown in free by her parents; packaged, enumerated, confining articles of hand-me-down wellbeing. This was the same predictable and safe existence that Rhonda Nudell lived to work for, and after her, Deborah Wentz tried to excite Alex with the vista of life together as zippy young professionals, owners of businesses (his) and properties (hers) that could get them into plush retirement by the time they turned thirty-five.

It wasn't even this anemic idea of bliss that drained the blood out of their romantic appeal. It was their parents; they adored him. All of their standards and ideals seemed to be awake in Alex, they recognized (they thought) the reliable values that animated their households. In short, they made assumptions about Alex so gratingly off target that the more he heard himself lovingly described by these moms and dads the less of a desire he had to get into bed with their daughters.

His quiet clothes, his comfortable manners, his academic success and professional plans, these were the surface features which encouraged three sets of mothers and fathers (four, counting his own) to assume that Alex was one of them. Alex knew he was camouflaged by the sports jacket and slacks and MBA, and if they had any inkling of the gambler, the thrill-seeker peering out at them they'd probably chase him off with a shotgun. No, Alex wasn't like them, he didn't hug the shore, he was swimming out there beyond sight of land, figuring out all by himself where he was, where he was going and how he was going to get there.

3   Other Life in the Tide Pool

FROM the day Alex met Alba Saldino and Baylor Lejeune, fellow guests at Gilbert's sister's wedding four years before, his friendship with them meant, somehow, that he was off the hook, here were people who would believe his side of the story, trust his alibi. But the separate affections he had for each of them developed quickly in different ways. Baylor could have been Alex's best friend in kindergarten and now, just as easily and intensely as they might have examined a perfect kickable dirt clod, they ranged over Alex's business plans and Baylor's artwork. Alba, by slow, inevitable osmosis it seemed, became more than his accountant. Alex ended up in the circle of her protection. She was his bodyguard, his spirit-guide through the tax year. Her clear sight and eerie sensitivity could put her in touch with the mitigating human side of any institution, including the IRS, an aspect of such things that Alex had trouble even imagining.

The door into the Fonseca Gallery is the same color as the unfinished wall around it, set back from the sidewalk in a lightless recess screened by a lounging pair of olive trees. The impression created by this pocket of shadows facing La Cienega Blvd is that the entrance can only be located by secret knowledge, or by providence. At night the effect is predictably more mysterious: it was to Alex, since he never had a reason to get out of his car anywhere along this stretch of the Westside, this clean mile of three-course restaurants, Armenian rug stores, specialty linen shops and modern art salesrooms.

Electric light gorged the tall oblong windows, strained through olive twigs over his head and freckled the terrazzo courtyard where

Alex stood still for a minute looking in . . . at the women first, wrapped in sheath dresses or controlled explosions of shiny fabric, bare shoulders, tanned arms, tennis muscles, ready smiles, that blonde head inclined in confident conversation for a few seconds . . . they circulate, they browse here, padded with enough money to buy any of Baylor's paintings, fancier than the original '5 boy!' posters Baylor gave him, art he couldn't afford. This coldly hypnotic thought fastened his attention on the men in the room, hair slicked straight back into a ponytail, safely bohemian, French suits over black T-shirts, the Harley Davidson bikes reined in at the kerb must belong to them, yup-yup, they say, give me the numbers, free to state their terms, cool and motile men who occupy their own square footage, who can afford to live on some kind of *large scale* . . .

They can sniff a weakling in the crowd, a runt is stuck with a runt's odor and Alex assumed that the clubby public of Alba's and Baylor's friends could smell him coming. He was arriving at a place where his appeal depended on rumors of success, of expansion, so Alex was preparing to be blandly disregarded, elbowed around and pushed into the margin. But in the middle of the activity where those substantial personalities throbbed out pressure waves, rings of social energy both signal and barrier, he also expected to be welcomed in for a few minutes, remembered and protected.

Alba blossomed from the edge of the crowd, and seeing her there finally tugged Alex through the door. With a hundred people around her, with a few words and a half-smile she could enclose anyone she wanted in a soundproof bell, intimate conversation that blurred a roomful of voices into the deep background, generous attention that became its own temporary conspiracy. For the moment, Alba was in secluded cahoots with a very tall Iranian whose appearance Alex thought he recognized from a profile in the *Reader* — a diplomat? an arms dealer? a collector? — who bent over Alba to bring his ear closer to her mouth, a stickman whose stiff resemblance to Baylor's sexless jumpin' and jivin' human cartoons nudged Alex to wonder how come Alba's husband never painted any figure inspired by her. She was a stickman's shame and hope, her compact round-edged body composed of circles and ovals; to see her walk across a room was to watch a march of female abundance, all the relief Alba could provide the men in her life she carried in front of her in those bobbling shapes, changeable in the fast narrowing of her eyes from maternal bumpers to the turbines of a sexual powerhouse.

This private view of Baylor's new work was the first chance that cropped up for Alex to wear the red cashmere jacket and Doc Martens slip-ons, jarring flashes in his Ivy League wardrobe supplied by Alba on impulse a month before. ('I want to buy you something.' 'You don't have to console me.' 'Every time I pass this store, I think of you. I want to buy you some Doc Martens.' 'What are they?' 'Classy shoes.' 'I don't need shoes.' 'You're getting shoes.') He struggled a little harder against the jacket. Alex told her red wasn't his color, he told her if he wore it to any restaurant in Beverly Hills he'd get car keys thrown at him by crabby diners who'd warn him not to scratch the paintwork. Well, two steps inside the gallery he was handed a glass of champagne, a plug of sushi and a copy of the catalog; it looked like he merited the same customer care as any potential buyer.

'Loosen up, Gordon! Say hey, honey – it's – a – party!' Baylor's voice bulged out of the crowd hum, permission from the mightiest swinging dick in the room for the big fun to start. Alex worked his way through the chains of drinkers and smokers and found '5 boy!' leaning his back against a freestanding Doric column just a foot taller than he was. The fake marble sculpture turned Baylor, upholstered in his red silk double-breasted, into a comic book caryatid peering down on the festive temple mob. 'Say hey, Alex.'

His arms stretched around Baylor's trunk. 'Say hey Willie Mays.'

'They look any different in here?'

Alex's eyes flicked over the hanging art. 'More expensive.'

'True.'

'They look sold.'

'Out, honey.' Hugging him close, Baylor ratcheted Alex around to face each piece. 'Red dot. Red dot. Red dot. Red dot,' and giving it his soul-funky bedroom walrus basso he dripped, 'I think you know what I'm sayin'. I'm sayin' on time and to the dime, honey.'

'A cruise around the world.'

'Nah, not that far. Alba wants to go to Zimbabwe. She wants me to touch Africans.'

'Doesn't she know any Africans in Malibu you can touch?'

'My people aren't beach people, my little white friend!' Baylor struck his heart with his proud fist, gazed across eons and oceans and Shaka Zulu held forth with the operatic, tortured English oratory of his ancestors. 'My people are of the savannahs. Men of the bow and arrow. Women of the yams. I must unite with them in the land of free parking.'

'When was the last time you united with your people in Boyle Heights?'

'They're all dangerous Samoans down there now, I thought.'

'I guess.'

'She wants to go to Ghana, too. And Mali. We're just going to tour until somebody in some clan somewhere claims me.'

'We're all supposed to be from Africa, if you go back a million years.'

Baylor kissed the top of Alex's head. 'You are my brother Kunta Kinte.'

'Umgawa,' Alex agreed.

'You've got the whole bible thang you can go back to. Don't you want to investigate Israel?'

'I live around the corner from Canter's Deli. I can touch Jewish people anytime I want.' Alex sucked up his champagne. 'Does it cost a lot to fly out there or's it more spend, spend, spend when you go touring around?'

'Both, I think.' Baylor shrugged a don't-ask-me apology that covered not knowing and not caring.

A bump in his lower back, a squeeze on his elbow. Alba reached up on tip-toes to kiss Alex lightly on his lips. 'Finished pissing and moaning yet?'

'Pissing, anyway.'

'When did you get here?'

'Ten-fifteen minutes. Did I see that guy's picture in the paper? That Iranian?'

'Why didn't you come over? You should meet this man, really, Alex, he only owns three-quarters of the Beverly Center.' She gave Alex a second for the wave of implication to reach him.

'I didn't want to interrupt you in the middle of whatever.'

'Just schmoozing. Hadi bought three pieces for himself and three presents for his girlfriends,' she said as she latched on to Baylor's dangling hand. 'All right, Bobba?'

'In with the in-crowd, yeah.' Sudden joy pumped into Baylor's face, expanded it from inside to its outer edges. His eyes were on the door. 'Yo! Frank! Frankie!'

Alex had to back out of the way or be trampled under the big guy's crepe soles. Alba picked up the story. 'Frank is his guitar teacher.'

'Every boy should have one.'

She turned back around to ask Alex, 'What's the news?'

'Same-o same-o. I'm trying to raise a chunk of venture capital for my Odo-bag thing. I'll get there.'

'Where is it now?'

'Well,' Alex let rip a self-ridiculing laugh, 'not there yet. I've been one-basketing. Not smart, I know that, right, but I *know*', he tapped his chest, 'that this guy would see the same future I can see for this product. So far I just haven't had the chance to get in there and pitch it to him.'

'Who is it?'

'The guy who owns about fifty-eight national companies. Dinu Cristescu?'

'Hadi knows him,' Alba said, looking around for the silky Iranian. 'Hadi's into some jewelry deal with him.'

A veiny hand fluttered in over Alex's shoulder and grabbed for a perch on Alba's wrist. 'I *told* Baylor to watch out or else he'd turn into a beach bum like me!' Plunging in behind the blue-webbed hand came a pink tracksuit bunched up with the uncontrollable bonhomie of a lanky man in his late sixties who, without a look around, wedged himself between Alex and Alba. He was somebody with a festive message to deliver and he was dragging it in at the end of his other elongated arm. 'Alba Saldino, I don't think you ever met my wife, Gloria.'

'Hi, Gloria,' Alba invisibly braced herself for the two kisses, continental style. 'Gary told me you sold, what was it, some famous house.'

'The Chaplin property. I *did*, I *did*,' squeaking that seemed to come from the skeletal jaw under her tight, tanned skin.

'Tweety Pie.' Old Gary gave Gloria's arm a crazy shake, cocked his head at her and grinned ain't she sumpthin'. Alex stood there hoping he wouldn't say it. Alba was hoping he would. He did. 'She tawt she taw a poody tat!'

A spark jumped from Alba's eye to his as Alex nibbled the rim of his champagne glass, staring hard at the fascinating little clusters of bubbles foaming under his nose. His attention had wandered back to Baylor's work when he heard Gloria say, with trembling gratitude,

'We *love* our painting. It goes *perfect* in our bedroom. I have to tell him how pretty it fit in . . .' And Alex sneaked a glance back at that couple in their matching powder-blue and powder-pink tracksuits, 24-carat gold necklaces, his *USS Coral Sea* baseball cap, the portable phone she wore gunslinger-style in a gold leather holster on her hip. What *was* it in the '5 boy!' graffiti portraits of hip-hop rebels and inner-city mayhem that *went perfect* in their bedroom? On the warehouse shutters of the Lower East Side under the oily clouds of bus exhaust those 'X-Babies' that Baylor daubed appeared to be some spontaneous, cryptic eruption of the underclass, but framed over Gary and Gloria Klein's bed 'X-Baby Wig Posse Don't P 4 U' has to look, well, a tad sarcastic.

Cramped out of the socializing for a minute, Alex worked on the question of this message by himself. Faced with a subtlety of marketing he'd never considered before, while he flipped back the pages of the catalog he decided that this was a factor in '5 boy!' promotion he ought to grasp. *What was the selling-point? What's really going on here?*

Baylor Lejeune's biography read like a rap sheet – truant, shoplifter, car thief, baby gangsta running wild on the streets since he was twelve, Haitian father (absent), Puerto Rican mother (deceased), defacer of public property, defiler of public morals, a delinquent genius adopted by Andy Warhol, a renegade talent who never let white America leak into his paintings – owning a strip of his mangy pelt was more than a privilege, it was a necessity to the Kleins. The selling-point is cave magic . . . In their house on Mulholland Drive or in Westwood or Woodland Hills the 'X-Baby' up on their wall was a taboo handprint, an aboriginal charm against gangbangers storm-trooping in from Compton and too pissed off to wait one more minute to get their hands on what the white folks've got . . . so they boot down the boudoir door and what do those Crips or Bloods or Rolling 60s find? It just takes one look at that genuine '5 boy!' hanging in front of him and the one with the pump action, with his Raiders hat on backwards, calls off the assault. 'Yo, they cool. Respeck to *that*.' Pictures of monsters on the wall to charm away the children of the night . . . Booga Booga Boo!

'I bet they'd put Baylor's head up over their bed,' Alex mentioned, watching the Kleins wade toward the exit.

'I'd make sure they'd pay him top dollar for it.' Alba plucked Alex's sleeve. 'What're we going to do about making a fortune?'

'Scary times. I've got to put something together by February.' He stopped there, he felt his voice cracking. 'Not a fortune.'

Her touch on his arm pulled him back. 'There's a safety net. Listen, are you saving all of your receipts?'

'You can start bugging me for real at the end of the tax year. Before I pay income tax don't I have to have an income?'

Baylor sprang up again, emceeing a merry round of introductions which sucked in Alba, Alex and a skeletal lurker who'd been standing motionless behind Alba for the last ten minutes. Under protruding, swollen eyelids his gray irises swam in red not white and the only other color in his face was the dyed black pencil mustache clinging to his lipline like a centipede on a twig. With his high-waisted, wide-shouldered 1930s English tweed suit all that was missing was the monocle. It was an image he obviously worked at, but Alex had to wonder who this man wanted to attract, dressed up as a lesbian in a Third Reich cabaret.

His hands stayed in his pockets when he said, 'I'm Teddy Fonseca. It's going very well, don't you think?' The accent wasn't German, it was the lazy nasal drone of the beach community.

'Oh, right.' Alex showed him he was on the ball. 'This is your dealership. Baylor says they're all sold.'

'Oh, that. Yeah, yeah. I mean the party. Lots of disagreements. A lot of arguments.'

'Who doesn't like what?'

'Yeah, right.' Teddy grinned at Alex's savvy.

'No, I mean, I was asking. Those arguments. What're they about?'

'Sorry, I didn't hear what you said. I've been drinking too many psychoholic cocktails tonight,' was his excuse and then he caught up with the party talk already in progress. 'This studio wife over there kept on trying to tell me art is never self-revealing. I think she was calling Baylor a con artist. She just watched her husband write me out a check for a hundred and fifty thousand. I thought he was going to throw his drink in her face. Or rip up his check. So I said the way you look at it is an individual expression. It doesn't matter if you scream and run away or run up and hug it, any response is valid. Then I walked away.'

'Maybe you should sell Baylor's stuff with a parts warranty.'

'They're guaranteed by MOMA and the Getty already. Norton Simon bought "X-Baby Mother". So, you know all these from his studio?'

'They look different in here.'

'Alba said you've got a few pieces at home. Which ones?'

'Those six AIDS posters he did last year? He, um — I own three of those.'

'The lithos or silk screens?'

'They're red and yellow.'

Teddy slipped Alba an aside. 'I enjoy your friend.'

'Alex is on his way to his first million,' she slipped back.

Alex didn't want to disagree. 'Maybe my career total.'

'I know different.' Alba was serious about it. 'You boys talk about the track,' she said, matchmaking before she dropped out again to confer with her husband.

Looking at her Alex sighed out a little breath. 'My mom away from mom.'

'Definitely. Alba's a world-class cooze.' Alex caught Teddy giving him, his shoes, his clothes, a dry appraisal. 'Which tracks?'

'Hollywood Park, usually. Usually.'

'We should go together sometime.' He handed Alex his card, with his home phone number underlined in ballpoint. 'The Oaks, after Christmas.'

Alex's pupils opened wide, his mind wasn't on horse-racing or on Teddy Fonseca's deepening interest in him anymore, he was stiffening up, staring across a dozen feet of floor at Hadi. Alex accidentally said out loud, 'I think I need to talk to him.'

'Hadi bought a Schnabel from me for ninety thousand,' Teddy leaned in to confide and confided more, 'when he was cheap. I mean when Schnabel was cheap.'

Drifting out beyond caution Alex went over and said hello to Hadi. He felt his skin tightening.

'We're going upstairs to look at the reserved work,' Hadi said, making it sound like an invitation.

A tide was running now, movement on every side. 'Coming up, big boy?' Alba gathered Alex into the group.

He felt Teddy's toe clip his heel. 'You're with us, Alex, good.'

Between opportunity and relief is a gap that insists on transformation: this was the thought forming out of Alex's hovering need to be included.

As soon as he fell in next to Hadi on their way upstairs to the mezzanine gallery his reasoning was clear, and right there it sharpened and punched through as a workable conversation opener. 'Hadi, do you think LA smells different from Tehran?'

4   Lost Foods of the Andes

IT wasn't the toned-down but sustained bombardment of letters, phone messages, postcards and faxes, much less was it Hadi's suave pressure behind the scenes that delivered Alex and his Odo-bags to Dinu Cristescu. The fixer who finagled the meeting, dinner at the great man's home no less, was Alex's mother. She had won the Cristescus' hearts and trust by negotiating the sale of their Wilshire Boulevard penthouse.

'Dinu's very happy to give you the benefit of his time,' she advised her son, support that came gift-wrapped, as practical as a cardigan and as lopsided with obligation as one she'd knitted for him out of her own hair.

'I've got my pitch down to a fine art,' his promise to her that he wouldn't make a mess of his chance to shine.

'Don't talk so much, go there to listen.'

Alex went to meet Dinu Cristescu with a posy of violets and angel's breath tucked behind his back, he was going there to ignite a tender passion, to stir this man's romantic imagination, to drop down on one knee if that's what Old World millionaires liked to see while their fingers were being pried loose from a measly hundred thousand dollars or so of venture capital.

The doors of the private elevator broke open on an empty corridor washed in milky light that condensed under frosted-glass panes beveled into the ceiling, a pale filmy haze that clad the monumental marble walls like icy moisture. The approach to the white double doors at the end of the hallway unbalanced Alex with the vague sensation of a downward slide into an igloo.

Dinu's wife Elizabeta opened the door at his second knock and met him with a frazzled apology. 'The kitchen is so many steps from the front door!'

'Hello, hello, Alex. Please.' Dinu composed himself further along the marble-floored entry hall, a ministerial reception that impelled more than invited his guest to step forward and shake his hand. His mother had more or less prepared him for Dinu's aristocratic manner so Dinu's black silk turtleneck and turquoise shot-silk suit, which put a wobbly spin on his courtliness, surprised Alex. 'Betta, this is Ellen Berry's son, Alex.' He patted the sides of his slicked-back hair, iron gray that the pomade darkened and polished, still declaring vitality behind the disciplined verge of his hairline.

Dinu sniffed the air. 'Do you smell that?'

The hallway smelled sharply clean to Alex. 'What am I supposed to smell?'

'You're a polite boy,' Dinu said, and explained, mildly cranky, 'we had to keep out of our house all day, for the pest control man. So we don't choke on his insecticide. Today he did half and tomorrow the other half. Maybe I should charge him rent.'

In the dining-room a glass of beer was offered, 'Belgian Chimay. You like it?' and accepted, then fetched for him as Dinu guided Alex around the collections showcased in the largest of his twelve rooms. The stodgy padded leather furniture, two Chesterfield sofas and matching library chairs, seemed to comprise their own display, a reconstruction of the smoking-room of a gentleman's club or the corner of a Czarist palace opened to the post-revolutionary public. In the informative tones of a caretaker Dinu's description of the ornamental pottery, key specimens of Lalique, Roman silver coins and cups, Venetian glass and art nouveau figurines hinted at some sentiment he reserved for this accumulation of stately artefacts that went beyond proud ownership; the necessary payments, the patient manipulations, his equity in the past was presented in these mahogany cabinets, the drama of his autobiography.

'Can you see what they are?' The opposite wall stood sixty feet away, fogged in its own shadow, and Alex thought he was looking at a row of family portraits. When he spoke up like a quiz show contestant and guessed that, Dinu had a quiet laugh for the two of them, then he said, 'Betta would say so, yes.'

A private gallery of self-celebrating works of art fit precisely into the image that Alex formed of his host, the cultured European architect and escapee tycoon who could spend five and a half million dollars on the bare shell of an address and, his mother figured, another two million on furniture and decoration. 'With all the power they gave him in his own country, Alex, they didn't appreciate him. He only wanted to come here.' Dinu had seen it coming, he saw what the Securitate didn't see because he looked out and around, not in and down. Hungary finished with Kádár the year before and it was only months until Budapest had a stock exchange, McDonald's, French TV commercials and sex shops. Dinu saw punks and skinheads in Bulgaria. In his own country he also saw that he lacked the lung power to convince Elena Ceausescu that oceanic change was rolling over the country and if she wasn't going to get out of the way then she'd better learn how to float. Instead of loyally supervising the bulldozing of seven thousand villages ('To pave the way', he chuckled to Alex, in Nicolae Ceausescu's voice and very words, 'for a system of agro-industrial centers you can see from the moon!') Dinu lowered the lifeboats and rowed his household west. The retail value of the possessions he brought out of Bucharest by way of Prague, Dubrovnik, Vienna, Milan, Geneva and Montreal, neither Alex nor his mother were connoisseur enough to estimate. More millions, probably.

The paintings weren't on display because they were masterpieces of their kind (which they might have been), they were the personal joke and subtle pleasure of the man who outsmarted the state apparatus from president down to border guard. 'Here I have two dozen, most of them show Krakatoa. Some others', he pointed them out, 'are Etna and Vesuvius. This one is very funny.' Dinu peered at the canoe-load of Polynesians paddling away from the lava storm into a nest of circling sharks.

Alex peered along with him. 'Kind of a bad call, there. I think I'd stay on the beach and get barbecued.'

'It's all blown up, the whole island. The smoke from it, the ashes, it clouded up the atmosphere for years. A piece of the world that broke off, can you imagine it?'

'I remember the earthquake here when I was nine, but, no, I can't imagine how bad a volcano would be.'

'You can see!' Dinu stretched his arms out in opposite directions, pitting the erupting volcanoes against the treasures in the room and the traffic outside. 'Earthquakes, floods, terrible disasters in the environment, a hundred times worse than styrofoam boxes from fast hamburgers and look: we are all still here. Has my secretary given you her lectures, too? Miss Weiss wants to save the grass and trees from businessmen.'

'She told me she doesn't eat anything with a soul. I thought she meant the fish.'

'But you listen, hm? You can look at her face and the ridiculous nonsense coming out of her mouth turns into *Madam Butterfly*.' Dinu called to Betta in the kitchen and she called back to him in English. 'Twenty minutes,' he relayed to Alex as if this needed translation, and flapping his fingers against Alex's chest he continued, 'Good. Betta can finish cooking. We can talk now, so when we eat we can concentrate on our food.'

The hallway leading back into the apartment was lined with dark wood, aged panels that might have been salvaged – or pirated – from a church, and lit by amber lamps dangling Turkish style from brass chains. Each room they passed on the way to Dinu's study seemed to push further east, carved furniture, brocade drapes, Persian carpets. 'This could all be a different country back here.' Alex might have been talking about the vastness of the place, but his eye ranged over the décor.

'Oh this,' Dinu denied its relevance with a wave of his hand, 'this is all for Betta. Ten rooms for her and two rooms for me.' On the other side of his study door was a hideout that existed in its own dimension. Cool cream walls, a glass-topped tubular-steel desk, two black leather chairs, and the atmosphere of a bomb shelter. 'This is where I belong. I soundproofed it in here. This is where I can read and think. And smoke.' His eyelids fell shut when the fat cigarette touched his lips and didn't open again until he'd puffed life into the tobacco. The heavy smoke he released slowly from the corners of his mouth settled in the air like a sediment, rich with the loamy odor of burning leaves and spiced with cloves. Alex sniffed it in. 'You'd like to try one of my Greeks? I'm sorry,' Dinu shook one out of the crumpled pack, reaching across the desk. 'I assumed you were not a smoker.'

'I'm not, no.'

'I enjoy smoking very much. These I bought last week. They have such an aroma, of coming indoors on a cold day and honeycake on the table.' A slow pull again, eyes closed in silent, almost dreamy, self-indulgence.

The lips, slightly everted, with a Napoleonic authority that plumpness made dainty, were a flamboyance underneath the hard, sharp beak. If his fleshed-out squirely cheeks suggested a decade or two of fussy over-privilege, the wrestler's torso and mechanic's hands were blunt statements of Dinu's stamina and ready physicality, he captured a guest's patience and held it poised on the verge of revelation. Some oration was being prepared for Alex.

Dinu blinked himself back to attention, catching Alex contemplating the only piece of art in the room, a large hand-tinted photograph in a chrome frame, stiffly bolted to the wall. Any car, bus, vegetation or pedestrian must have been airbrushed out, or just as likely uprooted and banned from the broad avenue, so nothing apart from the receding flat pavement and dwarfed streetlights was in view to give the building a reliable scale. Its central bulk thrust up from the horizon, a blocky wedding cake presenting its white cupolas and rococo cornices to the blank azure sky, a construction of Babylonian proportions, colossal enough to generate its own gravity. 'My first inspiration was from the Fontainbleu Hotel. You know it? In Florida. I wanted to make Ceausescu's idea, his House of the Republic, a beautiful place for everybody. A national anthem in concrete. It was almost a beauty, almost a wonder.' More than that, Dinu meant his design to celebrate Romania 'coming out of the Middle Ages' and in the earliest stages his personal initiative achieved something which still gave him a glow. 'With this building I could even go around communism, go around Ceausescu.'

In the same subdued voice, moderate pride gave way to serious regret when he spoke about the 'systemization' which pulled down 25 per cent of Bucharest. Alex commiserated, imagining the mudfields and splintered ruins, then a jolt knocked through him when he realized that Dinu's regret was for a job left 75 per cent unfinished. 'All of that neo-Romanian garbage mixed up with Gothic, and mixed up with neo-Gothic, even very bad Art Deco in some places, all a mishmash with no logical point. Cobblestones all over the pretty streets, very advanced for six hundred years ago. Very good for the ox-carts! Rubber wheels on their ox-carts and they say, "That's enough for now," and this is all the progress they want, all the development they can tolerate. Even the intellectuals, even the best brains in the country are so hypnotized they think they see stability where there's only stagnation.'

29

'What's going to happen back there, in two years or five years? Can you do something from here?'

'Oh, maybe the king of Romania will come back, then it will be like here.' Dinu rested his chin coquettishly on one fist and gave his head an unironic tilt. 'My king of America, I'll tell you who he is: Ray Kroc. Do you know there will be a McDonald's hamburger restaurant in Moscow by January? A genius king, better than Walt Disney. Teenagers from Iowa volunteer to go and train teenagers in Russia, you know, McDonald's gives them a tremendous motivation *to serve*. An artist of business, Ray Kroc, like Andy Warhol in reverse, with a limited edition of one hundred billion! In McDonald's the Big Mac hamburger is the same in Moscow and Honolulu, the paper cups are the same size, every milk shake and french fry potato the same, *also it is the original*. This product is a social contribution. People go into McDonald's in any city in the world and right away you have them on your side, they know exactly what their money is going to buy. The teenagers who work in there, they have confidence in the items they're selling, nothing is haphazard about it. On both sides of the counter people enjoy a certainty in a little fast hamburger! It can change the way they behave, you know, people behave in extreme ways when they have too much uncertainty around them. A beautiful hamburger that people can depend on can make a real difference in society.' His hands dropped back into his lap as he stopped himself there. 'I'm sorry, Alex, I'm sure you learned these things. Your mother told me that you studied business administration at your university.'

'And in the real world.'

'Of course, yes. Maybe I'm too fanatical with my admiration, but,' the ambassadorial charm crept back into his voice, into the unemotional smile, '*franchises*! God in heaven, how they've played out their franchises.'

'I can do that, Mr Cristescu.'

'Sure. Anybody with brains in his head.'

'I mean I'm ready to do that now. I've got a product, it's – wow, it's a beautiful thing. Can I show it to you?'

'Of course, Alex, yes, bring it in here. As long as our dinner isn't on the table. Let's talk about your international business scheme.'

According to the story he told Gilbert, before Alex swam into his Odo-bag presentation he visited the bathroom, an event that he left out of the account of the evening which he gave to his mother on the telephone the next day.

Framed in the bathroom mirror Alex probably thought, *He won't buy the product unless he buys the salesman*, locked arms supporting his upper body against the edge of the sink as if he were leaning on a podium and on the other side of the mirror, through the power of positive thinking, Alex faced the future throng of Odo-bag stockholders. 'Happy, happy, happy,' he told them, clenching his fists in the air, shoulder high. Surrounded by the gold foil wallpaper, iridescent blue tiles, the gold gargoyle spigot over the lapis lazuli sink, his grimace of willed optimism and go-gettem shake of his fists gave Alex the look of one of those miniature mechanical toy surprises inside a Fabergé egg.

He unzipped his fly and he must have had to stand on his tip-toes to pee directly down the drain, to keep himself from dripping into the high pile carpet. The bowl of the sink was a shallow slope and his last squirt and dribble lacked the oomph to avoid sprinkling the sides with yeasty gold drops. A fast douche of hot water sluiced away most of the mess, the little puddle on the lip of the sink he smeared off with a square of toilet tissue. Somehow, one bead of Alex's urine ricocheted up into the soap dish where it landed on a waxy petal of rose-scented soap. A drop of his own scent to leave behind and contaminate this wealth, to bring it closer.

Ready to do business in the small quiet study, Alex spread out the three prototype Odo-bags on Dinu's desk. Mesh, rice paper and linen. Dinu picked up the metal mesh sachet, weighed it in his hand. Alex said, 'Your nose can tell the difference between four hundred *thousand* odors. The sense of smell is our most primitive sense, and even if we don't have to depend on it to survive in the everyday world anymore, our animal instincts are still inside us waiting to be activated . . .'

And on through a sketchy but informed run-down of Odo-bag chemistry. He remembered to compare the wax beads in the sachets to lifesavers, and told Dinu how the fragrance is cooked into the wax the way flavor is cooked into candy, how the simple addition of heat atomizes the scent, transfers it to the fibers of fabrics, onto the skin or into the air.

'Upholstery, wallpaper, sheets and pillow cases, all impregnated with permanent, natural fragrances, beautiful fragrances like willow or sweet chestnut, aroma therapies that can change people's moods:

calm them down so they can sleep or wake them up when they've got to work, even soft kinds of aphrodisiacs, why not? It's a life-enhancing product, it does some good, so besides the wide mark-up we can allow retailers on account of our low bulk costs, we can actually feel good about the profit we take out of it. We've added something wonderful to the world, like your, what did you call it, your House of the Republic. Who knows how far we can take it.

'There's a doctor in Boston, George Dodd. He's been doing research on basic odors connected to individuals, the personal scents of their own mothers. It's amazing. When a baby is suckling, you know, on it's mother's breast, it's not only getting chow that makes it happy, it smells its mom's special odor, from her whole body, and that activates the baby's emotions, locks them in, it knows it's being loved and cared for. Can you imagine the impact of a line of Odo-bags that can re-activate those babyhood feelings? Of peaceful childhood, security and milk and whatever. Also, there's wide scope for line extension possibilities. I'd like to do a new range of scents every season. Say, in Year 3 we'll go with something like an ancient fragrance range — frankincense, myrrh, sandalwood, cinnamon, saffron. And we can go the other way into *future* scents, new combinations of odors that nobody has ever smelled before. I mean, this is a product that can extend forever, little changes once in a while, and Odo-bags will be in business for as long as people've got noses to smell with.'

'Oh, yes.' Dinu bestowed the compliment directly upon the mesh bag, contemplated it in the light again and painstakingly avoided the issue. 'Miss Weiss came into this room for the first time and she looked at my House of the Republic up on the wall and she told me her opinion of it.' The memory tickled him and so did his effetely camp impression of her New York accent. ' "Dee-noo, it's so on-*natch*-or-ul!" She told me square buildings are unnatural, they're against nature. Concrete is against nature. Well. Man cannot escape nature. Whatever we make is nature. We carry nature wherever we go, it is inside whatever we do. This, what you made out of wax and aluminum is nature.'

'Right. I agree with that,' Alex got in fast to sideline the philosophy.

'You want to charge how much for these? How much for one like this?'

'We'll be able to wholesale them for under a dollar, retailers can let them go for two-seventy-nine. But there's the industrial application to consider, too. There's an idea of the kind of numbers we can expect on page twenty – ' Alex found the chart in the business plan, displayed it for Dinu. Into the pocket of silence on the other side of the desk he pitched, 'The profit potential is there, Mr Cristescu, right in the second year. By the third year, personally I believe we'll be into licensing, and five years from the go, why not, Odo-bags could be fat enough to go public.'

Dinu's eyes flicked up. Behind a direct, distancing stare he said, 'From me you want what?'

'Start-up capital, that'd be for the equipment, materials, initial advertising, retainers for my technical people, running costs for one year, this comes in at ninety-eight thousand.'

'A hundred thousand dollars.'

'Out of the second-year profits your participation would be fifty per cent up to 98K and twenty-five per cent royalty on sales after that. That amount would go up to thirty-three per cent when we reach a 600K turnover.' Alex laid a spiral-bound copy of the whole indexed business plan next to the Odo-bags.

Thumbing the cover back, skimming the contents page, Dinu shook his head. 'This is a story for small children.'

Alex felt the oxygen leak out of his lungs, a swirling pressure in his stomach.

'Tell me why *this*,' Dinu went on. 'Why do you want to make this? Tell me the reason for this product.'

'It's the right time for it, that's what I . . . . If you look at the market research I carried out – um, on page ten it starts – it suggests, very strongly, there's a positive niche – '

'You think you'll produce this and make a killing,' Dinu flatly suggested, baiting Alex with a skeptical come-on.

'I want it to be a success. Sure, yes.'

'That's your reason?'

'Well, it's something new.'

'It's something you want to see on the market. Two years, three years, ten years, going on.'

'Isn't this how Henry Ford started out? Ray Kroc did it this way, I mean, I don't know another way to do it. There was a time when there was only one McDonald's in the world, until he raised his investment capital, then the whole future opened up for him.'

'*Transportation*, Alex. You heard it from your professors, you know this, cheap transportation and cheap food, hamburgers, your *national dish*. Your product here, you tell me, is what?'

'It can be . . . It can be attainable . . .' He fell back on the closing phrase of his prospectus, 'It will be an attainable distinction.'

'It's a soap bubble, in my opinion. This is what I think, it's a temporary thing, because what will happen to it when people don't have so much money anymore? Maybe you can make a big soap bubble in one year from one hundred thousand dollars, you can stretch it, but look at this soap bubble: it takes up space but it's very thin, look inside – no substance, all air. You want to create this? It's very trivial, that is my analysis, it's a precarious thing.'

'Everything is at the beginning, I guess.'

Dinu winced an apology and handed back the plan. 'I'm sorry, maybe my language is too hard. I don't want to make your mother angry at me, but if I was too soft with you maybe I'd disappoint her more.' Now, into the silence collecting around Alex he said, 'Connect your ideas to something bigger, look at the world from high up. Big changes are already coming. Here, Europe, Africa, you can see the connections.'

'Maybe you can give me some example of what – '

A chime rang behind them, three mellow notes, and a square blue light flicked on above the door. Dinu stood up, hiked his waistband and pointed the way out of the room. 'Dinner is on the table.'

Even with the earthy aromas billowing up from the gravy which bubbled like red mud in the terracotta tureen right in front of him, Alex had a hard time keeping his mind on the food. If one of the city's highest profile entrepreneurs, known for his imagination and audacity, a regular Cecil B. DeMille of wildcat speculation, if Dinu Cristescu turned down the opportunity to invest in Odo-bags then what kind of a reception could Alex expect from his neighborhood bank? He knew the first two questions they'd ask: 'How much?' and 'When?' and they wouldn't be talking about the cash flowing out of their pockets into his. He tipped out a ladleful of red gravy, his eyes saying 'Yum, yum' in a dumbshow effort to keep his misery from making him look clownish.

Out of a porcelain bowl the size of a chamber pot his hostess scooped out four small blue potatoes. When they landed on his plate

Alex stared at them as if they were ticking. 'I don't think your mother give you food like this ever.'

Betta spooned a goulash of cassava and brown beans into a mound next to the potatoes, the first helping for Alex, the second for her husband, serving them with the ritual respect of a Slavic geisha. Her shoulders were softly slumped, whether from hefting milk buckets or from the weight of thirty-five years' companionship with such a titanically effective man, Alex had to wonder. The duties she performed, in the kitchen, at the table, she took on for herself, though, without doting, without drudgery: she could do these things much better than Dinu could, and this way she did more than supply his epicurean needs, she satisfied needs of her own which were much more basic. In the trauma unit of the Hollywood Presbyterian, where she supervised the emergency admissions four nights a week, was it conceivable that any of the other doctors, or nurses, patients or grieving relatives treated Betta as a mere attendant? It was tough for Alex to imagine.

'I want you to tell your mother what kind of a fabulous meal you ate here,' Dinu said to him, pointing with his fork at the red, blue and brown food as Alex chewed a bite of potato. The waxy flesh had the aftertaste of a eucalyptus cough drop.

'Is this like a Romanian national dish?'

'No, no! This is Inca food. Betta made the whole dinner from old recipes from the Incas.'

Betta uncovered another tureen to offer Alex a helping of stew. It was sulphur yellow, thick as molten rock, with potato halves capsized in broth.

Alex looked at it. 'Weren't Incas the ones who ate people?'

'Aztecs,' Dinu taught him. 'In Mexico, Aztecs. One of their recipes tasted like this maize-and-potato stew. Very nice for vegetarians, but for Aztecs, no. *Tlacatlaolli*, maize-and-man stew. From a prisoner the priests have his heart, one thigh to the aristocrats, also his liver, his kidneys, his shoulder. His head they put on a skull rack. And the rest of the carcass went into the stewpot.' Chewing a potato skin, he said, 'They say it tastes sweet, human meat, like pork.'

'Dinu,' Betta censored him with a tired smile.

Dinu stopped eating to say, 'You eat pork?'

'Not, like, every day.' Then, Alex got the point. 'We don't observe any of that stuff, not very much.'

'In such a tolerant country there's no reason to insist you're a Jew,' was Dinu's theory.

'Your mother helped us very much, to sell here. I think she is very respected in her field.' Betta couldn't make the polite, personal turn sound like anything more than it was, a plain tactic to deflect another one of Dinu's arias.

'She's just got a hold of a serious listing in Holmby Hills.'

'Holmby Hills.' Betta nodded. 'It's very good for her in there. Every house has two swimming pools.'

'This one's got a disco and a bowling alley.'

'Good, then. She can sell it for a big price and she will get a wonderful big commission, then maybe she can buy a special present for you, maybe a Rolls-Royce car.'

'I wouldn't want her to do that.' That, or anything resembling *this* again, an audience she procured for him with a man who's only prepared to listen to a business plan for five minutes and whose only practical advice is to start over and think big. *Finally, to be left sitting there in front of him with my mouth hanging open, feeling like his pet monkey, happy with a peanut.* Alex could hear Dinu cutting up his food, fork and knife scraping the surface of the plate, he could hear Dinu chewing.

Without lifting his head, Dinu murmured a few words in Romanian, it might have been a blessing delivered straight to the potatoes but when Betta asked him, also in Romanian, to repeat what he'd said their eyes locked across the table. 'Too many stories, it might be boring to Alex.' From Dinu, not budging out of Romanian, complaint and a denying shrug. She answered abruptly, with a quick glance at Alex. 'It should be a meal tonight with us, not a French opera.' From Dinu: touchy indifference. 'My husband wants to cut my head off.' She roped Dinu into the joke, 'You want to cut my head off?' and kept after him in English, not to exclude Alex.

Alex excluded himself, climbed into his canoe and floated away from the noise and heat. His loss of heart didn't feel temporary, it wasn't a blush from the slap of rejection, now he saw just where Odo-bags figured in the picture of the world painted by the CEO of the multinational, five-hundred-million-dollar Falcon Development Group. Alex thought of his Odo-bags still sitting in Dinu's study, disappearing in the dark, absorbed into the vacuum, migrating into the past. He'd struggle on with Odo-bags for six more months, repaying the debts and investments with plodding dedication, but the choice to drop the whole idea was made here, over dessert.

Mountain fruits, Pizarro tasted this same sugary flesh, but no Inca maid could have presented a meal's climax with more expressive care. Betta conveyed respect for her guest through the respect she showed the food, nestling slices of pacaya, cactus pear and pepino on a bed of broad dark green leaves, fanned in tiers on a platter made entirely of ice. And there was more after this. As if the dewy pastel crescents of a purple-striped egg-shaped melon that tasted of mild honey and smelled of honeysuckle were as plain as potato chips, she said, 'Now you can taste something out of this world.'

Cherimoya, the 'pearl of the Andes', landed in front of Alex cupped in its own ice bowl, balanced on a thin silver dish so shallow it was no more than a platform. The fruit it held forth was as big as a softball, shaped like a hand grenade, wrapped in a dull hard skin that made it look as appetizing as a small meteorite. But its meat was custard soft, and it was bananas-with-lemon that Alex tasted first, then coconut, then vanilla . . .

'Your mother can buy them at Gelson's.' Dinu wasn't just passing along a neighborly tip, he was sharpening a point. 'A thousand years ago, this is what they ate, these, what you're eating now. Like ordinary ice cream to the Incas,' he dug in his spoon and twisted out a bite of cherimoya, 'but for us, luxury. A gorgeous luxury for twelve dollars each.'

'They're beautiful,' Alex offered his appreciation to Betta. A hand lightly touching his arm brought him back around.

'You can learn something from this food.' The small straw basket sitting in the middle of the table which Alex took for decoration was handed over so he could see what was in it. 'Quinoa. Better than soya, better than wheat. More protein than millet. More fiber than oats. It has iron and amino acids. I'm growing this in Canada. Not for here, not for Gelson's to sell quinoa bread. No, in a few years Hungary, Bulgaria, Romania and all the rest back there, they have to come this way, out of the cul-de-sac. They'll repair agriculture, also manufacturing, it has to go on for generations. Imagine the markets there for companies with broad-based products to sell them, something useful, useful systems, something even an Albanian can understand.' Alex received the message after all that Dinu Cristescu actually took him seriously. Dinu scrutinized him and said, 'Can I ask you for your opinion?'

'Go ahead, definitely.'

'When I get my citizenship should I change my name to Dino? Dino. Like your singing star Dino Martin. And don't be nervous, tell me what you really think.'

5   His Natural Selection

THE unforgiving conclusion that Alex dragged home with him was a part of the story he didn't tell Gilbert and couldn't tell his mother and father: this starstruck ambition of his to originate a product and launch it into the American mainstream was the plot out of a musical comedy.

At least this lesson was one dividend from his flat failure with Dinu Cristescu, a point in the plus column; so, he told himself, looking at net loss and net gain he'd finished one unit ahead. Alex had seen himself in a fable, taken out of his skin to be shown by the Force of Conscience or the Angel of Capitalist Greatness his destiny's true route. Just in time to rescue his life he heard the unearthly voice single him out and say to him, 'Try to make a living, don't try to make a difference,' and Alex was bent in gratitude for the second chance. He had to suck in his gut, polish his brogues and become another buck private in the demobbed army of MBA grads walking the circuit of corporate lobbies, knocking on doors, offering his youth, bargaining for shelter.

How did I keep doing this? he scourged himself, still amazed by the Technicolor home movie of his impressive future, *I've got to stop doing this, selling this line to myself.* Into the solitary hours of the next morning he stayed awake reading every project outline and contract filed in his black box, revisiting them as though they were souvenirs of defunct romances.

Prolonged expectation and abrupt futility, in a looping cycle, stood out as the prime forces that were shaping his life as a man. Trivial plans he used to think were visionary insights, unpatented gimmicks he used to see as universal necessities, all just soap bubbles, crude choices he'd made, pretty ponies he'd backed; one by one he let them go. Into confetti went the exploding-paint car alarm system, Odo-bags, Laser Busts, each lame prospect a weight unhooked from the iron collar of them. Out went the Designer Revolver, Heeto Teeto the cordless chemical pouch baby bottle warmer, and Alex felt physically lighter, moving on, out through an exit, past an ending.

Now he fell into his real work, dropped away from every dumb miscalculation, felt the distance open up between this new toughened maturity and that early faulty incarnation, the apprentice Alex who could be suckered by false promise. He sat on the edge of his bed shredding the cards, the blister of light from the desk lamp only filled half of his face but seemed to double his age.

One card survived the purge. It had a gravitational pull that brought Alex back to it, into orbit around a product that wasn't trivial, an item that wasn't a gimmick. *It's starting now*, the thing said to him, a single idea that wouldn't let itself be discarded by his mood. Alex couldn't shake free of the belief that he could make it happen. A secret structure was being divulged to him, a personal message forming piece by piece out of a different world; the sensation of being directed to this by wild coincidence, change and pursuit gave him the notion of destiny.

He crumpled the pink card, read it over, crumpled it again, didn't tear it up. As he fell asleep it was still intact, clutched in his palm, his fingers curled protectively around it. There he was like a new-hatched chick, caved in by hours of impossible effort, flat on his back as the sun started to come up, as I was absconding. One idea caged in his hand, Alex clung on to one staggeringly unreasonable plan.

6 Light in the Sky

DRIVING down into Topanga Canyon, Alex encountered a vision of Heaven. He saw the surrounding sky, hills, time, pour out their belief in him, luminous and massive behind the treetops, it summoned him with an emotion close to panic. As it rose above the asphalt road the illumination that spread like sunlight (but couldn't be) gathered Alex into the reward that would placate his parents, forgive his mistakes, repay Alba's and Baylor's confidence, end all of his hardship, crack through his city's indifference. The unreal cloud of light was no mirage, he was driving closer to it, an actual emanation out there, and in here it weighed with a pressure in his chest and throat, a knot of breath caught between his lungs and mouth now only a few hundred feet away from being shucked out of his limitations and parted from his imperfections, a realm opened up to him that had darkly shut him out before.

Through his dusty, bug-flecked windshield a halo appeared over the ridge of the dirt trail that zigzagged down to Chick's canyon home. It tinted the dusk around it, reddened it where the light fell on the scrubby brown hillside. Beneath the orange-red bloom, squatting in Chick's workshop, was an invention Alex knew could transform the lives of millions, the beginning of a line of continuous benefit to its producers and its consumers. Rooted in personal convenience, it connected people to their environment through their own household economies, good done to one was good done to the other – *multiply households into neighborhoods, neighborhoods into communities, communities into cities.* 'The world is a filthy, immoral mess,' Alex would tell them, 'and here is something you can do about it.' Front yard or farmyard, urbanite or peasant, First World or Third World, this was a gift to the self-reliant, a refuge to the grazing affluent, a marker of conscience and potential necessity in the life of any adult with enough imagination to look ahead a few years. 'Since it's been installed,' owners will testify, 'I can stand up as a good example to my children . . .' – *to anybody's children*, to presidents and popes! Holding the vision in front of him Alex understood that his summons was to manage its descent, before the Humpty Dumpster could enter – and alter – the everyday world, his undreaming will had to pull it out of the sky.

Almost underneath it, the light billowed out its ghost, a curtain of heat that slapped through the car windows and gusted over Alex's skin as he coasted around the oak trees where the steep trail spilled into the delta of Chick's rutted driveway. Above the woodframe bungalow a dire, mushrooming pillar of smoke erupted, spitting amber sparks and hot flakes of tarpaper. Chick's house was on fire.

On his feet ten yards from the front door Alex could hear the heat inside cracking the window panes and a prayer emptied out of his mouth. 'Oh God, oh please. Please, God . . .' I tell you I never loved him more than I did then, in his belittlement, defending himself with the sudden thought that his plans deserve God's immediate magic.

Without help from above, Chick stumbled out from the back porch dressed like a six-year-old's idea of a Space Age commando – his head encased in a welder's mask, his hands protected by a pair of oven mitts, a scuba tank strapped to his back and a plastic pipe six inches wide and three feet long tilted on his shoulder. A flame as big as a man lashed out of a window when he came around the side of the house, but Chick didn't even duck. It flapped over his head as he knelt down and, with the focused concentration of a golfer lining up a putt, watched the fire stretch for the roof, for more air, then he stood up, levelled the bazooka and moved in.

A quick, serious pull on the trigger loosed off a jet of water and a funnel of spray in a single burst that puffed out the fire like it was a birthday candle. Only a fringe of flame was left, hotspots the size of fingertips guttering across the lip of the sill. Alex stepped in and grabbed his friend's shoulder, yanking him back from the brink as Chick cocked a leg to climb in through the window.

'You want to kill yourself?' crazy with worry, Alex panted at him. 'Everything's on fire!' Whatever Chick shouted back was lost under the metal mask so it was impossible to tell whether he meant the sharp force of that split-second to protect Alex or himself. Chick danced him out of the way, shoved him very hard in the chest and was heading back to his burning house before Alex's rear end landed in the dirt. From ground level Chick's assault on the heat and smoke had a heroic look, even at the exact moment when he disappeared into the disaster.

Alex heard the blast of the water jet. And again. Gray-white smoke drifted out, a cloud of it, then only threads more like steam straining out between the shingles. In the spooky stillness the screen door out back banged in its frame, slanting on its one remaining hinge, and keeled right over when Chick swaggered through it with the bazooka slung nonchalantly over his shoulder G.I.-style.

'Couldn't see the door!' He tipped up the welder's mask, shook off his oven mitts and wagged a finger at Alex. 'You almost got into trouble. In the way of all the action!'

'You think you're fireproof? What do you think, you can't get hurt fighting a fire in your own house?'

'I put it out.'

'Nothing's burning in there? Are you positive?'

'I put the fire out. Three-four litres of water. That's all. Very amazing, huh!' Chick fiddled with the flimsy nozzle on the end of the plastic pipe. It was only a rubber cup sliced into flaps, previously employed to guard the mouth of his kitchen dispose-all. 'I can improve this. It doesn't keep enough water in. It dribbles.'

Something fell heavily behind the scorched walls. Alex pointed at it. 'Your house.'

'You know what happens,' the grin still reaching for his ears, 'when things get out of the experiment zone.'

'You should experiment on something a little less terrifying.' He eyed up Chick's singed boiler suit.

'I've got immunity, for real. From my dad's side, island fever. The Uchiyamas are all tiki doctors. Kanaka attitude to what happens. Spirit of Diamond Head watches over me.'

'Kamikaze scientist.' Chick's sudden fur-ball cough dredged up a gob of ash-black phlegm, shiny as patent leather. Alex suggested, 'Let's go to the hospital and X-ray your lungs.'

Chick held up his hand until he stopped coughing. 'This was amazing, I thought I used up all the air. Everything full of smoke, coming from the middle of my lab. I didn't know where the core was, couldn't see in, so I followed the heat. Weirdness supreme! I was in it, Alex, and the sonofabitching thing jammed, okay, no pressure. Out of control *supreme*, char-broiled Hawaiian Surprise tonight, but check this out: one pump and it unjams, first shot hits the core like it's *heat-seeking*.'

'Chick, I want to talk to you about – are you sure you feel okay? You feel like talking now?' He was hawking up more grainy spit, but nodded Alex ahead. 'What all got damaged in there? How bad is it?'

'That's the real amazing part. See, look. One litre in a room eight by twelve means water damage you can clean up with a sponge . . .' With a steady bedside manner Alex listened to Chick explain how the compressed air propels large droplets into the core of the fire and how the mist at the end of the blast cools the fuel and smothers the embers like a wet sheet, and how much better than a hose this water gun is because it's more fun for firemen to use. 'A Walkman version of a fire hydrant!'

Alex showed him a set of plans sketched out on a piece of graph paper, three years old now. Chick had sold the idea to him for sixty-five dollars and for twenty more he threw together a working model. 'Does this still exist?'

Like a rising drizzle, smoke blurred the air in the room where the fire was started. Ashes of the corrugated cardboard that Chick had used to kindle it ended up in a mashed, soggy ring around the skeletal remains of a charred wooden pallet in the middle of the floor. The heat had jumped high enough to melt the ceiling light and scorch the beam above it, and when Alex stood underneath it he caught a sugary whiff of burnt cedar. Where brackets got knocked loose from the wall warped shelves sloped or collapsed, the tools, jars, cans, hardware and assorted raw materials they held all dumped into messy pyramids on top of sprung coils of wire, stacks of plywood, sheet metal, strewn circuit boards, jumbled into trash and salvage. He could have been looking at the aftermath of wartime scavenging.

Buried someplace in the dark, beyond guesswork, it was waiting to be unburied, the ugly flat-topped object that had the power to give him back his faith in a radiant future. 'What's that?' Alex pointed out a corner of the lab that faced the open window, where a soft glare signaled to him. A corroded mirror propped up against the wall collected the last dab of light in the room directly over an oblong aluminum canister.

The flat lid had buckled, the front of it was scraped and dimpled, but Chick knew what he had there before he kicked it free. 'Eureka,' he sang out, then, 'Huh?'

Loud enough this time to carry across the room. Alex repeated. 'That's it. That's the one.'

'In six weeks I can show you a practical prototype,' was Alex's deal, if – '

'If,' Meyer was the obvious jump ahead, 'I put up the cash.' The serious face that reminded Alex, from the age of five, of the stiff-necked warrior-chief Sitting Bull, showed he could only be moved by detached and reasonable argument to invest eight hundred dollars in a machine that chomps organic waste into all-purpose fertilizer and compresses paper and plastic into pellets that burn 30 per cent hotter than fuel oil. The reasonable argument went: 'With a profit-resourced R&D program we can go on expanding our market by developing a range of variations adapted to local needs. For Eskimos, maybe, something blubber related.'

During April and May Alex put in calls to Dinu at the Falcon office. Nineteen attempts to make contact failed and on the twentieth attempt Miss Weiss passed this information to him: Mr Cristescu was in Canada, he had no definite plans to return to Los Angeles before the end of the year. A telephone number in Winnipeg went with this top-level disclosure but apart from the five times he got through to the answering machine either the line was busy or it was just left ringing.

43

Alex dragged Chick out of Topanga Canyon for a crisis meeting. With the money from his father firmly sunk into the construction of Humpty Dumpster 001 they only had to scrape up another $319,200 to swing into full production.

7 Time and Motion

THE twenty monitors of the Global's video wall presented Alex with the world under glass. While he glanced from screen to screen and contemplated the sweep of continents falling to advancing waves of Humpty Dumpsters, Chick doodled on the electronic sketch pad, waiting for lunch to arrive. Upside-down, the boxy drawing was as unreadable to Alex as the Le Mans circuitry of a microchip but when Chick rotated the ornate geometry 180 degrees Alex stopped breathing. 'Who're you talking to?'

'My pen pal in South Korea,' Chick said.

Alex pounced on the escape key and the screen went blank before one more micromillisecond of that schematic drawing could be beamed into the heartland of industrial piracy. 'I've got to worry about *this* now?'

'Look what you did.' Chick pointed helplessly at the computer.

'You want to put us out of business before we even get going? What were you thinking? Where was your mind?'

'If you're asking me a question – '

'Mm.'

'Information exchange. We show each other what we're working on, and that lowers the suspicion level, okay. My information,' straight from the Magna Carta, 'I've got a right.'

'You were sending him the blueprint, for fuck's sake. You could bankrupt us with your rights.'

Frowning under the weight of two platters balanced on her forearms, their waitress let them know with a 'Sorry, I don't want to interrupt, but can I get in here?' that she'd been standing around waiting to serve their sandwiches. 'You ordered two Four Corners?'

'Thanks, sister.' Alex aimed at light relief.

She parodied a curtsey, aping a demure maid. Demure was a

44

remote proposition for the girl in the dirndl skirt and motorcycle boots. 'My maximum pleasure,' overdoing it now, especially since Alex was noticing her scraped knees, so she gave him the playground toughie. 'If I was your sister, I'd blow my brains out.'

And just to show her that he knew his way around late night screwball comedies Alex bit back, 'If you were my sister, I'd load the gun. Boom boom.'

Deliberately vile: 'I spat in your sandwich.'

'A Sam Peckinpah movie, right?' which wrung a feeble smile from her as she clomped back to the counter.

'I think she likes you – a lot,' Chick nodded enthusiastically.

'I've always been attractive to women with mustaches.' Corner by corner Alex investigated the layers of his sandwich, but there were a thousand places to hide a bead of saliva in there between the slices of egg fried bread, Canadian bacon, turkey breast, peanut butter and garlic cream cheese. Still on his spit search, he asked Chick to look over a list of names he'd compiled. 'The numbers on the right are what I'll ask them for, not what I'm expecting to get. Can you think of anybody else we can hit on? What about Roy Disney? They get excited about futuristic things like the Humpty Dumpster, don't they?'

Huddling in, 'I never met Roy Disney.'

'So you don't have any ideas, do you.' He took the edginess out of his voice and tried again. 'Do you?'

'In this country?'

'As long as we keep ahead of the curve,' Alex worked up a new rational case for encouragement, '*somebody* is going to notice us.'

'This is so.'

'Somebody who can see dollars out from doughnuts in.'

'Do something for me,' she was back with their coffee. 'Move your plates over so I can pour. I know him.' She dabbed her flat thumb at Teddy Fonseca's name, the first one on Alex's list. 'Is that how much the guy owes you?'

'Not exactly.'

'Seventy-five thousand dollars?' she gasped. 'Woza.'

Heidi kept pace with their orders over the next hour and a half, carting over refills of coffee and the wedges of pecan pie and more coffee that punctuated the high-tension brainstorming. Each trip turned into an excuse to drop in for a chat and fragment by fragment she put together a muzzy picture of Alex's financial challenge. 'If it'll help, I'll donate my tip,' she'd say. And next, 'That guy over there's a lawyer. You want me to ask him if he's got extra money?' And she knew a few other names on Alex's wish list. 'Baylor Lejeune, he's a friend.' Alex blinked for effect. 'You know Alba and Baylor?' 'I mean I met him,' she soft-pedaled, 'through Teddy. At his X-Baby party last year, I went with my ex-husband.' '*You* were at that? *I* was at that!' 'Oh, yeah: *yeah*. I think I saw you talking to Baylor. Strange things, weird days.' And she hushed up with something easy to mistake for deference when Alex worried out loud about 'the cost of capital' and finding a secure place 'to warehouse our stock.'

'It's the end of my shift,' Heidi tramped back to say. She caught Chick squinting in the direction of a small brunette, her heart-shaped face a smooth match for his own. 'See her?' she lowered her voice and the tone. 'She's got a crusty gusset.'

'Supreme. What's that?'

'No washee. I saw her with no clothes on. She's real ugly-looking.'

'I was just trying to see what time it was.'

'Douche time. So are you guys going to pay me now? Unless it's too big a strain on your finances.'

'We're still, um — ' Alex wasn't a tramp in a doorway who'd move on at the first tap of a friendly nightstick. 'We're not finished here yet.'

'It's the end of my shift, though.'

'I think she wants us to pay now,' Chick said.

'Oh, you want money.'

'It's a sick society,' Heidi insisted. 'Can I put these down here?' Alex's hesitation was the gap that made room for her and she added two steaming bowls to the table clutter then followed them down, plunging into the chair next to Alex. Cracking two pairs of chopsticks out of their paper wrappers and pinching a set in each hand occupied her noisily enough to miss Alex's main point — 'See, we're still talking . . . ' — and she answered him with, 'Wanna see my trick?' Heidi didn't give him a choice. She clicked her chopsticks like castanets, one pair over her rice and the other she dipped into her stir-fry, lifting alternate mouthfuls to her lips. 'You guys go on and talk.'

Alex led Chick in a quiet round of applause for Heidi's food juggling, applause for this smart-mouthing badgirl who wears her parched shoulder-length hair (this week's color bone white) cut ruler straight across her eyebrows, an inch of black roots showing, heavy eyeliner, thick mascara, making a crude event of oil-dark eyes, a trashy

46

pop princess or sword-and-sandal Egyptian slave girl . . . Under the make-up she's fighting off thirty, her complexion is corroded, peach pit scars in the hollows of both cheeks, her laugh is sarcastic and flaky, there it is, Alex can let her go without punishing himself for thinking that he'd reject a woman superficially, strictly on account of her unappealing exterior.

'What happened there?' Alex pointed at the scuffed knee that was attached to the foot propped on the side of his chair.

'Koreans, man. The old women are *hellacious*. This one shoved into me at the bus stop, I mean I was on the ground under her feet and she was pulling dudes off on top of me so she could get in first. Just pushed me down out of her way.' Heidi tamped down the edge of her scab with a wadded paper napkin. 'Everett's cool. He gave up nine hundred bucks for our *Mice and Men* costumes.' Alex looked down at his lap. Everett C. McColl, Holmby Hills, was number six on his list. 'What're you hitting on him for?'

Chick's interest in the conversation perked up, with a lateral glance at Alex. Alex raised his hands helplessly. 'Censored,' he said.

'Like in porn?' If any baloney was being served up today, she was going to cut the thickest slices. 'The editor of *Screw* put his hand down my panties in the Royce Hall parking lot.'

'No, not like porn, it's – '

'It's more private,' Alex concluded.

'So how come you're talking about it in public? Answer that one and see if your condom stays on.' Her gappy teeth chopping up bamboo shoots, Heidi said, 'I know why you do. Boys like girls watching them. You're always acting out, whatever the thing is, it's all spectator sports. Watch a man buy a car. Most hilarious thing I ever saw. Talking RPMs and blue book price. Oh, *man!*'

'How would you pick a car, by smell?' Alex asked reasonably.

'Like going to the animal shelter for a puppy,' she said. 'Women don't act out, it's between *us* and *it*. Even when we do, we don't. You know what's going on, with RPMs and chrome headers and what-all, that's cool, it's what you guys do. But me and my girlfriends, we know what's really going on. We're left out of stuff from the get-go, so we can see what shape it is all the way around, which you hate, but that's why you want us to watch. Woman is nigger of the world.'

Without even a silent consultation and deciding too fast for him to consider Chick's likely reaction, Alex pushed his list of names in front of Heidi. 'Do you know anybody else who might have some capital to invest in a totally new thing?'

'Tell me what it is first.'

He said to Chick, 'This is different. This is here, it's promotion.'

Chick shrugged off any responsibility. 'What do I know?'

Charmed by Heidi's language, the language of the natural market analyst, Alex toppled over into trust. The risk itself incited him to bring her into the mystery, to test the Humpty Dumpster's sex appeal.

Her eyes flicked between the column of names and numbers and the sketch of the Humpster on the cover of the business plan. 'You don't have Jim Tickell on your list. He puts money into all kinds of weird stuff.' Eyes up now, pulling in the room. 'Owns this hole. A computer car-pool, some Jap hotel deal. He's into it for what-all he can get out of it.'

This was Heidi's worm's-eye view of the Reverend's business practices and her insight into his deeper motives was nonexistent. He listened for God's intention to rise, as clearly as he could hear it, out of the competing noise. Around the time Bobby Dyson won the Democratic primary, JT bet the integrity of his ministry against the chance of Bobby's election.

An organized arm of the religious right in California, a creationist pressure group active across the whole state, approached JT with a political proposition wrapped in a business deal. The Creation Science Institute energetically supported all people, places and things anti-Dyson and now they wanted to add Jim Tickell's firepower to their armory. My enemy's enemy. Their foot in his door was this: the opportunity to resurrect a defunct pig farm – the very hopelessness and farcicality of it would be a hot come-on to JT. What was there for him to 'get out of it' was another success against the odds, God's personal endorsement.

For people like Heidi and Alex who only notice an impersonal, distant effect of the religious among us, the most constant and undisguised human desires become irrelevant. This changed for them, and with lasting consequences for Alex, when someone moved by such belief crashed improbably through his life.

'You know about him, you mean,' Alex said, 'or you know him personally?'

A secretive smile was all Heidi gave him before she said, 'I could try and call him up. But something, though.'

'Not that it matters at this stage, only you'd tell me if you were, like, a member of his cult or any radical thing like that. Right?'

'No, Alex, relax. I don't know him in the biblical sense.'

'That's fine.'

'I'm going to ask you for something.'

'If we get any money from him, sure, definitely. If it works out.'

'Well, I won't be your drone.'

'Tell me what you've got in mind.'

'No. You say. Tell me what's fair. A per cent?' she speculated. Then, her aim a little steadier, 'Or a fee, if that's how you'd rather work it.'

'It depends on what he puts up. Let's say I'll give you a hundred dollars cash money, minimum, or one whole per cent if that turns out to be more, up to five hundred dollars. Can you live with that?'

'Wait a minute.' She called over to Chick's brunette, 'Cherry, put the vid on record for me a sec,' and next thing she got Cherry to freeze the house camera over Alex's table. 'Zoom in, zoom it in on us.' And there they were, Heidi and Alex, framed in the top center monitor. 'It's better than it'd be in writing,' she decided. 'Okay, say the deal again.'

'I, Alex Berry, promise to pay you, Heidi Knauer, the sum of one hundred dollars American cash money – '

'You're not doing it *serious* enough,' cracking up a little bit herself. 'You have to make it sound *legal*.'

'Let it be known seriously, here's the whole deal – you get the sum of one hundred dollars or one complete per cent if that's a larger amount, of any money we can screw out of Jim Tickell, God's asshole on earth. Happy with that?'

'Uh-huh, right down to my little white cotton socks.'

Cherry zoomed in for an extreme close-up of the harmonious handshake that set the seal on their video covenant.

8   Daughter of Darkness

ONE story that Heidi began telling when she was fourteen ('I wanted the school nurse to think I was an interesting case . . . ') was that the imaginary friend she made when she was six years old still haunted her. 'Haunted' was the word she picked for disturbing effect, she only meant that without doing anything herself to encourage it, the relationship had turned more serious as she got older. Anytime she had a choice to make he was standing just behind her, mouth to her ear, suggesting the smart decision. She couldn't ignore him, his thin, pale body was seven feet tall, his long, bony face only had color in the ice blue Nordic eyes. He always spoke in a calming voice, from the other side of confusion, a slightly raspy 'hissper' Heidi called it, which had the rise and fall of a gust of wind in high branches. He wore a luminous white kaftan, angelic but non-denominational. She knew his name was Triangulon.

Back when she was a little girl, he'd have something to say about which shoe to tie first or whether she could sneak yesterday's panties out of the clothes hamper and put them on without them being sniffed out by her mother. As the choices got to be more complicated, not only strategic but moral, and the consequences more tangled ('Should I break into Mr Van Gorder's house through the doggy door?'), Heidi started to realize that any idea of infallibility was way off the point, a choice was a choice: this advantage and this trouble or that trouble and that advantage. The job of Triangulon the Existential Angel was to blow the breath on the scale that weighted the balance on one side or the other. 'I am my world' he taught her to say in a dream she had the night before her appointment with the nurse. Heidi's mission to fascinate was accomplished in spades, she was happy to hear, when Nurse Caulfield summed up their session with the worry that Heidi's friendships with actual people, based on distortion and misapprehension, sounded chronically imaginary, too.

Triangulon hisspered to her at a crossroads she reached when she was nineteen and vegetating in every mind-narrowing class she didn't cut at August Le Winter Junior College. Convinced that the wisest course was to drop out, Heidi substituted exhibition for education and pinballed around the state as a one-nite-only stripper. The academic connection wasn't shed completely, though, canny references in her act to science and the arts hoiked her a notch or two above the Kandy Kanes and Pussy Katts she'd run across in the toilety dressing rooms, dim tarts she routinely got stoned with before (during and after) every show.

In Sacramento she stripped under the stage name Rosetta Stone, and on down the spine of California, the crasser the venue the more recondite the moniker. In Fresno her *nom de danse* was Vita Brevis, in Bakersfield she performed at the U-Kum-Inn as Anna Mirabilis and onstage in Oxnard she was Stella Maris. Once even, in Pasadena, a spit and a holler away from the Jet Propulsion Laboratory, she stripped down to her mylar G-string in the guise of Polly Peptide. For Latino audiences south of San Diego she appeared as the Midnight Gaucho, teasing them with an opening view of her lumpy midriff bouncing over the pinching drawstring of parti-colored pyjama bottoms.

All that year Heidi was a creature of the night, crawling into her sleeping bag or occasionally somebody's bed as the dark was shrinking to shadows outside. Her grainy complexion drained into dismal pallor as bloodless as Triangulon's, a portrait of proud lawlessness, the bawdy personal myth she intentionally promoted. She goaded men, especially, into treating her as an unreformed hooligan, backing them into a revulsion of her that she could interpret both as cowardice and quaking respect. Faced with the opposition of deceivers, users, losers and generally sick souls whose purpose on earth was to block any chance she had of material success, what else could she do except gamble, fight and run for it.

When her ante-bellum striptease as Fleur D. Lee was catcalled to a halt by tableloads of plasterers on a half-price dad-and-lad night out, she rooted herself to the stage, hands on her naked hips, and spat insults right back at them until she was drowned out by the rising chant, ' "Spackle! Those! Pits!" ' Every grimy index finger in the room was raised in the air, a bristling massed rank pointing Naziwise at Heidi's defiantly unshaved underarms. ' "Whaddaya got there darlin'? 'Nother coupla snatches?" '

The manager of Barney's Irish Tavern O' The Towne, an overweight Londoner called Darren, sided with the mob and refused to pay her or escort her through the crowd of uncontrollable drunks.

' "Looks like hedgehogs backing out of your armpits," ' he said, with lip-curled disgust, a reaction which didn't stop him after hours from doing his darndest to sweet-talk Heidi into favoring him with ' "an expert blow-job." ' He: Help yourself to some beernuts. She: I've got to watch my waistline. He: That's not a waistline, doll, that's a coastline. This pitched her into a squinting tantrum with Heidi windmilling heavy ashtrays and assorted glassware at Darren's head, scoring a knockout ('He didn't move fast enough . . . ') with a beer bottle. 'Seemed like the right thing to do at the time. It got me my way. It got me my thirty-five dollars and I didn't do anything I didn't want to.'

Nelda Grunwald was one of the few people who passed through Heidi's life, and maybe the only one, who never victimized her, betrayed her, denied her talent or blamed her for her own unhappiness. On the first day of their acting class Nelda announced to the troupe that she was a committed Christian. ' "The only way it's going to get in the way of my acting is if other people let it." '

Before Nelda was Heidi's friend she was her foil, in class and out of it. Heidi was the more natural actress, filling out the lines she spoke with personality more than character but also with an intimacy easy for her to project in the largeness of the theater. In Nelda's acting, especially at the early stages of rehearsal, there was always a sense of her barging into her lines. Off-stage the opposite was true, Nelda was at home in the open, Heidi a gate-crasher everywhere in the world.

Their hairstyles paired them up, identical except for color, both revisions of childhood: blocked straight across the brow and the rest combed long and straight, one length streaming down to the middle of the back. Nelda's was wheat-colored, Heidi's processed dirty blonde, farmgirl and bargirl. After the good-twin/evil-twin jokes were exhausted they found that the mutual appeal, genuinely present, was their shared amazement at how different two women could be and still find so much to laugh about together. Nelda's bursts of opinion and appreciation, Heidi's sullen discontent, Nelda's stalking personal anger at life's injustices, Heidi's undisguised me-firstism, Nelda's continual effort toward decency, Heidi's persistent efforts at decadence, all out of the same impulses, they realized.

Unlike Heidi Nelda photographed badly, for the same reason that the art of acting was such a struggle for her. On the surface, under the surface, behind the eyes, in her light limbs, too much was going on to be focused on a single point. Her body was constructed to lope across the Nebraska plains, long boned and sturdy, the perfect vessel for the Big Ideas she called down out of the sky to give her tendencies depth and enthusiasms weight. From weekly fasting to sproutarianism, theater to Christianity, there was a secret flaw, familiar and reassuring, unhidden from Heidi in Nelda's emotional, cartwheeling assault on life: moments of exhibitionism masquerading as innocence.

A few weeks after they met Heidi gave Nelda an opportunity to put her newfound Christian principles to work. She needed late-night rescue from her landlord, a 'trainee rapist.' 'I intrigued him. Told him about my tattoo. *Big* mistake.' The description was all it took to inflame a forty-seven-year-old father of three, who boxed Heidi against her bedroom wall and, breathing sourly down her shirt, urged her to think of him as a reasonable man when it came to the collection of back rent. He nearly broke her legs when her strength gave out and she fell to the floor where he went on pulling at her skirt, clawing at the waistband of her tights. She showed Nelda the welts on her hips.

In the middle of the night she turned up at Nelda's door, bedraggled, homeless, impoverished and alone. Heidi sheltered in the guest bedroom and stayed on as Nelda's roommate. That first long night though, fueled by cinnamon toast and coffee, trading past and present secrets, Nelda told Heidi that she was dating Jim Tickell. I can just imagine the impact of JT's gigantic certainty on Nelda's questioning spirit and fluid mind.

She didn't trust her attraction to him, she said, because before it started *for real* (Heidi assumed Nelda meant before she started sleeping with him), JT told her how his first marriage ended, when his wife and ten-year-old son were killed in a car crash on an almost empty road in the middle of a sunny afternoon. Nelda had trouble reading her own heart, which felt divided against itself, half wanting to be the woman JT deserved, who outweighed the tragedy, and half wanting him because he didn't really need her in that way. 'We were like sisters,' went Heidi's story. 'I always want the men who confuse me.'

Their sisterly closeness darkened into claustrophobia, at least for Nelda. In her photo album she used a note from Heidi as a caption under her snapshot: Heidi's hair is a nest of tangles, a cigarette is stuck to her lower lip, her eyes are half closed and her grungy flannel shirt is half open. The note reads: 'I'm sorry you made me suicidal last week. Can we talk PLEASE?'

Heidi inherited the apartment for six rent-free months when her roommate moved out to Jim Tickell's house in Burbank. The only occasion that Heidi had a chance to meet JT was the night he dropped by with a U-Haul trailer and a wiry little man called Munro, to help Nelda move her things. She offered him her concept of heaven. ' "It must be like a party, everybody having sex without touching. Something to make up for all the shit we go through down here." So he's like, "With God's help we can do something every day to change that situation." ' Heidi was a rock of unbelief. ' "The world is hell, is my opinion," I told him, "so what difference does it make how we act in it?" '

As an illustration of the meaty corruption of the human life-cycle and the only sensible reply to the dependable way that human experience never fails to disappoint, Heidi invited JT to look at her tattoo. First he wanted to know where it was on her body and when she told him he said, ' "Well, no, I'll pass. I'm not a prissy-assed man, but you'd better just describe it to me." ' The seven words in Roman capitals followed a gentle arc above the flat funnel of her pubic hair: ABANDON HOPE ALL YOU WHO ENTER HERE.

Chick peered at her. 'You've really got that?'

'I'll show it to you sometime.' To Alex she said, 'Do you want me to call him up right now?'

'Do you want to do that?'

'I need two more quarters.'

Alex fished around in his shirt pocket and located three dimes. He looked to Chick. 'Can you give Heidi a quarter?'

'Da kine, bruddah. Means no washer for my pump gun today.'

'Ask Gilbert for it. Moan while you loan.'

Heidi frowned directly at Alex, fenced out of the action. 'Is that a private joke?'

Cherry was busy on the payphone when Heidi got up to make the call. She stabbed a glance at their manager then whispered a short message in Cherry's ear upsetting enough for the girl to make a fast excuse and hang up the phone. Before Cherry made it back to the counter to hear, 'Problem? What problem?' Heidi was talking to the Information operator. Alex watched her jot down a number, jam in a few dimes, dial that number, jot down another number, dial that one

. . . On his way over to her he was more convinced with each step he took that this partnership was a dangerous idea.

He had a thought he wanted her to consider. 'Are you sure that Jim Tickell really wants to hear from you?'

'Be *quiet*,' Heidi shut him up. 'It's ringing . . . '

9   The Opposite of Oblivion

NELDA walked into the den, into the cell of a penitent. JT was up on his knees in the middle of the floor holding open in both hands the blueprints of a barely surviving, dilapidated, orphaned pig farm. It filled his view. She walked in on a scholar's digs, the unkempt shelves, the mounds of overdue library books and periodicals, research documents, drafts of reports, detached chapters of his unfinished dissertation lying loosely in reach, a crawl away. She walked into the nursing home cubicle of a by-passed writer, quarantined now, a compulsive magazine subscriber, or JT had turned his room into a beach cave where the tide washed in and deposited all of this wrack, the blankets twisted across the sofa and coffee table, the plastic tumblers and mugs on the desk, the dishes heaped into the well of the chair, and her husband's shipwrecked body, too.

'Pretty soon you'll need a map to find anything in here, huh?' She tilted down to peck the top of his head, describing her visit with an undemanding kiss. 'X marks the spot.'

'I know what's where.' To prove it, he pointed out the different heaps and bundles. 'Those are books. Those are letters. Those are more books. Those are books and letters in one pile together.'

'It's me, honey. I'm not the big bad wolf.'

'Am I ignoring you? You spoke, I spoke. We're engaging in a conversation.' He offered up a jangled smile. 'I'm sorry. Sorry. Okay?'

'I'm on my way to the market. Any special requests for dinner?' She was going to get through to him but she wasn't going to implore.

'I'm out of Fig Newtons.'

'You can't just live on cookies. If I brought home a barbecued chicken, would you eat that?'

Nelda felt pushed into being the sensible one, to haul him back. 'It's just food we're talking about, Jimmy, you're safe. Can you talk to me for a few seconds about what you want to eat? You have to eat protein, besides Fig Newtons.' Looking back at him through the door she thought that even his ordinary perceptions were different from hers, his skin must prickle from the pressure of her entering the room. The view she had of him, framed in his temptationless pit, was of a man not becoming but reverting.

With his eyes shut, focusing on the horizon of Heaven, approaching it across the black vacuum of space, he couldn't see past a glory of colored light. The piercing brilliance of it ignited pinwheeling shimmers in the corners of his eyes, fibers of silver-rose-amber-copper, colors of heat, webbed the rind of his skull . . . and with his eyes open he saw the bright fog descended, with a shape cocooned in it, something earthly, useable, throwing a shadow through the glare.

The noise that reached him from someplace outside was the telephone ringing on his desk. If he could see the bare wires, see the current pulsing through the phone lines, the fluttering trail of electric yes/no would have led him to the pay phone in the Global Video Café where Alex and Heidi were waiting for him to answer.

'Pick it up, Nelda!' JT called into the rest of the house. 'Pick up the phone, will you? Please, Nell – I'm not here!'

Stopping for a strict-nurse glance down at the invalid laid out on his back ready for therapy, Nelda answered it on the eleventh ring. With her hand muffling the mouthpiece she said to him, 'Yes you are, Jimmy. You're definitely here.'

Two

FOR THE EYES
ARE THE SCOUTS
OF THE HEART

1   Mercy Meat

IF Alex had struck a route to JT two years or even a year before, my
judgment is that their connection would not have lasted any longer
than their telephone call. Playing at the top of his game then, Jim
Tickell wouldn't have seen any heavenly gauntlet flung down in the
shape of a college boy scampering around campus, doing classroom
and textbook business. The Reverend was used to turning around
other men's commercial failures, milling profits against all the odds,
pitting his durable physical strength, his canny intelligence and taste
for extreme risk against God's faith in him and his in God.

Against everybody's advice except the Almighty's, JT sank every
penny of his capital into a bankrupt sportswear company. One year
later the jogging craze quaked across the USA. Department stores,
sports boutiques, mail order outfits, all of them made money with
Wendywear. Even the Japanese capsule hotel deal, which looked like
the shakiest speculation he'd ever walked into, turned out to be one
more reversal of misfortune. Every gamble that God beckoned him to
take only dramatized how JT was blessed and favored, each business
victory counted for much more than its banked gold.

The history of JT's slide into the unhousebroken condition he had
reached by the time that Alex entered his life began around the date of
his marriage to Nelda. It was only the most public and flamboyant crest
in a spate of changes which tore at stretches of his self-certainty and
washed over him with cleansing doubt. Perhaps without Heidi's
unflinching exploitation of Alex's search for investors, without Alex's
thirty cents for the phone, JT would have failed with his pig farm. Or
he would have gone off to be an astronaut or a beachcomber in
Borneo. No: history is what happened, free from any course that was
or wasn't changed. And Alex wasn't a bystander in JT's fight back, he
had a part in, and I'd argue he benefited more than anyone from, the
Reverend's short-lived revival.

Here is the history of JT's brave disintegration. It begins,
coincidentally, when I entered as a silent and impotent party to these

events. Perhaps converging momentum is an illusion and that is the only meaning. But Alex did tumble through graduate school, through Odo-bags, through Dinu, through Humpty Dumpsters, through Heidi to Jim Tickell, and down those same two years Jim Tickell tumbled through a rough landscape of his own to end up talking to Alex on the telephone about pig farms and Humpty Dumpsters. Before that conversation, two years before it, these things happened, the narrowing track of JT's way down.

Jim Tickell's audiences always behaved with the confidence of a majority, back-slapping insiders whose secret knowledge boiled down to a single law: if they only persist then the world outside will either come around or wither into the ground. I hovered at the back of the long room, transparent among the golf course retirees, elementary school teachers, franchise managers, businessmen and women, young husbands and wives who didn't have to struggle to say what's normal, the overclass, Los Angeles white folks. They welcomed each other as robust, finished examples of a living moral code whose noblest demonstration was this allegiance to Reverend Jim Tickell. Right-thinking, he taught them, raised them up to see over the heads of the stooped remainder of deluded humanity, and by a natural dynamic process gathered them to his church.

The regulars who filled the rows of folding chairs to attend his live telecasts from the Worldview Life Ministry studio were never very convincing as colonists of a frontier outpost, which was how Jim Tickell described his people to themselves. It was easier to see them as a happy ship's company, sailing toward the edge of the flat earth in nose-thumbing defiance of untested, conventional belief. The nautical suggestion may have entered my mind by way of the décor: the studio lights blasted forward from the side aisles and sealed any natural light behind the floating drapery of a broad bow window, so in his high-backed chair the Reverend appeared to be ensconced in the captain's quarters of a brigantine.

Forty rows away I could see him fidgeting with his lapel mike and picking through the clutch of newspapers fanned out on the floor around his feet. The two tiers of Faith Operators were already at their telephones answering pledge calls, but no monitor showed the activity, every one of the screens framed Jim Tickell in close-up. Not even that multiple presence, though, was his most wizardly quality.

The sound of his voice filled up the space, even unamplified, it heated the air, it comforted and challenged us with the Christian truth.

'I'm going to tell you about the rats scurrying around behind the headlines. What's in the world today that wasn't here yesterday?' JT flung back the front page of the *Wall Street Journal*, squinting at it through his half-moon reading glasses. 'Some people think . . . it's fine if I talk about the miracle of the Red Sea . . . but I get booed from the bleachers if I say water is wet . . . Say again?' The newspaper came down, the eyebrows went up. 'Are we going, Tommy?'

'On air, sir,' from someplace around the cameras and cables.

'I'm the last one they tell anything to. You better be serious.'

'Yes, sir.'

'You better be right.'

'Yes, sir.'

'You got your cameras switched on?'

'Yes, sir.'

'All five of them rolling?'

Five shots of the stage flashed up on the screens one after the other, three of JT and one each of the Faith Operators and the house band. 'Yes, Reverend,' Tommy said, lifted on the gentle wave of our clapping and cheers. We enjoyed the teasing as much as he enjoyed JT's cantankerous affection.

He fluttered his fingers over his mike. 'Is this on?'

'Yes, sir.'

'Do you know Jesus?'

'Yes, sir,' a few of us called out together with Tommy.

'Then, I guess we're going.' He didn't read from *Die Welt*, *La Stampa* or *Le Monde*, usually handy for foreign headlines or on-the-spot summaries of quirky articles; he didn't read from the *Financial Times*, the *Los Angeles Times*, the *Washington Post* or the *Wall Street Journal*, either. He spoke to us as if the idea just that second rising behind his eyes was part of a conversation we'd been carrying on with him since yesterday.

'Unless your last name is Mayflower you only think about the Pilgrims and Plymouth Rock around Thanksgiving time. I don't know what the Puritans were so pure about, purity didn't feed them or heal their sicknesses: *the red man did*. You'd figure God would have blessed them with favor more directly if the Puritans were purely good Christians preparing the world for the Second Coming of His Son.

Instead, He sent them the trial of a killing winter and deliverance in the form of the human compassion of the red man.

'We're in Malachi 3:6 today. *I am the Lord, I change not.* God's intentions toward us are *constant*, I want you to grab on to this one idea. It's the only predictable aspect of every event that's recorded in God's Book: He doesn't abandon us unless we abandon Him. The changes in the world today aren't any different from the changes going on in the world before we were born. Change is the constant feature in human life and it's where God wants us to find our faith, to see Him in surprising places. He surprised Saul on the road to Damascus, He shook up the Jewish world and the Roman world with the teachings and the Crucifixion and the Resurrection of Jesus Christ. How many could see God's hand behind those events at the time?

'He surprised the suffering paleskins by working their physical salvation through the unsaved natives. You get my point yet? The red man taught those people the trick of planting dead fish under their corn. That harvest was bountiful. The Christian colony survived and their descendants survived and only returned the gift of salvation to a remnant of the natives. In Salem, Massachusetts they had a trick to teach the red man. I'll quote you their exact words: "Voted: that the earth is the Lord's and the fulness thereof; Voted: that the earth is given to the Saints; Voted: *that we are the Saints.*" They did *that* instead of recognizing God's way of saving souls.

'The rock core truth that even self-anointed, self-appointed *saints* can't camouflage is God's presence in action, it's where you see God in the flesh, *after* the moral choice has been made. I'm asking you this question. Where do you think you see His presence strong enough to make you rectify your motivation?'

JT gave us three or four starkly quiet seconds to dredge up our private replies, then he trumped us with his: 'In marriage. Marriage puts flesh on God's main intention, it's the way human life goes forward, where it recreates itself in love.'

Three toll-free phone numbers rolled up onscreen while he stared out at us, a satisfied clarity settling in his eyes, watching his people catch up with his message. The softly brushed sable hair fountaining up from the crown of his head, rippling and crashing down over his ears, was a loose bouffant that would have looked effeminate framing a less majestic face. On Reverend Jim its effect, especially in close-up, was astonishing, it made him appear to be descending from the clouds. In his coarsely trimmed beard, that smoky bush, there was an earthier authority, enforced by the fun poked at it by the ironic sparkle rising to the surface of those steady brown eyes and by the tilt of his wispy eyebrows that quietly announced that he was uniquely undeceived and undeceivable. Then, the unexpected spontaneous smile to remind us that wisdom is a private joke that he and the Almighty, lofty pranksters, have been sharing every day for the past fifty-nine years. Before he said another word he cocked a black baseball cap on his head. On the peak, embroidered in silver letters, was the motto ZEITGEIST.

'Certain Christian ministers I notice were on the four o'clock news today, getting down on their knees. You think they assumed that position to pray to God, well *they did not*. It was only so they could keep their pants dry when they leaned over on all fours *like an ass* to shove their handsies and feetsies into some wet cement out on the sidewalk in front of the Chinese Theatre over on Hollywood Boulevard. Yes. Maybe they ought to lean back over the opposite way and put some more relevant aspect of their anatomy into cement for posterity.'

He let our spiky laughter die down, joined in with it mildly and shifted in his chair, with a brand new issue on his mind. 'I've got a special request to ask of you, I'm only going to ask it once, this one time. Tommy, pan over and look at Nelda. Go on. Get Camera 3 off of me and . . . Focus up, let's go, let's get there, Tommy, you're wasting my precious airtime.'

The camera found her for us, chin up, posing uncomfortably, her skein of girlish hair spilling down over a print dress that started as a lace collar under her chin and ended as a lace hem near her ankles. Nelda sat on the edge of the bandstand, right underneath the drummer's high-hat, kicking her heels the way she did when she was a little girl on a playground swing, back when Richard Nixon promised to bring us all together in his first term. Our memories of romance slopped out of us into a spreading pool that swamped JT and flowed thickly across the room to his best girl.

'I want to show you all Nelda, my intended bride. Not only intended as in going-to-be but intended as in *meant* to be. Let our wedding be a living example of Christian love, an antidote to pre-marriage contracts, empty hearts and aimless loins. Starting with this special event and with His blessing through our children, our family line, we're going to magnify God. Share it with us, that's what we want, we're in the business of building faith. Okay. Maybe you can guess how big our electricity bill is going to be for a location broadcast on this magnitude, so you can earmark your dollar donations just by writing the words – Wedding Appeal – on the envelope. Everybody wins, see, from God on down, if you say, "Yes, I want this to be the Christian commerce between us." Down in the world money is the meat of mercy and it's going to be a mercy in the highest if my family and I can enjoy your company at the wedding banquet. The sorry part is we can't set a date for it until we know we've got fifty-five thousand dollars in our Wedding Appeal and as of right this minute I know for a lead pipe fact we're fifty-four thousand and nine hundred and fifty dollars away from our goal. For every tithe of twenty-five dollars we'll send you a personal invitation to our wedding party, so, please come. Join us, will you, the other two thousand one hundred and ninety-eight of our faith circle who want to hasten the day. I'm finished asking now, I'm waiting. I want to hear from my Faith Operators that the first thousand dollars is pledged in . . . '

Publicly Nelda stood elevated in the Worldview crowd, honored first for her marketing innovations (the single-project Faithathon series was her idea and brought her to the boss's attention), while privately JT distinguished her from the small crowd of women who had secretly appeared and disappeared at odd times in the long wake of his wife's death. Choosing Nelda meant making a deliberate move in an unknowable direction, a conscious separation from the obligations of past tragedy as well as a swan dive back into it. Where her predecessors showed JT the cushioning, muffling pliancy that they assumed he expected, Nelda offered him artless, persuadable resistance that tested the emotions behind his ideas. With her the Reverend didn't have any choice but to think about his life as it wasn't, her questions, her own open-hearted needs kept JT's thoughts in motion.

Nelda's youth, too, attracted him strongly, tilted him backward across the starting line. Physically, Ruby Tickell (née Bethune) was Nelda's polar opposite – small and dark haired, her downward-slanting brown eyes carrying a permanent and misleading look of wounded disappointment – but in spirit the two women echoed the same shout of loving dissent from a man's inborn priorities. So Nelda was a reminder to JT of the young husband he had been, when he had a clear view of the kind of man he was because of the woman he had courted and won.

JT sank into silence, gazing into our hearts as the toll-free numbers came back onscreen. Behind him, off-camera, his band strolled through a bouncy jazz number of 'Jesu, Joy of Man's Desiring' while he made us contemplate his deliberate speechlessness. To the golf course retirees he was a son in a bind; to the franchise managers he was a brother calling for a crucial boost; to the young husbands and wives he was a stubborn father who'd only admit that he needed their help if it was a matter of life or death; and I ignored his bribe, I was cold to his emotional blackmail, but his bargaining touched me in such an intimate way that along with everybody else, I couldn't bear to disappoint him.

The Shrine Auditorium is a 1920s Hollywood pastiche of a Babylonian palace, a homage and fiction harking back to two imaginary golden eras, ancient and modern, and *ipso facto* the ideal backdrop for the Tickell-Grunwald wedding reception. Two thousand two hundred of us shuffled in through the lobby where, packed around the arches and columns, Worldview Life Ministry laid out its bazaar – commemorative plates, T-shirts and silk screen portraits of JT and Nelda, mass-produced keepsakes advertising the achieved destiny of their marriage as though it was the fulfillment of an ancient prophecy.

The souvenir I took home was the specially produced video tape of the wedding ceremony. In spite of the fact that their exchange of vows had been broadcast to the 1.7 million homes of the American Christian Network and any slacker with a VCR and a blank cassette might have recorded it himself, the added attraction of a twenty-minute video tour through all the private rooms of the Tickell family mansion truly justified the tithe of $55.99. Sometimes surveillance gifts drop out of the sky into our hands.

They had the tape playing on a 54″ screen mounted on a plinth in the middle of the lobby. There she was, reciting her verses again underneath a bridal veil that draped her like a mild snowfall. Only Nelda's hands were open to the air, otherwise she practically disappeared into her wedding gown, a massy architecture of crinkled satin and lace with the proportions and approachability of the Matterhorn. 'Love is as strong as death,' she told JT. His eyes held her captive, her eyes were doves, honey and milk were under her tongue, his lips were lilies, her lips were scarlet thread, her breath as sweet as apples, they enclose each other in the rapture of the body . . . And for the finale the view of the bride and bridegroom at the altar faded into

an image of a rippling American flag which faded into a portrait of
Jesus in glory. Lightheaded celebration, heavyheaded reverence, JT's
wedding, more than a thousand hours of faith drives, epitomized our
convictions and confirmed our assumption that for an unwavering
Christian today no concessions are necessary.

They arranged the high table up on the stage, under a white linen
canopy. The buffets around the auditorium, humbly uncanopied,
were set just as lushly with dramatic presentations of food. Bowls of
California dates and olives, raisin cakes, stacks of pita bread, honeycake, terra cotta urns of wine, plates of carp, mullet and perch, it was a
biblical feast that managed without a miracle to feed the horde in
authentic style: the caterer depended on an Israeli archeologist from
UCLA to prepare a menu of ancient home-cooking that would tempt
any first-century Roman or Christian in off the street.

Munro Fyke's eyes flicked between his plate – where he was mopping
up a puddle of olive oil with a heel of bread – and JT at the far end of the
table – where he watched for a gap in the conversation. 'I'm going over
to the Reverend for a minute, okay?' He was wedged in next to Aunt
Queenie, the eighty-year-old sister of JT's daddy, who was too confused
by her Cappadocian loaf and dab of lamprey roe to face any other demand
on her attention, so she just pretended to be asleep.

'What's this, now?' As Munro handed over a package the size of a
basketball, JT slid his chair out, almost kneecapping him.

'I couldn't get it to you on time.'

The pink bow was a sloppy ornament knotted around the pinched
neck of thick white butcher paper Munro used for gift-wrapping, a
dressy detail that only pointed up the hobbyist's practical priorities.
'Oh . . . Oh, hey, look at that.' JT was geared up for delight before
the glass-domed case was halfway unwrapped. 'Just look at what
Munro did for us.'

Seeing the thing, a startled laugh gushed up from Nelda's throat. The
hug that she wrapped around Munro's shoulders folded him inside a
good-humored, protective pity. 'You really tried, didn't you. I wouldn't
like this if it came from anybody else.' She tapped her mother-in-law on
the arm and nodded at Munro's gift of a pair of turtle doves perched on a
cedar branch. Ma chirped at them as if they were alive.

'That's the female, there.' Munro tapped the glass near the bird
whose sleek head was dipped as if sensing the approach of danger.
'And this one's the male.' Her mate's head was arched over hers,

steadfast, eyes alert but not alarmed. Here was Munro's trade and faith combined: Christian taxidermy.

The birds were meant, of course, to symbolize this husband and this wife, to evoke the ethereal purity of their love along with its earthly character. It was that last angle that broke up Nelda, who knew she was too much of a Valkyrie to blend in, even with her metal breast plates and horned helmet in mothballs, and the nervous fragility of the bridal dove only reminded her how hard she had to work at it.

'You got them at the peak of their love,' Ma said, dipping her own sharp beaky nose at them.

Munro was glad his artistic intention was so clear. 'That was what I wanted.'

'They look alive as anything,' JT said, jarring the table as he stood up. 'I'm going to go and mingle with the masses.'

Munro steadied the lip of the glass case. 'Hope you can find a nice place to put them in your house.'

'I'll let Nelda decide on that one.' Chuckling, JT effortlessly pried himself away.

'When Jimmy was a baby, maybe two years old or less,' Ma told them both, 'we had this terrible thunderstorm.'

Munro knew this chapter of the Tickells' saga. 'When the family was all in Indiana?'

'A real loud electrical storm in Indiana.' Ma handed down the oral history. 'I heard him squealing in his crib, raising a racket, so I went into the nursery room and what'd I see? Jimmy was standing up, holding on to the rail and pointing out of the window. He wasn't screamin' and cryin', no, you know what? Every time he saw a stroke of lightning he laughed right out loud at it, out of plain happy-natured joy. "God, Ma! God!" '

' "God, Ma!" That's right,' Munro backed her up.

'Pointing up at it, up at the sky. And after every big explosion of thunder, too. Very peculiar for a little boy.'

'Specially blessed.'

Nelda said to them both, 'I'll put our birds in the wrong place and he'll move them to the right place. He justs wants it to *look* like I make all the household decisions.'

'Munro,' Ma half turned his way, 'you're going to get bored stiff by this, but there's something I want to talk about to Nelda.' She didn't wait for any kind of answer from him before she launched herself into private conference. 'I've got a little worry, honey, that you can help me do something about. I know you don't get your ideas on clothes from French fashion models, but listen to me woman to woman, where the vital organs are concerned. Your turquoise skirt.'

'Ma, it's mid-calf.' Nelda wasn't sure what she was defending.

'The sneaky evil of it is you've got to support the weight of it all on your hips. It presses on your internal organs and drags them down. It's double the gravity on them and you know what's next: your abdomen muscles go weak, you curl over like an old lady, your lungs get cramped and then the door's open to pneumonia.'

'I feel fine in that skirt.'

'That's an invitation that goes right into Satan's ear.'

JT stopped at the bandstand to request 'Moon River' on his way down into the crowd. Gladhanding his guests one by one, stopping to accept a toast, then pushing on with a selfconscious urgency to plunge into another clump of friends and fans, answering questions about his honeymoon, the current strategy for Worldview's expansion and, obvious to me, dodging his father. Mister had been a gloomy presence since he arrived, saying very little but conveying the chilly sense that he had more than one reason to be with his son that day.

JT lifted his hands in goofy surrender when Mister caught up with him, allowing the old man to herd him into a corner behind the wine urns. 'Okay, Daddy.'

'Don't want to rain on your parade, Jimmy.'

'Wait on it, then.'

'When Bobby Dyson calls time out, I will. We've got to get something down on paper by ten tomorrow morning. Where's your head at?'

'Daddy,' JT looked out over the packed room. 'It's my wedding.'

'Let's talk about that. Who'd I have in the office last night?'

'Tell me who.'

'Oh, representatives of representatives. It's still informal. I traded a few ripe expressions with the boys who put the *inform* in informal. They showed me a copy of your catering bill.'

'They got that?'

'Just forget about any restraining order, and that's the time of day from Judge Bower direct. Our transmitter gets shut off voluntary or not at midnight on the thirtieth of the month.' Mister shook his head, dryly amused by a passing thought. 'They're mean and nasty but they're not real smart. I'll tell you what else I got from Dyson's pet hebes. He's running for governor in '90, so just think about how *that's* gonna stack up.'

'The only person two miles outside of Burbank who knows who he is,' JT said, finger on the knowledge, 'is his mother, and she'd vote for him anyway.'

'Jimmy, he doesn't have to win it to stink up the atmosphere. I think he wants to ride Worldview into the primary, jump up and down on our backs the whole way.'

'What did Lenhoff tell you? Is his station coming up with any airtime worth spit?'

'It's worth about that. If you would've come down to that meeting – '

'Can you give me the short version?'

'Four hours a week, late night Monday to Thursday, and that's gone up to sixteen thousand and change, but Lenhoff's not going to shake on it until we give up our d-lists.'

'We're not doing that.'

'I told him it didn't affect him at all, our problem is our problem, but he said he got some friendly free advice on the subject from Bobby Dyson's lawyer, and he got it before breakfast.'

'How did they know you were talking to Lenhoff?'

Mister said, 'Something else we got to work on,' his voice almost cracking with the effort he made to strain out any queasiness. 'Just want to keep a hold of it.'

'They're trying to scare us, draw the lines, Daddy. That's all they can do.'

'I want them to realize we're no kind of a rinky-dinky outfit they can just boss around.' Mister stroked back a cord of white hair that shook onto his forehead. 'Hebe Number One, that Olansky, he told me First Amendment isn't any protection against fraudulent solicitation. *Fraudulent*, Jimmy. I mean, what's the protection against a state official who misinterprets the facts *on purpose*?'

'Those words will turn to ashes in his mouth.'

'You know it.'

'We won't go down. Other people go down.'

'It's been that way.'

'There's easier times coming, Daddy. There were easier times for us before.'

Throwing a fast glance over his shoulder, a view that covered his family up on the stage, covered eighty years in half a second, Mister said, 'That's right, when the world was young.'

2   Moby-Pig

THE mud in the yard disturbed Munro's sense of justice. In the hottest, driest week of the year, when every scrappy patch of grass in town was a fire hazard and dust filled up the cracks split like lightning bolts in the sidewalk, the square flat yard of Hummingbird Farm swam in cakey black mud six inches deep. Cutting across it, the wheels of Munro's jeep churned up fresh furrows in the slippery paste, along with the sharp smell of slurry, brown juice that never stopped leaking out of the slotted end of the growing house. On a rough calculation he figured the daily waste matter of fifty pigs only added up to part of the wet mess, most of it must be seeping through breaks in the water pipe that fed the main block. If digging up that faulty pipe was too much of a job for Olin Mulley, who had been unwillingly deputized as foreman when the Creation Science Institute inherited the farm, why didn't he at least report the problem to the Water and Power people? Give us this day our daily waste.

Olin's new white Buick stood out like an iceberg where it was parked next to the farm office. It had to be Olin's car, tagged with the same bumper sticker on the back that he attached to every vehicle he owned: 'God Said It, I Believe It, And That's That!' With Olin just an uninsulated wooden wall away, it wasn't going to be easy to pack up the hide without being interrupted. Munro scuttled into the shed as smally as he could, just to get a head start on flushing out the preserving tray; he might even make it through the second rinse by the time Olin walked in on him to 'supervise'.

The skin fixed without a blemish, a true blessing since any crease or doubling would be twice as noticeable on a pelt as evenly white as this one. Because an albino Poland China boar was a rarity, Munro had to have the pink glass eyes custom-made and this was typical of the intricate care he invested in his best work. As he stretched out the whole skin on a clean plastic sheet he was already thinking ahead to the background he was going to paint for the diorama. It would definitely be a view of Hummingbird Farm, but if Munro came up with solid reasons to capture it as it actually was, two seconds later he came up with a host of different reasons to present the ideal farm it could be.

'Is that you in there, Mr Fyke?' Olin's slap-happy hello from the other side of the wall, followed by a frisky shave-and-a-haircut knock dotting his way across the room.

'It's me, uh-huh.'

'I was hoping I had a burglar in here,' Olin said from the doorway. 'So I could shoot him for trespassing. *Bang*!'

Munro looked over and found himself staring straight down the barrel of a broom handle. 'Careful when you put that down. If you kick up any dust it'll be real hard to clean it out of the nap.'

Hands stuffed apologetically into the pockets of his slacks, Olin tipped up a little on his toes, showing an interest. 'What stage are you at with it, Munro?'

'Far enough to take it home with me.'

'You can take the smell of those chemicals with you, too. The sheer odor of it, it's been getting me high.'

'What odor's that, Olin?' It was a clean smell of borax and it always reminded Munro of fresh, laundered linen, and the cleanly stinging camphor fumes underneath only carried the whiff of a liquid razor.

For a few seconds, while Munro concentrated on rolling up the five feet of skin neatly in its plastic sheath, the only sound they heard was the woofing and squeaking of the pigs across the yard. 'All week they've been making more noise then usual. I think they smell what's going on with Moby and now they all want to be immortalized, too.'

'Just a minute, Olin. Let me just do this.' In rubber gloves and an apron that would give practically anybody else the look of a surgeon, Munro looked like a butcher. He sank into his stature and even appeared to grow smaller as you talked to him, as if flinching away, retreating into the distance. His face led and his body followed, his gravedigger's face, too thin, hollowed out, unsurprisable eyes pushed unreachably deep into their sockets. He could darken a mood without trying and it was an effect he had even on his friends.

Packing up and joking over now, Olin said, 'You know it's Ving's party on the seventeenth.'

'It'll be done for that.'

'Want some money?' Up on his toes again, white belt pinching his chubby tummy.

Olin got his reply in a sparky little grin as Munro squeezed past him cradling the boar's remains high in his arms. Ten minutes went by before he correctly figured out that Olin wasn't coming to the car with his check, which made it impossible for Munro to weasel out of the longer conversation he had made a blunt effort to avoid.

'Next time maybe you could do us a couple like that.' Olin stretched his freckled arm toward a poster stapled to the wall behind his desk. '*Makin' Bacon*, shoot!' he read it out loud, the gag tacked onto a rib-tickling photograph of a boar humping a sow. 'Maybe for my and Carmen's wedding anniversary. Will four twenty-five do it for right now?'

Munro folded the check into his wallet. 'The other half COD, all right?'

'Whatever, sure. So what's the big man busy with these days? What's the inside news?'

'JT's sitting on top of the world.'

'I mean about the FCC complications. Is he yanking their chain or are they yanking his? Tell me the inside news.'

'He doesn't talk to me about it, not really.'

'Saves it all up for his wife, I bet.'

Munro looked away. 'Well, we don't talk about that concern,' he experimented with diplomacy where politeness flatly failed.

'Don't you talk about anything when you drive him around?'

'We talk about baseball, Olin.'

Olin respected the warning and relaxed. 'Is he putting money on the Angels this year or the Padres?'

'Oh, nobody. We just listen to the games.'

'He keeps his personal business to himself, I guess.' Olin gave this the whisper of a commiseration. 'It'd bug me though, driving with somebody else in the car and just listening to the radio, not talking about anything.'

'I didn't say we don't talk *at all* in the car.'

'It'd bug me, that's the only thing I'm saying, Munro. If I was somebody's friend and he kept his most important troubles to himself. Important enough to make it into the newspapers.'

'He doesn't ask me about *my* personal work. It doesn't mean a lot to me, Olin. It don't mean boo to a goose.'

The nickel he spotted on the garage floor, wedged halfway under a bale of excelsior, put a thought into Munro's mind as he walked over to pick it up, a thought he spoke out loud: 'For money's sake. It's five more cents than I thought I had.' And back at his workbench, picking up the scalpel again, splaying the macaque's arms and legs for a ventral incision, he said, 'You know it keeps the bills off my back. But I do love it, too.'

At any time God could tune him in like a radio station and that made any utterance a prayer. Nobody ever only talks to himself, he always has God's ear, so a Christian man is always on trial, minute by minute, every decision is a test of his moral fitness. If a stranger wandered into the garage (the way the man from the phone company did in 1985) he'd make the usual mistake and see a room full of death or some kind of a torture chamber, but Munro worked with the truth of it: this was the place where he restored life.

From a point below the ribcage to a point between the legs, down the straight length of the shallow cut, Munro's hand felt guided by vibrations under the skin. The pads of his fingertips on the scalpel's solid handle picked up the texture of separating tissue quivering up from the edge of the moving blade. *My sensitive hand.* In thirty years, thirty thousand incisions, it never split open a bowel, it never hit blood in an animal as big as a monkey.

Skinning is an ugly process, intruding into the passive anatomy, why pretend it's something else? With one of the legs popped out of the loosened vent, Munro scissored the knee joint, then again on the other side and freed the skin above the hips. The noose already hung at eye-level from its pulley, prepared for Munro to loop it over the flayed haunches and hoist the carcass by its rump another few inches in the air, abducted from the bench top.

Five fingers on each hand but I'm the one with the opposing thumb. 'That's why I'm up here and you're down there . . .' Munro picked around the base of the skull with the tip of his knife, unzipping the scalp, using his fingers to feel for the root of the ear. 'Snip, snap' – twice – and when the skin was peeled from the sides of its face he tucked his hand inside the tented hide and found each pair of eyelids, poked between them, sliced neat arcs around the edges and guided the cut downward to the lips, close to the teeth of the monkey's upper jaw.

'Animals have feelings but not souls. Humans have sin and crime.' Attached at the chin and nose, the mask of its inside-out face gawped back at its own skinned body as if harrowed by a need to speak to it, to howl at the sight of his shape inside, the shape of his own putrid meat, the squalor of the part of him that's rotting away to filth. *This ugly stage is just the foundation, a necessity that will get us to the beautiful finish.* Doting, Munro strained his vocabulary to locate the right word to sum up the jeopardy he shared with the macaque, deciding on 'companion' but actually meaning 'harbinger'.

'Any animal is more beautiful than any man or woman in one way: you don't know about time. You're innocent the way a child is.' Right after a half-hour break for the eleven o'clock news and with four doughnuts and a cup of instant coffee in his stomach, Munro laid out his tools for an all-night assault on the artificial body of the great white pig. The bones had been dried and wired to the plywood center-board for a week, posed on its sloping oval base next to the door to the kitchen as if it was the guardian at the gate of a pig burial ground.

The labor was sculpture in reverse: instead of hammering and chiseling the body of a pig out of a lump of rock, Munro reassembled each sinew and muscle out of soft wire and shredded wood, cartilage out of dental plaster. 'You'll be beautiful, boy. Better than when you were walking around.' He stepped back across the room for a full and final view of his six hours' work. 'You look pretty beautiful now,' waiting for its coat of clay, the fine modeling of flesh arrested in the middle of action. Munro's eye could catch and recall the twitch of a snout that was ready to sniff a mate or food or a threat. 'I'll fit your skin on you on Friday, there, Moby. And you'll be a whole pig again.'

(More whole than Munro thought, in fact. The special pink glass eyes were fitted by a small company in Van Nuys. While the animal was there overnight I spent three hours implanting a camera, transmitter and battery pack in its skull, a wide-angle quarter-inch lens in one of its eyes, a microphone in one of its ears and a six-inch antenna twisted into the pig's nasal cavity. The set-up had an effective range of a hundred-fifty yards, probably three times the strength of a pig's actual sight and hearing.)

Arrested action but not restored innocence, that's a supremely human beauty, and temporary. Munro saw it once in the flesh, bouncing a volleyball in a school playground, counting the bounces, her unaware, extreme clarity, *Six years old of age and blonde mop head curls*, only before he saw her in life he didn't picture her playing with a volleyball. *I'd model her exactly how she is, with her face turned up, the way how good girls listen to a teacher they love.*

'I couldn't do that.' Munro shook the tableau out of his imagination. He wanted to say that he didn't mean he couldn't do it because it was beyond his artistic skill, he meant to say he was fit to be a Christian, fit for God to console his doubt. 'Father, correct me with all of your power and force, rectify me. You know my wild thoughts. I just want to thank you for Thy mercy unto me and everybody, and just, I want to tell you I desire for it to continue. I want to say Thou comprehends my spirit even when I do not and how I personally love all of Thy creatures like they were my own, especially human children. Amen, amen. Amen.'

3 'Woe to the bloody city of Los Angeles!'

ONE visitation seized JT in public, on a Palm Springs golf course. Double vision and a cloudy, toxic ache in the back of his head dropped him to his knees on the seventh tee, and since his father had heard him say so many times, 'God doesn't care if I birdie this hole or eat my five iron,' Mister knew that he wasn't keeled over down there with his head in his hands praying for a putt. The first words JT said when he woke up in his bedroom four hours later were, 'God wants me to buy that electronics company in San Jose. Personal computers are going to be *real* big, *real* soon.' On the rock of those staggering profits was erected Worldview Church – its television ministry, its viable earthly franchise, its divine guarantee.

Apart from the first time, JT was always alone when he was visited by these mysterious fits, usually at dusk or dawn, when contrasts inescapably press in. Before the first sparks started whirling in the corners of his eyes, before his spit went watery and metallic in the back of his mouth, he breathed in the damp smell of grass cuttings from the wet lawn outside and when the pain started JT thought the smell of moldy leaves was coming from his skin.

From two bright points flaring at the root of each eye this pain reflected spines of light up behind his forehead. Friction, heat, the glowing circuitry veined from the back of his skull, visible in the darkness of his cupped hands, and when he stood up to reach for the ice bucket he saw the room around him, desk, chair, window, newspaper, fountain pen, all of it breaking up, obliterated by the pain.

With ten fingertips pressed against the sides of his head, spots as tender as rotten fruit, JT felt the movement of his breath in and out of his mouth, he pictured the physical reality of the thunderhead of pain foaming through the layers of brain tissue, an irresistible fact with a grip on his attention tighter than any coil of his imagination. A slight warmth covered him, a presence in the room as solid as the pain; as implications clarified into obligations the pain and the presence renewed his contract with them, *endure this and speak in the name of God* . . .

This was the new text. *The word of Lord God came to me* . . . I'm putting words into your mouth, because I'm smothering in pain. Each time I talk to you I want to howl out, 'Change this!' or else I'll leave you forever . . . Remember Myazumi . . .

The office was dark when JT levered himself up from the floor and the present reassembled itself: first in a highball glass half full of tequila and vanilla and then in the clear plan he now had for the one hundred and sixty-five unused insulated pre-fab modules in storage downtown, leftovers from last year's Japanese capsule hotel deal, cocooned in plastic, without a knowable purpose until today.

The call went out to the white buses, in ordinary times the milk-and-cookie fleet, to round up the curb creatures. At each stop between City Hall and the canyon beaches, limbs and faces poked out from the litter of cardboard boxes and greasy blankets heaped up in alleyways or strewn like storm damage across sidewalks and dirt lots, colonies of the displaced clinging to the face of the earth. The ones who refused to collapse into optimism, the stiff-necked veterans who'd watched clean-up campaigns parade out of the sun and then, drums beating, on into the sunset, resisted the invitation to climb aboard and believe that JT's Faith Girders were bussing them to a place just an hour away where everybody would get 'a mansion of his own'. Skepticism being the last foxhole and first principle of individuality, the new poor who selected themselves for the bus ride to Burbank arrived there relieved to hand over their doubt and fear of the future to the judgment of a good shepherd who was offering to take charge of their welfare.

'Do you want to use a toilet?' Ma's greeting to each bundle – man or woman – rolling out of the bus to stand blinking in the gritty heat of the Worldview parking lot. She poses the question in a way that makes it sound as if she's not sure that they know what a toilet actually is. 'Do you need to use the *toilet*, dear?' her arm lifted toward the row of chemical johns tucked around a corner of the main building.

Instead of (or right after) the toilet visit, Ma steered them over to the twelve-foot-high, seven-foot-wide, one-hundred-twenty-five-foot-long structure raised on the grass behind them. Top to bottom its façade was gift wrapped in a banner painted with the words, *What you bind on earth shall be bound in heaven.*

The parking lot was starting to clog up not only with the milling homeless, but with news crews from local TV and radio stations, Worldview's own cameramen and at least one network reporter whose feathery blonde hair-do Munro recognized from the back, a bus length away. Working a path around her, he caught the drift of her report on 'the most lavish of Reverend Jim Tickell's social action stunts'. Scanning the brownish tide of home-grown refugees slug-gishly pooling, she latched onto her angle and rehearsed her punchline. 'If the poor are always going to be with us, at least some of them can stick around in style. For Eye Witness News, I'm Chrissy – '

Mister stepped back from the office window to give JT a full view of the developing carnival outside. 'In front of the bus. See her?'

'Sure hope they put the emergency brake on.'

'Ricey Krispy didn't come out here to do us any favors, count on that!'

'Crespi, Christie Crespi.' JT fixed the name, bled out the triviality.

Munro said, with identical seriousness, 'Chrissy. Not Christie. She pronounces it Chrissy,' handing over the warm stack of Xeroxed press releases.

'I'll let her interview me. She's not too bad. I think her news gets a twelve rating and a twenty share. If they use it at six I bet it'll get on at eleven, too. What else, Munro?'

'There's just too many of them, I didn't have enough numbers.'

'I'll get those army tents put up on the back lawn.' Mister geared into the problem, waving for Munro to come along with him.

'No, wait on it. How many extra are we over?'

'At least forty-five or fifty,' Munro said.

'Uh-huh, well,' JT sized up the emergency and decided, 'that'll make a *loud* point.'

In the viewfinders, straight-backed, waiting to speak from the long steps of his neo-colonial headquarters, JT's poise demanded presidential comparisons. Nobody watching him from behind a camera or from the roof of a bus would have flinched at all if he had raised his right hand, sworn his oath of office and delivered a speech of prophetic conviction straight to the heart of the nation. That image only faded slowly while he spoke and never entirely lost the charge of anointed authority.

JT flashed a picture postcard at the crowd. 'I bought this in a gift shop in Century City. Here's what's on it, it's a color photograph of the cardboard ghetto, a ghetto of cardboard boxes *where people live*, and in big sunny letters across the top it says ''Greetings From LA'', can you beat that? Misery is a tourist attraction now. I'm going to mail this postcard to the state senate with a personal message on the back: ''Wish You Were Here''.' Riding out the applause, he handed the card to Chrissy Crespi and away from the microphone he said, 'Chrissy, maybe you can do me a favor and drop this in a mailbox on your way back home to Beverly Hills.' Then to the crowd he sang out:

'Woe to the bloody city of Los Angeles! To a place where the ones who fight the hardest to live are entombed in their degradation, woe to that!' 'You don't want to hear this, Californians, Los Angelenos, especially you homeless street trash, it hurts, this terrible knowledge. Good. Pain means that *something* is happening, it wakes you up. Pain makes you pay attention to what's causing it so you'll *do something* for relief. That's the time when the world changes, see, because you want the pain to stop. The way Jesus felt the torment of us all, so he went out on his ministry. He knew that frightened, hungry, homeless people can't reach any higher than their hunt for safety, food and shelter, there's no morality without all that. The state of California runs the thirteenth biggest economy *in the world* and every time you turn around you see more people on the lowest level, punch drunk. We don't live in a Christian society, not yet. We don't live in a so-ciety at all, it's a sui-ciety, thanks to the hairy knuckle brigade, the stiff suits up in Sacramento who don't have the nerve to expose themselves to any real pain and even if they did, they don't have brains big enough to do much about it.

'Daddy? You got that ready to go over there?' From the middle of the lawn Mister raised both of his arms, each one ending in a thumbs up. Worldview workers scattered to grab the half dozen ropes dangling from the wide banner strung across the module wall. To the lucky number holders corralled by Nelda and Ma into a muttering parade along the edge of the lawn, JT announced, 'Welcome home, welcome home!' The banner jerked, snagged, fluttered and fell, and the stack of hard-shell single occupancy 'homeless pods' stood waiting for its buzzing colony to pile in.

Seen from high ground the confusion fanned into a picture of crazed freedom as breathtaking as the Great Oklahoma Land Race, but down in the swarm where Mister and a squad of Worldview ushers were trying to match up numbers and pods, it was more like a game of musical chairs played by the deaf and blind. But further inside, in the beige sarcophagus behind the bamboo slatted opening the size of an oven door, with the single bed, air conditioning, ten-inch TV set, reading lamp and mini-bar there was a kind of stillness, a blind quiet that came close to privacy.

Munro heard his name barked over the PA. 'Bring those people over here to me,' JT cued him. The podless bunch pooled around the steps where JT met them. 'Lord. How many of you have we got?'

'There's forty-four, Reverend.' Munro handed him a list of their names. 'Thirty-three males and eleven females.'

'Somehow, *somehow* we're going to fix you up, all of you. Stay here with me. I'm going to make a few calls in a minute and see if I can get my hands on a couple dozen army tents. See, we're in a fight,' JT rallied them, 'against the do-nothing potato heads in government offices – city, state and fed, so let's circle the wagons. They're going to fight me on this, they just hate to get ashamed by somebody who they despise. Don't worry about it. I predict they'll send the goon squad over to rip down your army tents and unplug our homeless pods, but that's nothing, all they've got on their side is earthly power. God's moving through this.'

Camera rolling, focused in, Chrissy tackled him on it toe-to-toe. 'When did the city issue permits for housing on this site, Reverend Tickell? Do you have permission to set up so much temporary housing?'

'Would I have to get permission from a pencil-neck in City Hall to shelter people after an earthquake? It's *emergency* housing, get the nomenclature right. Let them clamp down on me with their man-made zoning laws or health and safety ordinances, whatever they want to try, and we'll find out what's *temporary*.'

'But if you know the city won't allow your shelters to stay up, then how do you feel about putting these men and women right back out on the street again?'

'I won't be doing that.'

JT stepped out of range, with Chrissy flinging her indignation at his back. 'It's not your responsibility, is that what you're saying? If you know in advance . . . ' and she found herself talking to Munro, plainly flabbergasted: 'He knows *in advance* these shelters won't be here *two days* from now.'

'Maybe he does, I don't know what he knows. But the reason he knows things in advance is because God tells him what to do and when to do it so it'll always come out all right.'

'All right with Jim Tickell on top, the people's choice.'

'Guarantee it. The Reverend could make a believer out of a monkey.'

Rational observers, and many of them only hereditary Christians far outside the Worldview community, watched the hectic parade of events that followed and read into it all convincing, vivid evidence of divine management. The connection was unhidden, the connection was Jim Tickell, and the demonstration was his glaring success. His Faith Drive netted $220,000 in under four hours of telecast from the 'tent city' crammed onto his back lawn, and after that newspapers from the *Los Angeles Times* to the Sacramento *Bee* ran as many stories about his direct action on homelessness as they did about his running battle with the Federal Communications Commission. Inside of three months the state initiated a pilot program in cooperation with the community of Palmdale in the Mojave Desert, a refuge for over three hundred of the Southland's dispossessed. The state treasury funneled money through TransCare out of a matching fund which also paid for all one hundred sixty-five hotel capsules, sold to TransCare by JT at cost. They were re-erected in double rows next to the same number of reconditioned mobile homes on ten acres of scrubland.

Another interpretation, less mystical, might be that these develop-ments were connected to a meeting in the office of Assemblyman Bobby Dyson, underway five hundred miles up the spine of the state in

Sacramento at the time that JT's Faith Drive was ringing out across the airwaves. Bobby listened keenly to my assessment of the situation but stopped me short of any deeper analysis of what might be the Reverend's hidden ambitions, satisfied that he could divine those himself from the tape edits and transcripts I let him see.

On questions of practice and strategy he took the counsel of Marty Olansky, a constitutional lawyer he'd met at a Democratic fund raiser during his maiden term in the state assembly. Their friendship was cemented by a strong feeling of common cause. Marty too was a Berkeley alumnus, one college generation younger than Bobby, who found his way through the protest years to the American Civil Liberties Union, from there to Fritz Mondale's staff, work on the Gary Hart presidential run and finally, worn out from the effort of straining nobility from the pulp of defeat, he joined Bobby who had chest-beatingly sworn to Marty after his third re-election, 'I'm going to keep on doing what I can do.'

As I was coming to the end of my synopsis, to stress the point about JT that he thought I was making, Bobby leaned across his desk, stiffly silent, and turned up the volume on the television so we could hear the Reverend's 'self-serving horseshit'. Bobby said, 'It's his personal shanty town. He put a shanty town in the San Fernando Valley. Burbank isn't Rio de Janeiro, it's not Ethiopia! He's just shameless.'

'Sub-standard, inadequate sanitation,' Marty checked off. 'You can start right there. The county can close it down and clean it up on Thursday.'

'Three more days of this?'

'Well, what else do you want to do about it, Bobby?' Marty stretched his lanky slat-slided legs under the coffee table. 'Wipe him out with a SWAT team?'

'Jim Tickell is *not* going to call this play.'

'The site's in violation, which is a local problem. You don't need to do anything about it.'

'And he'd hug himself to death over that,' Bobby said. 'It's immoral. It's a distraction, Marty. He's trying to win the case in public and drag us down into it. If I do something or if I do nothing, you understand?' Impatient with his own logic, he started again. 'I'm not going to give him what he wants.'

'Which might be what he wants.'

'That's wonderful.' Bobby caught his full-length reflection in the dark window, the lineless, beardless face scowling back at him, the body still slender and athletic, a cross-country runner's shape, looking young enough still to pass for a college boy under the rumpled unparted hair. 'I need a haircut.'

Marty had to keep his eye on the higher good (cheating the cheat, exposing the sham piety, the massive swindle, e.g.) to quiet his conscience when it came to my research methods. He said to me, 'How did you get that material in his office, Jack? I can't exactly feature you crawling into the building through a window.'

'It's just a matter of timing,' I said. 'Waiting.'

'But when you're inside, I mean when you break in, how do you find your way around in there so fast? Someplace you don't belong.'

'Marty, if I tell you I'll just spoil the magic. The main thing is to plug in and exeunt as quick as I can.'

'You don't like talking about it. It just seems to siphon off so much of your time and energy.'

'Jack doesn't mind,' Bobby said. 'It's what he does instead of fucking.'

'Is it?' I said.

Bobby dropped the subject. 'Are we finished talking about the Tickell thing?' We both nodded. 'Marty, you're going to have to let him know what we're in a position to do. To him and for him. It's got to go when and how I say.'

'I think that's the situation he's after,' Marty suspected.

'Jack, you can keep an eye on things in LA, right? Let's not provide Jim Tickell with any photo op of a ''goon squad'' marching around his property. I'd rather French kiss him than make any crackpot prophecy of his come true.'

4   Blessings of Sugarbush

GLANCING up in the middle of a phone call to see Nelda smiling to grab his attention, Mister stopped her with the feeling that she'd just walked into the wrong room. She pushed herself past that uneasiness by talking over it in a hurry as soon as he dropped the receiver back into its cradle. 'Can you talk to Tony Orr? He's acting like lord-god-king over every little bit of Wendywear Sports Day. You come up with ideas and he asks you to write them down and then he just thinks they're his from now on.'

'Is that what he's doing, you think?' Mister sympathized, with patient reason. 'He knows he's got to take final responsibility and maybe you're reading some wrong stuff into that.'

'But he just sits in his office all day changing the plans. We're not at Grant High anymore, as of this morning we're at North Hollywood High. I had to talk to the fabric lady because he didn't. And bills he told me we already paid I found out are overdue by a month, so now I'm not sure I can get all of my orders in on time.' Nelda could hear herself, the way she sounded to him, wound up and inept, her legitimate complaint unraveling into nervousness.

'All right, Nelda, I'll call him up. There's no problem.'

'The baseball shirts are so cute, Mister. With a patch on the back in the shape of a baseball and you know the stitching? It's in the shape of a Jesus fish,' she said. 'That was my idea.'

Before she was finished telling him that the discount she got on the flannel meant the shirts could retail for under thirty dollars, he said, 'Over at Wendywear you're standing for the family,' the unsaid sharpness of his point being, *Don't waste your family privileges.*

'Everybody's been raring to help me. They like to hear my ideas.'

'You'd just rather not work with Tony Orr, is that it?'

'When I start something I like to see it through.'

Mister scratched a few words on a notepad, a doctor writing out a prescription for a simpler way to participate in affluence. 'Are you done with your decorating up at the house?'

'Not the finishing touches yet. We're still waiting for the kitchen wallpaper. And the blue carpet for the stairs.'

'As long as Jimmy knows he's not living in a warehouse,' grinning the message into a kind of joke. He tore the page off the pad and tucked it into her hand, his grin softening before it faded.

'I don't know this one by heart,' Nelda had to admit, reading the title he wrote down. 'Thirty-one, ten to thirty-one.'

'Hey, don't worry, I'm not testing you on it. Read it when you got a minute. Proverbs might be my favorite book out of them all. At least I think it is whenever I'm looking at it. Read it over when you're settled down at home.'

'If I'm complicating things at work it's because – '

'Well, I don't believe you're doing that.'

' – it's because I can see what I can do. I mean that's different from – '

'I think you're almost perfect, Nellie, you're over halfway. You're out there on the forty-nine-yard line. I know you've got the good sense to run Worldview's balls in the right direction.'

Out of his audience, out of anonymity and into his arms. Nelda's romance with JT mirrored her feeling about Christianity, which mirrored back her precious knowledge of him, infinitely. Her secret worry, though, when she started with him, was that religious excitement oversexed her. In bed together all of her concentration was on the moment, which wasn't filled unless she knew that she'd narrowed all of his concentration into that inescapable motion.

On top of her, he pushes Nelda's legs apart with his knees, he nuzzles her breast. 'Neither shall they say lo here!' he intones, and he kisses her nipple. 'Or lo there!' He lurches up, strains into her. 'For the Kingdom of God is within you! Aah, Lord, Sugar!'

Before they were married he prodded her to chatter about her family, to rummage through the memories of her homelife. His questions helped Nelda remember how she'd felt about her father's weakness for female coddling, her mother's (and her sister's and her own) dancing attendance on him, selfless love tiring into self-mutilation. When the talk turned serious like that, it was a way, she thought, of showing JT that her papers were in order, that she wasn't another suburban dropout shopping for religious bargains at Salvation Mall. She had left her family to marry him, to follow Jesus, her Christianity was the genuine article.

Alone with him in their bedroom the semi-stardom of her public life with him drained into the background and Nelda felt the risky reward of marriage, strange knowledge of the unimaginable, distant and completed future reaching back into *this*, this moment of theirs. Somewhere out in the afternoon Tony Orr was tapping his computer keys, undoing more of her work while Nelda was out of that action, here with her husband, coated in the light that bled in through the living-room drapes, wrapped around JT, naked on the floor. The blue carpet set off the silverwhite hairs on his chest, it cushioned a grown body, a man's body twenty-three years older than hers. When she thought about his age, its bare number, it only made her think of time moving and then that because of him she had less fear of it.

With her hands on him, one massaging his chest and the other reaching for his cock, the coarsest part of her pleasure was the illusion of tampering with him. The flesh in her grip, the thickening bone, tampered with her — its hardness made definite demands, its own pleasure was unrefusable, outside herself. *Is my sweet pussy that way for you?* 'Let me feel you there — oh, uh-huh,' his dirty-old-pervert chuckle, 'there's dew on the bush . . .' Excited by what she was doing to him, she wanted his hardness inside of her now, to hang on to the fact of it. Nelda spread underneath him, grabbed his hips, guided him down, his breath over her face, 'You know I'm a fountain of love for you, my sugar baby,' arching up and rolling onto his back. 'You do it, the way you can do it with your mouth.'

JT already had the NaturaLamb out of its wrapper and Nelda let her mouth fall open, ready for him to feed it to her. Eyes wide, the skin-colored disk of the condom behind her lips, it was the head of an inflatable sex doll that fell on his veiny organ, and then it was his own Nelda rolling the sheath down, lips pushing, tongue smoothing, sealing him in. *He tells me I am his own.*

Looking away from her, he didn't know, couldn't guess, that all the time she was pulling him inside, wildly grabbing at the backs of his legs, clutching his back, stroking his face, gasping out the only words she needed to say, 'Look at me, oh . . . I love you . . . Kiss me, *kiss me* . . . oh, I . . . ' two overlapping fantasies were thrilling her. In one she was spread underneath him on the living-room floor, spilling words from her heart, stroking, clutching, wildly grabbing, pulling him inside, with no condom cutting her off from his bare dick. In the other they weren't alone in the room, a watcher or watchers pressed in on them, saw her do these things, heard what she said. *God wants to see His will incarnated, this purity is an offering to the Unseen.*

In Nelda's fantasy, an offering; in her understanding, acceptance. In my eyes, she was overacting.

5   Assistant God

MUNRO was suspected, he was sure, of leaking Worldview's
confidential donor and disbursement lists. He'd felt breakable
all week, just a shout away from an avalanche and now with the
Kimmels slamming their car doors outside, Olin was torturing him
with wrapping paper. Ving Kimmel was celebrating ten years as Vice
Chairman of the Creation Science Institute, Oswald Pogenpohl's
deputy, the Doctor's chosen successor. For all of the above reasons
(and for another one besides, about to come out), Olin commissioned
from Munro a de luxe tribute in the shape of an artistically posed,
handsomely mounted albino pig. Thirty feet of pink and blue crepe
paper *Congratulations!* surrounded by gold foil cherubs and bells lay
unspooled on the floor, junked in a heap in front of the alcove in the
living-room set aside as Moby-Pig's nook of honor. Munro kicked and
tramped a path through it, not sorry at all for the painful confusion he
caused.

'It won't look like a *present* if we don't wrap it up.'

'It makes him look cheap, Olin.' Munro, on his knees, nudged the
animal into the window-light where bright flecks of it caught in its
eyes.

Olin watched the front door. 'But then he's gonna see it right when
he comes in.'

Pointing at the foot-high maple railing that Olin carpentered into
that corner of the room, Munro said, 'It's not exactly a surprise, is it.
Okay, let's go with that four and a quarter. You've got to pay for your
pleasures.'

'Hey, are you going?'

'Yeah, bud. I've got barbecue spare ribs at home.'

'We've got food here, plenty of stuff. Macaroni salad, got a
raspberry Jell-O ring . . . ' He counted off the plastic wrapped dishes
lined up on the card table while he patted his pockets, frisking himself
for his check-book.

A second later the house was mobbed with voices. Ving's two little
boys, miniature adults in gray slacks and navy blue blazers, let loose

after four hours of church, sprinting over to ogle Moby, had to be corralled by their big sister . . . The women, Frances Kimmel and Olin's Filipina wife, Carmen, made straight for the kitchen, heads bent together to prevent a bad-mannered explosion of private laughter . . .

And then, 'Way hey, Oleo!' Ving roamed in bedecked with joy the way his living-room was plastered with crepe paper. He met Munro with a frat house chumminess, sort of showy and male. Like his flat-top crewcut and varsity handshake, it was a deliberately positive attitude that could be (but wasn't) a braying triumph over some crippling childhood disease. 'You've got a fine hand, definitely, Munro,' he said, petting the pig's snout. 'It's a marvel. It is, it's a killer-diller.'

Ten years of hustle in the service of the Creation Science Institute had taught Ving that the power to persuade rested in the outward respect he showed to outsiders. He pretended to remain open to their knowledge and judgment so that out of courtesy and fairness they would hold themselves open to his, a tactic he used in public debates against evolutionists around the country with a fair share of success.

Crouching down, Ving noticed the pastoral landscape that Munro had painted for the background. 'That's Hummingbird Farm in the back, is that right? All cleaned up?'

'I used my imagination a little.' Munro wanted him to see the storybook meadows, the grain silo, the gabled farmhouse and its hog-shaped weather vane, the oak trees, tractor and hay wagon and appreciate that this figment had moral substance.

But Ving read it unsymbolically at first, concentrating only on the farm, the thing that it could be in the world, in time. 'The damn place doesn't deserve to fail,' he said quietly, and honestly, Munro thought, because Ving seemed to be talking to himself. 'I'd like to know how you did it,' politely baffled, straightening up. 'It's a beautiful piece of work. God's got a sixth sense about choosing certain people for certain tasks.'

When Frances handed him the telegram that had arrived while they were out, Ving read it at arm's length so that Munro could see it at the same time. The Doctor sent *Fond love, sincere congratulations, eternal thanks to my favorite warrior*, the sum of his feelings wrapped up in ten words exactly,

'Is Dr Pogenpohl going to be here tonight?'

'Oswald's in Omaha this week. Sweet man, he's a sweet man.'

Ving smiled at Munro's interest, catching the hint that he knew something about the Doctor's work.

'I went to a couple-few of his speeches,' Munro said. 'I listened to him talk about the prophets, out in Van Nuys when I lived there.'

'Have you ever heard him teach on Genesis? On the Noachian Flood?' Munro never did. 'Catch up with us, we're doing some things. Not like you, though, not like Jim Tickell. He deserves all kinds of respect.'

'You said that right.'

'Even if those meatheads in the Missouri Synod want to lynch him. That's an *endorsement*. Those guys lollygag around as if Lord Jesus just endorsed *them* so what else do they have to do, right? Best thing would be if we were raptured out of here today and we left the world to the ones who are of it, but second best until then is doing something that makes our time worthwhile.'

'Jim says that.'

'Well, there you go: something we've got in common.' Ving hooked his arm around Munro's shoulders, gave him a pally shake. 'How does he turn that stuff around? Every single one, a bullseye every time. Man oh man, one success right after another one.'

'He's just blessed, in my opinion. They're his blessings.'

'I bought one of his computers when they came out. You couldn't beat it for the price, it was the best PC on the market. And Frances has got half her side of the closet full of Wendywear clothes. She must keep that whole company in business. What did I hear he's into now? Hospital supplies?'

'Two years ago. It's old news. Jim sold that off.'

'Right, after that. I'm thinking of the home-shopping thing.'

'We're out of that.'

'Maybe he can give us a hot tip on the stock market. He's a real investor, right?'

'Reverend's a financial whiz, sure.'

'I'd give anything to know what Jim Tickell thinks in private.'

Munro looked away saying, 'I'd like to know that sometimes, too.'

Of course he noticed her before Ving pointed her out, his lanky daughter, stilted between her little brothers who thought twelve-year-olds were grown-ups and the adults who classed her as a slightly over-qualified child. She served Kyle and Joey their snacks, mopped up their spills and came out of the kitchen again on her next assignment, offering around a plate of cheese cubes.

'Say hello to Mr Fyke, Kimmy.'

Her greeting was, 'Would you like a piece of cheese?'

'What you got there? Orange cheese, that's cheddar in my experience. What's the white one?'

'They're both cheddar cheese. Mom got them on sale.'

While Munro gnawed an orange cube off its cocktail stick, Ving more or less bragged to Kimmy, 'You see Mr Fyke's best friend on TV, honey.'

'What channel is he on?'

'Reverend's on Channel 40 at the moment. You watch him? Reverend Tickell?'

'Oh *him*.' Right away she understood this was pretty impressive so she bugged out her eyes for a second, stranded, acting amazed. 'He's your best *friend*?'

'Maybe if you ask him, Mr Fyke can get you his autograph.'

Suddenly on the spot, Kimmy leaned her head into her father's side to be spared any more special attention. Planting a kiss somewhere in the loose caramel brown strands, he teased her, hoped she wasn't going to melt into the floor, and this gentle off-stage push got her talking to Munro again. 'Would you, please?'

'Sure you don't want mine instead?' And Munro joined in, chuckling under Ving's raspy laugh.

Kyle, the six-year-old, wandered back for a fast hug around his daddy's knees before asking him for 'a ride on our new pig' and inched back silently toward Moby when he got the disappointing answer he expected. Olin flashed a goofy jack-o'-lantern face at him, routine therapy for depressed minor Kimmels judging by Kyle's happy yelp, and chased him back into the nest of women on the other side of the room.

'Olin's a crazyman,' Ving goodbuddied. 'Do you have any kids, Munro?'

'I'm not a married man.'

'It goes fast when you've got them. Kimmy's going to start junior high school in September.'

'It'll be a few years before she's got to make any big decisions, you know, about what to do,' Munro guessed.

'I already know what I'm going to be,' she said. 'A veterinarian. In Africa.'

'Lots of animals in Africa,' Munro sure had to agree.

'Means she has to study a bunch of biology and general science and I'm worried there.'

'*Daddy* . . .' She knew what she'd just opened up.

Frances called him into the kitchen, the ham was done, so Ving gave in for the time being, 'Don't get me started on *that*,' fending off the temptation, 'or I'll *never* shut up about it!'

'Kimmy is not, definitely *not* going to Africa,' Frances said for the record, tugging her husband by the elbow. 'In Africa the native children make dung toys. Can you believe it? They make little dolls of hippos and horses out of dung they pick up next to the rivers or water holes or whatever. Patty-cake with dung – yuch!' wrinkling her nose at the dismal and silly backwardness.

The dinner table was set for a formal event with wagon-wheel place mats and a creamy white linen tablecloth. Ving stood behind his chair and welcomed his family and friends to theirs, waiting for them all to do as he did before bowing his head. Eyes closed against even this wholesome distraction, he bonded with God. 'Heavenly Father, bless this day as I know you have already and this gathering of your people. I just want to thank you, Lord, for our food today and the ten years of blessings you've poured on me and my wife Frances and our children Kimmy, Kyle and Joey. Thank you for the loving guidance of Oswald Pogenpohl who led me into the ways of you, God. Also I ask your blessings over our brother in Christ, Munro here, who used the skills you gave him, of picture painting and taxidermy, to add more beauty to our world, and bless his colleague Jim Tickell who creates wealth where there was unfruitfulness, multiplying your blessings . . .'

The amens went up around the table as woozy eyes opened, Munro thinking he'd missed out on something; they all appeared to be waking up from a refreshing nap, smiling benignly at each other – and at him – as if they'd just stumbled out of a dark room. Ving stayed on his feet, carving the honey-roast ham, a sturdy, modern Dad in his diorama of Early American furniture, calico curtains, stacks of plates and spread of steaming casseroles, reigning over his household, the shelterer of his mate and nestlings.

'Who wants grape soda?'

All three kids pushed their hands into the air, squeaky liberty that prickled and deflated their mother. 'Oh, Ving. Not with supper.'

'This time it's all right. It's a special occasion.' And his more direct reply to her, 'I have *spoken*.'

Carmen passed the can of soda to Munro, who passed it to Kimmy; Carmen's plump, stubby fingers he compared to Kimmy's, cleanly tapering, very warm on the cold can. His plate of food was there in front of him when he glanced down, and with his thank-you, in the same breath he asked Ving, 'What does Dr Pogenpohl say about who's allowed into the highest heaven?'

Olin said, 'Hitler could be there. Adolf Hitler could.'

'Adolf Hitler?' Munro's mild dare, 'I never heard of that.'

'If he repented. Maybe he repented in the last five minutes.'

'It's not as if everything he did was wicked and evil,' Frances said. 'He helped toward the end-times. He turned the Jews to return to the Holy Land, which has to happen and it did because of him. The next Hitler has to turn them to Jesus.'

'There's an Arab Hitler over there, probably,' Olin said.

'How's an Arab going to convert all of those Jews?' Frances spooned up her apple sauce, working on the concept.

'Only have to convert 144,000. That's not so much,' Olin summed up. 'The rest get destroyed, so maybe the righteous Jews are all in this country and Israel gets it with a nuclear bomb.'

By this point Ving was finished listening to the discussion. 'I've got some of Oswald's books I can give you to read,' he said, looking down the table to Munro as if the two of them were the only sane men present. 'Now let me ask you something about Jim Tickell. How does he tackle the propaganda machine of the liberal humanists?'

Munro shied away from the challenge to nail down any strict policy on the subject and stuck to, 'Oh, he just, you know, socks it to the bureaucrats any way he can. Bobby Dyson doesn't give him headaches. Do you mean Bobby Dyson or the, um – '

'What I mean is,' Ving kept going, fueled by his own message, 'when Kimmy walks into Portolá Junior High School she'd be committing a crime if she prayed in her classroom and from eight-thirty in the morning to two-thirty in the afternoon she's going to be force-fed the religion of evolution.'

'I know of a good church school in Canoga Park,' Munro suggested as if this solution had never occurred to the Kimmels.

Ving made it clear that it never interested them. 'Why should I spend my money on a private school when I'm a taxpayer and there's a public school system? Why not try to change it, as the saying goes, we live in a democracy. Darwinists believe in spontaneous generation. And that a human being is just the highest form of animal life there is. My kids are going to come up against this big lie in school from all of their teachers and I'm worried about it. They'll hear how stupid it is to believe God created everything in six days, we're descendants of parameciums not the special creations of God, so don't worry, it's all right if you behave like an animal most of the time, you can't help it. Christian beliefs get mocked in public schools and the only thing they've got to put in their place is a very low view of human life. You probably know this already, the Bible says the world can't be more than ten thousand years old. Okay. Did you know that science verifies that fact but the top scientists won't let it out?'

He stopped there, pulling Munro into the gap. 'If they know it's the truth, they should say so.'

'They won't release the data. Before, it was the Big Bang. Now that's gone, that's a thing of the past. Now they're telling us all about galaxy clusters and galaxy clumps, so we're supposed to believe the universe is an infinite onion now instead of a doughnut. Thank you, Dr Einstein, for clearing *that* up! Thanks, Carl Sagan!'

'What? That's *ridiculous*!'

Frances dripped acid. 'They lie through their back teeth.'

A block of static buzzed between Munro's ears. He was being clobbered by ideas and conclusions that were stubbornly not forming pictures in his mind, they were beyond his intellectual reach, but the implications found the dead center of his emotional grasp.

Ving dropped his voice, spoke to Munro man to man. 'We could really learn something from your boss over at Worldview. When he sees the kind of social affairs dictated by state officials Jim Tickell really knows how to grab non-interested Christians and wake 'em up. With a bang and a boom.'

While coffee was being percolated and cake sliced for dessert, Munro quietly cornered Olin. 'Have you and your check-book been reunited yet?'

'Oh, right. Here it is,' he said, scratching in the numbers, sounding pained. 'I had it on me the whole time.'

'Cheer up, bud. You're not losin' your life savings.'

'I'm not – oh, look, it's not this. I'm thinking about Carmen.'

Munro craned around Olin for a look and didn't see her. 'She's lying down in the bedroom,' Olin told him.

'She looked a little vomacious halfway through her Jell-O.'

'She's pregnant, is why.' He cut off Munro's next comment with a smile of sudden innocence, aimed elsewhere. 'Hi-ho, Kimmy.'

'Hi-ho, Mr Mulley,' and that out of the way, riveted by the albino pig, she came right to the point with Munro. 'How did you make that?'

'You want all of the steps?' She nodded she did. 'Does your daddy let you stay up till midnight? I'd be explaining it to you all night.'

'Where's its skeleton? Is the pig's bone structure stuffed inside with the straw?'

Well, Munro had to take her seriously. 'When you model an animal you've got to take away all the flesh, all the tissue that rots, the muscles and whatnot, that's what bulked the body into its shape. You've got to build all of that up again. With a mammal this size, yeah, you mount the spine on a wood cut-out, connect up his legs with wire so you can pose him exactly how he'd be if he was alive. Then you have to get into plaster and rubber molds to do all the details of his body to make sure the skin is a perfect fit. You want to be able to lay the skin down so it doesn't stretch sharp over the joints. Like here, see?'

Kimmy was concentrating, bouncing her knee against the wooden rail. As Munro crouched down to show her the seam hidden behind Moby-Pig's hoof, her bare lower leg was only inches from his face.

'You've got the correct relationship of men to animals there in a nutshell,' Ving approved, arriving with the coffee. 'I wish our pigs understood it.' He made a sincere effort to sound spontaneous when he wondered out loud, 'Hey, speaking of that, do you think Mr Tickell would come and take a look at Hummingbird Farm? On a business level, give us the benefit of his advice on it, you know, spread the circle of his blessings?'

'He likes a challenge, for sure. It's his main enjoyment, but I don't want to say yes or no for him. You know his father used to raise pigs about a hundred years ago. Out in Indiana.'

'Maybe it runs in the family. Can you ask him?'

'I probably might,' Munro said, thinking ahead to his restored merit, his impurity forgiven.

6 After the Gadarenes

ONE lonely thought scampered around inside Munro's skull after Ving's party that night, it flashed in and out through the patches of light and shadow in the passages of his brain, frantic footsteps that kept him awake. As he sat up in bed reading (for the fourth time) the first chapter of Oswald Pogenpohl's *Steps to Scientific Creationism*, even his difficulty in understanding the technical arguments was a sign for him to be patient and ready, a sign in a web of signs that imposed shape on the incomprehensible: Munro was being pushed along at the head of a procession of events that included JT, Hummingbird Farm and Oswald Pogenpohl. The Sign of the Pig stood out as the clearest message homing in on him from the distant Heavenlies, and to accept the unforced interpretation required a brave act of realism.

It was April before Munro persuaded JT to drive out with him to consider the redemptive potential of Hummingbird Farm. In the car on the way he entertained the Reverend (and Mister, who rode shotgun as technical adviser) with a true story he had come across in Oswald Pogenpohl's book *Fools' Errands: Blunderful Wonders of Science*. The saga of Nebraska Man went back to 1922 when a rancher dug a fossil molar out of the sandy bed of Snake Creek. He sent the tooth for study to the chief of the American Museum of Natural History, a paleontologist named H.F. Osborn, who decided as soon as he got it unwrapped that it was the right upper molar of a human-like ape and, thus, proof of human evolution on the American continent. He proclaimed this great discovery every time he opened his mouth, he gloated over the backward Christians who were trying to hound Darwin out of the classroom. Only, it turned out that the old tooth fell out of the jaw of an extinct pig.

A toot-a-toot on the horn as Munro pulled in and parked flushed Ving and Olin out of the office. 'Hey there, gentlemen,' Munro called at them, rolling down the window. Mister told him to be quiet and listen.

'What is it, Daddy?' JT said.

Even before Munro cut the engine they could hear the noise of a few pigs raising thin voices into the bright air of the open yard. The crying spilled out of the dry sow house and spread like a reek across to the men. The sound of humans led the sows to expect their second feed which was by this time three hours late. They could have been whining to attract attention, to have their slops dumped over the rails of their pens, whining in pain or confusion, complaining to the sky, fretting to God.

'They're loud today,' Olin noticed.

At the far end of the nursery building an old man's head popped up above a partition, looked this way and that way, like a glove puppet. 'That's Anthony,' Olin said. 'He helps out around here most days.' He cupped his hands and shouted down the length of the building. 'Hey, Anthony. What's going on with the ladies?'

The shout came back, 'Got a dead one here, Mr Mulley.'

Mister didn't communicate any opinion to JT as they walked past the stinking pens, past the lardy porkers settled down on bare concrete in cool puddles of manure and urine. Their slurry clotted and dripped off the edges between the slots in the floor at the end of one pen and globs of semi-liquid filth clogged and crusted the gutters in the next one. The air was thick in the building, an invisible, eye-watering barrier of ammonia.

'They don't look too happy, do they.' JT stopped in front of a cubicle holding a dozen sows, four of them with their tails chewed off. Another one was backed up into a corner, haunches scraping the damp wall, fighting away from the mudstreaked cannibal twice her size.

Mister whispered to his son, 'A ten-year-old could run this place better as a *hobby*.'

Only one hose supplied water to the whole building and it lay leaking into a rusty washtub just outside the nursery pen where Anthony stood mopping up the slippery remains of an aborted fetus. 'She's all right,' he promised everybody, slapping the rump of the exhausted sow lying at his feet. 'You're all right, aren't you, girl. I'll do the feed now, Mr Mulley. Mr Kimmel and his friend want to see me do it?' He draped a square of wet burlap over the bucket that held the dead piglet. 'I won't give this to them, they'll choke on the bones.'

Ving invited JT to lean in close to see what Anthony *was* giving them to eat. Up on a dolly a metal barrel was half full of decomposing vegetable scraps and into this green and brown mulch he spooned a few family-size cans of cheap dog food.

'I thought up putting it on wheels,' Anthony said. 'So I can wheel it around easier from pen to pen.'

'Like in a hospital,' JT smiled back.

Ving took the sarcasm on the chin. 'Seems like everything we do around here just backfires. Mr Yardell should've bequeathed us a decent hog farmer, too.'

Lowered to its rusty wheel rims, a derelict LA County school bus formed the rear wall of the nursery and the entrance to the hog barns. 'See that house up there?' Ving pointed through the bus's windshield at a stone lodge on the ridge overlooking the farm. 'In the Thirties and Forties they put on German Bund meetings, so there's some history for you.' (And now I was in it, nested there with my stack of electronics.) 'I think it's up for rent now.'

The pig farm was left to the Creation Science Institute by Packer Yardell, a Seventh Day Adventist and pork king of Maylands, Iowa. It would remain in their ownership for as long as it was administered by Dr Oswald Pogenpohl or his designated successor. In the two years that CSI (in fact, Olin Mulley) had been handling things, the whole operation had been efficiently run down from the modest 200-head herd shipped from Iowa in fulfillment of Yardell's legacy, to the diseased, mentally disturbed 50-odd that JT found staring back at him through shit-spattered rails.

'The only part of this business we get right is trucking the finished ones out to the slaughterhouse in Vernon, but even with the break they give us we don't make anything. Now, instead of money going from here to CSI it's all going the other way around.' Ving leaned up against the dashboard and made his pitch from there. 'I sure know this doesn't look like much of a blue chip investment *per se*, Jim, but if you look at it as kind of a bunch of raw material.'

'Pretty raw,' Olin confided.

Munro cut in. 'I think this place has got a lot of life in it.'

'I still don't know what the deal is,' JT put to Ving.

'The deal is we'll sell ninety-nine per cent of the business to you for a dollar and you'll hold partnership in the title of the land, fifty-fifty, with CSI.'

'Well . . .' A limp shrug, a nod.

'Nobody expects you to make up your mind here, right now.'

'No,' JT said. 'I want to look at your paperwork.'

'Of course. No problem.'

'We're going to go home and pray about it.'

'That's the right thing to do.'

'And we'll have a hard talk about it, too.'

Though it was a softer talk he had with his father before they left that day, hived off from the others. At the gate to the weedy dirt clod field where five boars, two of them lame, scratched and snuffled around in the open, Mister sniffed the clean-dirty elemental smells, earth and water, roots, moss on the fence post, rust, damp wood.

'They trust you right off,' Mister remembered. 'You're their mother and father. For all they know you're just a standing-up kind of pig. I liked it when they trusted me, you see it when they look at you with those female eyes. Even the boars have 'em. Long white eyelashes. Mostly I'd forget about that soft-hearted stuff, usually, all I'd see was their big butts in my way when I was pouring their feed, or when I had to move them or whatever. But there was other times toward the – let's call it *the end of our acquaintance* – when I was loading them up into the trailers to go off and get butchered, I still saw that sweet dumb trust on their faces. ''Where're we goin' *now*, Mister? We goin' someplace *nice*?'' And I'd think about that place. A big electric shock and a .22 through the brain, throat slit, tied up by one leg on a chain, their guts tore out, their head chopped, their carcass hacked down the middle, their legs cut off into hams, their backs into bacon, their ribs on somebody's barbecue. Every six months or so that thought would hit me, over breakfast, and your mama she'd pester at me to say what's on my mind and I didn't know how to say. Finally it came to me, what it was.'

JT had to pull him back. 'Are you going to tell me or am I supposed to know?'

'How they never communicate the message, that was it. We don't kill them *all* and they're very intelligent animals. You'd figure in hundreds of years *some kind* of message would leak back about what hog farmers are up to. But uh-uh. They always climbed into those slaughterhouse trucks with that grateful trust in their eyes, like I was sending them off to summer camp.' Mister couldn't hold in his dry, hacking laugh. '*Funny* damn thing,' and the comedy of it kept him laughing, hugging his ribs, laughing at those lumpen boars, 'It just creased me up. Funniest damn thing you ever saw!'

JT didn't speak again until Mister's reminiscence chuckled away and in the pooling calm he said, 'I'd like to hear any opinion you've got so far.'

'There's a lot that needs to be corrected.'

'I know what I saw, what can you tell me on top?'

'There's no breeding herd to speak of. I mean, you saw the health of those animals. You're talking six hundred bucks per sow, then figure two hundred per pig for housing pregnant sows and boars and while we're on that subject, let's pretend you have to buy ten fresh boars. Rebuilding the pens, replumbing, modernizing the yard, and *then* what've you got?'

'It'd only be worth doing for the pathetic struggle.'

'Bank on a struggle about the size of a couple hundred thousand. I don't know *where* you'd see a profit out of this whole deal. What would you do with it, Jimmy?'

'Make gourmet sausages. Sell them to the Bulgarians.' JT looked back toward the farm buildings. Munro was on his way over from there.

'I don't know what's on the other side of this place, if there's anything beyond it. I don't know what Kimmel wants, Daddy. He's sitting on something, though.'

'Reverend?'

'We're done, Munro.'

On the slow walk back to the car Munro was concerned enough to worry, 'Ving asked me how long did I expect you to take to make up your mind.'

'Don't tell him anything.'

'I didn't, Reverend.'

'Don't say anything to him. I'm not sure I see myself in it yet.'

7   Belshazzar's Luau

A REMARK dropped by JT with passive interest when he handed back the Pogenpohl books encouraged Munro to think that the farm's rescue might still be a prospect. 'I know about Oswald Pogenpohl,' JT said. 'He looks like a man I can do business with.' True enough, Pogenpohl was a stand-up Christian minister who cherished the same hopes for the human race that JT did, but more meaningfully he could be the next trounceable contender for JT to engage in a deal. Either way, Munro didn't need to wheedle or connive to make sure that his best friend attended the dedication of the CSI library in August, it was the first chance that came up for Reverend Jim Tickell and Dr Oswald Pogenpohl to be in the same place the same time.

The uncolored facts that JT had filed away about the Doctor – his qualification in veterinary medicine, his fifteen years on the teaching staff of Peege College in Oklahoma, both professions laid aside in the early Sixties when he organized the study groups that grew into the Creation Science Institute – took on life in Pogenpohl's tidiness and public mood. The classroom exactness that was a natural feature of his days in front of the blackboard and around the operating table. No human condition was too complicated for straightforward diagnosis, souls are either sick or well, and Pogenpohl woke up every morning absolutely *peppy* with the haleness of his own eternal spirit.

If you saw him eating alone at the counter in a coffee shop, or worse, sitting alone in a booth (as I saw him one lunchtime), with his sparse white hair brushed up from both sides of his head, springy dry ends crushed across the bald strip down the center of his scalp, you'd have to stop yourself from going over to reassure him with a hug. As soon as you moved within range, his hazy gray unsentimental eyes would widen the distance again: they armored him. Their clear immediacy, a flash of it behind his bifocals, added to the impression that he was openly brainy, but the clarity and mental burden weren't intellectual; that look of his crystallized one night thirty years ago when his baby daughter was disfigured in a garage fire, a camping stove accident that ordinary foresight could have prevented.

For the preliminaries of the dedication we stood outside, spilling over from the brick steps onto the square of clipped grass that was as green as a country club golf course. Pogenpohl snipped the ceremonial white ribbon, officially welcomed us to the Packer M. Yardell Memorial Library then said, 'Now let's all get into the air-conditioned air.'

A second floor, really a balcony that collared three sides of the barn-sized room, overlooked the oak tables where we sat down and remembered the sound and smell of high school. That could have been the whole intention, I thought, watching the faces of CSI elders and their families, representatives of the Yardell clan, many of the authors (JT included) whose books and articles stocked the shelves.

Directly above him was the library's one decoration, a black marble plaque set into the brickwork above the librarian's desk. The Roman lettering on it flickered in gold leaf, visible from ground floor and balcony, entrance and exit: MY PEOPLE ARE DESTROYED FROM LACK OF KNOWLEDGE, BECAUSE THOU HAST REJECTED KNOWLEDGE. HOSEA 4:6.

Pogenpohl spoke easily, he made every syllable an emphasis, a blunt reiteration of his standing. 'Things are looking up. The new so-called guidelines coming down from the education board *advise* the removal of any reference in state textbooks to evolution as a *proven* scientific *fact*, so science teachers are getting the advice now to teach – let me quote this *per se* – "other reliable scientific theories . . ." ' Scattered applause for this progress and the Doctor paused to accept it before moving things along.

Holding up his hand like a wounded paw to keep down any more clapping Pogenpohl said, 'God is in this in a mighty way. His powerful hand is pushing our enterprises, as always. Before we all go up to my house for our special Hawaiian party, I just want to say we bear the name of the Soveriegn of the Universe, so we don't want to let Him down. He's done a lot for us, hasn't He? Let's try and do something He'd really appreciate.'

In the Pogenpohls' mock tropical backyard I stood at the dead center of the happy commotion. Even in the still bright late afternoon the stubby flames of the tiki torches added sparkle to the Aloha! atmosphere. Maybe their impact as props was boosted by the swishing presence of a squad of blonde leilanis, Young Christians from Pasadena City College who volunteered to strap on calf-length plastic grass hula skirts and funnel their bosoms into the cups of halter tops made out of kitchen string and a pair of coconut shells. Strangely, the flesh colored leotards they had on underneath made the outfit, if anything, *more* erotic since men were thrown back into the cave of their own imagination every time they lined up for a refill of Hawaiian punch. The girls ladled the pink juice into cups that were also coconut shells, not the smartest serving suggestion, as JT's mother noticed right off, 'Since we all know how a man's wanders and onto *what* . . .'

Pogenpohl and his wife Eleanor stood side by side by the patio door, a compact receiving line, welcoming each guest out to the luau area. She was at least six inches taller than her husband, an embarrassment she'd spent forty years trying to disguise by crooking into a posture that suggested she was constantly interested in anything anybody was saying to her.

Their daughter Carole sat clamped into her wheelchair, half smiling with her half-mouth. A woman now of thirty-two, she kept as close to her parents as a girl of five. The bristly hair, cropped close and growing only on one side of her head, was the color of the coconut shell I sipped my punch from, and the same texture. Somebody, probably one of the chirpy co-eds, festooned Carole's wheelchair with plastic leis, and she wore a corsage of plastic gardenias too.

When JT walked in Pogenpohl greeted him with, 'Maybe I can get you to inscribe my copy.' He held JT's study of the pharaoh Akhenaton, held the book out, chest-high, an offering. 'I'm not exactly sure you proved your point about him being the first of God's worshipers. I think Abraham still beats him by twelve centuries *and then some*, but on this other idea: do you really think there was such a thing as a pre-Christian Christian?'

'Tell you the truth, Oswald, I think there were probably more of them than we've got post-Christian Christians.'

Pogenpohl didn't bite. Looking past JT to the pit dug in his back lawn where the pig was roasting, where Ving, Olin and Munro were watching the smoke thread out from the layer of leaves, he raised his arms anciently welcoming, in benediction, and said, 'God *bless* this wing-ding.'

'God bless the pig,' JT added.

'I'm not trying to hurry you up,' Oswald tried to kid him, stiffly, 'it's just been, what, four months since you were up at Hummingbird Farm?'

'As soon as I know what I'm doing, I'll tell you.'

'When He wants us to know something He waits until we're ready to hear it,' Oswald said. 'The ring structure of the benzene molecule came to Kekulé in a dream. Did I pronounce his name correctly?' It was a historical fact that Pogenpohl had culled from another one of JT's books. He possessed a gift for making a new friend feel like a trophy, feel fine about himself in the basest way.

JT thought then said, 'Are those your hands sneaking up under my sweater?'

'I don't – oh. I . . . Very good, that's – Am I being too obvious?' He re-read the situation, fell back. 'And I'm glad *you're* back on the airwaves. Congratulations.'

'Oh, they aren't finished with me yet. Not till I promise them the life of my first-born son.'

'It's the same people, our opposition is the same people. If we can somehow, some way collaborate with you maybe you can collaborate with us somehow, for our mutual benefit.'

'Do you have a fix in with the FCC?' Pogenpohl told him no. 'No, well, that's where it is. The difference is, with me it's personal and a load of it is off the record. I've got a campaigning congressworm messing with my business and that's not official. It's official, but it's not *official*-official, so you tell me who's the anarchist.'

Pogenpohl shook his head, woeful agreement. 'These men are morally confused, people who don't conform to Christ. They don't have any basis to tell right from wrong, no belief to guide their emotions and if they acknowledge the truth of what we're saying they indict themselves. Bobby Dyson is just today's problem . . . Don't you think it's the right time to thin out the influence of the cultural elite? The ones who lord it over us ordinary mortals?'

The rhetoric, the uncommon defiance, showed JT that Pogenpohl didn't consider himself ordinary and the damp, lifted corners of his mouth hinted that he only considered himself mortal for the sake of argument. 'What conversation are we having now?'

'We're talking about human nature,' Pogenpohl answered him. 'How it's a constant thing. Terrible times lead to desperation, when any kind of behavior gets justified. Easy times lead to excess, when any kind of behavior gets tolerated. We're talking about the ones who oppose themselves to us, all the rejecters, the liberals who have no self-restraint.'

Asked twice by Eleanor to change his mind, Oswald stuck to the plan and refused to turn on the floodlights after sunset. Village fires, the tiki torches stood up in their own ponds of light, faint edges soaking into the open places between them where night came down. Thirty feet above, from the dark upstairs bathroom window, JT had a clear view of the two women who bordered his daily existence. If he'd been standing close enough to hear what they were saying he would have had Nelda's quiet frenzy to absorb, Ma's strain to tranquilize.

'Can we just stop talking about it now?' Nelda chewed a bite of meat and licked at the grease it left on her fingers.

'I'm going to ask for a knife and fork. Don't they eat with a knife and fork in Hawaii?' Ma didn't move though, and she answered the answer she imagined to her complaint. 'Pasadena isn't in Hawaii.' Finished talking to herself she said, 'I wasn't angry at you. That shortie dress made me unhappy for a minute.'

'Do you want me to scream at you, Ma?'

'I say okay now, it's okay. Let's forget I got unhappy over it before.'

'And if I forget about you being unhappy about the way I am, you won't think I'm small?'

'That's not the way you are.'

'If I was a mother, I'd let my girl dress the way she felt good.'

'How can you guess what a mother thinks?'

The gouge moved Nelda to tell her, 'It doesn't involve you.'

'I had to look at it.'

'You want to hear me scream? Do you?' she asked her dish of pork. Then, to Ma directly: 'Jim has to know I'm where he wants me to be.'

'You're too showy-offy with it. It makes me unhappy to see it.'

Nelda stared at the scrappy, bird-boned woman. 'Oh, *please*, y'know? Stop flapping at me. Let's pretend we're happy to be here.'

Out on the patio, Pogenpohl intercepted JT with a plate of roast pig, braised pineapple rings and mashed potatoes. He also brought over a late arrival, Howard Porta, California's Attorney General. 'A good friend in a high place,' was the way Porta was introduced. If this soiree had been thrown in Sacramento instead of Pasadena then JT would have heard him described in more precise language. In the restaurants around the capital, in the ones with names like The Tap House or The Colony Room, you'd think toasts were being raised to a double-barrelled English lord instead of the state's top law dog – 'To that Ballbreaker Porta!' 'To that Motherfucker Porta!' In the men's room of a bar that was a historic hang-out both for politicos and journalists from the *Bee*, every Friday night a satirical cartoon traditionally appeared inside the door of one of the cubicles; at the end of juicier weeks the political comment might be chalked like a Burma Shave ad across all four toilet doors and these (usually pornographic) insider views regularly featured the buttocky, bowling-pin shape of Howard Rudolph Porta. Oh no, this wasn't the sniggering disaffection of the overpowered and outsmarted, it was a gladiatorial tribute.

'Howard might tell you some things you didn't know about Bobby Dyson, can't you Howard,' Oswald pushed.

'How long he spends in the bathroom, that kind of thing?' JT joshed back.

Porta could have been serious when he said, 'What he does in there and how much it weighs.' When Pogenpohl excused himself to get them all fresh drinks Porta opened up with a joke of his own. 'Like Jess Unruh said, "If you can't drink a lobbyist's whiskey, sleep with his women and still vote against him in the morning, you don't belong in politics." '

'Say what you mean, sir. Are you banging Eleanor Pogenpohl?'

'The point is,' he said lightly, 'Jess Unruh was on Dyson's side of the arrangement. Republicans don't giggle when they give in.'

'Just Fay Wray in the big ugly fist of King Kongress. I'll bet.'

A sincere laugh. 'Can I use that one?'

'Maybe you should put me on the payroll. I'll write all your speeches.'

'I happen to believe in what Oswald is trying to do,' seriousness reclaiming his tone. 'We believe in each other all the way,' finishing off with a cozy grin for Pogenpohl who was back juggling three cups of punch.

'Howard lets the top people know that we're not as fanatical as we get painted out,' Oswald said.

'If I'm in a position to push things along, well, I can and I do. The better my position is, the better your position is.'

'I was kidding before, it was a bad joke,' JT said to Howard. 'Or did you think I really wanted to get on your payroll?'

The answer that JT got was just as unadorned. 'Your friend Bobby Dyson is going to be the pick of the litter next year in the primaries, he'll sweep 'em, you better believe it. He's going to be at the top of the ticket in '90. *Governor* Dyson. Governor *Dyson*. You think he's pissing on you hard from the Assembly, if he climbs up any higher you're going to need an umbrella as big as the Rose Bowl. Maybe you'd like to do what you can and help me stamp the little bastard out.'

JT didn't hear Nelda say his name, he didn't realize she was standing next to him until she spoke up again. 'Excuse me, Dr Pogenpohl?' She squeezed Munro into the group of men, explaining, 'Munro's been waiting all day to ask you a question, so is it all right?'

'It certainly is. I was *hoping* we'd get interrupted by something more important,' the line Oswald smoothly fed her.

'Yes, sir,' Munro stepped in. 'Can you explain it to me, what you wrote about the inhabitants of the Heaven of Heaven? How can my spirit be uncorrupted as a child if I have to grow up, sir?'

The Doctor took it slowly. 'Munro, you understand in the third heaven there're the ministering angels?' Munro understood. 'And they can cross down to earth, they can materialize into a human-like body, but they're spirit bodies who were never human beings. So they're outside the power of gravitational forces, mass-energy relationships or any other phenomena that can be observed by physicists or astronomers. The second half of your question, if you're . . . ? Help me out here.'

'I try to be like a child in my outlook, most of the time. I love to see children, I love them but they make me feel — they make me remember how far away I am from that kind of — I want to know . . . '

'If Jim Tickell wants you for his friend, I'd say your spirit is nine-tenths of the way there. On that particular evidence, if this is how your life turned out, your spirit was nine-tenths of the way there when God created it.'

JT turned to bring in Nelda. 'Tell Oswald your idea about creation.'

'It's not my idea *now*.'

Another grenade. 'No, tell him anyway, he wants to hear it. If I tell it it'll just sound like I'm picking a fight.'

'I was nine years old when I thought of it. I thought maybe God created everything this morning. Or an hour ago, a minute ago. He created everything in the world exactly the way it is right now, including our dead ancestors, the whole history of the world up to what we had for breakfast, every thought we ever had, too, all of our memories.'

'Well, that's not what it states in the Bible.' And *thus* Oswald refuted Nelda's idea. 'God doesn't want to conceal anything from us. He doesn't play hide-and-seek with His people.'

'That's right, that's it,' came from the Senator.

Then this, from JT. 'The problem with you, Howard, is you aren't moved by the public spirit.'

'That's a joke, right?'

'The trouble you make, it's the kind you can predict and handle. You don't have any public conscience.'

'I've got a public conscience, hell,' Porta levelled with him. 'I hate Democrats. And Unitarians.'

8   Ancestor Worship, Part 1

NELDA'S skin kept its normal eggshell smoothness for several weeks and then the hives erupted again. Granular scabs rose in a chain of dime-size islands across the backs of her hands, with flatter unbroken patches inside her forearms where it looked like she'd been scalded with molten wax. When those sores healed more flared up on her elbows and in her armpits, a cycle which peaked during holidays – Thanksgiving (Ma banned her from the kitchen), Christmas, New Year's Day – and on Good Friday she found the first outbreak on the upper part of her thighs. Calamine lotion didn't help anymore and JT complained about the obnoxious hospital odor of her prescription ointment when she wore it in bed.

She feared a time when she wouldn't be affected by her husband's moods, when she'd be washed ashore numbly to watch the great sea roll by in front of her. But JT's mood had been up lately, lively with talk of 'our farming family', and coincidentally Nelda enjoyed a let-up in her skin problem, enough for her to use the rosehip skin cream instead of the cortisone salve.

JT rolled close to her, kissed her shoulder. 'You're almost perfect now, aren't you.' He stroked her face and reached across to open the drawer of her night table.

'Jimmy, hey.'

'Hey, what.'

'Don't use one tonight,' she said, opening his hand, shaking the condom out of it.

He felt around the mattress for it, caged it in his palm, rattled it there the way he'd toy with loose change or a pair of dice. 'You don't have to do it. I'll do it.' But Nelda closed his fingers over it, shut it out of sight.

She told him, 'I know why you keep doing this.'

'Do you? Why?'

'I've been thinking about it, Jimmy. It's us now, you know? Things are supposed to be different. I'm not – '

'I still don't know what you mean you've been "thinking about".'

'You always cut me off in the middle.'

'I just want to make sure I've got a clear idea of what you mean,' JT said, 'if we're going to have a discussion instead of makin' whoopee for the first time in a month.'

'You just think the subject is all settled. The subject of Ruby and James, Jr.'

His voice was kind. 'You don't have to say their names like that,' parting words as he ducked into his bunker and sealed the hatch.

'You know why but you won't say it. I've thought about this and should I say why? I think you don't want to have a family with me because you're scared you'll lose it again.'

'Don't psychoanalyze me,' he said somberly. 'What's happened to you? You didn't used to have this whiny streak. You never wanted this, you said so.'

Nelda wouldn't spill her tears. 'I always wanted a baby with you.'

'I know it. I mean you said you'd make it so there wouldn't be anything we'd ever have to fight over. I remember when you said it to me. At that art museum.'

'What are you talking about?'

'The John Paul Getty Art Museum.'

'We never went to the Getty. I've never been to any museum with you.'

'We went out there when you had your apartment. With that girl.'

'Heidi Knauer,' she remembered.

'Her. We drove out to look at the art museum and you said you'd never bring any grief into my life, "I'll block it out, that's my job." I had enough of it, you said, enough grief and disagreement and trouble for two lifetimes.'

'Don't you want to do that for me, too?' He let her talk, without help, he watched the crying empty out of Nelda's eyes. 'You know what I'm – oh, a little life . . . I just don't want it to start and finish with us here, like this. You know, Jimmy, you *do* know what a baby does. I know what a baby does, it makes a mark on things,' she said, thinking about unslowable time.

JT sat up against the headboard to listen, also to dig in. Nelda glanced away from his face, looked down at the scab on her shin and pulled the sheet over it. 'Just tell me why you think a baby wouldn't make you happy too.'

'Sure it would. It will, when the time is right,' he said. 'Nell, what do you really want me to know? You're unhappy and you'd only be happy if we had a baby?'

'Something I think sometimes. I'm losing myself, I'm scared I'm disappearing.'

'Too much thinking,' he said sweetly, touching her. She shook him off, not sweetly. 'Come on, Sugarbush, be with me now.'

Nelda pulled back, to ambush and maybe vanquish him with his own tallest argument. 'You're interfering with God's desire.'

'Or at the moment,' he said, 'that rubber is God's desire and you're interfering with it. Let's see who wins out.'

His hardness wasn't brutal, it included her. 'I don't want anything to come out of a fight. I don't want to fight with you, Jimmy.'

'We're not fighting.' JT slinked down the mattress, pushing the sheets out of his way to show Nelda his flatteringly tensed cock arched up at her. 'I'll do it. Here,' slipping the filmy sheath on himself. Nelda buckled under his sexual muscle, quelled and quelling: she let go enough to soften underneath him, to give him what he needed from her. 'There,' he said, satisfied, victorious. 'See?'

In the afternoon when JT left the house to go off with Mister, Nelda rolled out of bed. She stopped daydreaming about how things would be if God wanted the situation to be different. She was living and breathing, alive on the earth, and so there must be a physical, worldly choice to make which reflected His choice. When it came to her it felt like inspiration, at least, the decision not to wait and see tilted her forward, she felt solidly in motion. Her method was as orderly as the alphabet – Nelda didn't cry over the drawerful of condoms, she punctured each one through the middle of its wrapper, invisibly, with a sewing needle. *Fine, it's fine*, she decided, *the best ones will squeeze through, the right ones.*

Because there was no running water in the dry sow house, because the end of the building had sunk into the ground because that side of the yard had subsided and torqued the water-main cracking open its joints, Anthony couldn't hose out the pens. Where the gutters were clogged because the drains had backed up he shuffled around the pigs with a broom and dustpan sweeping the green-brown impasto into a corner, scooping it up and slopping it into a bucket. It was the routine of a silent movie comic, the angelic hobo straightening his stiff back, hefting the umpteenth bucketload of the day. There Anthony stopped, to watch helplessly, dismally, as one of the sows spluttered out a fresh quart of loose crap on the square yard of the pen that he'd just cleaned up. He wagged his finger at her, called her a dirty slut, told her to stew in her own soup and asked how she'd like it if he went on strike. He dropped the bucket, crossed his arms on his chest and slouched back against the concrete partition – which fell away behind him like a drawbridge taking Anthony too, as if he was stapled to it. Mister thought they ought to go over and see what he needed, a Band-Aid or burial, but in a second they saw Anthony up on his knees grabbing at the legs of the happy sows as they trotted past him, squalling freedom.

'Tell me something.' JT scraped his muddy heel on the lip of a dry trough. 'Is there a circle coming around?'

'Indiana's a long time ago. I don't know if this is any kind of crowning glory.' But an unsuppressed smile broke as he denied it, creasing Mister's face.

'Tell me something else.'

'Okay, I did some research. Out of general curiosity. Hog prices are about fifty dollars right now. We're talking about a June to November crop for carcass weights of, say, one-eighty. What'd I pay for my pork chops on Friday? Two bucks a pound? Prices for producers are heading down, not up. You want to hear some more?'

JT nodded him on, hearing the first hint, *this could revolve around Daddy*, deciphering the message coded in the spaces between words, a whisper of the eerie glamour that God bestows on him every time JT rouses success out of an irredeemable failure.

'It'd be nine months before we'd be up to our first slaughter. *Whatever* we do we're just going to be a miniature producer, but I guess you can think about the second quarter of '91, that's when this farm might be shipping something like enough to justify our existence.' Mister checked behind him as if somebody out there had been overhearing, writing down everything he'd said. He gave them a laugh. 'Am I talking about this? I'm a white-haired old man.' With a look at JT's wilder, smokier, bouffant. 'We both are.'

'It's our prime, Daddy, we're in our primetime. Anyway, we don't need a year and a half, I might have a retail idea that'd speed things up

. . . If it's worse than we think that's just a wider door for God to come in and work through it, righty-right?'

'He'll have plenty of elbow room.'

'You think it's that bad?' JT speculated, brightly.

'Son, it's Tobacco Road.'

'Well,' came the wise shrug, 'the Lord abhors a formless void. There's something here, I feel it in my gonads.'

'They want to swindle you a little bit, that's what that is.'

'Pogenpohl? No. And Howard Porta? They only *think* they do. It's not about pigs to them. What's coming through to me is it *should* be about pigs, that's what's coming through.'

'Through your gonads.' Mister clicked his tongue.

'Yes, sir. And so far, it should be about raising pigs.'

Mister speculated now, 'Make it ours,' gazing around at the shambles, at the litter flung all over the yard, at Anthony clomping back and forth behind the bedlam of rioting pigs.

'I know.' JT saw it, too. 'You think it looks like a seed with a tree in it?'

Surrounded, outnumbered, overrun, Anthony squatted down on the rubble of the broken wall, covered his face with both shit-crusted hands and blubbered into them loosely, weakly.

'Jimmy, can you pick up that old mop handle for me?' Mister said, 'We'd better go help him.'

9   The Law of Falling Bodies Remains True Even When No Bodies Are Falling

IN JT's Worldview office on an afternoon early in December, silence replaced temperature as the most material property of the surrounding air; opening the door and walking in you'd feel it against your face. The source of this silence wasn't the Reverend, who sat kicked back in his desk chair leafing through the twenty-page memo from his lawyers, a progress report on the case still being assembled by the FCC. There were rumblings that Dyson was lobbying Howard Porta to run a state investigation of Worldview Ministry on top of the

FCC's. Mister waited on the rawhide sofa, sat there squarely as if he were on a long bus ride, traveling, staring into the miles ahead or at the back of the seat in front of him, an inward stare. That hour's silence didn't separate the two men, it contained them in its box . . . until, five minutes early, the telephone rang and an arm of the imperfect world crashed through.

'Yeah, Munro . . . ' JT cupped his palm over the mouthpiece said across to Mister, 'Should we make him wait?'

'Where's your head at?'

'Okay,' back on the phone, 'you better bring him in.'

Munro opened the door and walked in with a fine-boned, quick-eyed young man who divided an unawkward, 'Hi, hello,' between the Tickells. Charcoal-gray pinstripe suit, vest and gold watch chain, polished black brogues, an adult representative of a serious occupation who looked like he'd been dressed by his mother. The beat-up leather satchel that carried his documents (and probably a tuna fish sandwich for lunch) must have been handed down from his father or uncle, conferred on him the day he passed his bar exam.

'It's Mr Olansky,' Munro announced, as a piece of bad news.

A nod to JT, then Olansky made the journey over to Mister who didn't stand up to welcome him. 'Mr Tickell, glad to see you again.'

'Yeah, well,' refusing to roll over for him, 'can't truly avoid it.'

JT pointed to the low-slung cowhide chair in front of his desk. 'For your comfort and safety,' he invited Olansky to sit and invited Munro to let them get down to business. 'Thanks, Munro. We'll see you later. If you've got stuff you want to do at home, that's okay, just turn the message machine on.'

They all watched Munro until he tugged the door closed. Marty Olansky said, 'Is your attorney going to make this meeting?' JT disappointed him with the word that Gunter was busy doing a hundred more important things downtown. 'Well, I was really looking forward to meeting him, you know, since I've been hearing his voice on the other end of the phone for eighteen months.'

'You and Gunter can go on a blind date when this is all finished,' Mister offered.

Marty traded back, 'There's no reason why we can't be friendly.'

'It was a friendly suggestion.'

'I must have misunderstood you, then. My fault.'

'What's today's fad, Mr Olansky?' JT asked him neutrally. The sour undertone only crept in when he had to wonder about the motive of Olansky's boss. 'He wants us all to be friends now, is that what?'

'If it's possible. Why not? With some good will on both sides. The last time this subject came up Assemblyman Dyson told me that he's grown to appreciate how many Californians Worldview employs, either directly or indirectly. He recognizes that these people, dependent on the businesses connected to Worldview that operate in the non-exempt sector, might be,' Marty stepped carefully over the word, 'disadvantaged by a drawn-out court action which could kick off with the sequestration of your assets.'

'It's my good will', JT assured him, 'that keeps me from flying up to Sacramento and kicking *his* asset off into Nevada.'

'Threaten us some more and watch what happens.' Mister squinted directly at the boy lawyer.

Opening the satchel on his lap, Marty told them he wasn't there to threaten anybody, only to establish agreement on a few basic facts. 'So everybody knows exactly how things stand and how they can develop from here.'

He passed a blue file folder to JT, who glanced over two or three pages before enlightening Mister. 'Our d-lists.'

Marty said, 'We didn't keep any other copies. These are the same pages we received last year.'

'Then I bet you'd like these to follow you home,' JT teased him, unlocking his desk drawer and pulling out the originals.

While JT compared them with the Xeroxes, Marty claimed, 'The only important issue we want you to consider is what you know that we know. Like I said before, so nobody's confused about where we are or why we're here, it's all a matter of record.'

'This wouldn't be a cheap gimmick to swing my vote, would it?'

'Those are stolen documents!' Mister stood up to point at them. 'These private, personal documents were *stolen* and you received 'em!'

'We don't possess them, they've been returned to you. We've had sight of them, yes, I have to say that we did. I also have to tell you that we have affidavits from a man named Arthur Tagg – '

'Simp!' Mister judged and damned.

' – and Tony Orr – '

'Another simp! And a dishonest liar!'

' – past employees of Wendywear and the Worldview Church, who allege . . . '

'Did Tony Orr put in his affidavit how many tracksuits, warm-up jackets and T-shirts he stole out of the factory? I fired him for that, *I* did, for dishonest behavior because how can you say you run a Christian ministry if you tolerate lying and stealing. "Thou shalt not steal", "Thou shalt not bear false witness", that's the Ten Commandments, Mr Olansky, and they come from the Hebrew Bible, you should know that, minimum!'

'I *do* know that. And you know that Mr Orr was often, *often*, permitted access to financial records necessary to the administration of twenty-odd projects in this country and overseas, funded by Worldview. A toy factory in Taiwan . . . an orphanage in Seattle . . . a free clinic in Mexico City . . . a radio station in Costa Rica . . . This is a list that we *are* holding on to.'

'Licenses, we have good licenses,' Mister fought on. 'Contracts and licenses for everything . . . and we *pay* our employees, we pay them *salaries* . . . '

'Ex-employees aren't the only ones who've complained – on and off the record – about Worldview's practices and procedures, Mr Tickell. I think you should know that.'

'Bushwah! That's just plain bushwah!' A thick vein throbbed in Mister's neck and another one at the side of his head.

'Daddy, that's all right,' JT told him. 'Sit back down now.'

'For instance,' Marty shared with the Reverend, 'in 1988 Mr Dyson's mother became a Temple Apostle – is that the title?'

'Temple Apostle, is she?'

'And as a Temple Apostle, Irene Dyson contributed one thousand dollars a month, that's twenty-four – correction – twenty-three thousand dollars in the last twenty-four months. She stopped payment on the March check because she was down to her last nine hundred dollars in savings.'

'Now it's all coming out,' JT said. 'Oh, it sure makes sense.'

'Tony Orr would stand up in court and testify on *holy oath* that he just flew down from the North Pole where he was sitting all alone on the night of the crime and he'd bend over and show you the candy cane stuck in his butt to *prove* it!' Mister was up on his feet again. 'He'd swear it was the truth if Jesus Christ himself was asking the questions.

You should talk to my daughter-in-law on the subject of Tony Orr. She'd tell you how white he is, ask her, ask Nelda!'

On the other side of the office door Munro winced every single time he heard Tony Orr's name. He'd always read Tony as a sympathetic type of manager when he was at Worldview HQ, who showed the trust and confidence he had in the people who worked under him by doling out critical chores. He trusted Munro to Xerox the d-lists remembering not to leave the originals in the document feed where anybody passing by could just walk away with them. By the sheer grace of God Tony was the one who passed by and saved Munro from unthinkable, unspeakable torment by getting the loose pages back safely in their binder while JT was still preaching downstairs in the studio.

'Has he been outside *at all* today?' Nelda would have popped the door open and zoomed into the middle of it if Munro hadn't been on his toes.

He caught her wrist in mid-reach, stiffened a finger against his lips, smiled behind it as a fast apology for jumping her like that. He whispered, 'Pow-wow meeting with Bobby Dyson's personal lawyer. Down from Sacramento.'

Munro shepherded her (crowded her) out into the hallway. She kept her voice low, as if they were discussing an accident victim's chances of survival. 'How serious is whatever it is?'

'Reverend wants me to stop all his phone calls, et cetera.'

'What are they talking about? If he came down from Sacramento to say it face to face, what's *that* all about?'

A boyish shrug from Munro. 'I've been watching the phone.'

'I'm sure he'll replay every last word of it to me when he gets home.'

'Reverend's father, he's in there, too. Man, Olansky really works him up.' Mimicking Mister, mimicking a shout in a whisper Munro said, ' "*Thou shalt not steal!*" "*Thou shalt not lie!*" *That's the Hebrew Commandments, you assy jackass!* But I think they're trying to smooth everything out and come to a deal.'

Mister's voice, with pressure behind it, rose bluntly, muffled in the closed room. 'Oh,' Nelda filed this away, 'it's a yelling meeting.'

A civics lecture was in progress. Mister was saying, 'We don't have to release anything except what we want to, it's the law, carved in rock. No religious organization has to show their financial records to any government agency, not to any one at all.'

'I'm not here representing the government, state or federal,' Marty said, handling him. 'Mr Dyson only asked me to talk to you informally to see if we could strip out some of the dead wood that's tangling both parties up. As it stands now there are six suits and counter-suits filed, plus a class action suit pending and you've got the FCC on top of that with your license renewal coming up in June.' JT let him talk on. 'Let's say it's not completely necessary for us to agree on the relative values of the principles involved here. We'd like to look at it as a practical problem that's hanging around both of our necks, I mean your neck and ours. Let's dig down to the factual history, gentlemen, let's clear out the legal debris and simplify things. We can agree on matters of fact and record, so let's look at the facts that don't slip into interpretation, the ones that just need to be uncovered, and we'll all know where we are. If we can agree on that much then we can be clear about what we do *and don't* have to do next.'

It was a treaty that Olansky was trying to negotiate, hinting at mutual obligations and benefits that he wasn't ready to specify unless JT acknowledged the shape of the map. 'What kind of facts, for example, Marty? What kind of matters?'

'Besides your donor and disbursement lists?'

'Forget about those for now.'

'For *ever*,' Mister crushed any hope.

Marty said, 'Say, the eight thousand dollars earmarked to pay for an employee's dormitory connected to children's hospice didn't end up subsidizing a golfing vacation in Scotland.' He raised both hands in truce. 'That's not an accusation, just an illustration.'

'It's a way through the world,' JT meant the tactic. 'The principles of how we got into this don't matter and this talk is coming straight from Bobby Dyson's heart, is that a fact? And I bet you think *the resurrection* is stupid for a grown man to believe in!'

'If I thought you were stupid, Reverend, I don't think I would've bothered to leave my office this morning. No, I think if there was an opportunity to avoid the public and private damage of a legal carnival, you'd maximize it. Five-sixths of the argument, the named contributors who'd sue to recover their contributions, the ugliest part of it can be settled out of the spotlight.'

'How quick?'

'Weeks, not months.'

'Before June.'

'I think so.'

'Before the Democratic primary.' Now Marty found out what JT knew – and his opinion of it: 'There's only one thing more life-threatening than mediocrity and that's mediocrity with a mission.'

After he closed his satchel, neatly, and climbed out of the hammocky chair Marty pushed his final point; it could have been self-justifying or it could have been larger than that, a plea for reason. 'It's just a question of adjusting to the present conditions.'

As he left through the outer office he got another friendly suggestion from Mister. 'We'll send you people as many copies of the First Amendment as you want. In big print, with pictures if that'd make it easier to understand!'

A winner's grin bubbled to Munro's lips. 'Man oh man, you settled that all right,' he congratulated Mister, coming in to join the party. 'Right in his assets, he took it right in the asteroid, man – that was *beautiful*.'

Mister's face had the coagulated sheen of a plate of cold suet. 'If you're happy, Munro,' he said, 'you're just not paying attention. Jimmy, call Ma up, okay? Tell her I'm on my way home.'

'I sure will. See you in the morning.'

'I hope so, son. I'd like that.'

'Come on in here,' JT included Munro. 'I'm going to tell you some things.'

Munro dropped down in the rawhide chair, its seat still warm from its last visitor. 'Is Bobby Dyson going to send him back? That Olansky?'

'I love my enemies, I love how they work for my failure twenty-four hours a day, they *pray* for my downfall. But look: I'm still up. Up and up. I succeed and they fail. Sure, and if he doesn't come back I'll go up against his boss in his own ballpark. I'll take on the home team and you know what? I'll shut him out, Munro, I'll humiliate him.'

'Uh-huh, I'd like to be there to see that one. Do they know – '

'They don't *know* what they don't know. They don't comprehend the barest fact of them all because they haven't studied the whole record. The ones who compete with me, fail. That's it.' JT footnoted, 'They have, so far.'

Munro stayed avid to hear, to receive, to be cleared. 'What-all did he think he was doing, Reverend?'

Theatrically, 'He *threatened* me, Munro. Can you beat that? His assignment was to inform me that I was risking my money and property, oh, and by the way, my reputation, in a dumb lawsuit. He thought he was dragging me out of my cave,' JT mimed the chore of grabbing two handfuls of bear fur and pulling hard, 'but (I *love* this) I already was out there in the open. You know me, right? You see me live that way, exposed; way up here on the edge of the cliff so I can look out and see what's there and what isn't.' He showed Munro the Xeroxed d-lists. 'Know what these things are?'

Did Munro want to lie? (He didn't.) Could he try to deny it? (And add to the false impression that he could ever harm JT or want to?) Munro knowledgeably guessed, 'Your private lists?'

'Yeah, he *returned* them to me. Olansky told me, Scout's honor, that they didn't keep any copies.' Flipping the pages onto the floor JT showed how seriously he took *that* revelation. The contempt didn't stop at Marty Olansky's incredibility. 'He got a hold of them from Tony Orr. Tony stole them from us.'

'Did he say that? From Tony Orr?'

'Can you believe it? I think he wanted to knock me off-balance so he threw it into the conversation, a Sacramento smoke bomb. And we were just talking, the two of us, like we're talking right now.' JT flicked his finger back and forth between himself and Munro, then dropped the comparison, suddenly remembering to ask, 'Any calls while we were in here?'

'Nobody,' a little distracted. 'Nothing, no.'

'It's funny about him. Nelda didn't like Tony Orr. It grabbed me out of the blue, I didn't think it was possible, didn't consider it, but she really couldn't get with him. I should listen to my wife more often, which could be the lesson here. Whatever. It's a blessing from God, Tony's disloyalty, his dishonesty.'

It pained Munro. 'But he was trying to hurt us.'

'You're looking at it from the wrong angle. See, it's not a bad thing, it revealed something new, it gave me some fresh information. Now I know something I didn't know yesterday, it's changed my whole view, I can see what else is possible. It's *movement*.' He made it simple.

'If you're staring at a flat landscape that's the same as far as you can see – the middle of a desert, picture that, or the open ocean. It sort of solidifies, you lose your sense of perspective. Then something in it moves – a lizard skitters out, a bird lands – the view *shifts* and you can see heights and distances again. My eye's fresh, that's what I mean, I can compare how it is to how it was, I've got a new perspective on events. Things I didn't think of before, now I see what else is involved.'

Without getting it, Munro said, 'I get what you're saying. Exactly.'

'It's better this way, it's a clearheaded faith,' which made it necessary to ask, 'Are you still friends with Tony Orr?'

And it was necessary for him to answer, 'Jeez. No, holy . . . No, Reverend. We weren't *real* good friends when he was around. Just to talk to. To eat lunch with a few times. He was all right for that.'

A wave of electrical energy flushed through Munro, a prickly current connecting him to JT; he was being looked at. Out of nowhere (out of the hum pulsing in the back of his head, in his arm bones, throbbing on the surface of Munro's skin) JT was saying something important *to him*, ' . . . so if it's ever going to be fit for Jesus the world has to change. That's where God is, that's where you see His promise approaching, disrupting your life. Earthly life has a bunch of new edges then, splits and breaks, new spaces crack open where God's people can build up the things that God wants to see in the world. Every time there's a disturbance something might shake loose that uncovers what's been lying underneath all the time. It's movement onward.

'I like to see what's going on *from the front*. I like to witness it unobstructed, right from the brink because I don't want to live a deluded life. So I have my doubts about what I see sometimes, about what I hear, too. I doubt my own eyes and ears and I think about that doubt, I zero in on it. What does a doubt make you want? You want to annihilate it. Even if you can't, when you try to, that's movement, that's change, that's moving toward the truth. Only dead things hold still. You know all about that.' Munro blinked and JT tacked on, 'From your work, from your animals.'

'Oh, them. I've been working on a tapir all week. Trying to get his snout to hang correctly, that's hard and a half . . . '

Still looking at him, unreleased, 'Munro, don't you trust me anymore? I don't know what you think about me, in the middle of all

this hoo-hah. You have your doubts? I want to hear what you think.'
This silenced Munro. 'I'll help you with an example. Weaklings blame
it on the Devil when anything complicates their lives by being too scary
to understand. Anybody who used to say the Earth wasn't the center of
the solar system was just a mouthpiece for Satan, then the scientists
proved it and after that the order of the planets was one more gift from
God. Eventually everything comes back to God. Questions don't scare
me, answers don't scare me.'

'I believe it, I do,' Munro said, with no relief.

'One thing makes me afraid, I mean *mortally*.'

'Well,' happy to be strung along, 'I don't believe that.'

'I'll tell you what it is. It's the idea that someday God might lose
interest in me, that I won't attract His favor anymore.'

'I don't think I understand it, what you're saying.'

'Am I scaring you yet?'

'No, sir.'

'What are you afraid of, Munro? Ghosts? Punishment?'

'No, Reverend.'

'Of what, then? You afraid of me?'

'I just can't think of anything.'

'At night, I mean. A fear of something that makes you jerk your
knees up to your chest when you think of it in bed: drowning in the
ocean or falling off the Empire State Building, the worst thing you
could imagine happening, hot needles jabbed in your eyes . . .'

'Nothing in that direction.'

'If that's the truth, you're better than I am.' He went on prying up
the lid of Munro's conscience. 'Tell me what it is. I won't use it against
you.'

Munro told him, 'I'm scared of going to Hell.'

'All right,' slowly listening, surface calm.

'I'm scared I might have to because I'm not good enough for
Heaven. I don't know what's allowed there, what Jesus is going to let
me by with. I never did anything, not that was really my fault. And
when I'm working sometimes it hits me – God can do anything
anytime He wants, so then what if He got mad at us, say, and He
turned everything upside-down overnight and when we woke up we
were the ones in the zoo, you know, the animals ruled over the world.
It'd be cooked people on the menu. I don't like thinking of some

animal's fangs biting into my arms and legs, chewing me up for food.' But this wasn't enough. JT's infinite attention reduced Munro to a simple response, to entrust, to overspill. 'Women don't like me. They don't, that's all. I think about that sometimes at night.'

10   Ancestor Worship, Part 2

THE dishwasher could break down in the kitchen, the air-conditioning could stop working in the Cadillac, Mister could stub his toe on a piece of furniture and it was Bobby Dyson's fault. The hole in the Ozone layer, a tidal wave in Pakistan, eleven hot dog buns in a twelve-pack, 'It's Bobby Dyson's fault,' was Mister's sure-fire punchline. The round of cathartic laughs, though, was not part of JT's inheritance, only the joke, with its humor skinned away. 'It's Bobby Dyson's fault,' this time the cerebral hemorrhage that clubbed Mister onto the mortuary slab.

His father's death struck like an amputation, hacked the two men apart, and the phantom pains JT felt were the ordinary pleasures that Mister scattered unconsciously around his life. The smell of him after a shower and shave, the answering pressure of his handshake, the ironic silences. JT must have been in bed asleep next to Nelda when the blood vessel popped inside Mister's brain. Contain everything in that tenth of a second, the instant that included Mister's death: something entered the world that wasn't there before and something that was in it for eighty years was elsewhere, vanished out of reach.

After the ambulance ride, after the hospital, between the emergency and the funeral, JT spoke maybe ten words, all of them to his mother. If this was grief, it was separate from grieving at the cave mouth, at the ragged absence, this sense was a rotten sorrow over the limits of the body. A pinprick, a puncture in the tent of flesh and now his father was unreachable, one of the dead.

JT couldn't persuade Ma to stay with him and Nelda, couldn't pry her loose from her bed where she was able to see through to the bathroom, where Mister died. JT slept in the single bed next to her, the bed his father didn't come back to after his shower, and Nelda put herself on the fold-up bed in the living-room. Away from her, from the sweet antiseptic odor of her dry skin cream, there was room for JT to breathe in shreds of his childhood. The fresh linen kept the scent of Mister's drugstore talcum powder, sifted through thousands of nights, locked into the fabric of the mattress and pillow, it was like falling asleep in Mister's clean skin.

JT dreamed that he was dozing on his back, still there, his neck paralyzed, his joints numb, he couldn't even open his eyes. Mister stood somewhere in the room, also unable to move as the dark that had already crawled across JT's eyes was edging toward him. If he could force his eyes open, force himself awake to see Mister before he was lost in the enormous night, JT could keep him safe. A ball of air rose into his mouth, formed Mister's name and softly exploded, 'Bbbb-rhhhhh,' a strain violent enough to pull JT awake.

From his bed too he had a view of the bathroom. When he sat down on the toilet he looked again at the bathtub that eight hours ago had cradled his father's remains. 'A membrane, is all, it connects us and separates us.' JT saw a memorial holiness in the vacated room, as if the death rite had already been observed, the relics of physical existence – Mister's bottles of Old Spice after shave, the blue jar of Noxema shaving cream, his toothbrush, his washcloth – were funerary offerings now, containers of his private habits and of their last use.

The picture of Mister's body, naked, folded up in the bathtub, projected itself onto every wall, the same picture from impossible angles, from directly above, from inside the tub. They grinned through the early morning news report JT watched on CNN, film from the night before of the crowds in West Germany. Germans who weren't streaming through oblong gaps in the Berlin Wall were perched on top of it, swinging sledgehammers and pick axes, fracturing off big wedges of concrete right above the smiling *Volkspolizei*. Over there, God's hand erases a country's border, and here it comes down to the size of a man.

'Jimmy, what is it?' Ma didn't come in, she waited at the door and looked surprised to find her son in her house before dawn, as if (JT thought) she'd forgotten Mister's crumpled corpse and her midnight transformation from wife to widow.

He didn't want to frighten her so he said, 'I'm right here with you, Ma. You're not all by yourself.'

'My pills wore off so I woke up. I think I just fight them.'

'You're too strong for knock-out drops.'

'I guess so. You know me, I'll argue with anything.' (Mister's famous words of love, his endearment on every anniversary card.) She said, lifting herself onto the moment as if it were a piece of drifting wreckage, 'We can have a minute for us, a little minute. I don't want to think of him away in heaven, I want to feel what this feels like, I want to get used to it for a minute. You and me, we're who's left. We can pray for relief, as soon as it can come. Mister's all right where he is.'

Did she mean his body, in the mortuary? 'Do I remind you of him?'

'Not in any sorry way.'

'How do I?'

Without moving from the door her look floated an inch away from his face. 'You've got his white hair and his Roman nose. But you've got my scrappy manners.' The flounced hem of her nightgown splashed over her bare feet as Ma came in for one kiss, one hug. Before she let go of JT she said, 'We're such a small family now.'

At the funeral, at least in his eulogy, JT steered clear of any mention of Bobby Dyson or Marty Olansky except to suppose that it's everybody's fate one way or another to be a victim of homicide. 'Hell is here, devils live with us. And so do saints, who know something else about death. Our sin can divide us from God but death is the border where God's hand stretches across and touches us, see, beyond this there's a heavenly frontier. Daddy left sin so far behind so long ago that he'd've been a loving cup for the Devil if he wasn't already a chalice for God. He was my first teacher on the subject of the Lord's ways and Satan's ways and the first-of-all lesson he taught me about both of them was, "You'd never stop tearing your hair out if you knew *half* of what's going on in secret . . ."'

In the middle of a silent dinner four months after Mister's funeral Nelda remembered a wedding vow that JT made to her off the record. A courting vow, then, so romantic and at the same time so unbeguiled that it was enough by itself to restore her innocence, to throw her open to the idea that this marriage was going to make her happy. Shoes off, sitting on a red and white checked tablecloth spread out on her living-room floor, munching through a junk food picnic, JT got onto his knees to promise her, 'No silent dinners, not ever.' The next words out of his mouth were, 'God singled you out for me, Nellie. He paired us up and now what we've got to do is say yes.'

The explanation this time for his lack of anything to say over the peas and carrots was that composing his Easter Message exhausted him physically and mentally. Not the whole truth, but plausible; Nelda heard him rattling around his den until she couldn't keep her eyes open anymore and this had been going on for more than two weeks. Most times she was still awake at three in the morning but always asleep when JT came to bed.

Across the table, across the divide, he stared past her, his eyes unfocused, disconnected but not distracted. Nelda threw him a line. 'What's the weather like out there?'

'What?' automatically smiling. When she stroked the side of his arm he pulled away from her as if he'd been stung. He said, 'I have to do this by myself.'

'This what? I speak English, talk to me.'

'I've got to think. I'm concentrating.'

'I'm not just going to accept this.' It was familiar territory, placating a difficult (opaque) man. She wasn't starving in a ghetto or forgotten in a jail, Christian rules covering self-sacrifice shouldn't apply here: Nelda's idea of fidelity was to hang on to what JT started. She almost said, 'God didn't want you to marry me to teach me a lesson,' wanting him to know that the finest quality of her love wasn't the measure of her endurance. If she belonged with him, he'd have to remind her, so just to get him to talk she said, 'What can I do?'

She was a mouth the size of a room, sucking at him. 'You're doing too much. I'm right on the edge of something, I can't describe it to you, it's just *in motion*.'

'The pilot doesn't tell the luggage where it's going.' He kept quiet. (JT didn't see Nelda as luggage. Around this time he thought of her as a branch of himself, a thickening, warping branch.) She said, 'What did I do wrong? You don't let me do anything. What did I do?'

He let her stroke his face. 'You've got to stop that stuff.'

'You used to touch me all the time.'

'I've got to stop it, too.'

'Hey, I'm supposed to be the recovering Cathoholic in this house.'

JT concentrated on her. 'When I saw my father, the way I found him, you know, it made me think of an Egyptian mummy. He could've been dead for five thousand years, buried and dug up again, on display.'

'Oh, Jimmy. Oh, baby, you can pour your heart into him. I miss him the same way, I want him to be here, too. As much as anybody who loved him. You can go on loving him, Jimmy, is that — '

'No, that's only half-it. You don't feel it the way I do. You touch me and it's already gone, by the time the electricity jumps from my arm to my brain that touch is gone, that pleasure. It's out of reach. And it keeps you hungry for it, it's habit-forming, see? Nelda, I don't know, my skin feels like raw meat. I don't know if I'm getting closer to God, to everything, or if I'm sinking out of His sight. I've got to get to where I can see behind it. I have to get around the dark side of this thing by myself.'

If she heard his reason as a lie or a half-lie she believed the commoner truth it partly uncovered. Endangered, bewildered, she didn't fight back, only bravely said, 'I don't know why I don't make you happy.'

JT stopped eating regular meals. Instead, he grazed early in the morning and in the middle of the night on whatever food happened to be lying around. Lettuce and mayonnaise sandwiches, whole packs of salami slices, entire boxes of peanut butter cookies. He slept in his clothes on the floor of his den, most days until three or four in the afternoon, and the mood that afflicted him gelled into a stance which stiffened (exactly the wrong word) into monkish celibacy.

With his eyes shut, focusing on the horizon of Heaven, approaching it across the black vacuum of space, he couldn't see past a glory of colored light. The piercing brilliance of it ignited pinwheeling shimmers in the corners of his eyes, fibers of silver-rose-amber-copper, colors of heat, webbed the rind of his skull . . . and with his eyes open he saw the bright fog descended, with a shape cocooned in it, something earthly, useable, throwing a shadow through the glare.

The noise that reached him from someplace outside was the telephone ringing on his desk. If he could see the bare wires, see the current pulsing through the phone lines, the fluttering trail of yes/no would have led him to the pay phone in the Global Video Café where Alex and Heidi were waiting for him to answer.

'Pick it up, Nelda!' JT called into the rest of the house. 'Pick up the phone, will you? Please, Nell — I'm not here!'

Stopping for a strict-nurse glance down at the invalid laid out on his back ready for therapy, Nelda answered it on the eleventh ring. With her hand muffling the mouthpiece she said to him, 'Yes you are, Jimmy. You're definitely here.'

Three

MY DESCENT

1   The Invisible Hand, Part 2

HEIDI held Nelda on the phone for a quarter of an hour with a loose string of improvised lies. Criss-crossing the two years since she'd last been in touch, Heidi's monologue began with highlights of the day she was begged to take over the acting master class of their old stage workshop *and* to direct her favorite grunge band's video for Maverick Records, for ten per cent of the budget and selflessly, touchingly, 'for my best friend in the world, Dawn Elise'. Next, she ran through the cowgirl-in-a-pickup-truck screenplay she sold for 'rent money' to a producer who rewrote it and auctioned it to Paramount for eight hundred thousand dollars. This rotten luck walloped her while she was filming the pilot of her talk show for Fox TV, another championship shot sabotaged, this time 'by my director, who like, totally screwed up the shots'. Deft, opaque lies.

Flatly, nasally, but trying hard to mean it, Heidi squeezed out the syllables, 'So tell about your life.' Nelda's two-word prologue (or epilogue), 'I'm married', left room for Heidi to marvel at the channel-changing decisions that a girl's got to make sometimes. 'Yeah, so I'm finally like that about the industry. I mean, I've been in it for ten years and it's not the only thing I'm living for. I just got into this new business with somebody, like, this amazing project. Is Jim still investing in stuff besides his church or whatever?'

Staring down at JT, at the moment squatting on the floor, shawled in his blanket Big Chief fashion, Nelda puffed the exciting news about Hummingbird Farm. 'That's *fantastic* for us,' Heidi gasped, 'because Alex's machine is all about helping the environment. Nell, can me and my partner take a meeting with Jim so we can, um, so he can see if he's interested?' Nelda asked her if she wanted to tell him about it right then over the phone. 'Sure, definitely. Alex is better at describing what it does, so I'll put him on, okay? Nelda?'

Nelda was already pushing the phone into JT's face.

JT: Who's this?

Alex: Mr, uh, Reverend Tickell? My name is Alex Berry and I'm just wondering if I could come talk to you about a business opportunity.

JT: You're selling something.

Alex: It's a little hard to describe it on the phone.

JT: I'm going to ask you two questions. Can I use whatever it is on a pig farm?

Alex: If you've got any kind of waste material there, well, this appliance can recycle it for you on-site. It's a green machine with, uh, big potential, worldwide potential.

JT: A Big Green machine.

Alex: I'm looking for investment capital so we can move on from our prototype into a limited manufacturing run. All together I'm out to raise 285K, if that answers your second question.

JT: My second question is: Do you know Jesus?

Alex: Oh, um. I know who he *is*.

The horse laugh Alex heard belting down the line sounded good-natured and generous, it opened out to him. JT hoped Alex didn't mind too much if he cut the conversation short, blaming a 'baby *octopus* of a headache, man, it wrapped its suckers around my brain when I woke up today'.

This is Alex out in the economy; I saw it through his eyes, struggling with detachment. Stalled in his room, physically wrecked and mentally shredded after a week of broken sleep, Alex hacked himself free of every plan but one, flung the others into the never-to-be and released himself into the snorting insanity of inspiration. Out of nothing, something.

Out of nothing, the Humpty Dumpster – which dissolved the borders between the world and Alex Berry by projecting him into a kind of chronicle. In one unrealistic instant, expanding, boundless, he saw the world's place in his life. What else could he do then except move down into it, risking any idea he had of himself or of what he might turn out to be.

2   The Little Boy Pee-pee Dance

'YOU wouldn't believe it was the same property if you'd've saw it a few weeks ago. Under the old management all this where we're walking now used to be a big slushy lake of mud.' Munro swung his arm around in a fast arc over the yard, solid earth scraped dry and level. The clean, healed ground smacking against the soles of his shoes, the literal truth of it, charged him up with confidence in everything it portended.

He led the small delegation from their cars to the long low-roofed white hangar, the foursquare structure raised on the foundations of the dry sow house. The place got Alex thinking of prison camps, a stalag shower block preserved as a museum. A few steps closer and the illusion dissolved, it was as if the shady doorway had been hit with a spotlight. JT filled the entrance, in his three-piece white suit, smiling a silent welcome. More impresario than entrepreneur, more Barnum than Getty, Alex judged, with what he thought was canny maturity. But the direct smile that he collected with JT's serious handshake confided the assumption that any potential value they had to each other was unquestionably mutual.

JT lightly shook Chick's narrow boyish hand and with a shade less conviction but ample charm he told Heidi how wonderful it was to see her looking so healthy. 'Come on inside,' he said, chaperoning Alex and leading everybody else along the unlit aisle that connected the entry ramp to the center of the building.

The metal fenced subdivisions of stalls and pens had just been hosed down, water drained cleanly from the gently canted concrete floors to dribble off where the concrete ended in long rows of steel slats. Every surface fresh, untouched; prepared and empty confines that supplied JT with a tangible, immediate illustration of his higher motive. 'Here's my yes-vote on Prop. 128. I'm doing this for the land, sea and air, for all the generations we've got left.'

'Reverend was one of the first ones who signed up on the petition to get one-two-eight on the ballot,' Munro footnoted.

'And Munro was the first of the second ones.' Patting his shoulder as she said it, Nelda turned the joke into a small tenderness.

'You bet I was. Reverend 'ud murder me if I didn't!'

'Mr Berry, Mr Uchiyama, let's go on through. I want you to understand my plans for this place.' JT effectively muzzled Munro by way of calling attention to the roomy corrals for gilts and sows, the hog huts with their patch of pasture just outside for grazing and lazing, the almost discreet, partitioned servicing cubicle where boars had their virile mission to accomplish three times a week, the humane, cozily heated farrowing pens for new mothers and their babies, and out where the wrecked school bus used to squat, the unfinished nursery: in four months Hummingbird Farm's first piglets would be coddled in summer temperature day and night. ' "Happy pig, happy pigman" in my daddy's words,' JT summarized, showering this wisdom, for some reason, directly upon Alex.

Mistaking it for pressure to perform Alex answered resourcefully, 'Happy pigman, happy pig,' then shrugged at his own barnyard wisdom.

JT might as well have taken that verse to be his text for the day, which seemed to be the purpose of his quotation from the Book of Mister. 'What used to be here was nothing. Worse than nothing. Trash and confusion. And worse than trash and confusion, indifference. I said yes to a deal, then this happened.' He twisted his thick neck to look around again at the new buildings, inviting everybody else to see what he saw. The Reverend was sermonizing to a congregation of five, or ignoring Munro, Heidi and Nelda (as he was about to do), to his flock of two. 'What's the most beautiful moment in a business deal? When you close it? Closure? No: it comes after that, when something brand new happens. Because of the deal you made now there's something in the world that wasn't in it yesterday. It can be a ball-bearing factory or an insurance company, whatever you want to make, an opera, a rubber tire or a pig farm, when it happens it's connected to everything else that's happening at the same time, it gets folded into the mix, it affects the marketplace. It can inspire buying and selling, trading, you can start up a *trend*, you can succeed big enough to go public and then guess what – you look back at the world that has your business in it and you see that deal you made had a purpose. All along it did, but now you see it. You can make a difference with a useful product. At the end of next week, when our growing herd arrives, what's beginning here is the life cycle of the Hummingbird Farm Eco-friendly Sausage and our line of Eco-friendly Lunch Meats. We're going to be a showcase for eco-friendly pork production, make Hummingbird Farm an example to the world, let it shine. Maybe you fit into it, maybe you don't. I'll tell you this, a few people involved want to see me fail. They don't really think I can turn this one around, they think it's a hopeless cause and that's why they handed it over to me. That's why I took it. They're sure I'm wrong about what can be done here. Except I know something else, I know there's something beyond this. The size of it, that's obvious to me but the shape of it, that isn't. So show me how come you dropped out of the sky. Let's see what you've got beside big feet.'

Munro recognized the impishly goading tone, the flammable mood threatening a jolt of illumination, it was JT's pastoral voice translating the divine message into words that wouldn't challenge these people, language that was familiar to them. *The deal . . . useful product . . . affect the marketplace . . .* he was talking to them on the practical level but those rugged practicalities were the shadows of God's special intentions, the imprint of His weight descending on Hummingbird Farm. Squalor converted into wholesomeness, confusion into significance, indifference into faith, decline into revival. And so on, Munro reflected, rhyming what JT said with the private facts in his possession – *people involved want to see me fail . . .* that could only mean Oswald Pogenpohl, Ving Kimmel and Olin, high and mighty, but God turned His back on this place when it was in their hands. Their failure into our success, that was the sheer theology of the situation, their humbling into our blessing, as it's been arranged, right up to the arrival of this new bunch with their invention, *I know there's something beyond this . . .*

Strolling a few yards in front as they all circled back to the cars, Heidi and Nelda tucked themselves into their own conversation, heads bent girlishly together, their voices inaudible, excluding the men. The quiet comedy of Heidi's clothes also drew a frame around her alone, the cowboy boots, pleated calico skirt embroidered with a rodeo scene, frilly white linen blouse buttoned as far as the lacy upper edge of her bra cups, her straw-colored blonde hair yanked back into a loose ponytail, all the markings of a down home farmgirl, and the costume wasn't all satire. The private joke she was telling everybody showed them how free and willing she was to swing into the spirit of the outing and at the same time not really be part of it at all. If they caught her irony, fine, they agreed that Heidi was there on her own terms; if they didn't get the gag, also fine, also in her frame, their bland incomprehension was the punchline.

Thinking back to the day he helped crate up Nelda's books and records and move them into the Reverend's house, the concept of these two women living in the same apartment flummoxed Munro even more now than it did then. There must have been an imaginary line down the middle of every room to separate their lives, saved from unsaved, saved from practically *unsavable*.

'I thought I smelled a man,' Heidi breathed at him over her shoulder. Munro was only one step behind her, sleepwalking, he'd caught up with them without noticing. 'Can you get those latches?' pointing at the tailgate of her pickup truck.

Over the painful squeak of the dropping tailgate Munro heard JT talking boars and sows, growers and finishers, backfat thickness and loin-eye area, elementary knowledge of pork production urged on him by his father, fundamentals he'd memorized before Mister was gathered to God.

'Pigs are delicate creatures when they're born, you've got to regulate the temperature they're in to the perfect degree. Same as human babies, just the same. Soon as they're weaned they'll eat what we eat. I'm going to feed them on the best piggy cuisine, too, and I mean fruit, grains, eggs, cheese, fish, a little red meat . . .'

'Pigs'll think they died and went to Heaven,' contributed Munro.

'High negative costs, it sounds like,' Alex grasped.

'Well, no,' JT wasn't worried, 'garbage in, garbage out. Two years from now I'll be exporting gourmet sausages to Vienna. To all points east.'

'Eight-eighteen,' Munro vouched. 'Fulfilled and fulfilled.'

Alex let that drift past him and climbed up into the truck bed to start unbundling the Humpty Dumpster. Heidi passed Nelda a dumb look then said out loud, 'Is that a secret code for something?' Nelda could only come up with a lopsided I-guess-I-should-know-this-one-huh? frown and a quick, disengaging shake of her head.

'Remember the Lord thy God,' Munro recited to the ground until JT rode over him.

'Remember the Lord thy God: for it is he that giveth thee power to get wealth.' He leaned in toward Alex and said over the side of the truck, 'That's in Deuteronomy. That's in the five books of Moses.'

'Now I know,' not ungrateful for the information, but politely preoccupied with the main attraction. He handled the cast aluminum plinth while Chick walked the heavy cube of the Humpty Dumpster's body to the edge of the gate and leaned it into Munro's waiting arms.

It took the two of them to lift it down and heft it onto the base. Alex stood aside so that JT could take in a full view and to give Chick room to connect the leads from the two 12-volt batteries in the back of the truck. 'Better leave the engineering to the professionals,' saying something, holding himself back until he got the high sign from Chick. A motor whirred life into the machine. 'This is the working prototype of our waste recycling active energy unit,' opening his formal presentation, 'which is what we had to call it on the patent papers but we'll brand it "Humpty Dumpster".'

'Humpty Dumpster,' JT sampled the name.

Assembled, the unit stood at knee height, a compact anodized aluminum box as sturdy as a tree stump. Chick slid back the flat lid and scooped handfuls of paper and plastic trash from a shoebox into the Humpster's metal gullet. Accompanied by the robotic chewing and gurgling, Alex led JT through the efficient action that, in sixty seconds, pulled those shreds of cardboard, balled-up tissues, empty containers and other specimens of bathroom and kitchen refuse down out of the wide mouthed hopper and into the grinder where it's mulched, into the compressor where the homogenized mulch is pressed through a grid of quarter-inch cylinders and into the sweep of a rotary guillotine blade that lops off the extrusions into convenient lengths.

'Convenient for what?' JT asked him.

The first batch of finished product rattled into the flask, jackpot coins from the belly of Alex's slot machine. 'You can see,' he said, tilting open the drawer in the base, the cache of compressed, polished grayish pink pellets.

JT examined a few in the palm of his hand, poked them around with his finger. 'What can I do with these on a pig farm?'

'Oh, hey. They burn like crazy,' Chick certified. 'Believe it.'

'Burning's not a real big feature of life around here.'

Alex said, 'It's our domestic model, this one. Household trash maintenance. But there's a definite potential to scale the system up to the industrial level. Flexibility is the obvious point, the main selling point, since we can adapt the unit and apply it to a whole wide range of situations. Which is the area I'd like to go over with you step by step.'

He stopped talking when he noticed, a second after everybody else had, that Chick was feeding their lunch leftovers into the Humpty's hopper, ticking off each item as he chucked it in. 'Hamburger bun. Some hamburger. Tuna fish sandwich. Apple core. Hershey Bar.'

This tactic was baldly unrehearsed. Heidi put some distance between herself and any embarrassing screw-up by looking more surprised than anybody and speaking her mind. 'Gaahd,' underneath a nervous laugh, 'hope it works.'

Instead of derailing the demonstration Alex christened it with a flimsy joke about sacrificing his candy bar to science. A minute later the machine coughed out a few dozen gray-green pellets, some of them colorful hybrids of the food and paper-plastic residue. 'Mm, like bar snacks,' was Chick's report, munching a couple, spitting out the inorganic tips. Then, brightly recalling an earlier discussion and with innocent exuberance he spoke four words that doomed Alex's sales pitch. 'Pig food. And electricity.'

Unrehearsed demonstration, premature proposals, the strategy was shifting minute by minute. Gone, the careful development. Blown, the reliable perspective. The presentation plan they'd talked to death in the car on the way up might as well have been a plan for an assault on the moon. *Stage by stage*, Alex reminded Chick, the persuasion had to begin modestly with the common sense of the domestic appliance before it could escalate believably into a manufacturing and merchandizing prospect not entirely untouched by the romance of world domination, and he understood how to make that comically unlikely possibility plausible: only slowly, by describing the small, likely steps of his commercial logic, rising and powering forward on the swell of his investor's serious interest in the emerging picture, just fundamental business . . . torpedoed now by Baron von Frankenstein, by Mr I-Have-A-Dream. Alex had to ride with it, pretend this was the original scheme and he'd better look convinced himself because anything else would make his business plan look unrealistic (if not downright flaky).

JT focused hard on Chick. 'What's your machine got to do with electricity?'

'Pellets for fuel. Energy's locked up inside, see?' Chick held up one of the paper-plastic nuggets in the light, showing him the grain of energy sealed inside. 'Burn it in a micro-furnace, micro-furnace heats a boiler, boiler pipes steam to a turbine and this whole place can run off its own power supply. Six, maybe eight Humpsters for that. Four furnaces. You can be a big hero in the neighborhood, okay, you collect everybody's paper and plastic trash twice a week. Better than the city. Pick up their food trash, too. Four more Humpsters, make pig food fresh every day. I can integrate the system, ten – *no*, twenty machines, all interchangeable modules, very flexible, if you need more fuel pellets in the morning, right, use one of the food Humpties. And pig poop, I can do something with pig poop . . . '

He could? Well, this was some radical data coming in! Not in the car, not at the Global Video Café, not in the ruins of Chick's workshop, not on the telephone, not even in his dreams, *not ever in their relationship* did Alex hear that the Humpty Dumpster could work its magic on the squishy dumplings that drop out of a pig's butthole.

Expectant looks all around and into them Chick advanced, 'You'd have to dry it out first. Obviously.'

'Have you ever caught a whiff of pig manure? Out in the open with a hot wind on it?' JT added to the equation.

'Oh. Okay.' A new problem for Chick to attack, and he pressed his lips together, shut himself up, working on it already, prepared to find a practical solution on the spot, as his encore.

'I was going to ask him that,' Munro said, picking sides. 'It stinks so much it makes your eyes melt, that's right.'

'Fertilizer,' Chick said.

And Alex was pierced by the same keen shiver of inspiration. 'We can use everything. Fertilizer pellets, Chick can formulate them and we can sell them off in five-pound bags to local nurseries. Install a Humpty Dumpster system, integrated into every process going on here, and this farm won't produce *waste* products, just useable eco-friendly by-products. Reverend Tickell, I think, if I can say it, this can be much, much bigger than lunch meats and sausages.'

JT kept his eyes on the Humpty Dumpster, his mind fully on what was being said to him as though Alex's disembodied voice were speaking from that stubby silvery gadget. In a flicker of clairvoyance Alex saw reflected in JT's eyes a private treasure, cargo-cult cargo, an idea condensed into a material thing pulsating with charisma, exactly the way he saw it glinting at him out of the junk in Chick's back room, anointed by oil out of the air and sunlight dripping directly off the fingertips of God Himself.

Time slowed down for Alex, it slurred into a loosely expanding moment that held him passing through a clear mid-point. He had time to glance back in a nostalgic mood at his early years of struggle and then look forward to the panorama of his future rising to meet him. 'It doesn't have to wait a whole year, your eco-friendly sausages,' he said, transmitting calm certainty. In the same tone he asked Chick to time-frame his Humpty Dumpster system, built and installed, up and running.

'Inside three months. If I got some help.'

'I'll do the costumes and make-up,' Heidi helped.

'And you've got access to a kitchen?' Alex started saying to JT but slid the question over to Nelda.

'Our house came with one,' she lightly answered.

'Then you can be in business a week from today. Gourmet sausages, that's an easy first stage. We can firm up a customer base for Hummingbird Farm Eco-friendly Sausages before *pig one* even gets here. Let's buy in the best free-range pork from, I don't know, from wherever it already is. We can find out. Buy it in and use it to make your special recipe sausages, wrap them up in recycled brown paper and boutique the product. Santa Monica, Brentwood, Encino, the West Side, and be very selective about the stores that'll stock us. All the time the actual Hummingbird Farm pigs are growing up, the brand identity will be out there establishing itself. We'll get the product into gourmet sections of classy markets, and I'll bet we could get some press as soon as Chick starts installing the energy system. Think of the ultimate stage, think of this business six months from now: it'd be a showcase for resource efficiency – making its own electricity, cleaning up the community it's in, recycling its waste, producing tasty, nutritious, gourmet-quality meat products. I'm thinking, really, it's breathtaking what we can do here . . . '

Dropping back from the ferment, Nelda ignored almost everything that Alex was saying, but his personal theme reached her. He wasn't careful, this over-excitement wasn't a performance, he was selling *fervently*. Here it was, such a spirit, in such an unexpected package, this time with a Kick Me sign stuck on his pants. Nelda said to Heidi, 'Not the kind of boyfriend you usually end up with.'

'If I wanted him.' Heidi wrinkled her mouth. 'He's practically a virgin, I think.'

'. . . not only manufacture a Humpty Dumpster line, we could market *the system*. Directly to the emerging economies say, in Eastern Europe, or license custom-made systems at a discount to Third World farmers. Either way . . . '

If to Nelda Alex appeared to embody the fine young roaring spirit, to the other woman there his spiel reared out of a craving that was much earthier. 'But anyway, he just *lives* for his work. He's got so many really amazing ideas,' she whispered low, twisting the praise with a soft smirk into unblushing self-reference. She'd come to promote him, to promote the sale, to preside over it. Alex contributed his business sense, Heidi contributed her presence, she pretended to listen – strong manufacturing base . . . after sales service . . . centers in overseas developing markets . . . manufacturing bases outside the US . . . research and development . . . financing . . . franchises . . . local marketing and adapted designs . . . global branding . . . one world-family of lifetime customers . . . the words dissolved in her ears and she only wondered if Alex had started to hyperventilate. That egg beater in Heidi's stomach cranked around her worry that he was blowing this chance, and then when she spotted JT grinning like a lunatic and listening, still listening, it cranked around her happy panic that he was going to close the deal. If JT said the word she could count the changes that would come to them – the money . . . the travel . . . the consequence . . . the scope and scale . . . life beyond LA, life in Europe and beyond . . . beginning now, with this opportunity she'd created, this meeting she'd arranged, she was the hub of it, she brought together the ends and the means, none of this would be happening without her . . .

'Okay, let's do it,' JT said and time started moving again.

'We will, too,' Alex's motto over the handshake. 'We've got to come up with a name. ''Hummingbird Farm Eco-friendly Sausages'' is too much to cram into shoppers' heads. Too much for a label.'

'I can let 'em take a look at Moby-Pig,' Munro said, 'up to Ving's. They'd get some good ideas from seeing Moby in his splendor.'

'Ving?' Chick queried. 'Moby-Pig?'

'Pig Heaven,' Heidi said and everybody thought about it for almost a second and everybody knew it was indelibly right. 'Make it a pig with angel wings.' Smile jerked sideways, she half-apologized to Nelda, 'Oops.'

'No oops, girl,' Nelda said. 'I can draw it, I can do something with a flying pig. I'll draw the label. Leave *something* for me to do!'

3   'How do you think that makes me feel!'

IT was only in the note she wrote to Alex, neatly clipped to the upper corner of her drawing, that Nelda called her flying pig 'Pigasus'. (She couldn't have known – could she? – it was the name the Yippies gave to their porcine candidate for President in 1968; her 'little pagan joke' was theirs, too.) She'd given her heavenly porker a cherub's face behind its snout and a cherub's pudginess above its trotters; the runty wings planted on its back weren't doing much to keep that body airborne, in fact, Nelda had drawn him as *pig rampant*, forelegs kicked up, which made him look like he was floating in by parachute.

Along with the design of Pigasus which she asked Alex to 'critique' came a mock-up of the label, actual size, on a sheet of light brown butcher paper. 'It's all going on,' Heidi said, passing the smaller cartoon across the table, back to Alex.

He leaned the page up against his ice water glass, he reconsidered it. 'It's – too funny. No, it shouldn't be funny or clowny. The logo doesn't match the lettering. What do you think? The lettering takes our sausages seriously and the pig is clowny.'

'I say hire a real commercial artist to draw it, no muss no fuss.'

'Well, I'll talk to her and she'll change it.'

'Oh, swoon.' Heidi dropped into chorus girl sarcasm. 'Power over women!'

'Did I say it like that?'

'No, but that's how you meant it,' she said, mildly.

'I meant what's the point of running up our overhead when I can get what I want without spending one or two or five thousand company dollars on it, that's all.'

'I'm *agreeing* with you, Alex. Why pay for it when you can get it for free?'

Contracts, partnerships, are only superficially compromises; on the level where they are felt most sensitively, underneath the terms of price, obligation and liability they are instruments of dominance and submission. The deal that Alex cut with Worldview Enterprises made him a general partner with the Reverend and Ma Tickell in HD Systems Group. The Reverend's capital investment of something over $420,000 returned to Worldview a controlling interest in the fortunes of the Humpty Dumpster. Oswald Pogenpohl was satisfied with the 11 per cent share and CSI's limited partnership, and so was Chick with his 16 per cent after it was explained to him that as a limited partner he never had to worry about being totally wiped out if, for instance, one of the machines he'd designed accidentally ate a pet or small child.

Alex's new easiness settled in him before any negotiations began, he carried his solidity as if decorated with it, his chest and shoulders draped with future royalties on sales of both industrial and domestic models, his 25K advance, his 65K salary as Director of Manufacturing and Marketing. When the first rack of Humpty Dumpsters was delivered to Hummingbird Farm, Alex was talking to his parents about island-hopping around Hawaii over Christmas.

He slipped a white envelope out of his jacket pocket, fanned it over Heidi's pastrami sandwich. 'Gimme!' she breathed out and moved so fast that he thought she'd rip it from his fingers with her teeth.

Waitress at his elbow, Alex invited Heidi to order whatever she wanted for dessert. 'Lemon cheesecake. Cinnamon coffee cake. Cheesecake *and* coffee cake. Even though you're a rich girl now, I'm buying.'

'Right, right. Not enough,' she said cryptically, reading her five-hundred-dollar cashier's check.

As the waitress left with what she thought was the dessert order Alex said, 'Somebody to wait on *you* for a change.'

'I'm not waitressing anymore. I got fired. Who cares, right, I'm a rich girl, so what,' Heidi dismally waved her new wealth at Alex.

'Wait a second, when did all this happen?'

'They fired me because I had to go up to that farm with you. I had a double shift that day and all I could get out of was – oh, forget it, Alex. You care, right?'

'They fired you for missing a shift? I want to know. That's what they said? Heidi?'

'No, it wasn't just because I ditched my shift. That fucking nerdnoid rapist manager said he was firing me because I was *surly*.'

'It's not like you wanted to make food service your career.'

'I've been waiting five weeks for this money. I've got a month's worth of bills and rent to pay off. Five hundred dollars isn't *half* of it so listen, can you advance me about seven-fifty more so I can get to July?'

'Um.'

'You got your money, didn't you? Out of the deal?'

'I guess I can give you seven and a half. That's what you want?'

'Until July, or whenever.' Then she said, lodging a complaint, 'I was expecting more than five hundred.'

'Uh-huh.'

She kept quiet as Alex wrote the check, tore it out of his check-book and offered it to her. Then Heidi asked him if his accountant would accept her as a client when the rest of her money started to come in. 'I don't know anything about arranging my finances. I've never even paid any income tax before.'

'Alba's the tax terminator. I'll get you a meeting with her, sure. Tell me when's good for you.'

'When do I get the rest of my money?'

Alex recited the words, understanding as he spoke them. 'You expected more than five hundred.'

'Well, *yeah*,' as if anything else would be a mind-boggling injustice. 'Unless it's one per cent of what you scored from JT, which I know it isn't. I worked it out. One per cent is *four thousand three hundred*, not five hundred. Five hundred isn't even one per cent of yours or Chick's salary! *You* get a salary and I don't even get one per cent of it!' Then quietly, not calmly, 'You owe me three thousand and eight hundred dollars, man.'

Which mistake was going to have longer-lasting consequences? Meeting Heidi to celebrate the deal or picking his favorite table at Canter's for the setting? 'I've just paid you all of the money I owe you,' he said, steady and certain.

'One per cent,' she repeated, stifling any argument and picking a fight at the same time. 'We have a contract.'

'I remember, sure, I remember I agreed to pay you one per cent – '

'One per cent of what you got from JT.'

' – up to *one* hundred dollars. A ceiling. Not the sky, Heidi. Not one per cent of the world.'

'One per cent. I have it on tape. I looked at it again.'

'For making one phone call. You made five hundred dollars for calling up your friend and talking for ten minutes on the telephone. You didn't even pay for that call!'

'Oh, okay. Deduct forty-five cents from the rest of my one per cent.'

'There is no "rest" of any one per cent – okay? Stop it. On the other thing, the seven-fifty, I'm glad I can help you out the way my friends used to help me. Pay it back when you want to. Whenever.'

'You stink.' So much for decency. 'You can lend me money because I got Jim Tickell to start your business for you. You're lending me *his* money. Good business, Alex, taking advantage of me because I'm financially illiterate.'

'You sure know how to work out a percentage.'

'I can divide by a hundred! You've got *a life* out of this, you know, big money, and I don't get *one per cent* of a life!' Not only cheated but belittled. 'Pay me what you owe me, Alex, or I'll *sue* your butt.'

'Drag me through the courts. Outstanding. That'll teach me.'

'Alex, if I wanted to hurt you,' she said breezily, 'lawyers aren't the only friends I have.'

'Who'd break my hips, I suppose.'

'Yup, could.'

'Torch my house.'

'Yup, could.'

'While I'm inside it.' Alex smiled into the ridiculous steeliness of her pose. 'So you're a killer, is that the threat now? Are you *listening* to yourself?'

Arriving with lemon cheesecake in one hand and cinnamon coffee cake in the other their waitress found Alex sniffing and snorting over a very private joke, not shared, apparently, by his date. Heidi ignored the intrusion, fingertips pressed to her lips, eyes brim full of backed-up tears, on the crumbling edge of a mental explosion.

'We're done here,' Alex said, sliding out of the booth, still undisturbed enough to ask for his dessert to be wrapped up so he could take it home.

Heidi trudged behind him around the tables and over to the cash register, all the time murmuring her mantra. 'One per cent . . . one per cent . . . you owe me one per cent . . . ' If she couldn't make Alex cower in fear then he'd go down in public humiliation. 'One per cent . . . one per cent . . . ' she went on chanting, even to the waitress who handed her the pink box of cakes with a parting *Enjoy!* – 'One per cent, one per cent, one per cent . . . ' At least she didn't start hollering at him until they were out in the parking lot.

'I want my *goddamn* money, I *want* it from you goddamnit!'

'You got all you're going to get.' Every step he took she blocked, he turned around and Heidi was there.

'Fucking *give* me the *fucking* money you know you *owe* me!'

Now she was shaking the cake box at him, bouncing it in the air by its string. Alex hadn't been shrieked at that way by anybody his own age since kindergarten. What did it look like to the parking lot attendant, this couple? This self-conscious young man in gray slacks and navy blue blazer fending off this soft-core slattern, two inches of black roots showing in her over-bleached back-combed bale of hair? It looked like Alex was trying to sneak off without paying for his curbside blow-job. He was ready for Heidi to shove him up against a wall and mug him. Instead of that she put herself in his way again and attacked him on the forehead with the cake box.

'Drop it, you stupid maniac!' he demanded then and there, real police procedure. She whapped him again. 'Put – the box – down!'

'When you PAY ME the MONEY you FUCKING OWE ME!' Belting him on each beat as he grappled to disarm her, slapping at her arms when he couldn't grab the cake box which she was swinging at him like a mace.

A couple of teenagers loping by shouted out from the sidewalk, 'Girl fight! Ladies night! Woo! Take him, bitch!'

The fight was idiotic, the *position* was idiotic and Alex knew that no business ethic or moral obligation challenged him to stay there and deal with Heidi as an equal. Before she had a chance to start chasing him around the parked cars he held up his hands in a vague warning, told her he was going home and made a swift exit through the shrubbery.

Heidi followed him.

'Nobody needs this,' he said without turning around. 'Nobody *deserves* this.'

'I don't, for sure.'

'Right, I know. You deserve one per cent of my huge fortune.'

'I invented the name. It's not fair. I thought of "Pig Heaven" and I'm a one per cent partner when I should be a fifty per cent partner.'

'Oh, no. *This* now?' he asked the sky. 'No, Heidi. You're not any kind of partner.'

'I thought up the brand name!'

'Congratulations. You win a lifetime supply of sausages.'

'If Chick is your partner then *so am I*. That name was my idea. The machine was his idea. The deal was your idea. We should split the profits 50-50-50.'

'A grand total of a hundred and fifty per cent.'

'Whatever, three shares. *What's fair*, equal shares, Alex!'

'That's not what's fair. What's fair is paying you five hundred dollars and buying you lunch. Anything more than that is *charity*.'

'Calling up Jim Tickell for you, *that* was charity.' The implication suddenly inflamed her. 'You little *shit*. He wouldn't've even talked to you on the phone if I didn't bring you in. You'd still be scrounging around, you wouldn't have anything, *anything*.'

'Now we'll never know,' he replied easily.

Heidi halted on the sidewalk in front of Alex's duplex as he cut across the lawn and jogged up his stairs. Full of pity for him and hard knock wisdom she said, regretting everything, 'God, so I found out what kind of person you are, you user. Whyn't you just tell me business is business as if there's nothing personal going on? *You used me and now you don't want me involved.* Close the door on me, you fucker, that's how you treat women, isn't it! Oh, very sensitive aren't you! You think!'

If Alex had been suppressing a mightier self-defense, if he'd capped his defiance, this brought it geysering out. From the pulpit of his balcony he accused Heidi of jealous greed, of using and abusing *him*. 'I'm not your personal magic genie! If you hate your fucked-up life, that's not my problem. If you want it to be different, change it yourself, make something, do something, but don't try to force it all on me. You're *not* my responsibility!'

'You raped my idea!' she cried up to him from the foot of the stairs. Then feverishly, working out the unbelievable truth, 'And you can just pretend it's yours. Because of me you're getting everything you want and I don't even get one month's rent.' Crushed under the weight of final, shocking disappointment, Heidi had to sit, ruined, deserted, on the bottom step. 'I thought I *was* changing my life by getting involved with Chick and you.'

'Stop it,' Alex said with some softness, coming down to sit with her. 'I'd never take credit for your idea.'

'Well, I won't stop it, because we're friends. You're my friend and I want to keep it going, you know? I don't want to lose it, it should go on.' Her cheek quivered. 'I mean, I hear about your wonderful deal, your salary, thousands of dollars, Alex. You know what that is to me? You can buy clothes, I don't know, a new pair of shoes or a car or whatever. How do you think that makes me feel!'

She knows where I live was Alex's paralysing worry. In Heidi's version, he was the man who teased her with success and security and then egotistically deprived her of reward. He defiled her trust, retailed her optimism, made her a casualty of the kind of business he does, the kind of person he is . . .

'I didn't know you actually wanted to get involved in any of it after we got the company running. Not the day-to-day part *per se*.'

'Oh, Alex. I want to stop *living* day-to-day.' She dabbed a knuckle into her sticky mascara as if it were blood trickling from a wound. 'Will you let me go get a tissue from inside?'

He almost told her to keep the box, handing her the Kleenexes. Pouring Heidi a cup of coffee and not asking her what happened to the cakes from Canter's left him feeling like some kind of philanthropist.

4   My Argument Against Public Safety

WOULD he have put in an appearance at Baylor's 'Democalypse' show if the event hadn't promised him a couple of prime opportunities for self-promotion? In the first case Teddy Fonseca invited Alex to cater the opening with the full range of Hummingbird Farm sausages, which over the summer had won hip cachet with the pack that ran between AIDS benefits and art galleries; in the second case, there in public, away from the farm office, outside of his apartment, Alex could probe to see if the impersonal world agreed with his own idea of his personal substance (will he be sought out? will businessmen ask him about his business? will he intrigue anyone?

who?), a much more telling and critical test than generally measuring his progress by tax bracket alone.

Press coverage of Baylor's latest assault on our country's tenderest assumptions about itself stirred up acrobatic protests from the American Legion, the LAPD, Focus on the Family, and lone avengers who had to pretend that art mattered enough to be dangerous. Oh, they knew dangerous art, too, sure, because otherwise why would they notice it? Under their skin, Baylor's new residence: squatting there and multiplying the bacteria of his paintings, teeming germs incubated in the warmth of a National Endowment grant, released with the purpose and power to squirt toxins of doubt, pessimism, unrest and futility into the American bloodstream.

I'm pretty certain that the counterblast didn't erupt from any horror of the particular images photo-silkscreened onto different hunks of consumer debris. After all, pictures like these of murder victims, gun-toting nine-year-olds, drug raids, creeping squalor, child pornography and the perpetual Mardi Gras of the super rich showed up daily in the tabloids and nightly on television. These people weren't jumping because of the severed car bodies hung on the wall, or the trash can lids, suitcases, shopping carts, vacuum cleaners or refrigerator doors Baylor used as canvases; the message that reached in, grabbed and twisted was that life in Los Angeles really is this terrible, worse is on the way and the inert, insensible social order is all to blame.

The amputees and war-wounded paraplegics formed the moral and physical backbone of the sidewalk blockade. Pressing unchafed through the pickets, who chanted 'Hell, no! Don't go!' directly at each guest on arrival, Alex saved his placid, neighborly wave and smile for the army officer in the wheelchair who located and indicted him with the viewfinder of his PalmCorder.

A step inside the gallery he ran into the *objet d'art* that jammed the scummiest stink up patriotic noses. Baylor had an American flag staked out two inches above the floor, pegged by its edges to the walls of a narrow corridor. The only option allowed to avoid desecrating it with footprints was for you to inch your way along a sagging, unstable plank just a shoe-width wide, raised unevenly on bricks, a margin that ran the length of one of the walls. Alex tramped straight over the flag to whoops and cackles behind him which somehow echoed louder when he entered the main room.

'Smile happy.' Teddy Fonseca scooted in from the side, framed Alex in his Polaroid.

Alex swerved his face out of frame. '*Don't*, Teddy. I'm not here for you,' a pestered celebrity, denying him a shot.

'I won't believe your lies,' pouted Teddy *à la française*.

'Don't take a picture of me, I hate the way I look in pictures.'

'Because you pose. Don't pose.'

'I look stupid in photographs, so just don't, okay?'

'Alex, you don't look stupid. *I* look stupid.' Teddy spread his arms to demonstrate, to model his outfit – mauve plaid flared golf trousers cinched to his skinny waist by a white plastic belt, forest green checked drip-dry shirt, maroon doubleknit sports jacket and white patent leather pumps – Middle America dressed for slaughter, perky satire themed with the target of Baylor's new work. 'For the visitors book, Alex. For Baylor. Smile happy. Say *fromage*.'

The bare arm slinking halfway around Alex's chest was too fragrant and womanly to belong to Heidi, and if it had been her, of course, he'd be the butt of this sex kitten come-on instead of its honoree. He hugged Alba to his side and said to Teddy, 'Take one of *this*, I want a photographic record of this historic reunion!' Then to Alba, genuinely, 'We only get to see each other at occasions. It was your house-warming party last time, oh jeez, when was that – February sometime?'

Not as long ago as that, but for five months anyway, Alex's only contact with Alba had been by telephone. The raw material of those conversations tended to be his business reports and her financial advice, steady and practical and unavoidably insightful. Seeing her, touching her again was already a reminiscence which itself was proof of his persistence in her heart, of Alba's constant knowledge of him. A sly squint from her and he was reminded of, connected to, his truest, earliest intentions.

The schoolyard tenderness of their lip-to-lip smooch was fractured by the crack and wash of the camera flash. 'Too fine, too fine,' they heard Teddy congratulate himself, examining the picture. He didn't show it to them, he slotted it straight into the kitschy leatherette visitors' book.

Alba waved a cocktail sausage at Alex and by way of a compliment caressed it with her tongue and moved it in and out between her lips.

'You want to endorse them on TV?'

'If you make me chocolate ones for my birthday,' she said, biting it in half.

'We have the machinery. The chefess is supposed to be here. You can ask her yourself. Really you ought to come see the farm, it's the cutting edge of pork technology.'

'I know, *don't*. Somehow I got the idea that you buy a house and move into it. Do you want to hear my list? Mosaic tiles in the big bathroom, closets in our bedroom, Baylor's sound system doesn't work in his studio – I have to stop there or I'll make myself crazy all over again.'

'It's a big house.'

'It's ballast,' she accepted. 'We're completely, seriously here now, in the city.' That was meant to sound positive and forward-looking but only sounded irreversible. 'Hey now, Mr HD Systems, *listen*,' suddenly thrilled to spread the word, 'you'll be in a highly visible tax bracket next year.'

'Camouflage, I need camouflage.' His father's joke.

Alba looked past him, said in a loud hush, 'Is that it, Bobba?'

'The Sausage King of LA!' Baylor hailed and dubbed Alex and laid a flat package about the size of a glossy magazine at his feet.

'In a plain brown wrapper, hmm . . . ' Fingernailing the tape from the seam at the back Alex guessed, 'Could it be the September issue of *Girls Who Like To Buttfuck?*'

The gold leaf around the edges, the antique wood panel that it bordered told him no, probably not a masturbation aid. He was holding a flawless pastiche of a Medieval altarpiece.

'It's the Ascension,' clarified Baylor. 'See the pig losing his pink nightie?'

In Baylor's glorification of the Pig Heaven logo the angelic pig, drained of his earthly pink, was rising into the radiant azure cavern of the sky, his head haloed in gold, his face lifted to greet Paradise which appeared through an opening in the pillowy clouds, where his Pig Father and the choir of Pig Saints waited for him to be borne up from the world on his pearl-white wings, long and powerful, cocked back on their majestic upstroke. Stationed in the air below him, pig seraphs raised golden trumpets in exultant fanfare while a pair of pig cherubs coiled the tails of a silken banner around the shafts of the ta-rumping horns. Blazoned across the banner in letters red on gold was the motto *Sus Scrofus Domesticus*.

'It was worth getting up today,' Alex said, looking down at the painting in his hands. 'It's a beauty.'

The hollering outside died down for a minute or two and the single din of gallery chatter filled the room with low-level excitement, none of it, from anything I could hear, about the art. Mooing about restaurants, cawing about personal trainers, snuffling around the buffet table, aimless and vain name-dropping, but the awareness of Baylor's move away from graffiti cartoonishness and toward a new seriousness that was more rooted in the daily calamities of actual experience didn't run any deeper than two-word remarks: 'brutally honest' . . . 'shocking realism' . . . 'poetic force' . . . 'street politics' . . . descriptions lifted straight out of the catalog notes and studiously recycled to lubricate exchanges of *really* necessary information. Let one example stand for them all: 'This kind of, Baylor's kind of street politics equals rap music, it's rap music in a visual form, so let's show this stuff to Iceboi and he can pick one of these out for the album cover, any one he wants as long as it repro's sharp enough on a T-shirt.'

'*Hell, no! Don't go!*' the injured voices rattled back in, stoked up dramatically, freshly insulted.

In answer to Alex's unasked question Baylor pointed to the string of small p.a. speakers hidden along the underside of the balcony overhead. 'Teddy's idea of a soundtrack for my show, piping it in off the street,' a hyper-realistic accent that Baylor pretty obviously considered a waste of electrical engineering. 'He would've been happy with cars going by. Or a siren. He's just creaming himself over *this*.'

Those last six words of Baylor's perversely captioning for Alex the view he had of Heidi's entrance. Hiking boots, bare, scraped, boyish legs, dirndl skirt, varsity sweater closed by only two buttons, she trooped across the room as if it were the last stretch of her polar expedition.

'I just got my picture taken by some weirdo,' she needed to brief everybody. Also, 'Nelda and JT just got here, too.' Next piece of business, which made her suddenly, charmingly breathless: 'Are you finally going to introduce me?'

'Heidi works with us on the marketing side,' Alex placed her for Alba and Baylor. 'She led the sausage squad into our retail outlets.'

'They weren't our retail outlets then.'

He corrected the historical record. 'Absolutely, she brought in the key stores in the key areas. I don't even want to know how she did it.'

'Actors are the best sales staff you could hire,' she drawled, asserting the point.

Alba suggested, 'Especially if they've got strong feelings about sausages.'

'We can fake anything,' Heidi said.

Somebody had to obey the etiquette, and since Baylor hadn't formally joined the conversation yet, by law the job was his. 'You're an actress? That's what you do when you're not doing the sausage thing?'

'Hey, no. The sausage thing is what I do when I'm not acting. I've got a poster of one of your X-Baby pieces, it's my favorite thing. The one with the bleeding heart and the chicken head? *X-Baby True Love*? Maybe you could sign it for me or something.'

'Um, sure. Just give it to Alex.'

'I wish I could afford the original,' her piercing regret.

Alex said, 'When you sell your millionth pack of sausages.'

'No, my millionth *sausage*.' Which reminded her, 'Oh, Alba,' after five minutes as cozy as her sorority sister, 'do you think you can go over my money situation with me? My income is like from five or six different directions and I'm like *oh no* what am I supposed to do *now*?'

A signature from Baylor, financial counseling from Alba, a regular salary from Alex . . . and while he glanced down at his shoelaces, at the groove in the floor, anywhere except into his friends' carefully undisturbed expressions, while he wondered who or what Heidi's four or five other sources of income could be, Alex missed seeing Nelda inch her way into the room, balancing like a ballerina along the plank, tiptoeing past the flag.

Somewhere behind her, his shoulder hunched into the wall, JT attempted the same route, one large shoe in front of the other. Two steps in, plywood bowing under him, his best intentions lacking the gyroscopic power to keep him up, he wobbled and tipped sideways out of the safety zone. 'Whoh! I'm okay, I'm fine here,' a flourish, arms in the air, size twelves planted in the middle of Old Glory.

I don't think he could have noticed Teddy against the general movement in the gallery. If he had then I'm sure that JT would have charmed that snapshot away from him, he would have known in a second how such a photograph just cries out for a distorted and damaging interpretation, how it might be manipulated, publicized, circulated, maliciously exploited by people who were not his friends.

149

'Boy, the force of gravity sure isn't on my side today!' he drolly paid off everybody who was looking at him. That idly disbanding group didn't include either Nelda or Teddy – she'd headed out on her own to inspect the sausage arrangements and he'd skipped off to the visitors' book with his prize portrait of Reverend Goofy trampling our national emblem.

With a sober sense of his own initiation Alex towed Baylor over to meet JT and stood close between them as they shook hands – the referee between two heavyweights, conspicuously one of the men. And just as notably separated from everybody else, not only promoted in rank but declared by this fraternal closeness to be someone who deserves to be treated seriously. Alex caught the odd ray of momentary curiosity that flashed in at them on the weightless drifting glances of anonymous guests who'd never come over to interrupt, who respected the secrecy of man-talk-in-progress, who understood the terms of stardom.

'It's too bad y'know, my artwork keeps distracting everybody from your sausages,' Baylor generously mentioned.

Alex smiled slimily to JT, Igor to Baron Frankenstein, 'Our plan is working, Master.'

'That's right, we're on a crusade,' a fatherly pat on Alex's back. 'It's all part of our holy crusade.'

'Looks like it's happening,' Baylor said. 'If it's a crusade to make Alex into a meat tycoon.'

'The new ones went *real* fast,' Alex said. 'The sage and honey ones.' He confided to Baylor, 'It's the first one of our Fall recipes. We're bringing out two more new flavors in September–October.'

'Hey, Lex. There's your first million.'

'Sausages are only the by-product,' JT had to say, crucially refreshing everyone's memory. 'The main product of Hummingbird Farm is Hummingbird Farm. Man, if you'd've seen what a wreck it was before I took it over, it was Hiroshima. One ungodly mess and *nobody* else had the inspiration to see how it could be raised up. How *far*. Now we've got a whole futuristic system installed out there, we've got Almighty God in back of us pushing Hummingbird Farm all the way. Success against all the odds you can name. Tell you what, *that's* shocking a few people.' He brought the volume down, 'Jackasses who think they're descended from King David.'

'Anybody I know?' Alex asked.

'You'll run into them. It won't matter.' JT stared up at one of Baylor's pieces and came back to him saying, 'Do you know the work of the English artist Hogarth?'

'He can get a little cartoony, but, yeah,' Baylor admitted, 'he's got an attitude.'

'I enjoy his paintings. I bought a folio of some prints of his at an auction in London.' Again considering Baylor's Cadillac fender adorned with lynch mob silhouettes, 'Your work reminds me of Hogarth. In intention. Don't let 'em deny what they do.'

'I've got another one upstairs that's stronger like that. More like Hogarth if Fidel Castro paid him to decorate his bedroom with porno scenes of life in the White House.'

Alex wasn't sure how much of that was friendly art quackery and how much friendly hustle, but whatever it was JT buried it under a spontaneous concept of his own. 'They should see the rest of your stuff,' nodding at the picket line outside. 'Send 'em completely buggy, right? They don't even know what they're protesting about.'

'I don't think they're really interested in modern art,' Alex observed. 'They get more meaning out of monster truck rallies on TV.'

'You don't want to blank those people out, the work's necessary to them and they're necessary to the work,' JT lobbied Baylor. 'You ought to put your pictures on billboards all over Los Angeles. On the side panels of RTD buses.'

'Sure, give the shermheads a big target to hit that stops every four blocks.'

'What do you think provokes them all so much?' JT waited for an insight from the artist, waited for two seconds. 'What are they so excited about?'

'A big nigger telling them how it is,' Baylor smiled securely.

JT answered the smile and the directness. 'That's about half of it. You show them the genuine ugly details of what's around them, what they're in up to their necks, and from there, all by themselves, they can picture the exact opposite. You just measure the distance for them and they're scared because it's a long, long way between what it is and what it ain't. You exercise their imagination, you give them energy and they don't know what to do with it. They just ball up their fists, cross their eyes, clench their teeth and go argh, argh, argh. You've got to push them past being scared of all this because if they know how to contemplate the opposite they can *move* toward it. They rely on people like us, the ones who *do things*, to give them a little shove in the direction of betterment. Crack things loose first, there's the violent beauty you can force into their lives.'

In my non-medical opinion this wayward reasoning was another sign of JT's mental fatigue, a foreshadowing of the compulsion that twisted him so tightly when he knew he was dying. What persists in a strong mind aware of its own exhaustion? What emerges from its matter after every testable idea has been worn away?

Leafing through the visitors book, past thirty or forty different faces and then coming to his, I realized it was his language that seized me more than his argument, the prophetic exaggeration that shuddered out of his Christianity and seemed to catapult him further beyond it than anything I'd heard him say before outside the privacy of his home or office. Only later I had the thought that 'violent beauty' is the longing before the Crucifixion, before any martyrdom.

The Polaroid of the Reverend was only wedged into the spine of the book and that made it easy to palm. I slipped it into my billfold and bumped against Heidi as the billfold was on its way into my pocket. She didn't remotely notice me there.

'So he's like, well, why don't you just do this to the hilt for a year or whatever for the financial security and then I can go after acting work full-time. Nobody's casting right now anyway, it's dead until the pilot season,' the inside word she passed along to Nelda, 'so I'm like, fine, if I haven't found an agent I want to commit to by then, okay sure, let's talk about it again. And then I hung up on him.' Heidi laughed at that.

'You can get addicted to regular money,' Nelda advised, sanely.

'Not a habit this small.'

'Compared to how much you used to make waitressing? At least from – '

'Uh, no: compared to Alex's sixty-five thousand.' Heidi interrupted. 'He tried to buy me off for five hundred dollars, just, he's like, here's your money – goodbye. Forget any legal deal he made with me, he wanted to do what he wanted to do.'

'Who does that sound like? Hmmmmmm?' the hum a rising accusation.

'It's all *business* to him, that's how he makes you feel. He's worth sixty-five thousand and I'm worth five hundred.'

'You're saying that, Heidi. I really doubt if Alex thinks about it that way *at all*. He's not a petty person, he's got his mind on bigger things.'

'Okay, who does that sound like?'

Nelda had to turn around to see who it was that Heidi was singling out with her frozen leer, eyes squinting into the glare of the obvious. 'No . . . Is he like Jim?'

'He's a maniac for success.'

The maniac under discussion, sitting quietly alone on the lower steps of the staircase and tallying the sausages left over on the buffet table, was acting distinctly unmaniacal – soberly reasonable, in fact, agreeing with himself not to march into a conversation with Nelda unless she was off on her own or close by her husband. Either this or that, the window open or closed, heads or tails.

Open.

Almost alone out of the snacking, drinking, rubbernecking hoopla, Nelda moved slowly from piece to piece, intent on the art. The video loop that gripped her attention two and three times over was playing on a five-inch TV screen which Baylor had grafted onto the elegant enamel face of an Early American grandfather clock. He'd scissored the one-minute clip out of a home video made by a gang of muggers who recorded their crime and then sold the tape to a local TV news show. Over the flattened body of the Korean victim his attacker crooned to himself, 'Outta one punch, knocked the man *out*!' stomping around him, sweatshirt hood pulled up, pacing the championship ring. 'Knocked the young man out on one punch, oh shit! Who did that to the man? Punched him *out* . . . '

'I've got an order for two dozen chocolate sausages,' Alex greeted Nelda.

The non-sequitur must have added a Dadaist twist to her experience of that video mugging. 'This is sort of disturbing,' she said, darting a finger at the screen, her back turned toward it to conceal the gesture as if she might be seen by those little men.

'Disturbing is good sometimes, isn't it?'

Boosh. She looked away from Alex at the sound of fist crunching into nose bridge again and this time Nelda regarded the motive, the punch and the idiot dance of savage superiority from a distance of pity and amazement. 'What a man loves to do with his body,' head shaking in total dismay, 'it's wicked.' And she said again, directly to Alex, 'It's wicked, you know?'

He was half-caught reading the line of her hair, the upsidedown V made high up the back of her neck by the pair of braids she wore, Apache fashion, fastened at the paintbrush ends by rough strips of suede.

'Women just don't act that way with their bodies. It's not a natural thing for us to do,' Nelda was saying.

'Have you ever watched women's mud wrestling?'

'Women who work for men.'

'Some Saturday I'll take you to see it. I'd like to hear your opinion from a ringside seat.'

'You go to women's mud wrestling?' she inquired.

'Not *every* Saturday.'

Head shaking again, past Alex's joke. 'Our bodies weren't made for that, for hitting out.'

'They must be made for something else.' Alex knew when he said it that the dumb, unintentional locker room overtone was impossible to disown.

Nelda's smile widened with the dry pleasure that might congratulate a dyslexic's correct spelling of dog or cat. 'For taking things. For taking them.'

'I wouldn't try to sell Heidi on that idea.'

Emotional loot plundered from him by Heidi he was about to give up to Nelda without a struggle. He'd been swimming toward a decision semi-consciously all summer, nudged on at first merely by being a man around these two women and after that by his enlarging knowledge of their separate tensions and dangers. Heidi was a woman made of grudge and grievance, envy and suspicion, of blown chances and fruitless toil, explosive, tactless, fanged and taloned, a creature shaped by the forces of opposition and crisis, who demanded comparison with Nelda. Where Heidi was indignant Nelda was tolerant, where she had sarcasm Nelda had amused insight, instead of pose and posture the unaffected delicacy (as Alex read it) possessed by native maidens, although that impression could have been the effect on him of those long dark braids and ankle-length chamois skirt. Affections and confidences that would be squandered on Heidi and taken hostage he sensed Nelda would protect; she was pregnable to him in all the ways that Heidi was impregnable and where Heidi was flamboyantly available Nelda was married to his partner. Alex vibrated with the thrill of entering a place uninvited; virile mischief, risky surprise, vital ingredients of his big business success.

'Has anyone introduced you to Baylor yet, or Alba?'

A slow, lowing, 'No-oo-oo . . . '

'I'll do that thing. Her birthday's next month, so you think chocolate sausages can be a manufacturing reality by then?'

'Oh, you really want me to make them,' she understood. 'We'd have to experiment with a few recipes first.'

'We can use the kitchen after hours, we just have to hose out the Humpty,' another in today's series of probably lewd semi-accidents, which they both checked with archly polite coughs and turned the phrase into an instant private joke.

'It's my Home Ec project,' she said, reclaiming respectability. 'For extra credit.' Nelda stopped it there, lagged behind the fun and shared an inspiration. 'Alex, hey, it'd be so cute if we made candy versions we could sell right next to the other ones. Children would love them, I bet, *especially* children.'

'Well, let's talk about it some more. Could be an Easter item, uh-huh. I know a chocolate sausage would've made a serious impression on me when I was a little kid.'

'Me, too. I was totally miserable until I was sixteen.'

'I wasn't miserable until after sixteen. Probably for the exact same reason.'

On this Nelda was silent. 'It's funny seeing you someplace besides the farm. You're a little different.'

'Relaxed.'

'You always feel relaxed with your real friends.'

A shriek as harsh and bright as a Roman candle went up from Teddy, cutting off every private thought in the room. 'No! No! They are *not* coming in! They are NOT!' Arms stretched out behind him, stiffened with rage, upper body rigid too, tilting into JT who blindly ignored him.

'It's not so *scary*! Come on down!' JT at one end of the corridor was waving to the mob at the other end of the corridor who were jamming the entrance and hollering back at him about 'porno art' and 'gutter artists'.

Except for the new chant, 'Come! Out! Reverend! Reverend! Come! Out!' they were held at bay by their own flag taboo, the visible barrier was a moral boundary tangible enough for them to press their toes against. Glowering at defiers and defamers was an act of reverence, of Christian and American resistance against willful, temperamental individualists who charge around refusing to obey any of the normal restrictions.

And whom might *that* describe, eh?

'Come on into the lion's den, see maybe God's in here, too!'

'Reverend, you come out!' Softened with an implied plea to reason, the command issued from the officer in the wheelchair. 'I fought in Korea and in Vietnam, sir, and I'm here to tell you that American soldiers did not throw down their lives for social pornography like you got going on in there. I didn't fight for some hippy's so-called right to demean the American flag!'

'Brother Officer, that's exactly what we went out there to fight for. What else do you think the fight was *about*?' Somebody in the doorway pitched a whole can of Coke at JT, it thudded into his chest like a brick. 'Yeah!' he welcomed it. 'Now we're getting somewhere!'

When it came the change was so fast and complete. Out of shuddering disappointment, such hate against him. What used to be lovable about JT, when he was an extremist on their side, now, suddenly, was detestable. A minute ago he was their colossus, they expected to see his outrage and outrageousness boil over into some cleansing act, to evoke Jesus, Jesus the vigilante, Jesus the discipli-narian, Jesus the vanquisher of opponents, scourger of deviants, Jesus raising God's own uproar, breaking up the moneychangers' tables. They expected JT to wade into Baylor Lejeune's art exhibit with a baseball bat; instead, he stood there in the middle of the obscenity grinning out at them, daring them all to walk unprotected into the full force of the horrifying insult and open their minds and hearts to the severe truth.

Once the disruption started [the wording of my official report] *JT rode it into a demonstration that swallowed up the art and the protest together, he manipulated that event into a display of his moral fitness.* To support my view I showed Bobby Dyson a series of photographs shot outside the art gallery after the police arrived. In the middle of the scuffle JT stood solidly rooted, arms lifted in gentle authority, eyes calm and placating, and where he wasn't making peace he was fraternizing with the policemen, shaking hands and signing autographs. I didn't give Bobby the Polaroid, I didn't say a word about it.

But I did include the tape and transcript of a telephone call that

Oswald Pogenpohl made to JT from Sacramento early on Monday morning. After a few minutes of plausible interest in developments at Hummingbird Farm Oswald lurched into the real purpose of the conversation; reassurance.

Pogenpohl: I don't want to mess around with your tactics, Jim, only, you know —

JT: I don't have tactics, just illumination.

Pogenpohl: Whatever you want to call it. But I don't think Howard's going to benefit in any way at all from, uh, if you associate yourself with that liberal type of occasion.

JT: I bought one of Baylor's paintings for your campaign office up there.

Pogenpohl: Did you? Well, uh . . .[Self-conscious laugh.] On the serious side for a minute, you, you, uh, *do* want God's choice of governor to get in in November, don't you?

JT: Oswald, God's choice is going to get in. That's how we'll know he's God's choice.

Dangerous countersocial behavior of the kind manifested by Rev. Tickell should be encouraged [the closing recommendation of my report] *in officers of government bureaux and institutions at every level, federal, state, county and municipal. In an environment such as would be created, the entire population is sporadically forced to re-examine the core values, motives and consequences of their individual lives.*

I cited modern Italy as a prime example of this approach in practise.

'Why not paint out the traffic lights and street signs too?' Bobby argued with me. You're talking about anarchy.'

Three terms in elected office and that was the whimpering end of any sense of humor he ever had.

5   Road to Gloryland

POLITICAL action enlarged Bobby in his days of angry dissent, but state politics, its bloodless necessities and ground-level lobbying, made him small. What I could still recognize of the passion of his commitment to bring change, his agitation, his command, shriveled into the thick-skinned unpersuadability that finally made us strangers.

Of course JT lay at the heart of the rift. In spite of the moss of moral ambiguity that fuzzed the hard facts about how and on what JT spent Worldview Ministry donations, Bobby stuck with his first assumption that the Reverend was an out-and-out fraud. The next deduction, obviously, was that JT's every effort was bent toward bulking up his already gargantuan personal fortune. Worse, this fixed vision of him slanted out of a fiery instant of conversion, the moment when Bobby discovered that his own widowed mother had nearly pauperized herself to bankroll Rev. Tickell's high living.

The scattershot of freckles across his nose and cheeks, with that relaxed wing of sunbleached hair lolling across his forehead, gave Bobby the look of a teenager sauntering in for lunch with the extra dollar he earned from mowing the neighbor's lawn. What he'd been doing all week was almost as valuable to the community, campaigning up and down the Central Valley from the back of a flatbed truck, and when we met up at his mother's house he was still trilling from the rhapsody of hope he inspired at a rally of six hundred United Farm Workers.

His mother and I were catching him on the wing, a lunchtime breather before he was due in San Francisco at a two hour Q&A session with cutting-edge entrepreneurs from the millennium industries of artificial intelligence and genetic engineering. The fathers of these young women and men probably remembered Bobby with his fist raised in a Black Power salute, scary eyed and shouting 'Baby butcher!' at them. From his mom he only wanted a tuna fish sandwich and a glass of milk, and from me he wanted a quick rundown on the tape of edited highlights I'd selected from JT's non-stop Saturday-Sunday Faith-a-thon.

'His suits always look so handsome on him,' commentary from Mrs Dyson as JT left his band vamping on *Ain't Misbehavin'* to stroll across to his high-backed chair. 'There's nothing cheap about how he looks.'

'You probably paid for his gold cuff-links,' Bobby reminded her.

'I hope I did,' she said, 'he deserves beautiful things.' Not defiant, but sensible and fair. Her talents for sense and fairness were honed and hardened during thirty years in the public school system, eighteen as a history teacher and twelve as principal of the high school where her four sons won their academic and athletic honors. Any wrangle that she needed to mediate, any decision that stopped with her, Mrs Dyson settled with an unemotional appeal to civilized notions of mutual respect and simple human decency, effective standards which Bobby's lifework (1964–1971) seemed to have been dedicated so vehemently to subverting. And now I was sitting in the uncluttered living-room where Bobby's reprised values originated, where in hours of family discussions he learned the language spoken by the people who put people in power.

In her home the administrator's skills were redirected into maintaining a base camp for her scattered brood and, today, organizing a nutritious lunch – sandwich *and* soup, carrot cake *and* fresh fruit – for her over-energetic middle child. When performing as hostess Irene Dyson had the warmly formal air of a woman whose duty was her pleasure. Small and wide, she wore soft clothes, layered intentionally to bury her body out of sight. She played to the strength of her face, her wintery gray eyes set deep and wide, as if for stability, in the square clean-lined face which was clasped all around by a short, undyed bob, three more shades of gray, fine, obedient hair curving forward against the sides of her head and ending in two precise points at her jawline, a discreet reminder of the premium she placed on resolution.

Bobby jabbed his thumb at the TV screen and said, 'Oh this is a master. He's a master in action, Mom. This is the man who plays golf with God.'

'I went to bed before this part came on,' she said, watching with him. 'It's amazing how he can keep going and going. I lasted till ten at night and I couldn't keep my eyes open after that.'

'You didn't send him any more money, did you?'

'Not really.'

'Didn't we make a definite decision about this?' Bobby asked her, squaring up. 'He doesn't need your money and you don't have enough money to spend on – on what? What's he retailing this time? Korean orphans that glow in the dark?'

'Bobby, please don't *chastise* me. I only ordered one pack of sausages, they're making a special new flavor I want to try. It's not such a big difference if my Americard bill goes up by nine dollars.'

'On a credit card,' he said to me. 'That makes it easy. Mom, okay, it's not your nine dollars. It's nine dollars times five hundred thousand, times *a million*. He broadcasts all over the country and, trust me, his message has got exactly nothing to do with Jesus Christ, Mother Mary, the Apostles, God or even Christianity, if you ask me. No, Jim Tickell only has one message, you know what it is?

It's *pay me and I'll prove what a great man I am — pay me more, make me greater!*'

'I'm not stupid, I listen to what he teaches, I *listen* to what he says and the way he says it, and he's a sincere man. He wants people to come to Christ, Bobby.'

'To join the club.'

'Say it in those words, all right. What's so terrible about that?'

'It's a fan club, that's what. Tell me something – if he really is doing what he does for the glory of the same God you believe in, why doesn't he have any respect for people? *As individuals.* People are just his raw material. He herds them in the door at one end of his factory and they come out at the other end hundreds of dollars lighter. Around and around they go. He scares them and then exploits their fear, he shames them and then exploits their conscience. He's a fraud.'

'You came home from your first day of freshman philosophy, seventeen years old, and you used that word. You told me you finally knew that every religion in the history of the world was a big fraud. I'm sorry if you still think that. It means you can't understand a man who dedicates himself to God.' She turned her strong face toward the TV. JT sat with a *Wall Street Journal* open on his lap and he'd donned a pith helmet. 'He wants people to believe and be saved.'

'As long as they believe in him too,' Bobby rallied, '*and then* he can plug them into the ancient magic. Even if he honestly believes everything he says he's still a fraud because the whole extravaganza is really all about *him*. He wants to save people? I don't think so. He wants people to save *him* – from a low income, from a dinky, anonymous life. What he wants is money and influence, he wants political protection that'll make it easier for him to collect more money and pay less tax, and if he doesn't get what he wants he throws a public tantrum, he calls *me* dirty names. Jack knows all the behind-the-scenes facts, I'm not making up this stuff just to convince you. Tickell takes people's savings and he doesn't give anything back, nothing half as real.' His mother was finished defending herself from this barrage, she'd moved on to pressing the tin foil wrapper around the rim of the cake plate. Bobby tried again to drag me in on his side. 'Jack, help me here.'

I told him that if we only had an hour he should stop talking and pay attention to the video:

'All right, Tommy. Seen enough of that now. Can you show me the next slide? Advance it, are you with me? Just tap the little button on the right that says "advance". Okay, good, we've advanced . . .'

The color snapshots of Hummingbird Farm flashed up onstage behind JT, luminously projected onto an expanse of silver screen. From his storyteller's seat he narrated the farm's redemption in an unfolding series of scenes arranged to remind us of a journey from the deepest cavity in the pit of hell up into the clean enveloping light of destiny and salvation.

Ten or twelve famished sows gazed out dull-eyed at his studio audience from their wet-floored concrete barn, a picture you might use in a poster campaign for prisoners of conscience, more Paraguyan jail than Golden State piggery. 'That's another Before picture there. Look at those scrawny things. You couldn't squeeze six slices of bacon out of all those sad pathetic creatures put together.'

The gnarled muddy yard, the broken-backed school bus, the tumbleweed and dirt clod field where a few listless hogs lay scattered like skid row drunks, 'Just terrible. Doesn't that look like an atomic bomb hit it? All its future is behind it, that's how it looks from here. Rundown to nothing, bankrupt, godforsaken. Man oh man, I don't want God against me, He's too powerful! Look at what happens to a place when He just *ignores* it, it's degraded, it declines into slime.' JT contemplated the view of the collapsed sow house and the trash-choked gulley next to it. 'Nobody in charge who knows what to do or who'd know how to do it if anybody told them, a lot like the bug house of our glorious senate in Sacramento, see any similarities?'

And then the handover, as JT captioned it, a group portrait onsite with Oswald Pogenpohl, Ving Kimmel and JT in front of a bulldozer at the groundbreaking of Hummingbird Farm's renovation . . . rapidly, inevitably, followed by vistas of repair and renewal, progress and improvement – the Reverend in work boots and white hard hat directing the heavy machinery, welcoming truckload deliveries of corrugated sheet metal and copper pipes, timber and concrete, studying blueprints and pointing off to some new development beyond the edge of the frame, beyond the edge of everything that was visible to us, a pioneer father mapping the unforged trail . . .

. . . and like the mayor of a frontier town JT met the new arrivals as they trotted down the gangplanks, pink, young and healthy porkers, emigrants who stepped off from the corn-fed heart of Iowa, oinking with hope you'd think, to replenish the white palace that was the new dry sow house, the bungalows, veranda units, flat decks and cage houses, the Eden that was the rolling meadow of the boars' landscaped stomping ground . . .

. . . in the Pig Heaven kitchens Nelda and Heidi posed with the twin working Humpty Dumpsters, cranking out the premiere batch of hickory flavor sausages, and down by the shingle-roofed patio there was the thin, intense figure of the system's inventor standing at the front of a long double-decked row of – 'No, those aren't a lot of washing machines, they're more Humpty Dumpsters, and the ones that aren't making sausages are making fuel pellets out of garbage, and the Humpties that aren't doing that are making pig food out of a bunch of other stuff and the ones that aren't doing that are making fertilizer out of, well, some other unmentionable stuff. There's our resident scientific genius Chick Uchiyama who's done some revolutionizing work with an ingredient he extracted from the pulp of the yucca tree. He added a little bit of it to our pig feed and it breaks down all the ammonia and hydrogen sulfide in the unmentionable stuff I almost just mentioned. Hey, I'm not joking about it! Come on out and ask our neighbors. Hummingbird Farm's got the sweetest smelling pigs in all creation . . . '

. . . in the leafy neighborhood streets Anthony and Munro were out on their garbage round collecting paper and plastic scraps from curbside Pig Heaven bins, and then, there they were back again at the farm cramming that trash by the cubic yard into the line of Humpties. 'We're producing almost twenty-five per cent of our own electricity and we're only right at the *very beginning* of this. You can see God working here, everywhere you see something happening around Hummingbird Farm, He's not forsaking the place anymore. It's a miracle of reversal, so praise Him, it's God blessed. Keep your eyes open for the next ten minutes and I'll show you God's promise at work. You're about to witness a pretty miraculous demonstration. Watch this.'

The Reverend signaled with a small twitch of his fingers and that brought Munro out from behind the cameras. He hustled in with a wheelbarrow load of organic waste, hustled off the way he came, hustled back with a metal cart that cradled a Humpty Dumpster and its battery supply, and then he flitted away again. Walking over to the machine JT said, 'Here's my recipe for turning decay and corruption into something you save and use. I've got somebody who's come in especially today to make a guest appearance on our Faith-a-thon, he's taking time out to be here with us and there's only ten days to go before the election.' The applause ignited and flared before JT spoke the name. 'Attorney General of the State of California, Mr Howard Porta.'

Over the tail-end of the clapping JT asked how the campaign felt to him. Howard said, 'We're getting a fantastic response all over the state. Everybody I've talked to has been wonderful. Business people in San Diego, garment workers in Los Angeles, elementary school teachers up in Redding, they all want solid, steady improvements in their lives. Not radical, hotheaded solutions to imaginary problems.'

'California's got enough real problems to get rid of.'

'Well that's right, and about all of them are in the state senate.'

'You can get in some practise while you're here,' handing Porta a shovel. 'You'll be doing a lot of this after November 6th, after you take over the governor's office. Take all of this slop and slop it into the Humpty.'

'Am I working for you now?' He spilled in the first shovelful. 'I guess I am. Is this just general slop or a mixture?'

'It's a regular Caesar salad, Howard. We've got – ' and each ingredient raised a cringing moan from the crowd, *'compost . . . pig manure . . .* and *rotten vegetables.* Try not to drip any of it on your clothes.'

'No! Don't stop me now. I think I'm having a good time!'

'Looks like you enjoy doing the dirty work.'

'That's the crazy kind of hairpin I am, Jim.'

JT allowed Porta the honor of punching the on-button and the Humpty Dumpster whirred and whistled up to speed. A few seconds later the Attorney General held the first damp fertilizer pellets in the palm of his hand. 'Oh, wonderful, *wonderful.* There's no smell to it *at all,*' he relished, a true son of the soil now, crumbling the firm pale brown grainy pâté under his thumb.

'You can fertilize a desert with it. Turn the Mojave into one big golf course.'

'Maybe you could ship a few of your machines over to Kuwait. When the Coalition forces capture Saddam Hussein they can drop him in one and grind him up. At least that way his life can *amount* to something.' Fierce, euphoric cheers from the bleachers and a round of applause led by JT, support which Porta warmly received with his Grand Marshal of the Rose Parade smile, nod and wave.

'I'm sure we'll get over to the Arabs eventually,' JT said.

'Seriously, your work matters to people, Reverend, it makes a difference here in your home state and all the way around the world. Every success to you, every success.'

'You know, you can help me along that way. Tell me you've tried our Pig Heaven sausages.'

'I ate two of them for breakfast this morning.'

'And you enjoyed them better than any sausage you ever tasted in your life?'

'Yes I did.'

'And you went out and bought some more?'

'Yes I did.'

'Do you know Jesus?'

'Yes I do.'

'I know it, Howard. And we've got something like an earthly reward for you to take back to Sacramento . . . '

This time JT called Munro's name and Munro wheeled in another cart, the bulky object it carried hidden under a sheet. A bright, frothy arpeggio from the organ cued him and unveiling his handiwork Munro said, 'It's our Pig Heaven pig.'

'It's a pig with wings,' Porta mused out loud and stepped back to absorb the full impact of a stuffed pig the size of a small child with a pair of perfect white wings arching up and stretching out of its shoulders.

JT patted it on its pink snout. 'It's about all the chance that Bobby Dyson's got of beating you into second place.'

'A flying pig,' now Porta marveled at it. 'It must be the newest thing in evolution . . . ! '

Ten minutes on fast forward wound us to the closing moments of the telethon. I wanted to skip through the collage of film clips being chortled over by Porta and JT, but Bobby grabbed the remote out of my hand, rewound the tape and let it play. JT introduced it as The Little Bobby Archive, news coverage of Bobby in Chicago in 1968, rallying yippies in Grant Park, in the thick of the Hilton Hotel sit-in, making public declarations against the government and, by the sound of it, American democracy. Coming out of the footage JT said to

164

Howard, 'Compared to what he's feeding the voters now I think he's either a hypocrite, a liar or he's confused.' 'I'd say it's a little bit of all three, Jim.' 'And you know the man.' 'I know him well.'

'You see what I'm up against?' Bobby appealed to his mother, who knew the truth about his intentions in those days.

She said, 'I got the chills when you used to get on the news. I thought it would come back and hurt you someday,' clicking her tongue on the sharp point. 'He shouldn't smear you with it, that's beneath him.'

Bobby sped the tape on to the finale where, erect and perky, JT stood next to the flashing pledge board, applauding the numbers on display there, treating the Grand Total like a surprise celebrity guest. In thirty-six hours he'd raised over four million dollars in orders and pledges. I expected Bobby to pump me for any late information or revised analysis which might shed light on the converging interests of Porta and JT, but he was completely distracted by their 'moronic tap dance'. He said, 'I'm squealing like a virgin, is that what you're saying? I hear myself, I know, but that Cinerama entertainment, Jack, it's just confusion. People are going to pick up their ballot next week and they'll write in Bob Hope and Bing Crosby.' Even in that line of wild reasoning there was a relevant question he didn't ask, namely, *Meanwhile, where was Dorothy Lamour?*

6   Hygiene and Common Sense

THE noble spirit and heritage of Saturday afternoon brain death in front of the television lived on in Alex's life after Gilbert moved out of their apartment. Propped up by a loose stack of disarranged sofa cushions, pillows and blankets, he sat unwashed, unshaven, undressed and at four o'clock Alex's day wasn't even two hours old. He had filled it, loyally he thought, with JT's Faith-a-thon and nothing more distracting than a stack of toast. Alert enough to recognize that his mind had begun wandering into dangerous territory when he grabbed at the phone, into the dial tone he said, 'I'm not going to call her up.'

Nothing in the sociable tone of Nelda's voice on the telephone signaled to Alex that her instant invitation to come over for a visit suggested any kind of special availability. Her clothes, though, the care she took with her hair and make-up, the direct smile she met him with told another story. The batik sarong she wore floated loosely from the cinched waist and draped her legs almost to her ankles, the black leotard top uncovered with the fineness of a silhouette everything it covered, which was everything from her wrist bones to the high, sudden curve of her shoulders. The hair style was new, at least Alex couldn't remember seeing it on her before, brushed back on the sides and piled up from her neck, three dark waves, crosscurrents splashing against an outcrop of rock, something delicate and domesticated from something grand and savage. She dressed up for company, Alex thought, following Nelda indoors, she wanted to look pretty. 'I'm just goofing off today,' she said, when he asked her if she was going out later.

'Really should just make this swift anyway,' he said, then, 'Oh – food,' appreciating the display of china cups and saucers, cafetière, dessert plates and silverware laid out on the living-room coffee table, and under the drug store elegance of the fluted plastic cover there was, she told him, a blueberry pie. 'Did you defrost it yourself?'

'My mother'd spin if she heard you say that,' Nelda said.

'You're talking to a connoisseur of snack food. I can spot a Sara Lee Country Style Double Crust Blueberry Pie at a hundred yards.'

'Where do you think Sara Lee got the recipe?'

'Your nostrils twitch when you lie.'

'Fruit pies are way too sacred to lie about. I never lie about fruit pies,' strangely serious, a blurring into her next intimate revelation. 'I was thinking about you today. Just wondering what you were doing.'

'The usual thing. Plotting to take over the world.'

For the next twenty minutes Alex heard about the job Nelda used to do (and tried to do) at Wendywear. As an illustration of the resistance she faced there whenever she needed to make a command decision she showed him a framed photograph of Mister, his arm stretched bullishly around JT's shoulders. 'It's easier now,' her open answer, describing her life in general since her father-in-law died. She let Alex weigh up her ideas for organizing the kitchen at the farm to keep pace with the expansion of Pig Heaven's range and volume. She said little about JT, but what she chose to say so casually rumbled through Alex with the blunt concussion of a sonic boom. 'I take his food out to him in his trailer. He sleeps out there every night.' He could see through the big bay window to the driveway where a mid-size Airstream was parked, unhitched. 'Or he doesn't sleep, I don't know. I don't know what he does by himself in his clubhouse at night.'

He moved toward that honesty of hers, to console it and defend it, to attract it. Alex curled his fingers around her hand, he kissed her there and he saw in her sane calm that she didn't know what was on its way so she held still for it, and he stood up and kissed her again, her cheek first then her mouth.

Nelda kept her lips closed but she didn't pull away; she wasn't appalled, not yet, anyway, not cornered; rushed but not embarrassed. 'Your face feels hot,' touching Alex's reddening cheek with the back of her hand. She leaned in, held her own cheek against his, the way a mother might feel her baby's face and she let him kiss her less carefully this time, the tip of his tongue opening her lips. Nelda lifted her arms around his neck, after contact, connection: she knew what she wanted and she wanted him to know it, too.

Alex pressed the small of her back, felt the tops of her legs touch his, pulled in, she stayed firmly against him that way after his hands moved up across her long straight back. When he let his weight fold them both down onto the sofa she rolled him off of her onto the floor and then she joined Alex down there. His knees pried her skirt open in front and they humped each other friskily, as unmenaced by the responsible restrictive grown-up world as a couple of sixteen-year-olds.

Underneath Nelda's skirt Alex felt the softly grainy skin on the backs of her thighs and borders of fabric, seams, rings and flaps he couldn't combine into a picture of anything recognizable at all. She unhitched the tuck at her waist that held the sarong together, unwrapped herself and Alex encountered his very first garter belt.

'You want me to keep it on? Men like that.'

'What men?'

'All of the men I used to know. Men in general.'

'Am I men in general? Is that what you think?'

'No.'

'No,' Alex confirmed it, he hugged her to his chest, he closed his eyes. 'Don't take it off yet.' The real woman in his arms was not the voluptuous Perla model covering him in his imagination, not one of the fabulous unreal race of women who only inhabit lingerie ads, not a trophy Odalisque already adrift in a sexual trance; the woman whose white-stockinged legs he saw spread apart over him was a woman with a name and a voice he knew, with urgent motives he never guessed, an imperfect woman, a woman holding out complications.

'You don't have to go,' she answered the question he didn't ask. 'Do you?'

'When?'

'Stay with me tonight.'

'Tomorrow morning, though. I don't want to be here when he comes in.'

'He doesn't come in anymore.'

'Well,' Alex said, 'I should move my car.'

'He won't see it. He didn't even notice I cut all my hair off.'

He smoothed back an unsprung strand of it, tucked it behind her ear. 'I want to be careful with you.'

A brave, quivering smile. 'Are you trying to get out of this?'

'All I mean is I don't have a condom with me.'

It could have been a collection of precious family heirlooms that she was allowing Alex to see. She pulled the drawer open slowly and with intention. He felt the same twinge looking at that neat pile of condoms as he did when he imagined the concrete reality of his mother and father fucking, but no, these were the *relics* of JT's carnal life with Nelda, there in front of him, countable and uncountable were all of the times that he *didn't* sheath his cock and ease it or slam it into her when she opened her legs for him. Here was a rupture in their marriage, an opening wide enough for Alex to swim freely into this erotic stunt.

Quickly naked and in bed with her, he watches her shoulders dip and rise to the slow beat of her breath, her mouth around him, her head bobbing on the end of his cock, with him now, in her bed, guiding him through her knowledge of men. All of her movement is concentrated in her upper body, under the high arch of her neck, in her slim, muscled back, her swimmer's shoulders; below that, when she rolls onto her side, he sees the proud fan of dark hair dividing her wide hips, the tips of her bones there standing out like two soft points of light; he has brushed the side of her face, just to tell her that he hasn't gone away from her, but she stops and looks up at him.

'You like what I'm doing?'

'How does it feel, you mean?' he says. 'It's a strange sight.'

'Never how you think it's going to be.'

'I didn't picture this,' he lies to her.

It's a thin lie, delivered badly and she likes him for trying. Nelda tries one of her own. 'Neither did I.'

'Out there,' rolling his eyes to cover the vast curve of the world, 'I thought was separate, I thought I could keep it separate from in here.'

She leans up on her elbow. As she moves, the stumpy frosted crystal cross she wears shins down its jeweler's loop of chain. 'I couldn't ever – no, that's wrong; not always, but now I can't recognize myself in this house. I might as well go around wearing a tent and hide my face like a Moslem woman, and just deny I look like anybody special. I'm not saying I'm so gorgeous . . . '

'You are.'

'No. My face is lopsided. See?' She shows him, expressionless.

'It's a beautiful face.'

'Do you like me, Alex?'

Reaching for her, 'Is there anything else you like to do as much as talk?'

'Everything we do is talking. Everything else, this,' she rubs her cheek against his chest, she kisses his nipple, 'especially this, it's a conversation, isn't it?' He thinks about his hairless chest, where breasts would be he's tending toward sponginess, pale feminine shapes Nelda's mouth flutters over. Dry, tender pecks trailing down to his straightening cock are spaced between shallow bites and kittenish licks.

'How can you . . . look so sweet . . . and talk so dirty?'

She sniffs emotionally. She sneezes. She sneezes again. Another sneeze. Two more, three more after that, it's turning into a circus trick. More sneezing.

Alex braces her, Nelda bends away from him. And sneezes. 'Where's a tissue?' he says.

Nelda points at the bathroom. It's carpeted in white, as soft under his feet as alpaca. Cut-crystal jars, bowls made of blown glass as thin as the skin of a balloon, arrangements of glass animals decorate the tiled shelf around the sink and the wide tiled rim that yokes the bathtub. He's discovered the enchanted grotto of a fairy princess. The jars and bowls are filled with translucent spheres the size of large grapes, a different color in each vessel – jade green, silver, red-purple, turquoise, coral, yellow-gold — essences for charms and enchantments. He'd find out later the impression wasn't far from the reality, they were little globes of bath oil. At least in a strange bathroom for the first time you always know where to look for the toilet paper. Alex brings back a couple feet of it, folded into a neat pad. He sits on the side of the bed to nurse her, rests her head on his bare thigh.

Alex tells Nelda he wants to touch her. 'Show me where.' He rubs her with one finger, with two, slides a fingertip up and back along the watery crease. 'Tell me what you like. Nelda? Like this?'

'Wait,' — wait for her answer — 'let me listen . . . There. Very light. Feels . . . there, the best.'

'I like this, too.' He recites his love poem. 'Out there and in here with you.'

'Ssh.'

Every movement a physical declaration, a consent, and not only from this woman but from the outer world. The rolling momentum of his success out there hasn't broken here, it rolls on, announcing its direction as it goes.

Elegant and vulgar, Nelda's finesse with a condom. In the crook of her thumb and forefinger she unrolls it down the attentive length of Alex's standing cock: if those thick inches of him had the power of speech then out of that small tight mouth he'd hear the whisper, *acceptable! acceptable to her!* bragging a little. That small voice dies quietly in the red hot thrill of adultery — and theft, in the pornographic joke of using one of JT's own condoms to make this sex crime safe. 'I won't have to buy a carton of Exciters for a whole year,' he says. She gives him her sweetest dirty look. 'You think it'll take us that long?'

Tonight he screws his way through four of them . . . with this woman who knows what he needs and does what she can do! Fornication that moves the furniture, scratches the floor, splashes baby oil on the wall! Nelda turns herself around and lets him feel the cheeks of her ass bump under his legs, her strong back arch and hump up into his chest — the way bears fornicate! Or rhinos! She lets him curl over her so he was being done to by doing, the walls of his heart shivering, she pulls him physically into dazzling complication. 'Beautiful . . .' he strains to tell her, and she pulls away, twists onto her back, she needs to see his face, pulling him onto her again. Her eyes snap open, a little astonished, gone into wildness and she grips him, legs locked behind his, arms strapped around his back to keep herself from falling

170

through space; she comes into clarity, the curling warm fog seeps up from somewhere above her legs, it plumes under her ribs, ripples across and dissolves. This time, with Alex this first time the purpose in the frightening pleasure of sex with a man is divulged not delivered to her.

Gasping on their backs side by side like a brace of landed trout they stare into the air together. She dredges up the strength to feel herself with careful fingers, to say to him tenderly in awe, 'I'm melting down there.'

Nelda settled into sleep, Alex into electrified distress. He watched her from a distance that widened as he lay there, that made her a figure in the landscape of the bed: open desert where he woke up to find himself solitary and exposed. Nelda, she was the other survivor – the two of them grabbing this temporary safety after a bank raid, an hysterical getaway, surviving members of some underground cell and this was their first taste of life on the run. Would he have to depend on JT's ignorance or understanding to escape the minimum catastrophe? Forfeit his partnership, fight for his livelihood, lose it, bankrupt himself with lawyers' fees, plea-bargain a cleansing term of penal servitude, and these are only the consequences that Alex can *think of* . . .

The room was dark when Nelda sat up and found Alex exactly the way she'd left him, still on his back, glassy eyes still fixed on a point high overhead. 'Are you still alive?' Silence, nothing at all. 'Alex?'

'Huh, what?'

Abruptly relieved, she teased him again, 'Are you still alive?'

'I'm okay. How are you?'

'Sleepy.' Nelda sank down into his arms, nuzzled him.

To the top of her head he said, 'If Jim happens to ask you what you did today, what are you going to tell him?'

'He won't ask me.'

'Just if.'

'He won't.' Lifting her head, 'What if he asks you?'

'I was home all day. I'll tell him I was at home.'

Mock horror. 'You'd lie to my husband?'

'Don't joke around.'

'He's a *reverend*.'

'Right, see, that's what I mean. Check yourself. If you think you need to confess to him, I don't know, talk to me first. Will you talk to me before you tell him anything?'

Nelda arched away from him, aiming her blow. 'As if I ended up in bed with you because I'm such a little weakling. I'm so weak I couldn't help it. So when another almighty man tells me what he wants from me I'll give in to him too, just as easy. Did you listen to me? Wanting you in this bed isn't *easy*, Alex, you didn't trick me into it, you didn't *have me* because I'm too weak to say no. I'm as strong as you are, as he is, you're with me like this because I said yes, *I* did.'

'Stronger than God too, I hope,' Alex's real worry broke cover, 'if God puts pressure on your conscience. In your religion, adultery, isn't it one of the deadly sins?'

'Sleeping with you doesn't feel like a sin.'

'Does that mean you aren't necessarily going to tell him about this?'

She let go of a slow breath. 'I'm not in his life, I'm just not part of it. Jim's traveling out there, somewhere, like Halley's Comet,' she said and moved on from JT. 'I prayed for something to break and show me what God wants. I didn't know it was going to be you.' She squeezed his arm. 'You just have to accept what happens and stay alive so you can understand it.'

A cosmic statute too sadistic for him. 'The secret of life.'

'I sure didn't get it. And *that* was because I kept looking too close at every single experience. You have to look at your whole life story, then when you're ready you'll see what it means.'

'No, that happens when you're dying. In your last minute.'

'It happened to me when I opened my heart to Jesus. Really.'

Alex pressed his back flat against the headboard. A pillow covered his lap and he folded his hands on it as if it stood in for his office desk. 'You're not trying to sell me on anything, are you?'

'Jim says only God's got the power to open anybody up.'

'Uh-huh. What else does Jim say?'

'Things change because they have to. If you don't want this with me, whatever, Alex, whatever. It'll make sense later.' Trying again, 'You don't have to believe it.'

'I want this with you, sure, yes. Of course.'

'Whatever's going to happen, you should want that, too. God knew you wanted to come over here, He knew I wanted to go to bed with you and how I don't want to be the one who stops it.' She reaches under the pillow, grips him, emancipated from conscience.

'I'm not worried about God knowing.'

'Everything, *everything* goes in the same direction, it's all going in one direction, doesn't it feel that way to you *sometimes*? It's — ' fingers wiggling in the air in front of her, summoning stubborn indistinct words, 'oh, when you try to think about it it's the only explanation that makes any sense — the Creator who created everything else created me, so I'm not just Little Miss Nobody who doesn't count, as if it doesn't matter what I do. If doing this is wrong He knows I'll feel it. I'll be suffering and when I'm finished suffering He'll forgive me. Because if being with you is a sin or not, God's still leading me somewhere He wants me to go, so I'm not afraid of my choices anymore. All He wants is for me to follow Him and bring the people I love.'

Was it a concession to Nelda or the Whatever Beyond for Alex to admit that, *ye-es*, sometimes he felt that everything-everything in his life held together and moved with a reason, or at least in a created direction? He dangled mutely suspended between the grab of her native tenderness and the drag of negotiator's caution; he may feel the strength of an inspirational wind at his back but he'd choke before he'd say that was the personal urging of a Higher Power worshiped by gentiles.

'No,' this was *not* the message. 'No. I have the same ideas and I'm not any kind of Christian.'

She kissed his face, she moved the pillow away and leaned her bare leg against his. 'I just don't want anybody I care about to go to hell.'

'I'm not going to hell. There's no such place.'

The welcome waiting for him outside his door brimmed with the cheer of a prison camp autopsy. Heidi lounged in a patio chair she had dragged upstairs from the Nussbaums' porch. A handful of crushed cigarette butts decorated the Spanish tiles at her feet, the grimy charcoal of the tips stubbed and smeared into the clean veins of mortar.

'You shouldn't leave your window open if you go away all night,' she scolded him, minus the cartoon rolling pin.

'How long have you been sitting here?'

She shook her head, it didn't matter. 'Your phone's been going crazy. There's a ton of messages. A real exciting one from JT.'

'Am I supposed to go over to his house?'

'Oh, I don't think he was calling you from there.'

JT's voice crackling down the line on his car phone had a roughness in it, a *roughed-up*ness, as if he'd just been screaming and crying his throat to shreds . . . or, weary harshness was what you'd expect to hear from a man who'd been on his feet talking and broadcasting live for the last thirty-six hours. He was calling from somewhere north on Interstate 5, on the road to Sacramento. The state capital in the week before the election was an impressive and convenient setting for the entertainment of a delegation of pork producers from the Midwest, Oswald Pogenpohl's friends and supporters who were flying in to meet the Republican celebrities and hear all about the Humpty Dumpster agricultural system. 'You two fellas can set 'em up with science and I'll knock 'em down with morality.' Alex and Chick were going to be out of town for a week.

He spooled through the rest of the messages. Four of them were from Chick, instant updates on flight information, two hung up without a word and the last one Alex cut off in mid-sentence, Nelda saying, 'Alex, you're still not – '

'Aren't you going to listen to it?'

'It's old,' he said. 'It's from last week.'

Heidi patted the answering machine approvingly. 'I recommend this brand. There, see? I can do it.'

'What can you do?' Then quickly, 'I've got to take a fast shower.'

'Professional business. I can do management. I want to go with you guys.'

'Maybe JT left a message on your machine.'

'I'm too poor to own one.'

'That's bad management.'

Into the bathroom, right at his heels, she said, 'Stop for a sec, okay? Let me do more. You've got to let me. All I look at is sausages all day. I'm sick of sausages. I'm better than that, Alex.'

'Can we talk about this when I get back?'

'I hate doing this.' Finished wheedling she whined softly, 'I really should've seen it, y'know?'

The poor orphan, unheard, abused, misled, dragged herself to the living-room, to her sad chore. She slotted a cassette into the video. 'Can you come in here for a minute?' Heidi said to him, 'I have to send this to your boss. So he can see what kind of a cheating con-artist you are. How do you turn on the TV?'

The significant segment of the entertainment only lasted for twenty seconds so she replayed it to give Alex a chance to take in the incriminating subtext. Where have they gone, the unstained hopeful days of the Global Video Café? Full face, directly to the viewer: 'Let it be known seriously, here's the whole deal – you get the sum of one hundred dollars or one complete per cent if that's a larger amount, of any money we can screw out of Jim Tickell, God's asshole on earth. Happy with that?' She froze the frame showing Alex closing his mouth around his high opinion of JT.

'What's this really about?' he wanted to hear.

'About the fucking fact that you give me all the shitwork to do.'

'Well right now I've got to hump up to *Sacramento* and charm the balls off of a bunch of *pigmen* who wear plaid jackets, red pants and white shoes and think they're *dressed* up!'

'You get to do all the *fun* stuff.' She got him laughing with her, back on her side. 'Don't you think I can handle any responsibility? I just want to participate more. Let me have a trial week, okay? When I'm in charge at the farm. I'll manage it this week for you, Alex, I can do it. I'll supervise the whole business.'

Let her think she's in charge, he'd trade for that. She won't have the whole operation to herself, Nelda will be with her. How much upheaval can Heidi unloose in seven days?

7 Creation Week

Monday – Thursday

ATTACK of the Pig People, as Alex and Chick codenamed their upcoming encounter with the swine barons from Iowa, wasn't on the agenda until Wednesday. 'Let's take them by Oswald's, Munro,' was JT's answer to Alex's doubt that they could fill the forty-eight hours until then with any activity more stimulating than the Magic Fingers in their hotel beds. 'The Holiday Inn won't get up and walk away,' he prodded the boys. 'Enjoy the ride. You'll have entertainment galore.' Entertainment that was no distraction, entertainment with a vital theme.

'That's the Capitol Building,' Munro nodded at it, 'on the right,' as if the pale gray domed bulk they were voyaging around could be mistaken for a taco stand.

'Bureaucrap Central. Hold your nose till the stink goes by,' sour advice from the senior tour guide who brightened right up when the expanse of Capitol Park rolled into view. 'Here, look. The Palace of Learning.'

Dead in the middle of the broad, five-block-long stretch of lawns, in the shadow of the State Capitol, in snickering architectural mockery stood the mushroom shape of a circus tent – a brown canvas big top flying pennants around its rim and the American flag on its peak. Before its entrance, a gateway, a set of whitewashed goalposts lifting a banner into the sharp, clean air: *Creation Week Pageant – October 29 to November 4 – Free Admission*. 'If you want to have a two-way talk with anybody it helps a whole lot if you understand the other fella's language. Oswald's friends, these hog farmers, they aren't like me, you need to lock onto a different approach,' JT tutored Alex. 'By Saturday you won't be strangers to them and they won't be to you.'

The crash course in God, Pigmen and the World began with the first two nights of Oswald Pogenpohl's tent show where Alex and Chick only had to 'observe the big scene' and 'blend into the feel of it'. They were scheduled to enjoy each night's performance after that in the company of their new friends from Iowa, 'right down in it with them'.

'Pigs in a muddy puddle,' Munro described the hoped-for, cozy trust.

'Enormous, it's e*norm*ous,' JT said. 'Did I tell you on the phone how enormous this whole deal is? Hey, Alex?'

'You just told me it was enormous.'

'The inky-dinkiest of these set-ups is five times as big as Hummingbird Farm. As soon as we sell HD systems to them we'll pull in the rest of the Midwest, and that's our manufacturing base right there, that's our springboard into Europe.' Coming from JT, in his mood of inspired certainty, this orchestrated plan was the opposite of connivance, the opposite of shrewdness. 'We're on our way to a bo*nanz*a. This is our Golden Age, we're at the start of it.' He was saying this to the windshield, to the immediate future his car was closing on, its reflection visible to him in the paintwork of the hood, but he turned all the way around to say to Alex, 'Make them believe it the way we believe it.'

The mythology of success. To get that, do this. And what was this assignment now but to add his background to other prominences Alex had to hide or deny. A strange thought announced itself. 'Do you want us to pretend we're Christian?'

'Everybody else there will be doing enough of *that*,' JT promised. 'No, don't pretend about anything. Just stay awake and understand everything you can.'

'On Saturday, though. I'll just get screwed up, my presentation will just get screwed up if I'm censoring myself the whole time. It won't be clear. I can't think of anything new or different to say to them about Humpty Dumpsters.'

'God will put the words in your mouth.' JT faced front again. 'The first show's at midnight. Soak it all up with an open mind.'

Privately Chick said to Alex, 'The Nu-Art.'

Alex couldn't remember how many months it had been since he and Chick and/or Gilbert had made the midnight trek out to Santa Monica to watch some eccentric double or triple feature, *Eraserhead* and *Pink Flamingoes* or *Mondo Teeno*, *Mondo Bizarro* and *Taboos of the World*. 'This'll be weirder,' he said.

At their backs the soft cavern of the tent went on filling up with young parents in pairs and older folks in odd-numbered bunches, all with the same glaze of anticipation on their eyes, right up to midnight. In front of the VIP section (plastic chairs instead of wooden benches where Alex and Chick found their names printed on gummed labels attached to first row seats) a wide stage hived off twenty feet of tentspace. JT stood up there chatting with Howard Porta and generally ignoring the notables of the Creation Science Institute pantheon: Ving Kimmel, Olin Mulley and a tidy round-shouldered man who stood off in an empty corner of the stage apparently talking to himself. The beard, the skin the color of boiled ham, the independent flourish of a Paisley apache scarf, the look of an Italian tenor about to sneeze in the middle of an aria, they didn't need Munro to name *this* celebrity for them, this potentate of the early morning reruns.

'Quentin Nash,' Chick nudged Alex and broke into a floundering impersonation of Nash's highborn English-English, choking out the catchphrase that unfailingly tagged each episode of his network sitcom, his routine judgment of the twelve-year-old rap-singing orphan boy who'd hired him as a butler, 'You are a verrrry stew-pid boy!'

Loud enough for Nash to hear, to crack his concentration. Alex ducked away from Chick. 'Ssh, c'mon. We'll get thrown out.'

'In your dreams.'

'There's Dr Pogenpohl coming up,' Munro pulled them back to the action. 'There's Oswald.'

Alex watched him emerge from the edge of the friendly mob, lapped out of it by some gentle undulation, a man who looked a little bit like everyone else there, ancestor or descendant, chief of a clan of high school principals. Here was a man with no body heat, who sweated a clean fine white dust through his pores, but who drew warmth out of others. The beauty queen's concrete smile, practiced so keenly that to an audience of one or a thousand it never felt remotely artificial, the basking smile that returned their own warmth, favored them, showed them above all they counted, stayed plastered to his face as he greeted his friends onstage. Scattered hand-clapping followed him up and this applause rose into a pelting storm of welcome once he could be seen by everybody in the rows further back. Pogenpohl flapped his hands down at them to accept the demonstration of confidence and loyalty, then to stem that outpouring and contain the disorder.

He thanked all of us for attending at such a late hour, promised that the night's events wouldn't stretch past twelve-thirty and by way of introducing the 'very special men' sharing the stage with him he reminded us, 'Tonight's a *historical* occasion for many reasons. It's a celebration and a *consecration*, it's a *testament* and a battle cry, it's a rally and it's a *symbol* to *all* the generations *assembled* here. From *tomorrow* night you'll be enjoying the children of the Henry Road Christian Elementary School who'll be performing in our *pageant*, and I *know* you'll just want to cheer them on if you're one of the *proud* moms or dads *or not*, am I right? Tell me I'm *right* . . . '

Oswald's idea of oratorical style wasn't to create the illusion that he was speaking to individuals when he stood in front of a large crowd, it was just the opposite; he called to them all as though they were stranded at the bottom of a collapsed mine shaft and he was the local official sent to comfort and exhort. With the State Attorney General at his elbow the true picture came to life.

Porta joined Oswald at the microphone. Howard was sure, he said, that the many misguided Californians who oppose the teaching of creation science in public schools are led by honest conscience and thank God we live in a democracy where every voice can be heard. 'I save my anger for liberal politicians who fight to keep prayer out of children's lives and teach them it's their democratic right to go out to the playground at recess and burn the American flag. Those are the people I'm up against. They're out of touch with the majority, out of touch with the traditions that remind us who we are and how we ought to live. Let me leave you with a question, it's hanging over all of us:' — my eyes went immediately to the smattering of Porta for Governor banners dangling overhead, threaded into the fabric of the evening — 'Who do you want in control of our state curriculum, liberal politicians and absentminded professors or taxpayers and parents who pay for blackboards and chalk, buildings and books?'

His dignified gratitude was drowned out in a roar of support; a wave, a handshake, a wink and Howard was gone. In the softening ovation Oswald returned to his text, 'If a fellow holds a low belief about his *origin* he'll have a low belief about his *destiny*. It's the pitiful lack of any *believable* scientific teaching about where we come from that forces so many people to look for answers in so-called mind-expanding drugs, astrology, and the occult. There is knowledge, *certain* knowledge given to us to use as a shield, if we have the strength to lift it up.' Many heads in the audience bobbing in agreement, kelp buds bobbing in the current. 'Lord, we ask you tonight that we may increase so You might increase Your influence on society. As Your people we beseech Your blessing to understand Your will and follow Your ways . . . ' he went on unreeling the clear instruction, the reassurance of prohibition and edict, of rule. Above that tent across the sky a sparkling line marked the place where arguments disintegrate against the physical reality of Christian heaven, where in a mansion the size of Caesar's Palace and the mass of an eyelash the floorshow down below is the sad suffering excluded multicultural rump of humanity.

Alex felt insulated against Oswald Pogenpohl's spellbinding at this moment by his visitor's status. He was a tourist in a foreign city eager to observe the customs and ordinances, anxious to avoid mutual misunderstandings. As the house lights faded, dropping the whole space into total darkness, I caught Alex's feeling of separation, I shared it; and I caught JT's ache in my head, a grinding friction. I looked like I belonged there but Oswald's prayer delivered up a liberating shock – these are not my people now, if they ever were.

A low hum flooded out of large speakers hidden underneath the stage, a cosmic growl spiraling up into an ear-splitting thunderclap that cracked open in the dark air and unleashed two booming syllables. 'BAH-RAH!'

The vibrating wash of sound buzzed over my skin, a sudden field of grainy noise that expanded, rose, echoed then decayed through the roof and walls of the tent. Oswald's voice nipped in behind it. 'God spoke the universe into existence probably with the Hebrew word *bara*, which means *created*. This act of divine will, so generous and so typical of God, brought something where there was nothing. In the beginning God created the heaven and the earth. And the earth was without form and void, and darkness was upon the face of the deep. And the Spirit of God moved upon the face of the waters. And God said . . . '

Quentin Nash said, 'Let there be light!'

'And there *was* light.' A *ball* of light, a white flare blasted toward us through a scrim at the back of the stage. On the fringes of the glare I could see the figures of Quentin and Oswald, each at a podium, born in this creation but masterfully outside it too. 'And God saw the light, that it was good. And God divided the light from the darkness, and God called the light . . . '

'Day!'

'And the darkness . . . '

'Night!'

'And the evening and the morning were the first day.' That primeval glow flickered once then cut out altogether. Somebody must have tripped over the cable, I thought, jerkèd out the plug, but as the ordinary 150-watt bulbs strung between the tent poles flashed on again Oswald imposed the necessary closing solemnity. 'So it began. The foundations were laid for the future home of *human kind*, for *us*, for the only creatures who would possess *consciousness* high enough to appreciate creation and *praise* the Creator. Everything science has taught me magnifies this conclusion, and it is *by* science that we will eradicate the *dead end* theories *worshiped* by the humanist establishment, false ideas that drive *a wedge* between people and the fact of God. Come see us every night this week and you'll see us *beat* science at its own game because right here we're going *to prove* what you already know: the Bible is the absolute, factual record and Lord God is the absolute, factual source of natural and moral law . . . '

'Whoh,' Chick said.

'Really,' Alex agreed, head shaking.

'That was an aircraft landing-light, I bet. Some candlepower! I don't know *what* they were using for reflectors,' and he was out of his seat, off to investigate.

'I'll wait here a minute.' Alex stared out at the departing river of families and friends, scanned the faces, glanced over at the main entrance where through breaks in the crowd he saw Pogenpohl in a circle of men, listening closely, responding gravely. The only thing Alex wanted less than to be pounced on by JT was to wait there in the open any longer than he had to. He counted to sixty then squeezed out through the rear exit, a step in front of me. We'd made it to the end of the first night's show without cracking once.

If Quentin Nash had stayed in London to swing into the Sixties on the dangling vines of the angrier, riskier acting work being offered to him then he would have deprived a whole generation of TV-educated Americans of their knowledge about English butlers. In fifteen years he was never off the air and for each fall season, each revamped situation, he came back fatter, pricklier and more likely to spout the trembling cry of the exasperated, put-upon, genteel house eunuch faced with yet another pot-roast-in-the-laundry-hamper consequence of life with unsupervised American children, 'Oh, rhhhhheally! *Mas*ter Timmy!' Even though Quentin's October Surprise in 1980 was the cynical axing of *White's Knight*, a reshuffle of all the crucial Nashian elements which now cast him as a *valet* whose dotty Wall Street employer *loses him in a poker game* to a *single parent taxi driver* who lives in a *condemned tenement* with his *six* multi-racial children ('Oh, rhhhheally! *Mas*ter Alfredo!'), he still turned up at odd hours in commercials for dry sherry and in daytime reruns of every series that he ever made. Public appearances became rare and tabloid gossip about alcoholic binges and charity work with Vietnamese orphan boys very soon shrank to five-line items buried at the bottom of an inside page . . . until he bellied back into the lights and noise to announce that he'd been born again, this time as a servant of Jesus Christ.

But it was the Quentin Nash of *Dandy's Dumplings* (butler on the prairie), of *You Are Here* (butler on a Pacific atoll), of *Dear Earthlings* (butler in outer space), the Quentin Nash of yore whom Chick went stalking backstage for an autograph. He found the actor preparing for the night's performance, mouthing his lines, eyes shut against interruption, as distancing as a moat. While Chick waited for Quentin's trance to break he poked around a large piece of theatrical machinery that hadn't been there on Monday night. The black wooden box stood ten feet tall and ran the length of the stage, open at the front where rollers running along the top and bottom held shimmering strips of crinkled silver plastic looped between them. He turned the crank projecting from the side of the apparatus and the silvery wall shivered down a few inches.

'Hey son, can I ask you to return to your seat?' Oswald gestured at Chick's hand still on the crank, at his violation.

A step back, still inspecting the structure Chick said, 'It's a waterfall, huh, supposed to be a waterfall. Or rain or something. Like Niagara Falls, huh?'

'You'll see from out there.' Oswald pointed the way, showed him the rows of benches rapidly crowding up. 'Better go and grab a good seat.'

'Easy to convert this. Plumb in pipes and you can use real water.' One by one he solved the technical problems. 'Polychrome reflectors in the back, pump-and-sump system, two hundred gallons. It'd look a lot more realistic. Or maybe use glycerine.'

'This is about as realistic as we want it, it looks just fine from out in the audience. Sit somewhere in the middle if you want to see the full effect.'

'I'm sitting over there.'

Apart from Alex and the three reserved seats along the row from him, the roped-off VIP section was packed with a rainbow assortment of high school seniors whom somebody had seated boy-girl-boy-girl. 'That's fine, okay,' Oswald dropped the stiff insistence. 'You're in Dr Robertson's brigade. Tell him *from me* you've got a wonderful combination going, your Bible light and your hydro-engineering.'

'Shoot me *now*.' He waved over at Alex, linking up.

'Oh,' Oswald said, disengaging from the chat. 'You're one of Jim Tickell's.' A sigh, a dry chuckle. 'We'll have to work on you.'

Alex hadn't seen Chick since breakfast. Of the slippery jumble of worries he'd been struggling to contain since then the first one out of

Alex's mouth was, 'We haven't figured out what we're doing on Saturday, how we have to sell those guys.'

'Oh, hey. You missed the bitchenest tour. Russians used to colonize this place. A hundred years ago.'

'Not right now. Tell me later. I want to talk about Saturday now.' Alex fixed the priorities. 'Let's make a decision. Which order should we go in? Your visuals or my business plan? Humpster first?'

'Works for me.'

'Right, I think it'd be better if I gave them the overview after you show off the actual machine. Unveil it, it's sexier, you know, like the Car of the Year. Then I'll come in and – *whomp* – land on them with my business plan.'

'Whomp, that's good.'

'Has Jim said anything to you since we checked into the hotel? Have you even *seen* him anywhere around today?'

Chick showed two seconds of hard concentration. 'Today?'

'I haven't had a single conversation with him, not even a phone call. You know what I'm thinking? I'm thinking he's playing this on some other level, y'know, I'm getting this shaky feeling. Okay,' he laid it out, 'we need to co-ordinate Saturday with him and we haven't had one serious conference about the presentation. You know how it'll look if it all fucks up, it'll be on me. Worst case, he's got a fair excuse to reorganize the business. I was thinking about it last night, I woke up thinking what if I'm just a dumb part of some strategy of his that ends up cutting me out?'

Straining to understand the principles which operate in the mind of a businessman Chick said, 'Why would he do that?'

'Why does anybody do anything?' Alex answered him, deflated by the speculation. 'I mean, Jim's putting his Iowa deal together.'

'We've got days,' Chick said under the dimming house lights. 'Worry about something else for a while.'

The thin sweet barbershop fragrances of aftershave and hair tonic arrived a second or two before Munro ducked into his seat. Along with the fresh haircut he presented himself in a new white shirt and coffee-colored knit tie. Over Munro's shoulder, gleaming with the charmed satisfaction of a daily double winner JT mimed a greeting to Alex that said *Why so sad?*

Gradually the tent filled with the luminescence of the first day. Surrounded by that vaporous light and gripping the sides of his podium against the primal force that could somersault him into our laps, Oswald said, 'Last night, you might remember if you were here, God spoke the physical universe into being . . . ' The low harmonic hum of that terrible event spread into a full chord played on what had to be a circus calliope. 'And God said . . . '

'Let there be a firmament,' echoed Quentin's reply, 'in the midst of the waters. And let it divide the waters from the waters.'

'And God made the firmament and divided the waters which were under the firmament: and it was *so*!'

Alex tapped Chick's arm and leaned in to worry, 'Tomorrow, those farmers get here *tomorrow*.'

'Hold it, wait,' Chick's eyes intensely on the show, 'he's gonna *work* it now. Psych-out supreme!'

The plastic waterfall was in motion, a rattling cascade twinkling with blue light. And from both sides of the stage on came the children, twenty of them all dressed in aquamarine leotards, matching chiffon tutus on the girls and capes on the boys. Between them they stretched out the two halves of a floating swath of the same ocean-blue chiffon and meeting in the middle sank down underneath it, sat there Indian-style and arms waving kept the gentle swell billowing above them.

'And God called the firmament . . . '

'Heaven!'

'And the evening and the morning were the second day.' A flutter of airborne chords from the calliope triggered a round of applause and brought the girls and boys crawling out from that now lumpy cloud of chiffon. Oswald watched them gather into a neat semi-circle around him, a finger to his lips to settle them down. More to those children than to us he said, 'When you hear the word *firmament* you need to think of the *atmosphere*, an all-enclosing envelope of steam and gases . . . '

'Suspension,' Chick giggled out what sounded to Alex like perverse appreciation. 'Bitchen.' He knew. The atmospheric pressure of that hanging shroud would collapse it with such violence its mass would blow apart the ball of water inside it, boil it away into space.

'This warm and calm *world* reflected God's basically *peaceful* personality. The protective canopy above the waters kept the *entire globe* at one even temperature,' Oswald taught, 'it was as *mild* and *pleasant* as inside a shopping mall.' He broke off his talk to the kids and as an aside clued us in, 'I must've read fifty or sixty medical studies this year that prove hyperbolic pressures *can* reverse disease, promote good health and *prolong* life.' Oswald went back to his youngsters in lovable, open conspiracy and teased the end of his lesson into a cliffhanger. 'These upper waters were only resting there, swirling around in the sky for *thousands of years*, waiting for the day when God calls them to send *the Flood*.'

Twenty little voices squeaked up in automatic joy, forty hands wiggling in the air, fingertips mimicking the drizzle, faces looking out to locate parents in the clapping throng . . .

'He's a crooner. Didn't he just sing to you, Alex?' JT called over, bending around the back of his chair.

In mute reply Alex held up a handful of broadsides and pamphlets, Creationist literature he'd collected from the CSI 'Information and Education' stall by the tent entrance. 'Can you tell me what I'm supposed to get out of reading any of this?'

'Secret message is on every page.'

'Upside-down and backwards. I just can't figure out how to connect it up with selling a bunch of Humpty Dumpsters to a bunch of farmers from Iowa. I don't see it, Jim. I think the way to go is just let me sell the HDS off the back of Hummingbird Farm and let you take it from there.'

'If you treat them like a bunch of farmers from Iowa they'll treat you like a used-car salesman. They're Oswald Pogenpohl's friends. You can do that trick,' a general nod toward the vacant, still-bright stage. 'Tell them you traveled up to glory and you rode back down on a Humpty Dumpster. See,' he said, 'I mean you have to *tantalize* them.'

Alex had to say no to Chick's early-morning invitation to attend Oswald Pogenpohl's keynote seminar 'The Evolving Junkyard *vs* Predictions of Scientific Creationism in Relation to the Laws of Thermo-dynamics'. Input of that order would only overload his already faltering approach to the problem of how to base a Humpty Dumpster Systems presentation on his academic understanding of Christian expectations. With the main points of both subjects sketched on too many three-by-five cards laid out solitaire-style across his bedspread, after five hours of concentration Alex thought it would be easier to establish a natural correspondence between the Canter's Deli menu and the rules of cricket. Idling on a self-awarded coffee break he phoned Heidi and, in managerial control at least of this, asked her to give him a mid-week update on the general situation at the farm.

Heidi: Oh, are you checking up on me?

Alex: This is a totally friendly call.

Heidi: Did you talk to Nelda yet?

Alex: No, all I really, uh . . .

Heidi: She's here. You want to say hi?

Alex: Heidi, I've only got a minute. Can you give me a fast rundown?

Heidi: I'm a hit, what can I say? I'm a star. I closed two more hotel deals. The Beverley Wilshire and the Chateau Marmont. A two week try-out period, staring tomorrow. Plus, also I organized split shifts. I'm coping with every little thing.

A full month before the Cal/OSHA investigators released their official findings to the press, a few days after the fact, I was able to pull together a detailed picture of the catastrophic chain of events. My instinctive reaction was the same as anybody's, anybody, that is, who had not been directly harmed. You'd have to have sand in your heart not to be moved by such a calamity, you'd have to be in an iron lung not to laugh and scream until your ribs cracked.

Heidi's first act of ad-lib management was to freshen up the routine by calling in the sales personnel to trade jobs for a week with most of the day shift on the production side. She didn't have to explain the practical and psychological value of the exercise to her commission-earning ex-acting class sales troupe, but to the temporarily de-salaried sow house and hog barn regulars she had to promise, 'When you get back to your old jobs you'll have a total experience of the whole business.' Even though they loudly doubted the benefit to pig or man of spending their yardtime as sausage-mongers, orders came in and deliveries went out with no breakdown gyrating into a crisis.

Halfway through batch number 001030-2-B the Humpty Dumpster that had been cheerfully processing strings of sage and honey sausages began coughing out empty skins which closely resembled fouled condoms. Heidi's command decision was to send Greg Lerman – as handy with a socket wrench as he was with a scene from *The Rocky Horror Show* – to pick up an idle machine from the rack in the yard, adapt it for sausage duty and install it in the kitchen. Without ever seeing the mechanism before Greg reset the rotor, refit the service module, replaced the extrusion nozzle and got the new Humpster back at work on the second half of that batch in less than an hour.

If he hadn't skipped the final step of maintenance procedure he still would have made it to his Tiki Room audition on time, but Greg left the job of sluicing out the hopper with disinfectant to somebody else who didn't do it either. This wasn't just a checklist chore, in this case it was critical because the Humpty Dumpster that was now producing sage and honey flavor sausages had the day before been producing fertilizer; recessed chutes still held a residue of deodorized pig manure which, especially when forced into a sausage skin, looked and cooked just like sausage meat.

Alex: What've you coped with so far?

Heidi: Hey, this business doesn't run itself.

Alex: Just tell me if our real estate is still standing.

Heidi: I'm fine here. Okay? I'm in control of it.

Alex: Sounds like you're managing. Good.

Heidi: I'm a good manager.

Well, this is how things get to be the way they are: there's unpredictable creative power in the momentum of doom.

The gentle roll of his hips, the forward tilt of his shoulders, Alex entered the hotel bar on a sexual prowl, anxiously, passing nests of half-lit strangers' faces. Impressively overdressed in dark suit and tie, his symbolic display pushed ahead of him, eagerness to reassure combined with the aplomb of reserved knowledge, part prom-date and part head-waiter. Business started here, in a bubble of introductory trust, in the hopeful clichés of meeting and greeting that Alex traded with the three-man delegation from Iowa. With each handshake came the next abrupt opportunity to see himself differently, through these men's willingness to follow him from a Happy Hour cocktail to a million dollar transaction. Over the pitcher of margaritas he imagined something like the blossoming of romantic love, the possibility of a change in his life — and theirs — that decided the happier future.

They clustered around the end of the bar, JT as host sending Munro for a second bowl of tortilla chips, and Chick there as light relief, dressed down in Hawaiian shirt, blue jeans and open-toed sandals, no socks, elaborately re-enacting for the late arrivals the theatrical fun they'd missed on the first two days of Creation Week.

Frank and Roy Hornweid goggled boyishly at Chick's performance. Doughy-skinned redheads in their mid-forties, each one was the owner of a 2,000-head hog farm, Frank at the northern end and Roy at the southern end of the state. Plumped up with the oversized friendliness of conventioneers, any kind of stimulation – punchline or bar snack – let loose the same snap of excitement. Sacramento could have been New York City, Oswald's tent show could have been Broadway, and hearing about it all from a hyperactive Japanese devotee who'd been introduced to them as a genius offspring of Thomas Edison and Henry Ford was the acme of outlandish fun.

The twins' puppyish enjoyment of anything new or unusual had probably been a non-stop dull pain in Randall Edlund's ear since the taxi cab ride to the airport in Des Moines. The look he offered Alex was as steady as his handshake, both courtesies presented almost as tests for signs of weakness or strength. His dark blue eyes held a stillness that could tip over into hilarity as easily as into wrath, emotions as physically dangerous as a windmill in a gale. Edlund let a softness dimple the corners of his mouth and make a joke of his solid height, nudging six and a half feet, and of the muscles curved like tree roots under the long sleeves of his plain shirt. Thirty years ago, for one season, he was in the Cardinal line-up as a starting pitcher, and then, after surviving a mountainside car crash and ten months of traction, St Louis let him go. 'I didn't want to coach the dunces anyway. I get more satisfaction being around the honest kind of pigs, ones with four legs and a curly tail.'

Over dinner JT leaked barely believable stories from the Howard Porta campaign trail, less to do with slippery regional shifts of his policy on the environment or public school curriculum and more to do with the Attorney-General's taste in playfully obscene practical jokes. Wednesday's good sport was the wife of his campaign manager who paid two hundred dollars to a United Parcels driver for the special delivery of a boxload of confiscated German homo-erotic magazines, videos and computer disks addressed to her husband.

Twice during gaps in the chat and cross-chat Alex took a shot at man-to-man contact by floating his serious views on the state of the economy, but he was only asked by Roy to pass the creamed corn and after that he wasn't asked anything at all. Conversation bounced between sports and the California election, subjects which left Alex feeling vacuous, his contributions shallow and robotic.

'Just coffee for me,' all that Alex wanted instead of dessert, ordered in a quiet monotone, a male formality. 'Black, thanks,' even though he never drank it that way.

Munro sighed weightily, 'I can't decide if I want the banana split or the pie of the day.'

'Don't think we've got time to fool around here anyway,' JT said directly to the waitress. 'Nothing else for us now.'

'Oswald sure won't wait for us,' Roy said. Experience reminded him, 'He'll just start talking.'

'Oswalds waits for no man,' Randall agreed with Roy from a dry distance.

Chick said, 'Somebody else is on first.'

Frank perked up, shiny-faced, clapped his hand on his brother's meaty shoulder. 'Quentin *Nash*. He's live in person. From that Dumpling show.'

Sliding out of the booth with a courtesy that looked like self-protection Munro said, 'No, Ving's talking before that starts up. About where fossils really come from.'

'Dinosaurs couldn't fit in Noah's Ark,' Chick added miscellaneously. 'He thinks all the prehistoric reptiles got drowned, okay, in some underwater *landslide*.'

'Ving used to go out and do oil field geology,' Randall recalled. 'Never got fired for doing a bad job.'

Munro said to Chick, 'Dr Pogenpohl wouldn't let him mix up his scientific facts.'

'He doesn't know anything either.'

Everybody at the table heard the thin papery hiss of the dinner check being peeled off the waitress's order pad.

The earlier curtain time brought a younger flock into the tent, parents closer to Alex's age. The fresh dazzle of attention dancing around Quentin Nash – glimpses nearly promiscuous, bent away self-consciously whenever they were mirrored back – relaxed the borders of the occasion, let the Christian jamboree spill over into a sloppier celebration of all-purpose community beliefs. With a little shove of mental effort Alex joined that wider, safer, assimilated community, the TV audience, an instant connection which lightened the cumbersome sense he had of being an irrelevant outsider.

The same emotion buffeted him, the uncomplicated joy that channeled through the Hornweid brothers when they saw Quentin in the flesh ten feet from where they sat. Not only had he appeared to them out of the television universe, he materialized out of a collective memory, durable proof of human life going on beyond ordinary experience.

On the way down to their seats Alex muffed his chance to squeeze Chick out of the core of the group and he ended up wedged between JT and Randall. Damped on both sides, Chick might hold in any dazed, unsparing criticism. As Ving stiffly wound up his slide lecture with photographs of cave paintings in Zimbabwe – 'Clearly depictions of a variety of dinosaur types, in herds and as individuals . . . ' and from Paluxy in Texas, 'Undeniable human foot tracks you can see embedded in the same rock formations as dinosaur tracks . . . ' paleontological discoveries, he said, rejected by evolutionists out of professional fear and private envy – Alex only saw Chick shaking his head and staring down at the floor in amazement and solitude.

The hazy light outside still bled through the hay-colored tent cloth, twilight too fell on the stage. The commanding jut of Oswald's jaw overrode the affectionate swell of applause, he lowered the angle a fraction to cue Quentin with the words, 'And God said . . . '

'Let the waters under the heaven be gathered together in one place. And let the *dry land* appear!'

'And *it* was so!'

Under the vaults and arches of gothic church music children skittered in from the wings, the smallest ones bunching up the ocean of blue chiffon and the bigger boys and girls dragging out and holding up a shaky brown cardboard gorge that boxed the wriggling sea.

'And God called the dry land . . . '

'Earth!'

'And the gathering together of the waters he called . . . '

'Seas!'

'And God saw that it was good.' Oswald's ringmaster smile asked us to cheer the goodness of the perfectly unfolding performance. 'And God said . . . '

Loud throat-clearing, a squeak of feedback, Quentin returned, 'Let the earth bring forth grass, the herb yielding seed, and the *fruit tree* yielding *fruit* after its kind, whose seed is in itself . . . upon the earth!'

'And it was *so*!'

The background pulsated with new activity, all of the kids now lugging in cardboard trees and bushes, odd-shaped mats of astroturf herbage, and planted on an earth-toned hillock of felt, wax apples hooked to its flat boughs, unmistakable, the Tree of Knowledge.

Oswald confirmed it: 'And the earth brought forth grass, and herb yielding seed after his kind, and the tree yielding fruit whose seed was in itself after his kind, and God saw that it was good. And the evening and the morning were the *third* day . . . '

A flip of attention, a trick of concentration, I could blank out Oswald and only see those children in front of me. I made myself think that I'd been watching their own version of the creation of the world, the explanation they'd have come up with anyway, without adult help. They could have worked back to this story from a walk through a redwood forest, a hike up the spine of a mountain, ten silent minutes facing the Pacific Ocean, in the vast embrace of the physical world when they understood that they were children in it, just as their parents once were.

To his settled down circle of youngsters Oswald said, 'Those three simple words, *after his kind*, get mentioned *ten times* in the opening verses of Genesis. Translate that Biblical phrase into the language of modern science and you get three simple letters, *D-N-A*. Everything that's alive has its own DNA code, seaweed and penguins, oak trees and zebras, chimpanzees and people, an almost indecipherable sequence of chemical dots and dashes that add up to one thing: an organism that is designed and destined to reproduce its *own kind*. All you have to do is look around the audience tonight to see just how much *variation* there can be in *human kind*, blondes, brunettes and redheads and everything in between, Orientals, Caucasians and Negroid peoples, but if you survived for a thousand years you'd never find yourself living next door to a *new kind* of human being.

'Every ninety-six hours a million babies are born and they all come out looking a lot like their *parents*, the same way they have all through recorded history, *and yet* highly placed scientists, dyed-in-the-wool Darwinists, say it's more *logical* to believe that human babies and chimp cubs, acorns and penguin chicks descend from a *common ancestor* that didn't look like *any* of them – a deaf, dumb, blind blob of jelly drifting around an empty ocean. Tonight we saw the origination of the plant kingdom. You'll be with us *tomorrow* night too, I hope, and straight through the rest of the week, won't you? Then on Saturday you'll see how we recreate the sixth-day insects and what a sight *that's* going to be, what a demonstration . . . '

All open arms and hands, open mouth and eyes, lavish glee from Oswald as he acted out the social pleasure of reunion with the Hornweids, momentarily pried them out of the background and let the formal process of the reception line haul them on to Ving and from Ving to Quentin Nash. In place, one on each side of the pipe-puffing celebrity, the twins wanted their picture snapped and Ving found their Instamatic shoved into his hands. Frank and Roy could hardly hold still for the shot though, looking at Quentin then at each other then back at Quentin, half-surprised that they couldn't poke their arms through his non-televised physical form. Ungreeted, Munro and Olin fell into swapping anecdotes and advice about Holiday Inn room service, while Oswald's unfussy hardball mantalk drew in Randall, JT and Alex . . . friends and associates sorted out and placed by their specific gravity, judged briskly into castes. Gatherings within gatherings. At the center with Oswald, everything said was based on a separate understanding: we're the men who know what is, we're doing the work.

After circling once Chick stopped as if he'd come to an opening in a hedge. Across Alex he said to Oswald, 'I've got a question, can I ask you, please, *Doctor*?'

'Oh,' remembering the face, the connection, Pogenpohl inched ahead. 'Sure, yes. What is it?'

'Can I go and see your lab?'

'You could if I worked in a lab. I don't work in a lab.'

'Wherever you do your fieldwork. I could go there. In my car.'

'There's no place like that you can come to. Sorry.'

'Where do you do your science, see?' Wincing his slanted coffee bean eyes, 'See my question? What's the science, okay, what kind of experiments you do at home?'

'You're just making me repeat what I told you this morning, son. Creation science is the same as any other orthodox science. You can believe it or not.'

From someplace behind them Quentin's fruity counterpoint sailed in. 'Oh, rhhhheally! *Mas*ter Frank!'

The interruption released Oswald who turned away to take it in. Alex yokked along, brittly sucking in a breath. Chick said to him, 'Boss's joke,' and reached for Oswald's sleeve to get his attention again.

Stop him . . . quick calculation, quick tactic, Alex batted Chick's arm off-target, forced to cope with him the way he'd cope with a drunk date, the ordinary assumptions of friendship abruptly suspended. Unprotected, realizing it, Chick held still, speechless, appalled, eyes demanding, *Him instead of me?* And he tried again, blocked by his friend's back then by Alex's silent warning, a searching appeal, *Get your priorities right*. If Pogenpohl had witnessed any of this he would have seen that Alex was not reluctant to deal toughly and on the spot, that he acknowledged the cold and overhanging imperatives of business.

Leaving out details he classed as trivial, Bobby told me at our routine breakfast meeting that he'd been in contact with JT indirectly, he'd been approached by a third party. 'Little gawky guy. You know who I mean. His assistant. Igor.' 'Munro Fyke.' 'Munro. Him. So Munro hands a note to Mr Ed, Ed frisks him, escorts him to the men's room. I'm invited to a personal meeting with the Reverend.' 'You said yes?' 'What would you say?' 'I'd like to be onboard.' 'He wants to repent of his wicked, wicked ways,' a motion proposed for debate. I told Bobby he shouldn't raise his hopes and I said, 'He's on a selling trip. Hedging, at least. I'm sure there's something else.' My day's assignment, starkly obvious, only waited for Bobby to impose a motive. 'Where's the actual benefit?'

Indignation used to drive him, furious dismay, outsized emotions cropped by public office, pacified into a manageable desire for a neater world. Republicans, Democrats, candidates, incumbents, the power to determine events in this country is only the decoy ambition; the power to decide the meaning of *whatever* happens, that's the first cause of political adepts. Bobby used to agree with me about this, now he denies it's true. Transition complete.

Traipsing around behind JT all day clouded my mood with a hint of useless fatigue. Six shoe stores, fittings at two tailors' (one for shirts, one for a dove-gray Western suit), an expedition halfway to Nevada to find the perfect Stetson, a 'town meeting' in Sonoma where JT, subdued, distracted, seemed to be there more as Howard Porta's bodyguard than spiritual herald. The single phone call he made to Nelda lasted for sixty flat, empty minutes, JT directing her scavenger hunt through his trailer for a sealed folder he wanted with their attorney.

By night-time all I wanted was rest, to turn my face away from them, to cover my eyes, but I didn't do that, I went back to them, to

Oswald's audience. *The Children*, *the children*, posed around Oswald and Quentin, politely sitting onstage, selected, observed, waiting to listen.

Over the blue chiffon ocean surface, the brown felt heaps of finished continents and the tottering corrugated sheets of risen mountains, Oswald's narration struck and held. 'And God said . . .'

'Let there be lights in the firmament of heaven to divide the day from the night!'

A yellow paper sphere, a glowing lantern the size of a Volkswagen, descended from a rigged boom over Oswald's head. Above Quentin (to sighs and clapping, not all of it by the under-fives) a silver foil orb half as big dangled in a wobbly arc.

'And let them be for signs,' Quentin ordered, 'and for seasons and for days and for years. And let them be for lights in the firmament of heaven to give light upon the earth . . .'

'And it *was* so! And God made two great lights, the *greater*,' Oswald cast his eyes up at the yellow lantern, 'to rule the day and the *lesser*,' a glance in Quentin's direction, 'to rule the night. He made – the *stars* – also.' Specks of green light peeped on, a net of midget bulbs energized across the shadow gathered under the tent roof, Oswald gestured up at them for us to behold. 'And God set them in the firmament of the heaven to give light upon the earth and to *rule* over the day and over the night and to divide the *light* from the *darkness*. And God saw that it was good. And the evening and the morning were the fourth day . . .'

What kind of science begins with its conclusions, trusts unknown processes and supernatural miracles over natural law as an explanation for evidence of the past? All for us, as a humane act, God prepared a world piece by piece, Oswald said, divided the palpable from the mysterious, created division itself for us to use, divided the universe into light and darkness, 'Translated into scientific terms that means the day-zone and the night-zone were of approximately *equal length*, the same twenty-four-hour cycle we experience today, the *optimal* durations for rest and activity.' The ashes of science.

I recognize the militant stresses, the stagnant certitude, the pulp of special and absolute knowledge, the old rising cry of the Weather Underground and the Black Panthers, of national security zealots. It's an attitude that offends my democratic spirit, my libertarian instinct to allow life to be a constant unfolding to test for what is and what isn't, to dissent and uncover a subtler honesty and then to dissent from dissent. Oswald guides his crowd elsewhere, his happy destination is a buttoned-down born-again theocracy with its capital in Washington, DC, he's carrying a Christian manifesto under his arm, a supremacist manifesto that breeds terrorists.

In my dream that night I saw myself walking through a cavern, a passageway in solid gray rock. My body glowed dimly so I walked in a pocket of phosphorescence. A few feet of cave-dark distintegrated each time I took a step and at my back I felt the feathering pressure of a mild draft: it was the tunnel sealing up behind me, inches away, moving with me as fast as I could walk. The mechanical click and whirr of the recorder triggering under my bed didn't tip me out of sleep, I woke up hearing Alex's voice on the line to Nelda.

Alex: I just don't want . . . I don't mean to unload it all on you.

Nelda: You aren't doing that. Tell me. I want to hear everything.

Alex: Heidi's running her own program, isn't she.

Nelda: She said you talked to her.

Alex: Tuesday, yeah. I got her on the phone for five minutes but I'm not sure I had any real kind of conversation with her.

Nelda: Heidi's shift on Tuesday one of the machines broke down.

Alex: Did it? She didn't tell me. Talking to her is like talking in an echo chamber. I want to be back there. Can you get on Heidi's case?

Nelda: I want you here.

Alex: Jim hasn't said much to me since Monday. I don't know what's going on. Chick's kicked over into weird mode, he's no help. Over-invested, Nelda. I feel over-invested. All we need is for those guys from Iowa to start thinking the business is run by a bunch of flakes.

Nelda: I talked to Jim. There's no big –

Alex: Nelda, maybe I'm a flake too.

Nelda: Oh. Then . . . oh. What does that turn me into?

Alex: We can't keep it going. Not this too.

Nelda: Alex?

Alex: It's . . . I don't get what it is. Everybody's got their own plan. And the plans overlap in small areas. And I can't get any overview here. It could all be falling apart in secret, you know? That could be the hidden trend.

Nelda: Don't sink, Alby. When you get back. Hey, I'm holding you.

Alex: I know. What do you have on? Tell me. Those things?

Daily and nightly exposure to the surrounding certainty of God's governing presence had a subtle effect on Alex. New impinging arrangements were developing out of his reach, a rocking undercurrent stiff enough to compel him to wake Nelda in the middle of the night with a phone call cramped with every gnarled worry he could put into words, and he found words for all of them except the last one he needed to add to his trouble; that he wanted her. He didn't hang up the phone immediately, Alex kept the receiver to his ear, his ear to the faint electrical hiss, listening for a voice in the ether, hovering there, the one waiting to be asked for a clear explanation of things, somebody with the complete overview, somebody listening in.

Friday, Saturday

At the last public sounding Bobby's pre-election lead had opened up to six per cent, and going into the weekend Howard Porta was concentrating the energy of his campaign on enclaves of natural support, conceding to his 'tax-and-spend, day-dreaming' opponent all of California's hardship and grievance votes. The crudest, most obvious rationale for JT arranging a private meeting with us, Bobby said, to trade grime on Porta for a post-election truce, was also the most probable. The real question that required a working answer was: what was the Reverend's state of mind? Was this a maneuver or an act of principle?

'I've noticed a drop-off in flamboyant gestures.' Bobby threw the point open for discussion.

'He's been quiet,' I said. 'He could be coming over to acquire something for Howard.'

Bobby considered this, rejected it. 'Direct? Whatsername, his media co-ordinator — '

'MacKinnon.'

'Karen MacKinnon would've gone sniffing around Marty. She was in the same law class at Harvard. No, I think it's Tickell's last tag. He's allowing the possibility, he's entertaining it before Howard goes down and there's nothing to put on the table.'

'He knows it could happen.'

'I'm giving him ten minutes.' I squinted at the tough front and he dropped it. 'That's what I'll say, anyway.'

The diplomatic tone and emphasis that Bobby found to introduce me to JT, to ask his permission for me to remain in the room, effectively exacted the courtesy. 'Mr Ketchum looks like an honorable man,' JT said, shaking my hand clasped in both of his, ceremoniously, as if the invitation and not the acquiescence came from him. 'I really expected to be seeing Marty Olansky here, too.'

'It's all pretty crazy for him right now,' Bobby said, 'helming the campaign. You probably know all about that.'

JT let go of my hand with a firm nod, seeing (I think) what I saw, our frightening physical resemblance. The same height and coloring, the slight bow in our legs, similarities I'd noticed but implications I didn't absorb until we were facing each other and I had nothng else in my view. Our thumbs were identical, elongated and squared off, this was the monumental thought I carried with me over to the sofa on the other side of the office.

Bobby leaned back in his chair at the head of the table. 'How much can you tell me in ten minutes?'

Looking at him with eyes half closed, with a stilted caginess JT slid a photocopied page out of his jacket pocket. I could see the shape of the printing, it was a newspaper article. 'Would you believe me if I said once upon a time I used to stick up for you against all my friends? Nineteen sixty-eight, Chicago. Somebody'd point to you on the news and say you should just be shot, you're a subversive and I'd tell them you were more of an American than they were. I opposed the Vietnam involvement, too. That was *not* a popular point of view on the campus of a Bible college in Orange County. I resigned over it.'

'You did the right thing then.'

'The conflict was immoral. The bureaucratic lies were putrid. We knew, people didn't need the Pentagon Papers to make up their mind, we listened to what people said and heard the reasons behind what they were saying. Got more and more obvious who you could believe, who was showing the right kind of courage. You spoke up and spoke out.'

'The sides were as clear as they were in civil rights. It always seemed that way to me. Two choices.'

'See that? That's what I mean. You knew what was crooked and wrong in the world, something gave you a clear view of it and whatever it was – '

'Conscience, Reverend.'

'Let's call it that. Your *conscience* gave you a clear view of what *ought* to be.' He read the dateline of the newspaper story, agency copy from the third day of the '68 Democratic convention. The quotation he read out came from an impromptu speech Bobby delivered from the roof of a Dodge Dart a few minutes before he was hauled off for inciting to riot. ' "Somebody with compassion, somebody has to come down here and be with us . . . we need to be in there! Your ******* government is **** without our compassion . . . " ' JT presented the page to Bobby. 'Gone are the days.'

'And what does that make Howard Porta? The second coming of the Days of Rage?'

'I'll tell you one thing about Howard. Out on the street, when he talks to people there's no eye contact. He looks at them, they look at him, they could be watching each other on TV. Turn the channel and forget about it. All of the questions right after, except for the planted ones, they're directed at me. So for Howard's sake I've been dropping down in the back seat.' Twinkling with humility JT confessed, 'They just don't respond to Howard on the personal level.'

'You pull them in, don't you, you double his crowds. Triple them. Maybe we should hire Oral Roberts. Or who was Reagan's God guy?'

'Senator, you pull in plenty all by yourself. Seven thousand at North Valley High last night? I heard that on the news, they came out to hear what you had to say. You said things about me, repeated a few statements that're just about a cough and a spit away from slander.' Not an accusation, an in-joke. 'Smearing me is a pretty low-grade campaign strategy. Low yield too, I bet.'

'Are you saying Howard's associations *shouldn't* be exposed to a little examination? They're questionable, Reverend, I think they're misguided. It's not just you, is it,' Bobby said directly. 'It's Oswald Pogenpohl. The CSI brigade. You remember that bumper sticker? America – Love It or Leave It.' A glance across to me, then back to his point, 'I can't start dealing with anybody who has broken – anybody suspected of illegal practises or activity. Do you understand what I'm saying?'

'There's only one ex-con in this room that I know about.' JT recited from memory, 'Two times in '64, two in '65, three sit-ins in '66, civil disobedience, misdemeanors galore.' If I'd have opened my mouth those would have been exactly my words.

'What do you want to say to me, Reverend Tickell?'

'The feeling you had then, being right with the big thing. Moral. Right with God. First I'm asking you, do you know God?'

'Not the way my mother does.' He pulled back from the table, from the subject. 'If we're going on now's the time to be more informative. We know the top and bottom of Howard's backroom interest in Tentmark Academic Press. Unless there's something extra you want to tell us – '

'Oh . . . ' A self-amused smile, revelation. 'No. *Oh.* No, this isn't about Howard. I came over to settle a personal issue. I want to give you a chance to state the real truth. What you say in private, say it to me. Untelevised. Unrecorded. What you say to your friends, say it to me because we're opponents, understand? You have to know what you're opposing,' the heartfelt appeal of a trial lawyer imploring an unfriendly witness to part with testimony that carries the weight of a verdict. 'It's just the two of us talking. You *saw* my d-lists, you *know* the black and white facts. Now tell me what you really think I've done, my actual motives. God is my motivation, that's what I say. What do you say? Tell me. So when I see you on TV next time I'll know what's driving you for real, what's all the way behind those words you use. What I mean is I want to know who's talking about me.'

Bobby wavered between the strength of silence and the passing chance to hit out with some strong language of his own. He said, 'Oh, you better believe we're opponents! Do I know God? I'd know him if I saw him. You're a *brilliant* point of reference. God motivates you? Personally, I don't think so. Your donor lists are where we *begin.* How about sharing a few other fine examples of your private religious writings with a wider audience? If God is listening to us, if he cares about *you* in any special way at all – and this I doubt – then he also hears me pray for your financial ruin, for one chance to cut the ground right from under your feet. Let me have one chance, that's my prayer, to dig into your business affairs, your sex life, your associations, expose a few inconsistencies for you to reflect on in full view of the cameras – before the banks and the FCC shut you down forever. *Then* maybe we'll all be able to agree on what your "actual motives" are, when you're in recovery. I can tell you this – yes: I've formed an opinion based on what I know about you already. Is that what you're asking me? Fine. Okay, here: it's my considered opinion that there's a sick predatory compulsion behind everything you do. And if I thought that you could answer me honestly, speak *honestly* for five minutes, I'd ask you the same question. *What is it?* What's driving your egotistical, self-deluded hammy life? What drives *anyone* to go out and live in a trailer parked in his own driveway?'

Both of us thought that JT had only stepped out of the room, without a word, for a short break but he didn't come back. From the door squeezing shut on the empty hallway behind him Bobby wondered loosely, 'What was it?'

We trawled through the alternatives. It was a provocation, baiting Bobby into showing off the magnitude of his threat . . . it was abuse by satire, a malicious practical joke . . . it was a display of chest-baring nerve, a shaming rebuke . . . he was acting out a schizoid fantasy that heroic submission could win Bobby over to his side . . . Why would any of these hypotheses be closer to the truth than their refutation: it was just as JT presented it. He'd met Bobby to be clear about the terms of the feud, to agree with his enemy-of-record on the extent of plunder at stake.

'He was trying to be impressive,' Bobby argued.

'Well,' I said, 'he impressed the hell out of me.'

A tetchiness I heard him turn on Alex and Munro, an impatience he'd subdue and cover airily with a joke when he was playing host to the men from Iowa, an abstracted intensity that withdrew JT's eyes to pinpoints, this marshaling (as I saw it) was the only noticeable difference in him since the morning meeting. No change in his agenda, no development to follow up. My reasons for sitting through a fifth night of Oswald's *son et lumière* were separate from any practical procedure, divorced from Bobby's vendetta, unclear at first but solidly present, nagging at me to take a seat one row behind JT.

'And God said . . . '

'Let the waters bring forth abundantly the moving creatures that hath life and the fowl that they may fly above the earth in the open firmament of heaven!' Quentin nodded the proceedings back to Oswald.

'And God created whales and every *living* creature that moveth, which the waters brought forth *abundantly* after their kind, and every winged fowl after his kind,' standing back, making room, enunciating the cue. 'And God saw it was *good*!'

From behind the plastic waterfall, around the edges of the cardboard mountains, right and left the children pelted onto the stage.

Two or three underneath wobbling pairs of paper-and-coat-hanger wings, one brown herringbone lion, one bedsheet polar bear, cats and dogs, a chicken, a pig, two lambs, a monkey and a cow, every one of them raising a racket after his kind, barking, squawking, mewing, baaing, shrieking, pawing the air, trampling the scenery, tripping over their costumes.

'All right, all right.' Oswald clapped his hands to break into the excitement. 'All right, can we — ?'

No effect on them at all. Long experience of kiddie frenzy told Quentin how to meet this challenge. He leaned into his microphone, stuck two fingers between his lips and forced out a whistle as loud as an air-raid siren. Even adults talking in the audience stopped dead.

Watching the children settle down in their places, arrange themselves into assigned groups, Chick rolled his eyes, commented to Frank, 'He says every species is designed by God, right, perfect designs, they show God's love. The rabbit has to eat its own crap for breakfast to digest the protein it just dropped. Shows God likes practical jokes.'

'That's what they're showing now, I guess.'

Randall turned his silent face toward Frank who read the polite request for quiet, whispered an apology and joined him in respectful attention as Oswald started to speak.

'From their DNA on up,' he was saying, 'plants and animals were *fixed* forever in their individual kinds . . .'

'Kinds of what? Kinds of carnivores? Kinds of mammals?' Chick nudged Frank to consider, 'He said if I couldn't tell the difference between a dog and a turkey he didn't want to eat Thanksgiving dinner at my house. He's confused. Thinks I'm Chinese, Chinese kind.'

'C'mon, now,' Randall said, openly annoyed.

'Chick,' Alex urged, 'this isn't important.'

'He's up there, okay, *bullshitting*. He says he proved everything with science, alakazam, pigs and chickens out of nothing. Very scientific! Ask him about human and chimpanzee alpha globin chains and you get a bucket of bullshit dumped on your head!'

'I'm asking you, Chick. Don't make a missile shot out of it.'

'Hey, gentlemen?' Randall tilted forward, coolly directing each clipped syllable, 'Ears open, mouths closed. That's how you learn.'

Chick half-surrendered, one hand in the air. 'Okay. No problem.'

'Can any other notion of life's beginnings be as beautiful', Oswald marveled, 'as the loving command of God going out across the young earth and *filling it* with living creatures? Stocking the sea, the air and then the land with *millions* of life-forms the way a grocer stocks the aisles of his grocery store! I defy anybody to rival the true beauty of that perfect beginning . . . '

What do I become if I can imagine a rival beauty? Imagine this. On the ocean floor three billion five hundred million years ago the first change occurs around the spouts of hydrothermal vents. Around the rim of the in-flow hydrogen sulfide reacts with iron sulfide in the sea water, the reaction produces pyrite and electrons. Crystals of pyrite build on each other and the surface metabolism binds organic molecules to edge and angle, a repeating process and structure, a lattice of instructed, replicating material powered and determined by the inherent tendencies of chemistry and physics. Imagine this is true, that an unconscious pattern rising out of smart mud is the most ancient past of a conscious creature whose brain can envisage its own origin, find meaning immanent in its physical order and purpose in its natural history. And you share the world today with vestiges, primitive strains of bacteria which carry traces of pyrite inside them, grains of pyrite, fool's gold, emblem of romantic speculation that leads on to severe knowledge.

As soon as the house lights were up it came to me, the reason I'd been sitting there: I wanted JT to see me, to be aware that a personal connection existed between us, unconcealed contact I never contemplated with Alex. Filing out of the aisle I let my knees bump the back of JT's seat. He pretended not to recognize me, neither of us spoke, it was good, I felt closer to him.

'Let me introduce these sausages to you.' JT's announcement to the gathering in the conference room formally signaled the start of brunch and of the morning's presentation. 'This is our pork pageant, isn't that right, Oswald. It's our Festival of Pork. Three flavors you can step up and taste and two of them aren't even in the stores yet.'

'We're the guinea pigs,' Roy Hornweid ribbed him. 'I get it now.'

'*Honored* guinea pigs. My wife humped these out to the airport last night, flew them straight up from the farm.' Bathing his face in the aroma rising over one of the warming trays JT said, 'Hot and spicy ones in here. What did we decide these are, Alex? Creole flavor?'

'Creole,' Alex corroborated. 'Chili, pimento, ginger. Authentic

Bayou recipe.' He helpfully removed the tray lids as JT continued along the table.

'In here you've got chestnut and onion, and here,' inviting Roy to dip his head down for an appetizing whiff, 'shut your eyes and tell me what enters your mind.'

'Sausages and', a wild stab, 'red cabbage?'

'Sage and honey.' JT broke it to him, 'The prairie!'

'Ninety-five per cent of Americans are influenced by what they're told about food,' Oswald noticed clinically. 'The health food industry rakes in a billion a year from health food nuts.'

'I hope it's the same way with Yugoslavians. We put our first two shortwave masts up there last week. I'm trying to figure out how I can work Creole sausages into my broadcast on the Feast of the Tabernacle. Today Iowa,' JT smiled broadly at the Hornweids, 'tomorrow the Soviet Bloc. I'm going to turn Sarajevo into a suburb of Jerusalem.'

Earnest talkers and earnest listeners, sellers and buyers congregated around the buffet, two camps gamely present for each other's direct benefit, that was the proposition . . . ignored in favor of the food, the common pleasure of eating. 'Bring your plates over to Munro and he'll serve up the grub,' JT officiated but Oswald stood out as the grand convener. His patronage drew the Hornweids and Randall Edlund halfway across the country for this, a one-hour sales pitch; he provided Ving Kimmel and Olin Mulley in the same way that JT provided the glossy brochures showcasing the HD System, as an illustration of the primary corporate program behind the product. Any competitive tension racking JT was bound to be relieved categorically and soon enough: either they'd buy from him or they wouldn't.

Big round shaved head, pale eyelashes, boyish manners, harmless vapid eyes, Olin trundled over with his plate. Munro stared past him. 'Dr Pogenpohl? Can I get you some sausages and hash browns?'

'I won't, Munro, thanks. I don't eat much this early in the day. Just a cup of coffee and one of those slices of toast.' Oswald tilted his head back toward Olin and the line of men behind him. 'I'll donate mine to feed the famished.'

Ving opened a place in line for Alex. 'What I want to know is do you eat your own pork sausages. That's the quality test.'

'Sure,' Alex said. 'I'm my own best customer. But I buy at cost.'

'I didn't think you did. Like you'd get sick of being around them six days a week.'

'It's Ving, isn't it,' a feat of memory, a deliberate compliment. 'Is Ving a nickname or . . . ?'

'Yeah, I don't know *what* my mother was thinking,' fondly outraged. '*Ir*ving sounds so Jewy.' He released a thin, stingy laugh.

Alex felt a fatherly arm across his shoulder. Oswald joined them, holding a plate with a triangle of dry white toast on it. He thought he'd weigh in and detoxify Ving's humor. 'That's envy. The non-Jewish world *historically* envies your people's survival skills. I've witnessed it first-hand in Israel, it's something special.'

'I've never been over there,' Alex said. 'I don't think I could even get an egg salad sandwich with all the Hebrew I remember.'

It's possible that Ving really wasn't aware of Alex's tribal background. His posture slackened apologetically. 'Oh. I'm sorry there, buddy,' he said, manful and contrite. 'Shake on it.'

'I thought you said something else, anyway.'

In the tidy lull Ving stepped back to the buffet for his second plateful of everything. 'I'm trying 'em all,' pointing at the sausages, smiling across to Alex, his new friend.

'Are you ready to go with your big show?' Oswald questioned him.

'I'm all set. Could use your sound system and lighting, though. That'd get the message across.'

Oswald nibbled his toast delicately. 'Run down the agenda for me. You're going to present the financial structure of it, is that the gameplan? Jim's proposing some kind of leaseback scheme, are you guys jumping ahead with that?'

'I want them to know we're dealing to deal, but I'm saving the contract options for one-to-one negotiations. Today we're just going to tantalize them a little.' Alex concluded again, 'Tantalize them a lot. Chick's got a practical model of a Humpster so first he'll demonstrate how the thing works. I think he's using cornflakes or bran flakes to make the pellets so Frank and Roy and Randall can actually, you know, *sample* the output.'

'Chick. Is he flapping around here somewhere?' Oswald tightened up, as if they had suddenly spoken of the undead. 'He's the king of the oddballs, he worries me. I can't tell when he's being serious.'

'I'm with you on that,' Alex said. 'He's crazed but we all have to put up with him.'

'Okay. Glad you're aboard,' Oswald said without feeling, then moving away, 'I mean it.'

The food had gone, the guests had leafed through the brochures and drifted into a clump in the middle of the room, a pre-game huddle that rumbled out a cloud of male noise. Technical questions about the Humpty Dumpster System were batted adroitly over to Alex who expected Chick to cover that area any minute in his opening presentation. The area Chick was covering at the moment was his hotel room and he was covering it with pieces of the model Humpty that Heidi failed to pack snugly enough for its helpless life as a piece of air freight.

Machine parts lay on convenient surfaces – desk, bed, TV set – all in easy reach of the room service trolley where the reconstruction was going on. 'How long, Chick?' Alex said, staring. 'They're sitting down. They've been sitting for ten minutes.'

Chick stopped working. 'Want to know where I had to go to find a three-eighths socket wrench? This place isn't Hardware City.'

'How much time are we talking about?'

'You want something to eat?' He pointed at the basket of half-eaten croissants on the floor.

'I ate already. I'm finished eating. *Everybody's* finished eating and they're waiting around up there,' staccato jabs with his finger raised toward the ceiling, 'for *you* to show them why their trip out here was necessary! *Customers*, Chick. Our championship shot, we're going to make it happen so, please, would you *please* stop farting around now, bolt this thing back together and concentrate on what you're going to say to sell it.'

'They're not worth it,' Chick said. 'They don't deserve a Humpty Dumpster, okay, they don't respect science.'

'Kamikaze,' Alex blamed him and asked himself, 'Why do I have to deal with this unbelievable shit?' He swiped the wrench off of the desk and held it out for Chick to take. 'Fix this. I'm not making any more excuses for you.'

'I'll stay here.' Chick dialed room service, ordered himself a three-course lunch. Behind his back Alex was clankingly busy trying to fit the components he recognized into the aluminum frame. The shove from behind twisted him off-balance and he dropped sideways, banging his elbow on the edge of the desk. 'My machine, okay. Don't touch it. I don't want you to *touch* it.'

'Your machine, okay.'

'Cutting me out again but you tell me "fix this" and "sell it" when you want me to – '

'Right, right.'

' – to do what *you* want. Using me your way.'

Rubbing his arm, stunned, wounded, 'Is it okay if I stand up?'

Chick grabbed Alex's unhurt arm and pulled him up, looking away. He quickly occupied himself with the reassembly and said, quietly defensive, 'You made excuses? About *me* to *them*?'

'What would you do?' Alex said honestly. 'I just want to hold it all together. Nobody's using you. Nobody who isn't using me, anyway – and anyway, we're using him. Them. For capital. Everybody's got a plan.' A temporary invalid, he lowered his body onto the bed. 'I have to rest for a minute.'

He watched Chick work and envied the work, the engineer's fine dexterity. No doubt at all, the device in front of him was Chick's, minutely explainable and unambiguous in its mechanical principles, the action of those principles, the product of that action. As Chick assembled the twin escapements, the screw-drive ram, the overload sensor, he magnified the clarity of each mechanism's function. 'It's . . . I can't keep track of everything that's happening,' Alex spoke but he wasn't sure Chick was listening. 'Facing . . . I don't know what, something I can't see all the way around, I can't see the shape of it. I back up and it just gets bigger, I can't get far enough away from it to see what the whole thing is. Before we left LA – Chick? The day before we left LA I went to bed with Nelda.' Work stopped. From his analytic confidant Alex received a smirk of dry, ungrabbed skepticism. 'For real.'

Chick crouched down to eyeball the rotor alignment. He spent a few seconds adjusting the pitch of the blade. 'So are you going to do it with her again?'

'As much as she wants.'

'Weirdness,' Chick said, turning sullen. 'Why do I have to know about it? You stuck it in *my* head now. Supreme, Alex.'

'Cut me out, pay me back. Swear to God!' The stiff shock of it sat him up. 'I just told you what's going on in the scariest part of my life, I only got *started* on what's wrecking me, and you, what, you slam the *door* in my face? I want to tell you about . . . about why she – '

'You want me to say, "Good, okay. Sneaking around, that's some fun!'' What do I know about it? You told me, you pulled me in, so now that makes me a liar around here, too. Like them, Oswald and *them*,' his turn to point irately at the ceiling. 'I'm not a liar, I don't lie about the facts of life!'

Alex's failing wish, 'A little help.'

'You can't push it back, can't tromp it down if it's there. Tell Jim, okay, don't tell me. Or tell Nelda to tell him. Because he'll see it sometime, he's going to.'

'I can't do anything while we're here.'

Alex picked up a washer and a hex nut he saw slip onto the floor and plunked them down beside Chick's hand. Chick smoothed them both between his thumb and forefinger and then set them on a threaded pin jutting out of the blade axle. 'If this washer had a defect in it,' he talked it through, 'the vibration would rattle the nut loose. Centrifugal force of the blade would spin it out of alignment and if it wobbled off the axle it'd rip the guts out of the mulch trough.' While Chick fastened the last screws into the plastic housing Alex phoned the conference room and alerted Munro that they were on their way upstairs.

The clear plastic housing of the half-size model allowed a view from every angle of the machine's internal structures and processes. 'The Visible Humpty Dumpster,' Chick dubbed the object and asked pedantically, 'Can everybody see it?' He took the watchful silence to mean yes they could, although in addition it expressed some hedged fascination at the sight of Chick wearing a suit and tie, his straight dark hair neatly combed off his forehead, presentable as a Baptist missionary. 'Okay, we're going to turn low-grade organic scraps into high-potency pig food.'

A warm co-operative note hummed out of the Humpster when he flicked its power switch and a satisfied growl churned up from its core when he tipped a bowl of damp muesli into the hopper. 'Pretend we put in food group by-products plus twenty-five per cent regular dry feed. Gets mixed around, chopped and blended, pow-pow-pow, fifteen seconds.' He tapped the clear front panel instructively as the oats, nuts, raisins and dried fruit were granulated behind it. Chick rested one hand affirmatively on top of the machine, and in a delivery that Oswald was intended to recognize he went on, 'We can *use* the Humpty Dumpster to examine a supreme *scientific* question: is it a unique *kind* or is it a specially *adapted* machine that *evolved* from the wheel?'

Across the table from Alex who sat chewing his lower lip in a darkening trance, Oswald showed with a poised smile and by tapping his fingertips together in merry little bounces that he could be entertained right along with everybody else. Professorially Chick described the action continuing in the compressor bin and then in the receiver tray, out of which he scooped a handful of the shiny flesh-color pellets, sprinkled them into a cereal bowl and passed them down the line. 'Bar snacks,' he said.

'Boar snacks,' Frank snorted to brother Roy, in the fun spirit. After a munch or two he said, 'Tastes like doggie biscuits,' and told Randall to be a man and go on and try a bite.

'Very delicious,' Randall granted, 'for pig feed.'

When the bowl reached Oswald he nudged it away without a look. Chick, apparently, wasn't finished lecturing. 'If the Humpty Dumpster *is* a form of machine kind is it a *basic* kind or is it a modern species of some ancestor machine? What *is* a kind, anyway? Let's look at it. A Humpty Dumpster *isn't* a refrigerator or a fire extinguisher. Look — see? Obviously! And it isn't a lawn mower or a tow truck. But look closer, look *inside*: parts of it look like parts of a food processor and other parts look like parts of a trash compacter. Hmm. So what? So *the* question we want to answer is are they *genetically related*? Could be! According to the standard definition,' Chick prepared to read from a paperback textbook, a work authored by Oswald Pogenpohl, 'let me quote, ''The basic unit is the *kind*. Dog kind includes the coyote, the wolf, the jackal and all household dogs since all of these various species are interfertile and produce offspring.'' Then so, if they can *cross-breed* that makes them the same *kind*. Okay! But — oh, no . . . ' Heavily disappointed as he remembered, 'What about the *fruit fly*, the different species of *Drosophila* that *can't* breed together? Is *this* fruit fly a different *kind* from this *other* fruit fly?' Shallow sigh, helpless shrug. 'We haven't got any *serious* definition, we *still* don't know what a *kind* is. So how, where and why,' Chick pondered on, 'does the Humpty Dumpster fit into the world?'

The bubble dance wasn't over. Enduring it, pinned, Alex counted his options. He could interrupt Chick with a question. He could distract him with a glass ash tray heaved straight at his forehead. He could fake a heart attack . . . but, no: any attempt to stop him would just be a sign of disarray. Let him go, Alex thought, as he heard the creak of a trapdoor opening under his chair.

On the other hand, Frank, Roy, Randall and the rest seemed to be an easy audience for this burlesque, enjoying it as a loopy gimmick to highlight the product's design features and maybe even as a comic toast to Oswald, who of course didn't see it that way at all. He'd tired of riding out Chick's spunky sarcasm, which now lurched to the brink of its climax.

'The *evolutionary* history of the Humpty Dumpster we can say began with the *earliest form* of machiota, the wheel. Around every corner of the ancient world a new adaptive zone opened up where wheels could branch out and make a *living*. Wheel populations modified and diversified by random mutation and natural selection to fit into *vacant niches* of the environment. Some developed teeth and became cogs and gears, some wheels *elongated* into hinges or the barrels and tumblers you can see today living in combination locks and slot machines. Another line led to the family of *vehicles*, the chariot and trolley car, the tractor and skateboard. But the Humpty Dumpster is descended from the wheels that moved into the *kitchen environment*. The rotary motion of its mulching knives is inherited *directly* from its ancestor the egg beater. Its grinding action is shared with the garbage disposal, but it's much more *efficient* and the pressure to recycle has favored the development of a pelleting function from the *clumsier* bulk output of the household trash compacter. The critical *advantage* this species has is its indoor-outdoor flexibility, it can produce sausages or pellets: food, fuel or fertilizer and in a generation or two Humpty Dumpsters could colonize the *whole world*.' The sharp laughs around the table crackled out of the false impression that Chick was mocking the theory of evolution. Oswald knew what was being mocked and it was an effort for him to sit still. To spurts of ignorant laughter Chick classified the Humpster species for them. It belonged, he said, 'to the genus *Boxidae* which includes paper shredders and food processors, in the family of domestic appliances, in the order of portables, in the class of electrical devices, in the phylum of hardware, in the kingdom of machines.' Still, he hadn't scored yet. Crassly stepping on the hilarity he said, 'You think *that's* funny? It's *more* scientific than your cardboard, bogus scientific idea of basic kinds!' Their laughing crumbled in front of him and fresh silence clotted behind him as he crossed the room to sit in the seat next to Alex. 'Your turn,' Chick said, implicating him.

Softly, strenuously polite, Oswald turned to JT for the time, he had to obey the strict demands of his schedule. 'I've got to run,' he excused himself and stood. 'Ving can give me a full report.' He didn't leave though, not quickly. Arms stiffened against the back of his chair he leaned in toward Chick. 'Can I correct one small point for you? A basic animal or plant kind means animals or plants that come out of a single original stock. Or – '

'That's the total *argument*,' Chick fought back. '*Which* plants and animals are related to the same bunch of ancestors!'

'Let me finish what I'm saying, you had your chance to talk. *Or* if they're obviously the same morphological type, if they interbreed or not they're the same kind according to the logical axiom which states that two things equal to the same thing are equal to each other. Try and mate one of your fruit flies with a tarantula sometime and see how far you get.'

A geological epoch ago, when the hotel waiters setting out the chafing dishes were the only others in the conference room, JT bolstered Alex with a thought-for-the-day. 'Our competition isn't some other product, it's lack of imagination. Like always. *That*'s what you have to supply for them, supply them with enough imagination to see what they've got going now is obsolete . . . '

The lump in his stomach Alex pictured as soft and white, a marshmallow ball squatly foaming in a puddle of acid. He shut his eyes only for a second, two seconds, pictured instead the distance he had to close between proposal and acceptance. Chick's grand insult left the ground scrambled with rubble and over it Alex had to go, wading forward with an armload of gifts. Three seconds. He pushed each distraction out of view so that nothing except what he had to say waited to fill the moment: going in he knew that any personal quality he projected was bound to be read as indicative of the company and any company trait representative of its product, therefore . . . 'Gentlemen,' his unrattled approach prepared them for honest declarations, his diligent presentation spoke for the value of his merchandise, his effectiveness its viability, his bright health a radiant sign of corporate integrity. 'You can read the cold facts in our brochure and your experience can tell you what they mean – overall productivity statistics, seasonal profit margins, details of specific economies we've made on operating overheads, the market niches we're positioned to exploit with our home brand-line of meat products, you can see all this in black and white. Names, dates and numbers. Should our figures, our results, mean anything to you? Not as much as five minutes of your time on site where you'd see how the Humpty Dumpster System changed Hummingbird Farm *forever* . . . '

With missionary candor Alex offered them knowledge of the system that was a cosmic principle in material form, a secret that they had been selected to learn. A feeling close to family affection expanded in his lungs and fanned out into the room as he talked on, gathering in the Hornweids' pinkish balloon faces, softening the rigid angles of Randall's brow and jawline, convincing these men, becoming one of them himself in the split second he knew that they were willing to believe him. Oh, the gigantic, thunderous miracle of reversal, a rhythmic point Alex shuddered across, potently aware that he'd dragged his lost customers back out of the cratered wilderness where Chick had dumped them! Randall and both Hornweids agreed to extend their trip and spend one day in Los Angeles touring Hummingbird Farm (and Universal Studios) to confirm the glamorous claims. *Access*, *impact*, *penetration* – if that pretty well described the effect he'd just had then Alex wasn't wrong, he was not in line to be another one of capitalism's ejected losers. Such an Olympian award made it easy for him to buy into JT's earliest contention, that the God behind all the good in the world, the movement that shapes life's direction, crouched behind the jackpot of this transaction.

'Oh, mountain oysters, Oswald! Judge ye not. What if God sent you Mr Uchiyama to measure the sincerity of your compassion. Don't you think *any*thing is funny?'

The sympathetic hearing that Pogenpohl didn't wring out of JT with his prim complaint of Chick's 'unkindness' he received from Alex without a fight. 'Absolutely,' he nodded, grimly enthusiastic, maturely approving Oswald's decision to bar Chick from the pageant tent precincts. 'And I mean starting from right now,' Oswald breathed the diktat and mossy air into Alex's face as orderly daily business trickled on around them in the lobby. Pogenpohl turned away from the reception desk, tucked his chin and said in a voice softened only in volume, 'He's a walking disruption. I just *don't* want to be disrupted by him in public again. There's a limit to being understanding.' 'No, absolutely. Chick went way over the line. I'm sure he'd want me to apologize for him.' This, Oswald doubted. 'What's his thing? Is he some wild kind of anarchist?'

Nothing as coherent as anarchy was feeding Chick's behavior, so it knotted Alex's mind even more to puzzle out what pressure had turned his friend and partner into a suicide bomber. Before this week he'd always remotely admired the way Chick could be frantically inventive with his dozens of projects and at the same time, away from them, socially docile. As a matter of fact, in groups of more than three people, whatever the discussion, Chick typically exhibited all the resistance of a windsock. Still on the phone with him half an hour after serving him with Pogenpohl's notice, Alex strained to keep Chick on the single subject of that morning's near apocalypse.

Alex: What would you call it? A cry for help?

Chick: I call it if they know what they're doing then they're cheating liars and if they don't know what they're talking about then somebody should tell them to shut up.

Alex: Not you! Not now! What difference does it make to anything if they believe what they want to believe? They aren't hurting anybody with it.

Chick: Okay, right. Making people stupid isn't hurting anybody.

Alex: It's not hurting me. Fucking up a major sale, that would hurt me. It'd hurt you.

Chick: Let's all go live in caves, okay? You'd sell a ton of Humpsters to Stone Age guys in caves, huh?

Alex: I'm hanging up.

Chick: It's *how* they think about things, man, it's how they do their thinking. You know the front steps of the Natural History Museum? Granite or limestone — anyway, old steps. And you know how going all the way up, okay, the steps have a sag in the middle? So, I say to you those dents come from hundreds and hundreds of thousands of pedestrians walking up and down there for the last hundred years. But then Gilbert tells you I'm full of shit because nobody has ever actually observed the friction from a pair of shoes rub away a *millimeter* of rock like that. His explanation for it is that a long time ago, one night when nobody was looking, a flying saucer fired a heat beam at the museum and it melted a dent into the middle of every step in its path and *that's* why it looks that way. Okay, how do you decide what story to believe?

Alex: Your thoughts, y'know, your profound philosophy really had a wonderful impact on Oswald Pogenpohl.

Chick: Yeah, I know how cruddy it all sounded in there, but I figured out a better way to explain my point.

Alex: Chick, he wants you – *I* want you – to leave him the fuck alone.

Chick: I'm not going to let him alone.

Alex: Stay out of his way. Go back home. Stay out of *my* way. It's over for you here. You're over with this.

Chick's small brown face wasn't the only absence that night in the nest of VIP seats. Frank and Roy Hornweid lay sweating and shivering in their hotel beds, flattened by a mystery sickness that Oswald diagnosed as twenty-four-hour flu. Olin Mulley's place was vacant too, and for the same reason. In the shrunken contingent who were present no one was sparking very brightly. Ving sat hunched and strained, his square torso folded forward as if he'd cinched his belt too tight; JT, Munro, Randall and Alex filed in like a chain gang, dull headaches and queasy stomachs dropping them into their chairs, and for Alex, on top of that, a percolating clamminess which minute by minute made him less sure he could get through the rest of the evening. He was grateful for the low lighting and the almost solemn anticipation that subdued the crowd settling down before the climax of Creation Week.

Even the stage was covered in that charged solemnity. The plastic waterfall was gone, it had given way to a backcloth painted with a fabulous vista of the Edenic world, a rain forest stretching greenly to the horizon, parted by the glittery blueness of a river that broadened and flowed out of the flat scenery on into the narrow chiffon sea last seen jumping and yapping with fishlife. Its surface was calm, the fringes of its waves lapped, as of old, at the heels of Oswald Pogenpohl and Quentin Nash.

'And God said . . . '

'Let the earth bring forth the living creature after his kind, cattle and creeping thing, and beast of the earth after his kind!'

'And it *was so!*'

The astroturf drapery that framed Eden flapped apart on both sides of the backdrop, opening for the children's parade back into the show, in seemly procession tonight, disciplined and paired, hand in hand – a cow and a bull, a ram and a ewe, a lion and a lioness, a hen and a rooster, and two slouching apes, the little-girl-ape's femininity prettily declared in the thinness of her facial hair.

'And God made the beast of the earth after *his* kind, cattle after *their* kind and every living thing after *his* kind. And God saw it was *good*!' A small tremble in Oswald's throat, forcing the pace uncontrollably, 'And God said . . .'

But Quentin dragged out the rehearsed pause, collected all of us, each of us, into his over-awed hesitation, lifted his face into the gaze of the light, into the impending passion of history, and then crashed through his own silence with one towering, quivering proclamation. 'Let us make . . . *man* . . . in our image, after . . . *our* . . . likeness . . .'

Backstage, working the fishing reel and piano wire, covering Olin's job, Ving wound back the loam-colored felt squares that blanketed the center patch of the stage – a jump ahead of Oswald who rushed his reading to keep up with the action. 'And the Lord *formed* man out of the dust of the ground and breathed into his nostrils the breath *of life* and *man* became a *living soul*!'

Out of the navel of Creation, welcomed with a barrage of German choral music, up stood Adam, humankind in the shape of an eight-year-old boy blinking against the spotlight, blond hair perfectly combed, peach fuzz cheeks clean and pink, dressed for prep school in his navy blue blazer, gray slacks, white shirt and striped tie. Adam looked around at his world, stiffly dazzled as the square of loam right next to him peeled away and Eve stood blinking there too, in her dollish white dress, white patent leather pumps, waist-length hair the color of his, the same shade of blonde, her skin the same white-pinkness. Newborn, untouched by expectation or disappointment, by speculation or suspicion, human parents undefiled by carnal knowledge, by *any* knowledge except what they were told directly by their five senses and the unambiguous voice of God.

'And let them have dominion over the fish in the sea', Quentin said unambiguously, 'and over the fowl of the air and over the cattle and over all the earth . . .'

Permission and mandate which sent young Adam and Eve rooting around the scenery, plucking cardboard fish out of the crinkled sea and handing them to the lions for food, likewise cropping fistfuls of grass for the sheep, corn for the poultry and bananas for the dependent gorillas.

'And over every creeping thing that creepeth on the earth!'

A crisp nod from Oswald to Ving and a tug on a dangling lanyard broke open the nets suspended over our heads. Everywhere in the tent for a few seconds the air swarmed, it quivered with a snow of cut-out paper insects. They fluttered down, they corkscrewed down, glided and nosedived, rose-pink mantises, yellow bumble bees, indigo butterflies, giant brown ants, lavender dragonflies, they sprinkled into laps and hair-dos, into a heave of shared, chattering delight. 'And God saw that it was *good*!' I'm sure I saw Oswald swipe this line at JT, triumphant proof that yes-he-*does* have a madcap sense of fun. The pleasure smiling out of him was generous, wise and conclusive, it was itself the meaning he wanted us to take from the closing verse, 'So God created man in *his own* image, in the image of *God* created he him . . . male and female,' – Oswald half-turned toward the pair of eight-year-olds waiting in the spotlight for their final cue, the ceremonial moment when they unveil from its sky-blue velour shroud God's providence, a wicker Horn of Plenty disgorging its cargo of wax fruit – 'created he *them*!'

Pink hands scrambled at the veil and the folds zigzagged to the floor and the gold-tinted spotlight splashed against the boxy plexiglass robotoid half-scale model of the Humpty Dumpster.

The dizziness that swirled into Alex's head flushed up out of his stomach, and his stomach collapsed into a sucking vacuum. Wherever he looked he was hit with a different view of the surreal circus. Munro stroked JT's back, fussing tenderly, maternally, over the Reverend's physical pain while JT cradled his own heavy thumping head in his hands strangely, one hand at his forehead, the other on his neck. Right beside Alex, Randall sat gripping the back of the chair in front of him, his face hanging between his arms, sucking in his discomfort, in need of a sick bag, swallowing his rancid spit. Off at the other end of the aisle Alex caught a fractured sight of Chick flitting through the darkened margins of the tent, a wispy Asian sprite, followed by an impression of Ving grabbing Chick by his shirtfront and swinging him into the side of a PA speaker column.

Excruciating weakness spread into Alex's arms and legs, he heard the scrape of his shoe on the metal chair leg, he tasted the aluminum, and then the shuddering dug through him, switched on like an electric current, enough of a battering for his body just to give up. Thick muddy juices gurgled in the loops of his intestines, the unstoppable mess sloshed out of him with its cloud of personal stink, the bitter smell of burnt rubber, of sour cheese, foaming into the air as the puddle soaked through his jockey shorts wetting the seat of his slacks, bubbling there when a jet of rotten air blew into it so he felt the lukewarm glue squirt between his ass cheeks. He wanted to stand up; he couldn't. JT was looking at him now and speaking but Alex didn't know if JT was speaking to him. JT indicated something with a gesture, his hand in slow dreamlike motion.

Alex had no memory of getting to his feet. Munro must have helped him up, it was Munro's skinny shoulder under him now, walking him in doddering steps to the fire exit. 'Do you think . . . anybody . . . noticed anything?' he slurred like a drunk and stayed conscious long enough to hear Oswald begin his further, undamaged, reasserted exaltation.

'What a special creature is Man! When you look in the face of any other human being you see the *reflection* of God, you see His wonderful *likeness*. And yet God is as *different* from us in His mental potence and lifestyle as *we are* from all the animals! So how can I state that He is visible in every human face? His *image*, if you look for it, is in the unique set of *emotional expressions* that only *homo sapiens* is allowed to possess. Signs of moral conscience, awareness of time, appreciation of physical beauty, all of these advantageous traits *together* are the sign of the longing soul. We *long* to find God because in His existence we can *comprehend* the ultimate reason and daily business of our own individual lives.

'God entrusted us with supervision of His precious creations in exactly the same way He supervises us. Supervision – literally *above-seeing*, watching over . . . Horseflies, houseflies and fruit flies, flying fish, flying squirrels, flying lemurs, every form of wildlife you can name manifestly *lacks* the one spiritual characteristic that raises us into our special relationship with God himself, they lack *a soul*. They lack a soul for a good reason: so that we realize the great difference between soulless *animals* and *ourselves*! The chimpanzee and his kind, the gorilla and his kind, as wonderful as they are in their habitat or in our zoos, they *weren't* born in the likeness of God! What gibbon monkey ever wrote a Shakespeare sonnet? What silver-backed gorilla ever passed a high school algebra test? Is there an orang-utan anywhere that ever went to the Louvre to admire the Mona Lisa?

'Look at our faces,' Oswald wagged his hand under his chin, 'they aren't animalistic faces. They're designed to look upward! Our brains, tongues and larynxes are designed to produce clear language which permits us to *speak* what we *know*, the way *I've* been speaking to you all this week. *We've* been given the chance and the choice *to use* our separate, human gifts to *worship* the eternal God, our own loving Supervisor . . . '

Yes, and Oswald stood there as the prime example of spiritual achievement, an incentive for the people. JT, in his painful distress stayed to listen, pretended to roll along on Oswald's bandwagon, as gripped as I was by the enveloping sleet of applause and by the mortifying, bodeful realization that of all the guests at the presentation brunch that day Oswald was the only one who providentially escaped food poisoning.

Sunday

The half-darkness Alex awoke into had the same liquid texture as the half-darkness he passed out of in the tent, his dizzy exit could have been only minutes ago but the whole night had disappeared into his past. Most of the morning had also spun by. He groaned heavily, pinned under the limp weight of his own body, shredded inside, as fragments of the last twenty-four hours crowded back and massed into a congested picture of infantile disgrace and last-minute fumble.

'Should open the curtains. Twelve o'clock.' It wasn't a thought, it was a voice in the room. Chick's voice. 'I ate your breakfast.'

'Yeah,' Alex answered neutrally, squeezing a glance sideways to locate the round face that drifted, grayly haloed, toward the foot of the bed. 'Why are you in my room?'

'I waited for the doctor in here.'

'There was a doctor?'

'Checked you out last night. First she wanted to pump your stomach out. Then she said whatever was rotten in there probably already gushed out of you, one end or the other.'

'I don't remember a doctor.'

'She told you you can't eat anything until tomorrow. Water. You have to drink water.'

Chick carried over the copper-colored jug and poured out a glass of ice water. Alex propped himself up on his elbow, waited for the drink. 'What time is our plane?'

'Next one we can get on is four-thirty.'

Alex swallowed slowly, drank it all, held out the glass for Chick to fill again. 'Am I supposed to stay in bed the whole time?' Chick nodded, endorsed the order. 'Well. Either they'll go for the deal or not. What else can I say to them?' He sank down into his pillows and kept on sinking into a pool of dull, distant pain.

'It's not like they're out looking for us,' Chick twitched.

'Who?'

Quickly, 'Anybody.'

'The main work was good. It was good.' Alex struggled back up to his elbows, sweat-damp strings of hair flopped over into his eyes, a sud of spit wedged in the corner of his mouth. 'Chick?' he said, 'How do you think we really looked to them?'

In a hospital room personalized with pairs of fruit baskets and doubled flower arrangements, a forty-minute walk from Alex's hotel, Randall sat between the twin beds and the still groggy Hornweid brothers just as Chick stayed by Alex. His physical constitution (or his uncomplaining humor) equipped him to tolerate the insult of whatever poisons had incubated in those contaminated sausages, and now from his well of strength Randall lobbied for the same grace to be shed upon his stricken friends, supplementing their doses of antibiotics with hourly prayer. Gentle appeasement and supplication, his familiar words hammered at my ears; his self-important humility disturbed me, it shrank a grown man into a deserving dependant with no more than his submission to offer for the personal concern of a watchful power bigger than the world. No intention is outside the world. Randall saw himself facing outward, upward toward the open universe but I saw him facing in, facing its smallest part, dragging down the Monster of Good into his room, this minute, into his Christian magic and the Hornweids' bowel trouble.

I heard the words inside Randall's prayer, his real prayer, that is, for relief from the fear of his own irrelevance. Seeing him that way frightened me. I felt it happening to me again, slipping too far inside myself, into the emptiest dark, sliding away from material reality. Alex didn't hold me anymore, his perception of his work was reduced to the square area of profit and loss. Bobby didn't hold me anymore, his political scope reduced to the scale of his office. I felt less alone when I stayed close to JT, partial appearances and deniable deceptions had worn him out too. Just the two of us were left straining, testing, risking security for the sake of total clarity.

I followed him over to Pogenpohl's Sunday service of thanksgiving. Flanking Oswald on the platform, Howard Porta and JT sat together, and next to them, no matter how sick they might have felt, Ving and Olin led the parade of Creation Science Institute branch chairmen and their wives. Quentin Nash lounged in his seat at the end of the row, chunky legs crossed, showing a few inches of hairless waxy white calf above a drooping sock, peering down at the public as they filed into the tent and smiling benignly on them, evidently still in character.

'Hey, so,' Ving grabbed JT out of his silent distraction, 'did you fire that little twerp?'

'Sorry, I didn't hear what you said.'

'Load him on a slow boat to China, that twerpy loonytoon. You'd be better off if you cut him loose. The whole program would.'

'Uchiyama's my partner. He's part of the program,' JT explained slowly and without apology. 'I can't fire him.'

'Crucify him.'

'C'mon,' Olin cut in, flagging the near blasphemy.

'In a figure of speaking,' Ving butted back. 'Every action ought to have a reaction, that's all I mean.'

'Ving, I'll tell you what, then,' JT said, 'I'll give you Chick's address and you can sneak into his bedroom and hide a frog in his bed.'

'He'd probably ask it to marry him.' Ving sat back, let it go.

JT remained unbadgered for all of five seconds. Porta tapped him on the knee. 'Stage fright?'

'What, Howard?'

'Off your own turf. Out of your own arena.' Howard tilted his long lined face, struck a doctorly pose. 'Throat muscles can just seize up all of a sudden, when you don't expect it. Are you in shape to speak to these folks today?'

'Today's Oswald's show. I'm just a quiet dignified presence here.'

'The wooden Indian,' Howard said. 'Same as Thursday. Same as Friday night.'

'Did you want me to do a striptease at your town hall meetings, is that what? Just tell me next time, Howard, and I'll pack my Gypsy Rose Lee costume. You don't know *what* I did for you Thursday and Friday.'

'No, I don't. I wish I did.'

'Play out the string and see what happens.'

'You don't surprise me, not really. But if your attitude is different

219

from what it was a week ago I'd be a little interested to hear what bumped it out of line. Where's the large benefit?'

'Go on, let the bloodhounds loose. My attitude's out in the open where it was last week and where it is right now. See it? Shake on it.' JT speared Porta's hand with his, pumped it hard. 'Let them talk. I don't care what they say about you, Howard. You've still got my vote.'

'Well, you know how it is around here. They'll tell you any old b.s. you want to believe, all the way up to election day.'

I asked a bow-tied usher to point out the reserved section for me, a commanding touch that squelched any doubt that I belonged there. His instant impression must have been that I was one of the grand-parents or teachers chaperoning the herd of school children who were climbing into, under and over the special rows of seats which were their reward for performing so spiritedly in the pageant all week. I took an aisle seat directly in JT's line of sight, thinking as I watched him up there how isolated he was among those people.

'Good view from here!' Munro's nervous apology for tripping over my feet on his way down the row. 'You can see the whole thing.'

'Every hair on Oswald's head, that's right.'

'You must have good eyes.'

I said, 'It just figures. The last day of it all is when I finally get here early enough to make it to my seat. Every other time I got stuck somewhere back there.' I twisted around as if I were trying to spot the far-flung place I'd been unluckily occupying each night.

'I've been sitting right here for the whole shebang. Boy! I tell you,' Munro took in the tent's rough spectacle before he told me, 'it's been a special thing to see.'

'They should make it a compulsory national holiday.'

'I'm with you on that.'

Porta nudged JT with a remark that I couldn't pick up. Whatever he said forced a diplomatic and uncomfortable smile from the Reverend who nearsightedly looked in my direction then broke off the momentary contact with a swish of his hand. Munro waved back to him. I said that I'd been following Jim Tickell's ministry since he started on television, that I was an unshakable admirer.

'Have you ever met Jim in person?'

'Now that would be something. You sound like you know him.'

'I know the Reverend,' he said with the woundable shyness of a flattered wallflower. 'I work real close with him.'

'You probably go to sleep at night raring to get up in the morning. It must be an exciting time for you.'

Munro introduced himself and invited me along to meet JT after the service. I said that would be a thrill for me and he took my respectful appreciation as his personal achievement. 'He doesn't usually, but I can get you his autograph.'

I nodded gratefully. 'I'd enjoy that.'

Oswald's gleefully combative spirit bounded ahead of him to his lectern where it seemed to hang and wait for him to step forward and fill its shape. Buoyant and feisty, he answered the shouts of affection ringing from wall to wall with victorious overhead waves of both arms and a playful lightness in his step, the white golf shoes he was sporting even had the look of ballet slippers on his small feet. Gravity, though, he reserved for the spoken word, his words today and he spoke each one not only for the record but from it. 'You *know* when God speaks to you. He puts the thoughts in our minds that agree with the Bible. That's a high qualification *sine qua non*. You can fight the un-educators *and you can beat them* with a dose of their own weaponry – hard facts shot down the barrel of a straight, reasonable argument. In the first fractions of the opening seconds of Creation Week the same cause that determined the emergence and order of matter, energy and life in the following six days also caused us to be here, thousands of years down the line, recreating those all-important events. So we recollect our heritage. We are born out of the same ancient act of creation, our presence in this life is *intentional*. Accept that bullet-hard fact and you stand on the unmovable foundation of unchanging truth. We're a lot more modern today than we were in Biblical times. We can reinforce our belief with scientific evidence and investigation, natural doubt can be canceled *out*, but it's our primary acceptance of the historical relationship between God and humankind that cuts through theories and theories about theories, *faith* has the power to guide us out of confusion and argument. Faith in the plainly written word of God turns God toward us and in that loving look He protects us from the daily terror of being lost and the nightly dread of our soon-coming death. What sane person would *not* want to be rescued that way? It seems to me that's practically a test of your mental health! And even so, put in those terms, *still* when you go into the schools or into the offices of public school officials you meet humanists of this type, choking on their arrogance, refusing salvation, flaunting their petty authority, barbarians with fountain pens forcing us into the same fight our people have been fighting for two thousand years; namely, the battle for our civilization's body and soul! Nothing less! Modern institutions conspire to drown out any godly influence on society, *our* society – from the scientific community to the education establishment, from state committees to the movie and home entertainment industry, the top people dictate policies that deride our morality and belittle our ideas. They just *hate* us! And you should be proud of that. They hate us for our gifts of faith, our piercing faith. *And why?* Only because of what its message tells them about the sham of their own lives. Jesus faced exactly the same opposition from the same type of person. Materialists want to hang on to the world, they think it's *theirs*, and they'll fight us wherever they can. Where they can't fight us they'll deny that we matter much anyway. And where they can't ignore us they persecute us, it goes on every minute of every day. Christian children are being persecuted in California school rooms, ridiculed for their totally valid creation belief, force-fed on the state religion of evolutionism. Evolution, a *false* history based on *selected* facts strung together by *weak* theories, giant-size leaps of logic and *warped* imagination! Compared to the elegant descriptions of Genesis, evolution is about as convincing as a human face painted by Picasso, you've seen them: with a nose up here and three eyes over here and one ear stuck away over here. Compare that to a beautiful Gainsborough portrait or even a snapshot you can take at home with your own camera. Our sick society is full of Picasso-type monstrosities that so-called experts and intellectuals hold up and tell us are mirrors. They aren't mirrors! We don't look in a mirror and see a billion years of evolution any more than we see a face with green skin and three eyes! Do we get to the root of it if we say this victimization is at the top of the agenda of secular humanist fanatics, that our children are innocent victims of liberal fetishism? No, we don't. Are we any closer to the truth if we say that *fear* motivates the resistance, fear and envy of the calm power that God radiates through us? Closer, yes. Democracy has become a lottery, education a form of hypnosis, science a broken lamp. Like all disfigurement the twisted concept of evolution oozed from one source. As sure as God's touch brings law, Satan touches the world with disorder. Evolution has been his greatest and most successful innovation, a materialistic thought-system that has no need for God and maroons the human race without hope on a dead rock of fatalism and gullibility. Satan attacks us through our self-esteem, he targets us above all creatures because we specially embody God's love. What would Satan accomplish by confusing a colony of gorillas? Apes don't have the ability *to choose* to follow God's word, no, that gift, the *individual* conscience is written into our DNA structure and it is visibly *absent* from the DNA of every other kind of creature from fruit flies to the great apes. It's *obedience* that Satan has been demanding ever since he first whispered the deception of evolution to the elders of Babylon. He convinced them they could build a tower to heaven, one more ridiculous act in his rebellion against his Creator! He has convinced ambitious politicians over the years, philosophers, historians, scientists and revolutionaries, persuaded them to promote Satanism in many disguises – communism, logical positivism, libertarianism, social Darwinism, all of these movements are built on the anti-God foundation that concrete matter is all there is, *it's all we are or were or ever will be* and everything else is just dreamed up by our unconscious minds. *Be aware* of it! The Satanic rape of humanity is an unfolding plot which is blatant in its secrecy. I have assembled, collated and scrutinized evidentiary data, my findings are published and not reviewed by a single major newspaper or journal. You see? What they can't fight they deny. Satan's influence has to be *confronted* before it can be defeated. You don't need a wristwatch to tell what time it is! It's high noon in this state for the stupid and the lazy who don't worship Lord God and recognize, fear and adore His Begotten Son, Jesus Christ! It's time for Christians to stand up and take this place *back* from teachers and officials *who defile it*. Abortionists have turned our land into a moral void – let's take it out of their blood-dripping hands! Illegal immigrants marauding up out of the south are eating away the wealth of this state like termites chewing through the foundations of a lovely old house – let's *take it away* from them, it's consecrated by God to *our* use, *ours*! Imagine the clean-running co-operation of a society with Christians in charge, carrying out God's plain instructions . . . I want you to go to work in your local party, work for the victory of Republican candidates who are God-approved and target anti-God incumbents, work to *vote them out*. By the power of Jesus Christ you live in a democracy where you can *choose* a Christian government from the White House down to your local dog catcher, Jesus Christ *Himself* puts that power in your hands. Use it on Voting Day to honor the Christian source of the freedom everybody enjoys here and tell those people in office that you know what's good for California! Confound them with the CLEAR-AS-A-BELL truth of the Bible and in the face of their guilty denials ask them one question: If the Bible doesn't record the true history of Creation why did God allow the inspired men who wrote down His words to foist on humanity such a tragically mistaken picture of its origins . . . ?'

'Right,' Munro nodded along. 'Why would He?'

'Why did God allow the massacre of the Huguenots?' I asked him.

'Who?'

'Maybe ignorance is a more subtle kind of suffering. More suffering that God can't prevent.'

He seemed to appreciate this. 'Reverend says things sometimes I can't understand either.'

If I'd waited I could have found some less conspicious place to speak to JT, the two of us alone somewhere out of the spotlight, but the avalanche of ignorance, sneaky distortion and high-minded deception tilted me into motion. Motion to call a halt, a temporary stop to comprehend the flux. It was JT's feeling all through his meeting with Bobby and now it was mine. Sometimes this happens. I'm overpowered by a stirring need, something like an ambition, to break into the open (*for once*, I think) and breathe the same air as everyone else. I remember the few times I did this in the past, approached certain people on impulse, told them I had moved into their lives, said everything I needed to say to wipe out any ambiguity. I felt the passionate impact of my decision and then stood back ducking the shower of debris. What do I ever learn? I flare up, I have this loud heartache instead of anger; or heartache is the form that anger takes in me. Now I wanted to tell JT that I knew everything about him and believed him to be a good man attempting to live a dangerously saintly life.

Munro's pleasure in conducting me over to the elite circle was also his boast, exhibiting his (he assumed) distinguished catch to Rev. Tickell, Dr Pogenpohl and Attorney-General Porta and likewise the titans of his life to me. We reached Oswald in mid-flow as he was summarizing his onerous election-day agenda, a schedule so crucial it entailed the use of a chartered Learjet. Recognizing the rule of precedence and seniority Munro introduced me first of all to the occasion's patron, and he had a bouquet of his own to lay at Oswald's feet.

'That's kind of you to say, Munro. You enjoyed it,' Oswald beamed back the compliment, 'that's what really counts.'

'At the big climax those little ones were so perfect!' Munro elaborated. 'Boy, that Adam and Eve, they acted beautiful. I just wanted to wrap them both up and take them home with me.'

'Weren't they *good*,' Oswald said, not pursuing the point any further. 'All the children did so very well.'

Munro backed out of the conversation physically, he stepped out of the way to let me in, making his introduction on the move. Oswald pronounced my name as if he'd heard it muttered recently in a disgusting connection. I faced into his coolness and said lightly, 'You don't seem to rate teachers very highly.'

'Going on what my surveys tell me, no, that's right. I have to give them a low rating in their scholarship. Especially in California.'

'Oh, especially? Can you tell me why you lean so heavily on hierarchies to explain things? Sounds like a backwards process to me.'

Even after days of it, minutes after his full-scale operatic oration, Pogenpohl still flamed with energy, jumping at the chance to press me under the solid weight of his ideas. 'A hierarchy is a strong structure. It's a natural structure. God put the Seraphim above the Cherubim, Thrones above the Dominions, and so on. He showed us how it's done, how it is, and he gave us the tools of science so we could do it for ourselves in the earthly sphere.'

'Man above the apes.'

'Man above every animal. He wrote the difference into our DNA as plain as words on a page to anybody who can read.' Oswald was really talking about his own closeness to God, his own verifiable personal resemblance.

'The way I read it,' I said, 'the genetic differences that you say don't count at all with fruit flies you blow into gigantic categorical distinctions when you want to separate humans and apes.'

' "Pongids" is the correct word you want.' Then he let me have it. 'I don't think you're qualified to judge the question.'

'He is, sure he is.' Howard stoked the sputtering fun. 'Jack's a professor. Among other things.'

Oswald faked a revived interest in me. 'Oh, yes? Is he?'

'USC made him an emeritus.'

'I haven't been in a classroom in a year and a half,' I said.

'You don't retire from life,' Oswald pronounced. 'You're still active.' He swiveled his eyes indiscreetly from me to JT.

By now JT had seen all he wanted to see of my attempt at public intimidation. He started to edge away but Munro's spidery fingers landed on his elbow, held him back. 'Reverend, Mr Ketchum is a super-big booster of Worldview.'

JT grinned with the strain of pleasantness. He said to me, 'How much can I put you down for?'

'If you're still working on the homeless problem,' I said in all sincerity, 'you can count on me for a thousand, Reverend Tickell.'

He congratulated Munro, 'You brought me in a new Temple Apostle, say, how about that! Start at the top,' spreading the congratulations to me, 'right at the top.'

Howard blew the whistle. 'Why don't we just cut this horseshit out.'

'If this funny act is for our benefit,' Oswald told us, 'it's just not doing you any good so drop it. Hypocrisy makes me sick, *sick*.'

I only spoke to JT. 'Good to see you again.'

'I know what you're doing,' he blazed at me, and repeated it with the cold anger of a victim refusing point blank to pay a ransom. His hair had gone shaggy, his eyes were watery, sleepless.

Oswald said, 'Now that we've got both of you here maybe you can agree on one story about the ultra-private meeting you had with Dyson on Friday.'

'Hold on a minute,' JT said, taking control. 'Can't you figure out what he's doing right now? One more dirty trick. That's probably his specialty!' Howard was laughing softly behind him. 'Trying to raise a stink around me.'

'Jim, do you want to say you didn't have a meeting at eleven o'clock on Friday morning with Mr Ketchum, here, and Bobby Dyson?' Howard's lawyerly invitation to be freed from the pointless strain of lying reached JT and drilled in slowly.

I attempted a rescue. 'To be honest, when we asked you to come in we expected you to stand us up. Bobby was fit to be tied when he realized you weren't going to help him with any fresh filth on Howard.'

'Hey, I don't want to help that jackass at all! I wouldn't empty my bladder on Dyson if he was on fire. Do you understand that?'

'It's what I'm saying. You met him under a white flag.'

'He's just another bureaucrat today. Slinking around behind my back.' He said to Howard, 'My reasons didn't have a thing to do with you. I'd stay away from the sneaks who handed you the information. If they were worth spit they would've told you what-all I told the man.' Calmer or just tired of this JT came back to me. 'What you do in the dark, sneak, always shows up in the light. Always does.'

He elbowed a path through the sluggish pools of browsing families with Munro skedaddling after him in some confusion, stammering apologies to the back of JT's suit. Before I could get away myself, Oswald had his own reality enema to administer, the bully in him finally winning permission to come out. 'Emeritus *liar*. Emeritus *political operator*. I don't know what else you might possibly be – '

Howard knew. 'You're a Unitarian, aren't you, Jack?'

I made it to the street just in time to watch Munro careen the big Jaguar up onto the curb, power JT around the bottlenecked traffic and surge away down Capitol Avenue, a one-car motorcade. Standing on the sidewalk, whole sentences I'd prepared to say dissolved into alphabet soup and in the next breath I wasn't so sorry that I'd missed the chance to explain myself to him. I don't belong out in the open, it's not where things are clearest. 'Things are changing,' I heard JT lecture – and baffle – Munro. 'Slowly, but everything.' I understand this. A sense of gnawing incompleteness survives in the heart of being human.

8   'There's nothing frightening going on here, is there?'

CHANGES secretly planned and publicly sprung, changes by agreement, changes by accident, changes known and manageable, unknown changes forcing up through time like the stalk of a spore erupting from the dirt, Alex's lifeless eighteen-hour sleep screened out all the mayhem. His own bed in his own apartment sank to the bottom of the ocean. When he rose to face the bright afternoon he groggily reminded himself that instead of flying down to marvel at the novelty of Hummingbird Farm, as soon as they were back on their feet

Randall Edlund and Frank and Roy Hornweid flew directly home to Iowa. Instead of writing up a million-five of new business Alex returned with nothing except the prospect of crippling lawsuits and damning publicity, possibly just days away. Instead of overseeing the functioning routines, mechanical and clerical processes already in the trained hands of a settled workforce, Heidi spent her week as caretaker incubating an epidemic.

He found the lights on in the farm buildings, cold white windows squared against the thick shadows draining down through dusty scrub and collecting in the bowl of the surrounding hills. Night-time pouring in early, refrigerated by the expanding purple sky, the yard held the stillness of an ammunition dump. As Alex crossed it a lone figure materialized from the direction of the pasture, a man of about Alex's age dressed in long baggy shorts, t'ai chi slippers and a fisherman's sweater the color of burlap. The cuffs had unraveled and belled out over his wrists and the confused threads of yarn had the same look as his bushy brown hair, hassled by order and management, grabbed into a haggard ponytail. He spoke lazily with an English accent (real or affected Alex couldn't decide) and, asking if he could help at all, said that he worked there, that his name was Mudpuppy. Without elaborating Alex told him who he was looking for. Mudpuppy slouched back, friendly, welcoming. 'You work for Heidi, too?'

'Not yet,' Alex said momentously.

'I don't know if she's hiring till like the end of next week.'

'She's not hiring from now on, but I still want to talk to her.'

Mudpuppy thought he saw Heidi 'go into the place where they keep all the pigs'. The hazy memory solidified. 'Yeah, a few minutes ago, with the wrinkly. The wrinkly dude.'

'She's with Anthony?'

'Is Anthony the wrinkly dude?'

'What, uh, part of the farm do you work on?' Alex kept his surgical curiosity muffled, kept it polite. 'What do you do around here?'

Mudpuppy laughed at himself, at his non-existent skills. 'Whatever!' looking Alex in the face when he said it, a joke between them, a common truth, that employers deserve to be bamboozled. 'Tell Heids I had to leave early today. I have to get to Pasadena by five o'clock or else the clinic won't give me my treatment.'

'I'll tell her.'

'Thanks, man. Nice one.'

Closer to the boar pens Alex heard Heidi's voice. Her tone was soothing, almost musical. What could she be saying to Anthony with such tenderness and concern, with such flowing, hypnotic sympathy? What could she want to get out of *him*? Alex watched her from the far end of the pen. Heidi wasn't aware of him standing there and he let her go on cooing that way, on her knees, one arm thrown around the boar's shoulders, her other hand gently raking the bristles on his snout.

'What are you saying to that animal?'

Heidi unhanded the boar and gave Alex freshfaced attention. 'Hey, hi.'

'I looked for you in the office.'

'Anthony needed me down here for fifteen minutes.' The pink snout that was sniffing between her feet jerked up between her knees just as she said, 'I'm getting involved in everything now . . . aah! *No más*!'

'He wants you to wear a dress.'

'When Anthony starts wearing one.'

'Heidi, nobody's in the office. Where's Mrs Sieghardt?'

'She quit. Her sister had a heart attack so Lily had to go take care of her. She said she was going to write you a letter about it.'

'Mrs Sieghardt quit?'

'She'll write you a letter. No big deal.'

'The phone was ringing off the hook when I got there. Nobody's in the office to answer the phone.'

'Did you answer it?'

'That's not the point. What are you doing in the service pen anyway? Curtis is supposed to be helping Anthony. Where's Curtis?'

'I let him go to band practise. He promised to make up the rest of his hours tomorrow night.'

'Anthony doesn't need Curtis to help him after hours. Anthony goes to *sleep* at seven o'clock.'

'I had to make a decision,' she said, challenging him. 'He faced me with a decision to make and I made it.'

'Okay, all right,' right hand up to swear, peacefully. 'We're just talking. Tell me about this new work-schedule you started.'

The tall flaps of plastic that curtained off the outdoor end of the pen chevroned open to let in the prancing bulk of a sow followed by Anthony shooing her into the nearest corner with a large square of chipboard. 'She knows where to go!' he grinned at everybody. 'She's in the know!' The chipboard slipped out of his grip, smacked onto the concrete floor and the loud clap when it hit startled both pigs into a burst of panicky squeals. 'Can you get that back for me?' he asked Heidi, waving his arthritic fists in explanation and apology.

The boar and his mate-to-be calmed down in the watchful human quiet, he approached her again sniffing in her odor, nuzzling her flanks. Carefully Alex said to Heidi, 'Can I talk to you now?'

'I'm doing this now,' she said staring down at the sniffing and nuzzling.

Alex talked past her. 'Anthony, can you wait on this for a minute? Heidi and I need to have a talk.'

'Well, I can really use somebody's help while we're in motion here,' he said, corralling the sow headward into the corner.

'Maybe we can catch Mr Mudpuppy before he gets to the front gate.'

'Who?' said Anthony.

Heidi said, 'I'm not going anywhere, Anthony.'

'I'm teaching the girl how this gets done.' Anthony said to her, 'Don't stand too close to him. He'll get there, just give him room.' It was a move in a strange square dance. Heidi and Anthony stepped back, the boar shouldered in again, this time lurching up onto the sow's back. He pawed at her, his forelegs stiff and jerky, his lower half wide of the target pumping the air. 'Oh, no. That's wrong, of course.'

Shaken off by the sow he circled away from her. Heidi guided him back. 'This is his first time,' she said over her shoulder to Alex. To the boar she said, 'Isn't it, baby. You'll be good, baby. I'll help you be good . . . '

'There's no substitute for experience,' Alex agreed.

Anthony said, 'He's just gettin' the hang of it. He's sweet talkin' her, it's normal. You just don't want it to keep goin' too long or they'll get tired and cranky. Oh, there. He's up!'

He was up on tiptoes, sloped over her back but this was a repeat performance of the air humping. Before the sow got another chance to demolish that young boar's self-esteem Anthony decided to intervene. He had to use both of his mummified hands to hoick up the sow's tail. This was exciting for everybody in the room.

'See how it's goin' under there.' Anthony clung onto the pig's tail like an old angler reeling in a fighting pike. Heidi crouched down to observe nature in action and Anthony asked her, 'Is his thing out of his sheath? The sheath's that covering over his thing.'

'I know what a sheath is. Uh-huh, it's out.'

'You want to make sure his thing – '

'His dingus, Anthony. His dick-prick-cock-penis-boner.'

'It's got to be good and healthy.'

'Always.'

'You're lookin' for marks on it. Or lumps and bumps or whatnot.'

'Oh, no. No, baby!' Heidi stood up, laughing all over her face. 'He's trying to put it in the wrong hole. Oh, Gahd! Shades of – '

'Have to use hand assistance,' Anthony advised with calm urgency.

Both of the pigs forced out noises that were easy to read as grunts of frustration and snorts of exhaustion. Heidi added to the racket, 'I'm supposed to do it, you mean?'

'C'mon, Heidi. I'm holdin' her tail. You wanted to get up close.'

As she leaned her shoulder and head milkmaid-wise against the boar's heaving side Alex wondered, 'Shouldn't you use gloves?'

'Be quiet a sec, Alex. I'm concentrating.'

The boar's rhythm changed, his wiggling haunches moved in, sped up, worked at the sow's flanks, his jowls sopping on her back, drooling a white lather, wheezing. 'Now we're goin',' Anthony cheered quietly, patting Heidi on the arm. 'Now we're makin' bacon, makin' bacon for the boss!'

Listening to her talk about it afterwards you'd think Heidi had volunteered to carry that boar's genital in her teeth twice around the farm, stark naked, crying out, 'Look at what I do for love!' Her heroism in the servicing-pen was another bizarre anecdote she was rehearsing, a monologue that celebrated her devotion to the cause and that deployed her initiative, deftness and sheer guts as a climaxing flourish on the epic of her glittering managerial début.

In the slow walk from the boar pens to the office she warbled and fluttered through every register of self-promotion, from solemn humility ('my chance to show you how good I can be') through heady swagger ('What clinched the Bel-Air Hotel was I went over to convince him *myself*) to thumping, bare-knuckled enterprise ('so much good done in a week, think how much I could've done in a month'), a *tour de force* for a one-man audience by the PT Barnum of emotional pressure. Alex played dead, waiting for Heidi either to land incidentally on the story of the defective Humpty Dumpster or else for her just to talk herself out.

Any model formality that Alex half hoped to summon up by posing behind his neat desk was sunk by Heidi pushing his phone out of the way to make room for her to slide her rear end into the area right in front of him. 'I want to look into your eyes,' she said *à la* bar-room tramp. Under the thin skin of her pumped-up enthusiasm for a new active part in the business, behind the Barnumism Alex guessed some unnamed retaliation was being kept toxically in reserve, a threat held over his opinion, his judgment. Her hands-on experience, she wanted him to appreciate, her demonstrated expertise proved that she had a laureate's grasp of capitalism, its structures, priorities, objectives, practise and rewards, and this hard-won hardfaced knowledge, combined with her unique contributions to the founding, operation and potential of Hummingbird Farm and HD Systems Group, justified the proposition that ('before things go too far') she and Alex ought to hammer out a firm and honorable contract between them 'and put all of our problems to bed'.

'Sure, that's a discussion we can have,' no argument out of him. 'Can you bring me up to speed on any problems, any glitches, any . . . ' – was there a less provocative word he could use? – nope, 'problems you ran into?'

'Yeah, there *weren't* any problems, Alex. That's what my whole point is,' Heidi said, rankled, rising to it. 'Last week we wrote a bunch of new orders, *hotel* orders, we trained new maintenance guys, a few new reps, I planned out a better roster, everybody's way happier.'

'Who wasn't happy before?'

'Besides me?' She plucked at the rubber band that was holding her straw-dry tinted hair in a vertical column on top of her head, a distressed gold leaf sheaf that collapsed into a brattish mess when Heidi shook it loose. 'All you have to do is look hard and there's all kinds of improvements you can make. Say I'm the associate manager. If I'm here at a regular time I can keep any daily problems out of your way. Alex, really, I mean, I can be a great associate manager. If I'm just in the kitchen, y'know, my insecurity is only going to wreck my performance.'

'Were you in the kitchen when that sausage Humpty broke down?'

'Fortunately,' she said, snottily.

'Step by step, tell me what happened. Tell me what you did.'

Heidi seemed to inflate fractionally, in automatic defense. 'There's nothing frightening going on here, is there?'

Careful not to stampede her, Alex gave Heidi an unthreatening, even inviting, shrug of his eyebrows and a passive, 'Tell me.'

She read this as an oral test, a final exam, and she played along. 'The B-machine got jammed in the morning. I replaced it right after it went down.'

'You replaced it yourself?'

'No, obviously. I organized one of the yard guys to do it and I kept checking on him until he finished the job. Okay?'

'Has it been replaced since then?'

'Hell no,' the implication stung her. 'It works fine.'

'Do you know the number of the replacement machine?'

'The *number* of it?' with a look that said, This is the level of junk that occupies your little mind? 'Anal-retentive, or what, Alex.'

'Not good.' Then, a rattle of despair. 'You loose fucking cannon.'

'Excuse me?'

'Number eighteen, that's the number of the new machine. Heidi, Humpties ten to eighteen are the fertilizer processors. You have to remember the details, step by step. The sausage machine went down, and . . . ?'

'He disconnected it. He took out the, those module things and fit the new ones in no problem. And it worked, it started working.'

'You put the sausage template in . . . '

'Put the sausage template in *and* the rotating thing *and* the hopper *and*, Alex, we only lost half an hour of sausage time. Want to know what that meant? It meant we got all of our hotel batches out in time for first deliveries. Bel-Air and Chateau Marmont, they know they can rely on us! On *you*! And by the way, I got that machine running in time to do the extra run of that morning batch so *you* could have fresh ones for your big fucking, fucking important brunch! Y'know, maybe ''thank-you, Heidi'' would be better than – '

'I need to get this clear. You washed out the hopper and the mulch tray. You disinfected them.'

'Every night. Shirley was on cleaning that night.'

'I mean, you washed the other one, the replacement parts from the fertilizer machine before you started rolling out sausages again.'

She sniffed a trap, disguised hesitation as intense recollection. Then, 'Sure. Of *course*,' Heidi sounded untroubled but this was her technique, folding open the clear conscience of the habitual liar. 'Alex, you're *always* doing this to me, saying, like, whatever I do amounts to zero. It's just menial, my work, I'm your donkey.'

'Here's what you did. Everybody who ate those sausages, that's everybody at our big important brunch, our fucking fucked-up brunch, came down with food poisoning! I did, JT did, our customers-to-be – forget that! – our customers-who-won't-ever-be, *they* ended up in the hospital for two days! We're in the toilet now. We're positively in the shit.'

She said, 'Not because of me,' militant on the point.

'Did I leave Shirley in charge for a week? Did I leave Anthony?'

Infuriated now, 'Not because of me.' Her words were hardly audible, her lips stayed peeled back in silent but unrestrained obscenity.

And it was this self-dramatizing, self-obsessed, vindictive child, this fury, this ten-thumbed reckless alien who Alex left as custodian of his hand-reared business! 'You're a plague, Heidi. You're unbelievable. Everything you touch turns to shit.'

Without any visible hint of the churning rage gurgling inside her she hopped down off of the desk, minced back around to Alex and slapped him so violently in the face that his chair sprang back from the power of the blow, thudding his head against the wall. 'You goddamn monster!' he yelped at her, his cheek creased with a raw, reddening scrape. He bent both arms up in front of him to take the punches and slaps that came fanning in next.

'You bought this! What the doctor ordered!'

'You need help, you crazy psychopath!' ducking her fists, kicking free from the chair. 'Get out of my office, Heidi, get off of my property or I'll get the police down here!'

'When they're here I'll tell 'em you tried to rape me!' she said between wild jabs and knuckle punches. 'You get the credit, I get the blame!' She went on chanting this murderously, cuffing Alex's ears, drumming in her singsong protest.

Alex, standing up now, dropped his arms and let his own hysteria coat his wet eyes and swell into his throat, a wall of wreckage for Heidi to butt against if she had a taste for blood – and that looked likely, but Alex forced his strangling grief into the shock of one long loud emptying Kung Fu yell, blasted straight into Heidi's face. He aimed a loose fist at her jaw but she flinched the wrong way and it crunched into her nose. 'Crying now? Good. Terrific evidence! You're not going to lie to the police. You're going to tell them the truth. You won't *have* to lie, Heidi,' he whispered, making an evil grab for the high front of her collar, she trapped his arm and bit his wrist.

'Try it,' her panting disgust. 'I want you to try it. Try and do me.' She slid his paperweight, a brass ingot, into her hand.

From outside the building their standing forms appeared to me magnified by the clear air, by the strong fluorescent light. Heidi moved first, attacking his collar bone with the ingot, sobbing, and Alex, sobbing, jabbed her ear, her upper arm, the two of them boxing like shadow puppets. I shut down the receiver, I didn't need to amplify their name-cursing and blame-spreading, or take in any more spillage from their mouths. Specific concealments and disclosures, breathless accusations, gasping denials, all ceased to offer me any content, failed to add a single thought to what I already knew. But I didn't turn away from the sight of them mutely tearing at each other, I looked past them, past Heidi and Alex to their temporary shapes in the window.

9 'If you really want to martyr a martyr, let him live'

MY over-extension into Alex's life didn't produce the only (or most compelling) impetus to sprint back to Sacramento. I needed to return to cast my vote and I wanted to be there for the election's aftermath, however it left Bobby, as California's commander-in-chief or unemployed mascot. The support I gave to his candidacy, in the polling-booth and out of it, couldn't have been decisive but as the tallies piled up through the night with the split between Bobby and Howard narrowing, I teased myself with the theory that if I'd made a different mark on my ballot the political scales would have slanted the other way.

When it finally arrived at two in the morning, the result delivered (exclusively to me, it seemed) a trivial convenience and a pregnant irony. Bobby's victory party was staged in the refurbished Capitol

House Hotel, conveniently a block away from my suite at the Hastings. On the short walk down the street I meditated on the irony that the Senator's elevation to Governor pulsed with a symbolic glow as intensely for him as it did for Jim Tickell.

Drunk-tired, and by this hour honorably drunk campaign workers hoisted lifesize photo cut-outs of Bobby high into the arched windows of the ballroom. These were props held back until Howard Porta's official concession, candid photographs of Young Dyson in his student mutiny days which the cadres hung facing the street outside, taunting Howard's demoralized loyalists across town. It was the ghostly image of a dead era floating impotently behind the glass of the hotel's new ten-million-dollar façade and Bobby's first order as Governor was to have those effigies cut down and destroyed.

The celebration band serenaded him, his wife, their friends, with an unaccented medley off that decade's soundtrack, lyrics and chord changes that also reached out to the crop of college kids in the room, tunes they claimed for themselves as forerunners of their own house style. But open rebellion, flight from reality, contempt of power, mockery of maturity, every cocky attitude except whatever inflection remained in the name of the band had drained out of the music half a lifetime ago. *Eight Miles High* – The Byrds, *For What It's Worth* – Buffalo Springfield, *All Along the Watchtower* – Jimi Hendrix, *Somebody to Love* – Jefferson Airplane, *Born to be Wild* – Steppenwolf, hollow shells for them today, tonight in this aquarium filled up with the collective moments and agreed sentiments of recovered youth.

Youth recovered unfortunately without its physical co-ordination. In his three-piece suit, collar button popped, tie unknotted, there was Marty Olansky holding down the middle of the dance floor, jerking his spine, splashing his orang-utan arms around, brainlessly frugging to *Along Comes Mary* with his shimmying little-Dutch-girl wife, Mary. Their song, their dance. Their round of grateful applause too, which dominoed into a clattering free-for-all cheer as attention slid to Bobby onstage, sitting in on the drums for a spin through *Wipeout*. His wrists remembered the clusters of beats and blasts, the jungle tom-tom call to hit the beach and ride the surf, but in his tense neck and stiff shoulders, in the knowledge collected like cold rainwater in his eyes, there was the neighborhood dad who wanted his little girl returned home by dinnertime.

On the dance floor, first with his wife Charlotte and then for a waltz each with his two eldest daughters, Hayley and Ketra, the white cone of the spotlight landed on Bobby like an announcement from heaven. Hope emanated from it, and a princely romance that lit up the mass of faces around the circumference of the ballroom, it haloed him when Charlotte was back in his embrace, her Indian maiden hair lifting pennant-like behind her as they twirled each other gracefully to a finale. Even Bobby's mother, whose afternoon bridge games were plagued by The Doors and Canned Heat blaring from her son's bedroom, was shuffling in place to *Light My Fire*, snapping her fingers at random, modestly unglued by a nostalgic pride in the boyhood that unfolded into such a manhood. Bestowed on the boy and the man by the majority of California's electorate was a generous trust in his character and a fair chance for his social programs, the leverage of popular approval. The weight of the Governor's office rolled solidly behind Bobby's state-wide plan for the homeless, for instance, and his ballot box success vindicated the faith (not to mention the grinding toil) of his family and campaigners.

That night especially, everyone present felt eligible for something wonderful, wonderful and just. Out of ancient fixed points in the sky a brand new constellation had been mapped, Bobby Dyson aimed his finger upward and rendered the lines visible between those stars. The sudden realization, the astonishing conclusion was that the big pattern had always been there hanging above us waiting to be pointed out. Starlight was falling in Sacramento, inscribing the ground with a diagram of new foundations for progressive institutions, that's how he wanted us to feel about it and most of us did. I had trouble giving myself up to the democratic triumph; it wasn't the jubilation or the secure relief of a winning home team I felt packed around me, it was a vacancy.

Out of the background gabble of congratulations and career-jockeying, Irene Dyson said to me, 'I never thought I'd have fond memories of that music.'

We had our eyes on Bobby and Marty bopping their heads in time to *La Bamba*. 'You might be hearing the new state song,' I shouted back, voice raised over the guitar solo.

Irene plugged a finger into each ear, sheltering her eardrums. 'What a racket!' Then she said, taking my arm, leading me somewhere, 'If you can't beat 'em . . .'

I'm not a dancer and I don't like to be handled, or really I don't like anyone making assumptions about me based on their own moods. So I didn't budge but she danced a little step all by herself, showing me up, and I had a chastened look prepared for her when she footed back again. 'Refusing a dance with the Governor's mother would've gotten me beheaded in merry old England.'

'I don't get out much,' a confidential aside, self-consciously aware of her over-excitement. 'There's never much to go out for, nothing worth a new dress,' fluffing the broad pleats of the coppery green designer toga picked out by her daughter-in-law, apparently to give Irene the suggestive presence (and bulk) of the Statue of Liberty.

'You adorn this sad bunch, Irene. All you're missing is the gold tiara,' I said. 'Bobby should rent you one for the inauguration.'

'Oh no, Jack!' She took this as serious flattery, she could imagine the sight. 'I'd give all the fuddy-duddies a heart attack! I think Bobby would *enjoy* that, sweeping out the old things. He'll sweep me out next.'

'Lifelong gratitude is what he owes you. You're a terrific asset, Irene, his ambassador-at-large. So now you honestly believe he's just going to crate you up and ship you home?'

'He only let me wave a little bit, on those whistle stops.'

'You waved like a professional. You were the best waver onboard.'

'Jack, you know, he didn't want me to talk to those news people tonight. My proudest night, proud for Bobby, he's going to be so good for things, and I think he was afraid I'd embarrass him. As if I'd tell them about the nudie magazines I found under his mattress when he was in high school.'

'That wouldn't embarrass him, it would endear him. *There's* an unappreciated political reality. He told me that story, except the way he told it it happened when he was in *junior* high school.'

'Maybe it was junior high school. I threw them in the trash. He never mentioned it. He put all of that energy into playing his drums.'

'Now he can put it into running a multi-billion dollar economy.'

With their arms flaccidly strung across each other's shoulders, Bobby and Marty crossed the dance floor, stopping to hook onto the Attorney-General-elect Ty Guthrie. Ty's resistance to audience participation was almost as principled as mine, and where I could rely on my mandarin stature to ice any funster's approach, he depended more on the chilling combination of Southern manners and a linebacker's solid mass. Guthrie was a transplanted Louisianan who had lost most of his fine blond hair but not a single lolling note of his native accent in thirty-five years of West Coast public prosecution. Something more than his warm, throaty vowels and persuasively underplayed eloquence, though, singled him out in courtroom and DA's office; he never offered up an opinion on any legal issue, statutory or case law, until he thought through to its deepest moral implications. After he'd done that scrupulous work, Ty was not diplomatic. The Baptist absolutist in him remained in his hard belief in the existence of ultimate justice, but by that same humane rule the terrorizing threat of damnation, unearthly degradation and torture had been flitched from the ideal. Consequently, he dedicated his natural gifts and mature skills to pursuing fairness and routing cynicism, both of whose representatives in the actual world paraded unclad in front of him. Tough on crime but toughly opposed to the death penalty, compassionate in his fight for victims' maximum compensation, an unintimidated agitator against off-shore oil drilling, an enforcer of civil rights laws and petitioner for mandatory prison sentences for 'hate crime' thugs, Guthrie's constant and unambiguous support went to the deceived and exploited, the abused, the endangered, making his own decency a tangible reason to be convinced of the elemental value of human life in general.

'Oh, honey,' Irene sighed in a gentle lunge at Bobby. 'It's just like at your wedding, I've had the same teary feeling all night.'

In a realistic mood he said, 'This honeymoon won't last half as long.'

'You're going to be so busy now I'll *never* see you. Think you can fit my appointment in with all your bills and programs?'

'If we get our budget. And they won't *give* us our budget,' Marty said. 'We'll go to the mat on it but we'll be damn lucky if they don't claw the heart out of public works, conservation, education – um, what else?'

'Not all of Bobby's hate mail', I told Irene, 'comes from the opposing party. He sets the goals, assembly sets the limits. Of course he can always send in the National Guard.'

Marty remembered another budgetary item on his sacrificial list. 'You've got to let your homelessness program drift into 92/93, and that's soonest.'

'That's cruel, Mr Olansky. That's too rough,' Ty ragged him. 'We need to get Howard settled in a halfway house as soon as he leaves office. He won't survive ten minutes out on the streets, his friends won't recall his face tomorrow. Man, those Falangistas eat their young.'

'Howard'll be all right,' Bobby knew (thanks to me). 'January 7th he's the new chairman of Tentmark Press. That's the way the Puritan belches.'

Ty asked me, 'Did Oswald Pogenpohl put Tickell into Tentmark?'

'Porta would've thrown a holy fit.'

'Well, that skunk's been shunting his liquid assets all over everyplace. Jack, you'll love the latest,' – in other words, prime information about JT that Ty didn't get from me – 'he's just deposited four point five in a business account at a bank in Durban, South Africa. The paper trail is twistier than an acre of crookweed.'

The lip-smacking contempt in this attitude stunned Irene. She turned wide-eyed to Bobby. 'But you told me that the Reverend smoothed out all of his problems with you. He went to you *personally*.'

'I told you we talked, Mom. I said he gave me a clear idea of his personal position, that's all.'

'You said that you cleared the air with him.'

Gallantly, Ty reassured her. 'Tickell's got problems with me he didn't know he had last week. I honestly can't say if we can get back all the money you paid in, Mrs Dyson, but – '

'I donated to support his church and honor his mission.'

'Well, I'll make it tough for him to hide those funds from you.'

'Leave him alone! Can't you do that?' Irene's brittle appeal snapped from Ty to the rest of us men.

Bobby gave me a glimpse of himself as a curfewed teenager. 'All right, Mom, all right. We don't have to talk about it anymore.'

'*Can't you let him do his work?*'

'Jim Tickell's a vindictive bully, Irene, that's the truth,' Marty said. 'If he was up and we were down, how do you think he'd treat us?'

'Like a Christian, you know? That's how,' she answered back. '*Do you know?*'

My qualms about Bobby Dyson's upcoming administration weren't rooted in my inside knowledge of his priorities, not even as I watched his personal philosophies and emotional biases merge into official policy and then glare and throb with executive power. *Status quo ante.* Personality into leadership, vision into agenda, necessary for the public perception of events moving forward, Bobby's political success conformed to these conventions – freely, proudly. Not even this was shocking; if anyone had asked me twenty years ago I would have predicted it. But one custom he took on and made his own really shattered my heart, listing an item on his inaugural agenda that sprang from the dank old moldy ground of political superstition, concerning in particular the voodoo powers of known enemies. Vengeance, let me tell you, is not mine. My remedy is to drift away without fanfare into my own churning pillar of gloom.

I followed him out into the lobby where, behind the braided gold rope barricades, a scrimmage of amateur and professional photographers roared for a picture to remember. Out of lens-shot I could see each frame as it snapped through every camera, each print as it was going to be seen in newspaper, magazine and family album: Governor Dyson with his wife, with his mother, with his children, new tenants of the mansion, a profile in courage. And I was like the rest of them, I couldn't take my eyes off Bobby, his pruned vigorous hair, smooth cheeks, the bashful athlete's smile, and under the boxy American elegance of his suit the lanky body of a cross-country runner, his thoroughbred vitality irradiating the room, stoking everybody's gamble on such fragile change. I saw this at its peak and I thought, *Where is he going with all of this invigoration?*

In the middle of his victory gala, with inauguration ahead of him, a state congress to be roped in, a sprawling bureaucracy to motivate, Bobby, Marty Olanksy and Ty Guthrie were plotting their strategy for the legal destruction and disposal of Jim Tickell.

The news from Los Angeles reached the Governor-elect in the middle of breakfast with his transition team, meeting in the same hotel conference room which hosted JT's and Alex's home-catered presentation two weeks before. Bobby recited the memo to me over the phone, a word-for-word justification of his most cynical suspicions about the corrupt nature of the Reverend and his business.

The first cases reported were guests at two illustrious hotels in Beverly Hills. A pair of senior vice-presidents at Sony, an English ingenue actress, a plastic surgeon, his wife and three Air France stewardesses, all of whose fifty-five dollar deluxe grilled breakfasts turned vicious on them – manure decked out as wholesome meat that wrenched their internal organs, liquidized them and splashed them burningly out into toilet bowls, sinks and cupped hands. A gift, Bobby thanked heaven for it, a concrete, indisputable issue. ' ''Incidents are widespread across the Southland,'' ' he quoted coldly to me, ' ''totaling fifty-six confirmed or high-confidence diagnoses. After speaking with Mr Alex Berry, general manager of Hummingbird Farms, the LA health service estimates the minimum of diseased substance incidents at seventy-five and the maximum at two hundred twenty five.'' He peddles toxic sausages, what do you know about that.' 'Sure, Bobby. It's poetry.' 'No. Poetry would be if he'd've been selling baby food.'

At a kitchen table in a small house in Studio City a young family sits down to eat breakfast together. The wife and mother serves up a dish she thinks of as a wholesome indulgence, worth the extra three dollars-ten every week. This time she's brought home the new flavor of Hummingbird Farm sausages for her boys to try. A pale parchment label on the wrapper, a foretaste of the honey, is edged and lettered in dark green to hint at the sage. The winged pig hovering in the center, famous to the children and familiar around the house, is a nursery-simple pleasure to her eye, a packaging detail that tells a complex story of folksy personal attention and neighborly pride in the preparation of this food mixed with the confident imagination and sophistication it takes to appreciate an eccentric delicacy. These are qualities they'll consume right along with those six tubes of spiced meat. She peels away the plastic wrapper, lifts out the snug package of clean folded butcher paper, relaxes into her secure expectations of the meal she's about to provide.

Inside half an hour of each other, before the lunch-bell rang, both of the boys are curling over in their chairs, stomachs squeezed and gnarled by cramps. Any babyish animal moan out of them, they know, will only bring on the jokes and slashing whispers so they clench against the twinges until the last one opens them up. The gagging laughter when it comes from the other children is a burst of relief that whatever's happening isn't happening to them. Naked adults is what children are, their drama of disgust and mockery throws clean space between them and the shuddering disgrace. The nine-year-old is thinking that if he'd just raised his hand in time he'd be in the lavatory now instead of backing into the corner of the room with his underpants leaking slippery diarrhea down his leg. The smell of it springs out so sharply that the girls sitting next to him bolt out of their seats as if they can see the rancid fumes clawing through the air. His teacher walks him down to the nurse's office where his brother sits shivering on a bench, frightened, humiliated, a baby who can't control his own body.

Thoughts like these are also piling up in his father's mind. A feverish headache crowds in first, then the knuckling in his gut. He ignores the pain, goes on with his monthly report to the senior buyers and when the flash flood breaks he's in mid-sentence gaping at the men and women he'd just been assuring with his capability, his drive. He drops back against the office door, bare-assed in the spotlight. No jokes follow him down as he faints and slides to the floor in a dependent heap, incapable, unreliable, succumbing to *too much*. Somebody's assistant dials 9 1 1 and turns him into a medical emergency.

Back at home his wife is waking up on the bathroom rug, damp vomit in her hair, a mouthful of it caked on her lips and chin. A cut from the rim of the sink is still bleeding under her eye. 'What is it?' she says, trying to lever herself off the floor. She depends on her health, she's used to her ordinary strength but it's drained out of her arms and she's shocked by her body's flimsiness. 'What *is* this?' The phone has been ringing. She hears the second emergency message from the operator who breaks in on the call from the school. As she jerks through the afternoon traffic, wrung out and aching, she can see her sons' faces waiting for her, tortured puppies, and she thinks of the streets that connect the school to the hospital, wildly wondering how much of her family will still be alive at dinnertime.

Multiply this by ten, forty separate alarming attacks, mornings broken into, broken up. Double that, eighty kitchens, classrooms, employees' washrooms, eighty people in the first five days. Double it again, one hundred and sixty different screams, gasps, panics – fears of botulism, AIDS, coronary, stroke. Add another thirty-three, widows and widowers in luxurious, catered retirement in Palm Springs, one hundred ninety-three sufferers of the mystery sickness across the southern half of California by the end of the month.

Marty Olansky's compass of authority as Bobby's staff chief

included, by the look of things, the hand delivery of official faxes vital to the momentum of state government. 'It's in,' he said to us, 'it's *fantastic*!' trooping into the office, flourishing the curled-up paper then proffering it to Bobby as if it were a declaration of war, which in an obvious way it was.

'What is that, Marty? You're too thrilled with yourself, even for you,' I said to him while Bobby unscrolled the document and read it over.

'It's the Cal/OSHA summary,' Bobby said without lifting his eyes off the page. 'Report on Hummingbird Farm, Jack.' In the absence of a response from me he flashed the inky sheet in my face, the columns of nearly two hundred names, grinning a little insanely behind it. 'See? There *is* a God.'

'And he's off the bench,' Marty chorused. 'He's calling the play!'

Bobby said, 'With the Sherman Code, how far can we ream the guy?'

'All the way up. I just ran it by Guthrie. We've got the Rev on manufacture, on delivery, on holding or offering for sale. And sure as shit, if the class action doesn't crucify him, there's press and our prosecution that could establish prior knowledge.' Marty put to me, 'He was in touch with his wife sometime that week, isn't that right? Long, long call. Is there a transcript you can dig out for me?'

'You ought to know there isn't.' Elaborating with a sour comment, 'Look on my works, ye mighty . . . '

'How can he defend himself? What's his first defense?' Bobby gnawed his lip, concentrating hard. 'Talk to Ty about that, too.'

'Right, right. Fantastic. My mind's on fire with this, I mean, it's on fucking *fire*.' Marty crackled on, 'The thing of it is, the actual joke of it is, Tickell's going to get his rocks off, the hack martyr's going to *perform*. Dance around with nails through his hands, chew the scenery up, down and sideways. If we handle it right, you know, Bobby, when this is over he'll just crawl away into the elephant graveyard.'

'Don't um . . . don't force it. Keep his hopes up. If you really want to martyr a martyr, let him live. Jack, how can we do that?'

Thumbscrews? Oubliette? Death Of A Thousand Cuts? To wound JT: here was the emerging line, to listen to him holler and go on hollering in drawn-out agony. That's the Catholic in Bobby breaking cover, and against his mood — salivating at the idea of Jim Tickell roasting slowly on a spit – I was silenced, my numb reply to his ugly glee.

I let Bobby and Marty talk on around me, the two of them on the edge of their seats facing each other across the coffee table, hunched manfully forward, elbows on knees, sports coach position fleshing out the toughened mentality, that job-to-do male language, 'going balls out on this one', 'every swinging dick in the department', posture and slang that Bobby's narrow back and orderly vowels made even more affected and lamentable. There must have been meetings like this in Stalin's dacha, in Joe McCarthy's backroom, in Richard Nixon's oval office, first the denouncing and then the serious business of kicking the s.o.b.'s sorry butt; it's not an abnormal development in career politics.

Climbing out of my chair, I told them that I had to leave and Bobby immediately wanted to be told where. 'Out of town,' I said.

'Los Angeles?'

'I want to get away from Sacramento.' I asked Bobby, 'Can your secretary bring in a glass of water for me?'

'Is that what you want? Marty can get you a glass of water.'

The fingertip grip I had on my small container of aspirin slipped and the tin box fumbled onto the floor. I handed it to Bobby. 'Open this for me.'

He sent Marty the long way around for my water and as soon as we were alone in the room he asked me, 'How soon will you be back?'

'Oh, you'll see me lurking around again before your campaign to re-elect is on the road.'

'Is there something we need to talk out? Last night Charlotte accused me of ignoring my own children. Three or four hours' sleep then I'm ploughing through paperwork and I'm out of the house before the girls are out of bed. At least I'm ignoring my family before I ignore my friends.' Then he said, 'You won't leave. You wouldn't give up your suite at the Hastings.'

'That's the joyous freedom of hotel living.' I rattled the aspirins in my hand.

'But now? You want to leave now? We're finally entrenched, finally. We're not a pocket of resistance anymore.'

'Sure, Howard's the resistance these days. Or anyway, somebody like Howard, minus his sense of humor. Minus his intelligence. Pat

Robertson is organizing another assault on the White House in '92. You can be the resistance again.'

'When was winning *not* the object of the exercise?' Bobby said.

When he had a use for my angle on things, my critique, in those remote days, he'd talk about works of art to test his perceptions about people – it's what Bobby had instead of an entre-acte revolutionary political philosophy and it made him the only authentic and original revolutionary on campus. He didn't regurgitate the slogans, prison diaries or tracts of Italian anarchists, he didn't go to the Cubans, Russians or Chinese or to the ghetto poets of the American underclass. He went to Jackson Pollock, to Edward Hopper, to Géricault.

Raft of the 'Medusa' could agitate him for hours. 'Extreme conditions – famine, war, shipwrecks, revolution, whatever – ' (his words, inscribed on my affections, which I should have quoted back to him verbatim), 'let loose the things we all have to be if we want to go on living. Whatever we're not ashamed to be afterwards . . . ' The religious brutality of it cut into him, that pyramid of sallow human bodies, naked, discarded, raw, tormented and failing, sacrificed, cannibalized, leaderless, heaped on a disintegrating platform of debris, the attachment to life so powerful that it sweeps the survivors upwards, rallying, lifted above their swamped grave in an answering swell of hope, signaling to the horizon, to the rumor of a sail or it might be the blue-gray peak of another furious wave, signaling with torn shirts in the blowing wind, rags mimicking the shapes of the clouds and as distant from the view of any rescue ship as the clouds are above the raft. This picture of epic desperation inspired Bobby, it made him generous for a while.

If I'd thought it would have had an impact I would have dredged this up to reach him somehow, but nothing I could say then weighted the balance enough to change Bobby's mind about JT. He listened to me for a few more minutes with indulgent, shallow attention, the gaze of a society hostess plastered over the conscience of a locust.

'Any particular plan?' he asked lifelessly. 'I can't picture you back at USC teaching full-time. Maybe you could give William Manchester a shove and write my campaign biography. *The Making of a Governor*, I'd like that.'

'You'd like the title, that's about all,' I said. 'No, quiet pursuits for me, now. Birdwatching isn't such a preposterous waste of time. You can learn a lot watching birds.'

I wheeled away from him, his gang, away from the granite boxes of government, at the end of my work in the mezzanines, away from the capital, its heirs and bastards. I flew down to Los Angeles, in solo orbit (my heraldic motto).

10   In the Trough of Earthly Night

BURIED below the threshold of Anthony's awareness, but dumbly perceived by pets, livestock and most of the ground-dwelling animals in the LA Zoo, awesome and unanswerable change was bowling out of the instantaneous future, its subterranean force colossally bearing down on the local area. At Hummingbird Farm the tail-twitching, caged, feverish pacing, necks straining to locate the open ground, snouts lifted to sniff the rising breeze, this tingling panic as it spread through the herd had the look of precognition.

Stubble on a hog's jowl might tremble with the fluctuation of electrical charge in the air, a sow's molars might vibrate like tuning forks with the inaudible friction of rock sheets grinding past each other twenty-five thousand feet underneath the foothills, something like the way that the tiny receptors I'd dotted on the farm office windows resonated in sync with the micro-ripples that shimmered over the surface of the glass when people were talking in the room. The sharp, frozen, fatalistic silence from the entire herd might be the collective reply to the silence of animal life outside; whatever it was, it was this unbreathing stillness that shut off my tape recorder at 6:38 AM.

A minute before, Anthony must have been pacing through the long barn like a hospital orderly, wheeling the morning batch of feed down the middle aisle, stopping for a chat at each pen. But the pigs huffed away from him, flinched at his limping step as if it meant torture, snouts nervously angled up, nostrils flexing, sucking at the air. In this pen he'd find the sows huddled against the railing and in that pen they'd be scattered, pecking at each other, clearing lozenges of space to stand in, ignoring Anthony and the food he was dishing out.

'What's wrong with you girls?' he hung on there to inquire. 'You're acting pretty snooty to me today.'

The sensitivity has to be keener in individual pigs. I'm sure now that a few of them felt a more definite trembling, say, in the hairs in the cleft of their trotters, their own jumpiness auguring the danger, its closeness, to their ungifted companions: prophets on four legs. In the stupefied silence they were the ones who understood that vigilance will be no help, knowledge of what's about to befall them will be no help, Anthony will be no help, safety has gone, they are going to be slaughtered and swallowed whole by the onrushing, inescapable catastrophe.

'What is it? You can talk to me.'

A few miles away at Worldview, Munro folded himself into the Reverend's big chair in the studio as a stand-in during the lighting and camera preset. He had the *Wall Street Journal* butterflied open in front of his face and Tommy the floor manager had to tell him over and over again to keep it flat on his lap. JT waited for his call outside in the strong morning sunshine, concentrating on the bucket of golf balls he'd carried out there, putting them across the shaved front lawn.

And in his apartment behind the deli fifteen minutes away, Alex lay asleep with Nelda in his bed, 'their' bed as she called it now, the right she gained sleeping there more nights than she slept at home. He curled against her under the messy stack of blankets, she tucked herself into him, a snug fit, his front to her back, as familiar and unremarkable as a pair of teaspoons stowed in a kitchen drawer.

It arrived as the sound of an underground dam breaking, sixty-two seconds of torrential roaring, a ferocious current of boulders and crumbling soil coring through the dark earth. Anthony tumbled onto his knees, the concrete floor unknitting beneath him, the skin of the planet shrugging him off. Fractured slabs of flooring jerked up and slid over each other like crusts of arctic ice.

Somewhere over his head firecracker bursts punctured the thundering presence of the quake, six-inch bolts shearing between the walls and metal joists. The sides of the building torqued, thin as cardboard, fighting away from the roof, lumps of concrete and breeze block ripping electrical cables free. Sprays of wires snapped loose and showered sparks down into the flying dust and grit. The open, gushing heads of cracked pipes periscoped out of the ground, Anthony saw them spike up and then fold under a rain of rubble, blocks dropping out of the wall in twos and threes, mortared together, falling into the pens.

Sows, hogs and piglets rioted toward the gaps that opened in the middle of the building. Still lost, still squalling outside where the ground was gashed open into pits and ravines, they sprinted away and sprinted back, fell, were trampled. Anthony staggered out of the same exit, one hand covering his head. He looked back at the ruins of the farm – fences torn up or flattened, the mayhem of pigs running as far as they could, running anywhere, tripping over the ledges of dry fissures, the long barn battered apart, the front half of it sunken, torpedoed, disappearing into the dust of the yard.

Most of the yard had spread open into a crater and on the rim of it the farm office squatted, half its height, in a nest of snapped framework, smoldering planks and splinters. All three of the Humpty Dumpster service sheds collapsed roof first, the slate-shingled pitched frames pancaked onto the machines. So many of the square white modules were knocked out of their racks that the destruction took on the final symbolic form of a mouthful of broken teeth.

The first seconds of the earthquake bounced Nelda out of bed. In her half-sleep she shrieked Jim's name, then, jarred awake by the violent shaking, she grabbed at Alex. He dived on top of her, curling her head into his lap, bent around Nelda, covering as much of her as he could as the windows crunched broken glass over them, the plaster walls quivered, furniture toppled over, his homelife savaged by a shattering physical presence, a devouring act of God that drummed one thought into him, *this is the only reality, this is the only time.*

Worldview rode out the worst of the calamity, surviving with a web of hairline fractures in one wall of the studio. It was the first aftershock that brought the lamps down, dropping like grenades from the lurching scaffolding. Munro crawled out of hiding, left the shelter of the upturned chair and hotfooted it out of there to find the Reverend, ducking a drizzle of plaster chips, dodging the falling lamps as the tremor shivered away.

The passenger seat of his own Jeep wasn't the first place Munro searched for JT and he only saw him there when JT yelled across the parking lot to him, waving a golf club out of the sunroof. 'Get in and drive!' As Munro jabbed at the ignition with his key JT told him, 'I have to get out of here.'

'Nobody got hurt in the building, Reverend, not very. Tommy almost got a camera knocked on top of him but he's okay from it.'

Absently, JT said, 'Which camera, what number?'

'I believe it was Camera 3.'

'Harm's coming to everything I love in my life.' He wound down his window and stared out into the street, anxious to leave. 'He can punch the holy heart out of everything, I'm afraid that's been done. The vessel of all my love, Munro, the body that holds my love of God to the earth, smashed to pieces, killed off.'

'No, Reverend. We all got through it. Good thing I drove in so early. We'll probably need the four-wheel drive if those hilly roads up by your house are messed up. You want me to swing by your ma's place first or Nelda?'

'The farm, Munro! I want to go to the farm!'

Even the canyon's atmosphere felt ruptured. In the yard, under the landslipped hilltops, ragged air fluttered over the farm's wreckage, boisterous wind blowing in gusts and hesitations. From the lip of the crater JT saw the mounds of cement, wood, brick, steel, wire, pipe and glass that used to be standing structures, and he saw the end of construction and order, the end of containment.

I could see him from a window in the half of my bungalow that wasn't cantilevered over the gouged brow of the canyon rim. I probably had only an hour or two to pack up my equipment and vacate the place before the police cruised by to enforce safety orders. I stayed long enough to witness this:

Head bloody, Anthony wandered out from behind a severed corner of the sow house, picking his way toward Munro and JT over the knee-high furrows of dirt, rocks and debris. He only got as far as the edge of a trench that zigzagged across the middle of the yard crater, there he dropped down on his knees.

Munro thought that the crying he heard was Anthony's, whining, strangled, but when he reached him Munro found the cries were drifting up from the trench.

'I'm sorry, I'm sorry,' Anthony sobbed out, driblets of muddy tears running into his mouth. 'I'm sorry, I was here,' was all he could think of to say.

JT handed Munro a pack of travel-size tissues and said to Anthony, 'You're a tough old boy, you got through it. Something cut a slice out of your scalp, that's all.'

'I was here, I was here.'

Some of the pigs at the bottom of the ditch were already dead, others struggled there with broken backs, some heads or hindquarters stuck out above the quicksand of fresh cave-ins. A few of the wounded animals were caught on shelves of jutting rock, sows, boars, screeching in pain, in common fear, close to death. A piglet lay pinned and squirming under a dead hog. Munro crawled halfway over the sifting edge and tried to lift the infant out but before he had a grip on her she kicked free and flipped backward into the trench. Her fall led his eye to the rest of the carnage, snapped forelegs, lacerated flanks, veins nicked open and dribbling blood, broken shanks knifing through red muscle, pink meat and pink skin.

'Look at this,' JT said.

'We can rig up a sling out of canvas and a rope,' Munro answered him. 'I know where there's some canvas, if I can get to it.'

JT wasn't listening. In a transfixed monotone he said, 'It's all divided in front of our eyes again. One more time. Twice in my life. It's a Sabbath. It isn't a conflict in front of us, this is peace, this is the peace of knowing.' To the hog that squealed up at him from that mass grave JT said, 'Doctors can already transplant heart valves from pigs to save the lives of people suffering from coronary disease.'

'Reverend? Are you all right?' Munro asked softly.

Just as softly JT told him that he felt healthy, clear in his mind, that God just shot him through the head with a crystal arrow, with a shattering diamond light. 'I'm taking the Jeep. Did you leave the keys in it?' Munro said he did. 'Didn't I tell you to never leave your keys in the car? Take them out and lock the doors or it's an open invitation to somebody! It's an open temptation for anybody to sneak in and steal your Jeep right out from under you,' he moralized, trudging across the loose ground. 'Do I have to think of everything?'

'What should I do?'

JT turned around and pointed straight at him. 'Don't forget what we talked about.'

'About *this*, Reverend.' Munro glanced behind him and then side to side. 'What should I do?'

'Stay put.'

'Do you want me to do anything?'

'Stay here, Munro, and do what you can.'

Munro tensed himself by pretending that he'd just heard the last thing JT would ever say to him, that this was his last earthly sight of the Reverend – reversing the Jeep into a pall of dust, gears stripping, cranking it over ruts and rocks, up the steep road to the highway, engine noise fading, gone. What could he do?

He watched Anthony peel the wad of soaked tissues off of his cut. The old man stared at the blood stains, felt his scalp and started crying again. 'Ssh, ssh. Oh – there, oh,' Munro cooed to him dabbing at the rubbery flap of skin with a clean tissue. From somewhere in the trench a tormented wheezing drifted out of the rise and fall of yelps and moans. Stooping over Anthony Munro could see that the pitiful noise came from a sow stretched out like a sunbather on a pebble beach, her throat split by a gash deep enough to lay open her windpipe. 'Oh – there, ssh . . . quiet, now . . . ' Moved by mercy he lugged over a block of concrete so heavy that he couldn't raise it higher than his waist, and Munro heaved it down onto the sow's head. Her skull cracked, blood seethed, but she went on screeching in startled agony that reached up and gripped Munro too. 'Oh, ssh, no, quiet . . . Gather us up . . . ' He started a prayer, words dissolving in his own powerless tears. 'He will come to gather us to Him, oh – there, come to us, so, and gather us up,' prayer and weeping both out of control.

11   Father of Rain

ON the car ride to her son's house Ma told Munro why she wasn't crazy with worry over JT's disappearance. Even after a week and a half, she could think of a hundred reasons for him to leave without the breath of a word to the ones who loved him most. Going over the list of possible explanations again she remarked, 'Jimmy was a strange child to raise. I think he was the one who raised Mister and me ever since he was a little boy. He was always somewhere doing something. We'd find out about it later and he'd help us look back on whatever it was and see how God's hand was in it.'

Munro's confidence sounded forced. 'Reverend's somewhere doing something, I'm sure about that, too.'

'I wish I knew what, that's all.' Ma smiled at her own annoyance and spineless dismay. 'It's only us against the haters and traitors, right?'

'Right, uh-huh.'

'Mister and me always appreciated your family loyalty, Munro. To Jimmy and to us. That you'd do whatever you needed to if it came down to where you had to keep us from getting hurt, Jim or me.'

All she got out of him was, 'I hope to say.'

'Did Jim ever confide you with the fact he had a sister?' Munro tilted a little in his seat, knocked gently by this piece of news. 'Now's the right time to tell you about her, then. For three years when he was little he had a baby sister. We had Emily when he was four and he hated her on first sight.'

Ma caught Jimmy dangling his father's sweaty socks into Emily's crib, ordering her to smell them. There were encored acts of trivial, boyish cruelty he invented to remind Emily who was there first and first in their parents' hearts. With baby Emily locked in her high-chair he dropped dead flies into her cereal bowl and told her that cornflakes tasted twice as good with raisins mixed in. Sometimes Ma found the little girl crying, her cheeks pink and tender, inflamed, as if she'd been slapped. Once they had to grab Jimmy off of his sister's chest where he sat bouncing on her until she started to choke.

'I always thought he'd be a bachelor his whole life,' Ma entrusted him with this secret, too. 'You know him like I do, he just gets so single-sighted on what he's doing. God sure came to him early enough, he just about changed into a miniature man after Emily was gone.'

'Doesn't she stay in touch with you anymore?'

'What happened was, I told her she had to have a nap before her birthday party. She was three years old of age and all excited about her presents and the party favors and all, she was raising a racket, so I tucked her in bed for an hour. She was lying on her back, eyes wide open when I went to get her from her nap, she was all purple in the face. It turned out she suffocated on one of Jimmy's polished rocks from his hobby collection. I saw it, it looked like a piece of butterscotch candy. Jimmy hid in his bedroom closet for two days and when he came out the first thing he said to us was, "God wants me to make you happy again." Jim always knows something extra that's hidden from us.' But Munro obviously didn't, so Ma reeled in the bait and searched for hints in the phone call from Gunter Thorsen, JT's lawyer, requesting the meeting up at the house. 'Gunter knows something, so I guess we'll find out what it is.'

JT's legal proxy was attached to rituals of efficiency which he awkwardly disguised behind casual clothes and an amiable preference for informal meetings outside the precincts of his law office. Nelda hostessed in a blouse and skirt self-denying enough for any Sicilian widow, Alex arrived in jacket and tie, Munro in the department-store charcoal-gray suit bought for him in Sacramento and Ma, on this scorching afternoon, came drenched in black flannel. As for Gunter, anything as starchy as a tie would have been caught and eaten by his Hawaiian shirt and a belt would have slumped off in stodgy shame from the happy bloom of his surfer shorts. Two summers ago he sacrificially lopped off his Cherokee braid to become the youngest partner at Greenglass, Fenn, Leitner, Sandland. When Francis Sandland died JT shifted the responsibility for all of his legal affairs over to Gunter, mainly, it seems, to confuse his enemies and scare the bejesus out of his friends.

'We're all here so let's do it,' Gunter addressed them from the head of the dining-room table. He dealt out identical manila folders to everybody with a preliminary explanation. 'Yesterday morning I received a message – well, basically it was a signal – from Reverend Tickell, instructing me to notify you of certain deeds and gifts he's decided to settle on you.'

Gunter read from a document that was dated November 7, the day after the election. He drew everyone's attention to a page attached to each copy of his text, a Xerox blow-up of a smudgy public notice inserted in the classified ads of the bi-weekly specialist periodical *Tropical Animal Health and Production Bulletin*: 'James Gamaliel Tickell (Rev.) is as of this date no longer a principal in businesses trading as HD Systems Group, Hummingbird Farm Foods, Ltd., Wendywear Clothing Co. or Worldview Mission World Enterprises and associated companies. 11/7/90.'

Into Ma's name passed sole, uncontestable stewardship of World-view projects and accounts and into Munro's went full title to JT's Jaguar sedan. Hummingbird Farm reverted to the proprietorship of the Yardell estate and the farm's administrators, namely Oswald Pogenpohl's Creation Science Institute. JT signed over to Alex Worldview's holdings in HD Systems along with his ministry's interest in the eco-friendly meat business, which made Alex the majority patsy, as far as he could tell, a barn-size target for litigation, the owner of defiled assets and ruin of a kind unseen in the world since the sacking of Rome.

'My son probably's got a good strong reason,' Ma said, 'if this is what he wants to do. The main thing', she added, looking at Alex, 'is we have to protect Worldview.'

Privately to Nelda, Gunter said, 'My take on it is Reverend Tickell wants you to be totally free of money worries and he wants to kick loose from heavy entanglements. So here's a way that he thinks you two can go on it.'

The letter he handed to her asked Nelda to let Gunter take care of the paperwork for their divorce. The house had already been put in her name along with all of their stocks, bonds, shares, cash, jewelry and real estate, all he was taking with him was his trailer, his coin collection and Munro's Jeep; there was nothing she had to contest unless (he added in a postscript) she wanted to file a counter-suit and cite God as a co-respondent.

Nelda refolded the letter. 'Do you know where he is?'

'Can I get you to initial that for me?'

'His health isn't good. All I want to know is if he's all right where he is. Do you know if he's all right?'

'If I answered a question like that then you'd have good grounds to think I personally know where your husband can be located.' Gunter weighed up the implications. 'Ouch. Bummer *über alles*.'

He contemplated the end of his material security. Alex sat rooted in bankruptcy's slushy path, stuck in the high-backed chair where the exact terms of his commercial death and mutilation had been broken to him by Gunter hours ago. Its glacial shape crawled toward Alex from the shadow of the orange tree outside the dining-room window, reaching across the lawn and into the house. Gunter's moral support and offer of a half-price consultation on the class action suit settled one thing in Alex's mind, anyway: he was talking to the wrong man if he needed weighty defense against the scythe-rattling, torch-shaking, rampaging peasant mob that was heading his way. He needed an *heroic* defense to stand beside his (his alone!) titanic liability. Clarence Darrow! Daniel Webster! Alex kept Nelda with him at the table where they helped each other get used to the new reality in force, both of them too drained by guessing about the future and arguing about their guesses even to think of turning the lights on.

'Just please don't try and tell me what's happening to me is all God's idea, Nelda, don't, or I'll *never* be able to think my way out of it. I'm sorry, I just can't take in any Christian mumbo jumbo at the moment.'

'Step back a step, that's all I'm saying. You said to step back and look at the big picture.'

'My life isn't at the mercy of supernatural forces! This is a standard business screwing! Something else is going on here, something we don't know about yet but *that doesn't mean* I've been singled out for special attention by the King of the Universe. It's like this – ' Alex demonstrated by holding a plate up between them. He pushed the flat of it at Nelda and dialed his finger around the side facing her. 'This is a clock. See the numbers? See the hands going around? I know what time it is but I also know that back here there're hundreds of little parts I can't see, all ticking each other around. What you got from Jim was one enormous birthday present, honey, and what he gave me was a royal shafting! Aren't you curious at all about what made him want to pull this stunt?'

In a tone of numbed amazement Nelda said, 'How can you compare us that way? You haven't been married to him.'

'So I keep snapping back to the idea that Heidi told him about you and me.' He waded into this theory. 'She could've told him anytime. Maybe she knew about us from the beginning.'

'Heidi didn't tell him. She for sure didn't know anything,' Nelda said unshakably. 'Unless she heard something from you.'

'Heidi and I weren't that close.' Alex let out a mock sob. 'But put God into it and how does that clear everything up?'

'Maybe you'd find out the life-purpose of it and you'd feel more relaxed.' Alex studied her, tensely. She said, 'Everything you don't know also includes what's going to come out of this. It might be something wonderful.'

'No, no,' Alex moaned from the brink. 'I can see the purpose of the whole thing very clearly. The purpose of it is to save Jim's butt from the shredder.'

In touching contrast, Ma's immediate worries weren't over the implications but the practicalities. Settling into the back seat of the Jaguar as Munro gunned the engine she declared simply, 'I don't want to run Worldview and I bet he knows that. I can't do it like Jimmy does. It belongs to him. I don't care what it says on a legal piece of paper.'

'Reverend must think it's the best thing.'

'He didn't ask me what I thought about it. I want to go there, Munro, to where he is, I want to talk to my son.'

'I don't know where he's at. I don't, Ma. I'm being honest with you, I can't tell you anything else.'

'Pray on it, then,' she said. 'We'll pray on it together.'

JT's people wanted to find him and I wanted to see him when they did, when he was face to face with the ones who saw their lives refracted through his, sure they'd see the clear, complete image of themselves by asking their questions and hearing his answers. I include myself in that hopeful, apprehensive bunch.

12   The Flood

SINKING into his apathy and self-abandonment, Alex taught me where I'd brought on my own emotional death so many times in the past, by mistaking isolation for refuge. He needed shelter from claims on his life that he didn't have the power to answer – from Gunter's almost daily requests for a statement of Alex's net worth (an index which Alba had drawn up and submitted in triplicate twice already), from Heidi's threatening phone calls, from pre-dawn suicide fantasies – shelter he didn't find by barricading himself into his apartment. Unplugging the telephone only attracted hand-delivered, mostly pessimistic, updates from Gunter's office and the not completely demented worry that after weeks of bluffing Heidi was going to appear at his door with the police flaunting a warrant for his arrest on charges of theft, assault, battery, kidnap, torture and attempted rape.

Let her show up. Let her vandalize his windows and walls. Whatever Heidi had the nerve to do, Alex was sure that she couldn't track him down to his parents' house; their phone number was unlisted and Nelda didn't have to be asked not to pass it on. Even if by some tricky means that he lacked the strength to imagine Heidi *did* stalk him all the way to Pacific Palisades, Alex knew he was in a place where he belonged and she didn't, his family wouldn't let her root him out.

In his old bedroom he lay beyond persecution, crumpled onto his narrow, solid, maplewood bed with the will power of a pile of dirty laundry. Waking up from two days of fetal sleep, Alex lapsed into a nocturnal cycle that didn't help to steady his mental balance:

unconscious from dawn to late afternoon, a trip to the kitchen for a fresh supply of Coca-Cola, peanut butter sandwiches, dry cereal and chocolate-flavor instant pudding, then back to his room to sit blankly in front of the TV until he fell asleep again. First, normal hours, and next personal hygiene was the social convention he dropped to widen the gap between himself and the outside world. Bad diet turned his skin fishy white under the sparse stubble; washing, brushing his teeth, combing his hair and changing his clothes were all forgotten routines and Alex moved around the house in a humid billow of his own sour air.

At a feeding point some way into the cycle his father sat with him in the warm safety of the kitchen to remind Alex that he could rely on any kind of practical help he needed in this situation, any support short of admiration. Meyer had become more talkative with his family since he retired from the twenty-five-year headache of management trouble-shooting for IBM. He dived into a pool of neglected pleasures – collecting odd pieces of pre-Colombian pottery, listening to Mexican music, reading fifteen magazines a week, astronomy to news reviews to interior design, and he paid more attention to physical fitness than he had since his college quarterback seasons. This, especially, made him sensitive to the dullness in his son that Alex began to drag around with him like submissive middle age.

'Write up a list,' Meyer nudged him. 'Write down where you want to be in a year. A year isn't such a long stretch.'

'In the words of Al Capone's lawyer.'

'That's all wrong. Can I give you my input on the problem?' He was talking to a soft lump of wax, a dismal sound of futility wrapped in a stale T-shirt and sagging pyjama bottoms. 'If you don't start thinking very soon about how you'd like your life to be after this is over and done with then you're just going to dig yourself into a hole and stay there. I'm talking about severe depression, Alex, and it's not a million miles away. According to Janice the symptoms can flatten you overnight.'

Alex answered him in the trembly monotone of a chemically subdued mental patient. 'I'd be insane if this situation didn't depress me. Next time you discuss my case with Janice maybe you can score me some Prozac.'

Slowly unreeling the question (and amazed it forced itself on him), Meyer asked, 'Are you on anything now?'

' "On" like what?'

'Did you bring drugs into this house?'

'The thing of it is – drugs, Dad? If I was hooked on *cough drops* right now I couldn't buy one! You want a professional opinion on how depressed I should be? I'll give you Gunter's number. He'll tell you how many years it'll take, rounded off to the nearest lifetime, before I'm out of debt. Before I can run a company again. Before I can own a *credit card* again.'

'Is that what your lawyer says?'

'It costs me thirty-five dollars every time I talk to him on the phone for five minutes.'

'Okay,' Meyer said, abruptly cheerful. 'What are your options? Let's examine your options.' Out came pen and note pad. He labeled the pocket-sized page 'Alex's Options'. 'Give me an estimate on how much you'll end up paying out.'

'Legal fees, just those, if it goes on for two-three years . . . Say, quarter of a million?' Alex could only guess. 'Three hundred thousand? Four?'

'So much?' A gasp, the sound of Meyer deflating. 'I didn't realize it was that steep.'

'Dad, I can't make my rent anymore.'

'Move out of that place. This is your home, you can stay here as long as you want to. Your mom would like that. I can feed you and keep a roof over your head.'

'I know. You told me.'

'But I can't pay your lawyer bills. You know, your mother and I don't have that kind of money.'

Alex slumped back, heavily, dragged down by the unmanning need to introduce himself to his own father, to argue with flat words, inadequate words, his adequacy as a man. Before his business crashed and burned the question didn't come up. 'You think I don't know how much I went in with? I wanted USC, you gave me USC. Then I did the work and not the minimum. I pushed it all the time, I wanted to see if I had a limit because if I did I was going to push that, too. I went in with all my nerve and intelligence, Dad, I know that's how I started.' He was caught, falling upward in an emotional spiral. 'I was the one who was going to market a classic, not some hit-'em-quick disposable piece of trash but something original and worth my time and energy, worth other people's money, *a classic*.'

'You don't have to be a multimillionaire,' his father said. 'With what you've got on the ball you'll land the right job, I mean it. No more of these big ups and downs.'

'Dad, I never hit my limit. Back at SC I could see what was on the way before anybody else did. All the signs, you know, however you can tell about your real chances said *my* risks were going to pay off. All these glorious things, my brains, my head start, my work, the signs, they were part of this trap. They *are* this trap! All Jim did was slam the lid shut on my head. What am I now?' Plucking at his shirt, wafting a pulse of salty, locker room warmth across the table.

'You over-estimated your partner. He trusted you with the company, so you thought he was a trustworthy man.' Meyer snorted at the idea.

With resignation Alex said, 'He was a professional.'

'A professional Christian. I remember them from my three years with holy-holy operators like him in Wisconsin. Alex, I worked with them my entire career. They see you're smart, ambitious, you get ahead. Of course. You're a Jew. The first chance they get they'll throw you to the lions.' Freed to speak now by Alex's liberation from Tickell, Meyer delivered his stifled warning as an epitaph. 'It was idiotic to go into business with a man whose main livelihood is bilking people in the name of God, people who can't help themselves.'

'He didn't bilk me, I didn't screw up anywhere and, believe me, this disaster didn't happen because I'm Jewish. Jim would've done the same thing to me if I was a born-again Baptist.'

'Maybe. But he wouldn't have felt the same about it.'

'I don't know how he feels,' Alex said. 'Free and clear, I guess.'

'No more big ups and downs.' Meyer tapped his pen on the still-empty page of Alex's Options. 'Let's think.'

'Can I use your car for a couple of hours? I want to move my TV, video and stereo out of the apartment.' All he really wanted was to avoid receiving his father's advice and permission to aim lower, expect less and leave self-fulfillment to the gurus.

This was pretty much all the active resistance Alex could muster against abject emotional collapse: avoiding any discussion, even contemplation, of recent fatal mistakes or alternative future plans. He took Meyer's stodgy widebody Oldsmobile twice around the block and then, eventually, off in the general direction of his apartment.

Plowing along behind Alex in my van, I had to make a detached effort to comprehend his empty-minded drift without falling into it myself.

In the wandering embassy of the family car – the interior brushed with the medicated scent of his father's shaving cream, front seat littered with Meyer's news and science digests, his mother's dry cleaning bagged and folded in the back – Alex fell back to a place where reminders of his independent life couldn't get at him. Those glimpses of Alex cowering made me afraid for him. Stopped at a red light he let his mouth hang open, his gaze floating somewhere ahead, lost so deeply in the maze of his commercial failure this time that his ego seemed to be flushed out of him. He existed more in my memory then, yipping over the elegance of a business plan, howling in pain over its rejection, *alive*. Now, with conventional weights strapped to his ankles, I could see Alex sinking out of sight, reconciling himself to a daily attendance in a facsimile of a satisfying existence with 'no big ups and downs'.

He didn't want to remember but I did. When Odo-bags failed, his absolute belief in that child of his imagination only changed shape: it turned into his absolute belief in Humpty Dumpsters. Alex revived, his creativity sparked, his resilience and adaptability swept me into the surprising future he hammered out for himself minute by minute. He proved what he knew – that he was a rare one, one who imprinted his features on the life going on around him.

Now impersonal life had landed on top of him, now Alex wasn't howling. He flattened any yearning into an embarrassed memory of how he used to be and soon, it occurred to me, he'd be incapable of remembering how it felt to find unexpected approaches, to lay himself open to unforeseeable opportunities. As much as he wanted anything, Alex wanted to be blurred, softened at the edges of his ambition, accepted and accepting, unafflicted by imagination, talent or insight. I let other traffic merge into the lane ahead of me.

A fading radio signal is an eerie noise. A human voice disappears into the static soup, drowns under the rushing crumbling surface, unreachable, turns ghostly in the final seconds when any separate indentifiable sound is so faint that it is half heard and half remembered and then not there, sealed into hissing silence. I listened to Alex die away, audio channel locked open, holding onto him as long as I could keep him in sight. He dabs at the button on the car stereo and the preset slides out of *se habla Español* patter, he dabs again and the Latino car dealer slews into salsa music. The next words that come over my headphones are, I think, the last ones I'll hear from Alex: 'No fucking escape!'

Unmistakable, this clogged growl. 'A river of mud has burst its banks . . . ' With a cool tone of friendly aggression, the overmastering nerve of a hypnotist bearing down on his subject, with pre-recorded inspirational broadcasts he called 'faithbites' the Reverend was fighting back on the air. Thanks to Meyer's hobbyist enthusiasm for all things Hispanic, Alex tuned into the second edition of JT's nine-times-a-week radio spot on the 'salsational' high desert station KOSO.

'Good night, thank you and fuck you,' Alex coughed at him, belted the face of the radio with his fist and, wheels squealing, gunned the Olds through a red light.

I fiddled the FM dial as if I were cracking a safe, tuning in JT, and when I found him again his voice froze me into my seat.

' . . . On the ground out on patrol there's got to be a point man who sees what's coming first, but he gets it first too. Thus saith the word of the Lord. Now this point man saith *his* word *to* the Lord. Every time my headaches crack my skull open Your head aches. Right at the same time, I know it. See, God used to be with me around the clock. At the beginning of Worldview, He was there. When I took over Hummingbird Farm, He held me in His eyes. *I do know You*! You sat in the room with me and Governor Bobby in Sacramento and You heard him pray *for my financial ruin*. He wanted the ground to open under my feet, he prayed to shut me up and shut me down, You heard him ka lehlu hama shenna bana uhlas koruli ba somiel gedi labas ho lehlu . . . '

JT's spasm of glossolalia may have made him sound temporarily unhinged but otherwise every taunting word he spoke was rooted in reality. Did he know from the beginning that he was under surveillance? This was one annihilating revelation! This was a fresh sensation, the breathtaking knowledge that all along somebody had been watching me – or watching for me. In that case, how much of what I saw him do was unrestrained? How much of what he said was for effect? If JT was convinced, or if he even suspected that I was recording everything he did, then it was a cloudy image I had of him, a false picture my records contained. How close a view did he allow me of his undramatized conduct? As he talked on, everything that I'd seen happen to him or because of him up till then became scrambled in my mind and slowly collected around a different, unclear meaning.

' . . . God used to occupy my home. He used to see what I saw, hear what I heard, think my thoughts with me, chew with my molars! My walls, ceilings, floors and windows *heated up* from His scrutiny. You know me inside-out so You know I'm waiting here for You to find me again. Are You any closer to me today, are You?

'Did I pray as the hypocrites do? That I may be seen of men? I did not. God comes down into the world, understand me, through His people and we're *all* His people. We're Your hands, aren't we! For You to reach down into human lives and feel the shapes of our ambitions. Building, breaking, anything that happens to us moves You the same way, comfort or pain. His ways are higher than our ways, listen to me, we fill God up with human emotions. Every human feeling You have belongs to me . . . '

Oh, this direct accusation, ignorant and unfair, knocked the wind out of me. I never hid from JT – *or* Alex, *or* Munro, Nelda, Oswald or anyone else – to put distance between us but to close the distance as much as I could without interfering. The prickling doubt JT jabbed into my conscience was that if he suspected I was there then I already *had* interfered. My invisibility, my silence, just further proof to him of my constant, biased presence.

' . . . "How long will You leave me, God?" King David says, and God tells him, "Forever." "How long will You leave me forever?" It just didn't matter to David that God stopped talking to him. Find 2 Samuel 23 and there's David on his *death bed* saving his last words for God. He wanted God to know he knew godless men are all like desert thorns which are never gathered by hand. No one touches them, he says, unless with iron or a spear, and then they're burnt on a fire. It doesn't matter if You turn Your back on me now, I'll still render up what You want. I'll gather them in and be gathered in with the first word amma lo kara leshunna ba heema. I'm going back to the beginning, where You started with me, in my *organs*. Out of the vilest stench and corruption You promise the most glorious rescue. I've seen Your face, I know it, I *have* seen Your face.'

My thoughts reeled back to Alex. There was nothing else for me to do except violate my own fundamental moral principle and tell him what I learned about his life from keeping him in my sights for the last two years. From my fatherly vantage point unencumbered with family history I felt I could restore him to himself, assure him that the trail of choices which landed him here weren't naive mistakes, that he was not unfit for the rough and tumble of American commercial life, that if he only kept moving he'd be freer of self-indictment and clearer of perspective than his ex-partner was at the moment. I asked myself if this impulse of mine was the reaction of someone empty of emotion, of someone benignly latent in the course of other people's lives, profanely remote from any human response beyond impotent sympathy. The answer was as exhilarating as it was obvious.

He'd packed up his video and stereo equipment and gone by the time I'd made it over there. After a fruitless tour around Canter's I doubled back to Alex's parents' house and found Nelda's convertible parked behind Meyer's Olds in the driveway. Both cars' engines were still warm, they had been there for less than ten minutes. I wouldn't label it fate but just when I was most compellingly touched by the need to come face to face with Alex the presence of others forced me to seal myself into my van and view him from a distance, on a ten-inch portable television.

Next to Alex's complexion which was the shade of tapioca pudding (and in patches also the texture), Nelda's skin fluoresced with health. Her forehead and cheeks, clean and rudely freckled, her pale eyebrows and paler lashes, her coloring spun Meyer into a tender reminiscence of his favourite aunt. Nelda, he said affectingly, was Bertha's echo.

'If you're anything like her,' Meyer prepared Nelda, 'you'll still be hitting a tennis ball when you're eighty-two. *Is* there any Polish in your family?'

'Maybe somewhere. It's German, mostly. And Irish.'

'Oh, the Celts, yes. That's a wonderful background to come from. Stories and music, just like us.'

While Alex grunted through the clutch of mail that Nelda had picked up for him earlier in the morning, she was given the official tour of Meyer's pre-Colombian pottery. His ancient terracotta figurines of thick featured peasants and warriors squatted in a semi-circle on an eye-level shelf of the living-room bookcase.

'Can you see the details on that ear of corn? Perfect little kernels some actual person painted on there.' Amazed all over again, Meyer said, 'Somebody who was alive in Mexico four hundred years ago.'

Because it stood at the center of the display, totemically, as if it were a ritual object of Aztec worship, the family menorah was given the same curatorial attention. Nelda learned the whole history of that silver candelabra – symbolically and probably blasphemously broken up into its seven branches by Meyer's grandfather who then entrusted a branch each to his seven children when he packed them off to America, one at a time, starting with Aunt Bertha in 1919. It was Meyer's father, a jeweler, who reassembled it at last when the Berenstein children all were safe in Philadelphia twelve years later.

'He's been doing this to my friends since I was in third grade,' Alex apologized.

'No,' Nelda stopped him there and primly assured Meyer, 'No, I want to hear. It's like a Bible story.'

'You know how we use the menorah?' Meyer ignored Alex's cranky heckling and placed the candlestick in Nelda's hands, offering it to her as if she were a little blind girl.

'Dad, it used to be your paperweight.'

Nelda ignored him too. 'It's for the Festival of Lights. There was a miracle, right? With, was it the Maccabees?' She rattled off the essential points with eager, bookish sureness. 'The Romans had them trapped and they sent for help. They only had enough oil in their lamp for one night but it burned for a week.'

'Festival of Lights!' Meyer patted her on the arm. 'Hey, she knows her stuff, Alex.'

'I didn't know it a month ago,' she admitted.

'We'll be in my room,' Alex told his dad, tramping upstairs. 'If that's not a major problem.'

His bedroom door clunked shut behind the thud of Nelda's long body being pinned against it. Alex led with his lips, swung his face into hers, one hand against the side of her face, an emblem of tenderness that also kept her from turning away.

'Alex? Sweetie?' Nelda's delicate tone and cornered squirming only inflamed his urgency to show her that he was a man who'd stop at nothing, if he could just get started. Her whispered warning that she could hear his parents talking in the kitchen below he answered by sloshing his tongue in and out of her ear.

'Where have you *been* for two weeks?' dropping sleepy-eyed kisses on her bare shoulder, his tongue slackly prodding under the strap of her sundress.

'You know where I've been.'

'You haven't been here.'

She pushed at him, got Alex to stop what he was doing long enough to say, 'You haven't asked me anything about Wendywear.'

A whiff of perspiration in the sea-salt hollow of Nelda's neck dragged him out of any further discussion. 'Visit with me,' he said, tugging Nelda bedward and when they landed together on the mattress the metal frame underneath them bounced out a shocked squawk. She went rigid listening for Meyer's voice, a reaction that to Alex was as good as surrender. The bed-noise toned down to the squeaking of an asthmatic mouse, quick and shallow, the percussion of Alex rubbing himself against Nelda's leg.

'What's happened to you?' Serious concern from her.

Dumbly aware, he said, 'I'm dying. I'm dead.'

'Alex, I can't talk with you on top of me.'

He slid his weight off her chest, prying her knees apart with his, clearing the hem of her dress out of his way, brushing her thigh, the solid, knowable, consistent physical reality of Nelda's flesh under his hands. But it wasn't safety he gripped onto, not welcome, pity or immunity, it was more resistance. She was a pile of warm sand under him, a bale of hay in his arms!

'Tell me when you're done,' she said. Alex lay his head on her stomach, he sagged there, washed ashore. Nelda touched his hair. 'It's just, you're pulling me down. I can't do this now, I'm in the middle of a lot, Alex. Work, plans. Things are happening. You have to hear this stuff, there's a bunch I've got to tell you.'

'And *I* can't process any more data. Really, Nelda, my head's going to explode if I try to cram one new concept into it.'

'Barook atah adonai elo-haynoo melick holum layolum vah-ed.'

'What?'

'My pronunciation is stupid. I don't know how the accent's supposed to sound yet.'

'Say it again. Slower.'

This time the words weren't so lumpy in her mouth and in answer to Alex's okay-what's-the-punchline expression she said, 'It's from the prayer you say when you bless the candles on Chanukah.'

'You don't really pronounce the *ch*.' Alex demonstrated the correct Hebrew sound, the authentic Temple Israel dry gargle recommended by two thousand years of dads and rabbis. 'Imagine you've got matzoh brei stuck in your throat.' He leaned over the side of the bed, came up waving the postcard from Heidi that Nelda had carried over in the week's batch of mail. 'Did you read this?'

'She's been leaving messages on my machine that use up the whole tape. Just as tacky. Whining about you and blabbing about all the hot video deals she's got going.' Heavy on the knee-slapping irony Nelda winked, 'She doesn't hate *me*. I think she wants me to give her a job at Wendywear.'

The front of the card was a black and white photograph of a small boy in a high-chair, in a raging tantrum, his tiny fists balled up over his head, food thrown everywhere. Three red strips cut across the picture bearing the slogan: Admit Nothing – Blame Everyone – Be Bitter. The back was unsigned and Heidi's personal message began without a greeting of any kind. She wrote: 'Maybe you can get a job as a door-to-door salesman. That's all your "talent" is good for. How does it feel now that you don't count for shit? You'll never make any money again. You're too sensitive for business.'

Nelda shook his shoulder as if to wake him up, anyway, to bring him back to the reality that mattered. Alex reached for her too, for her breasts and groping them he hauled himself back on top of her. 'I *miss* this.' It was the bedframe that wheezed and mewed out Nelda's complaint every time he rolled his hips into her. 'Visit with me,' his last surviving ambition, *visit with me* and dole out this one comfort, permit me to be in raw, infant need, to be granted just one hour of mercy in the hammering battle, to lie salvaged in your arms . . .

'Your *bed*, Alex! It's making too much *noise*.'

A useless argument but a proper consideration – damn! – just when he'd tricked himself into forgetting Mom and Dad were in the house, even that it was their house he was doing this in! Alex thudded onto the floor with her, rummaging under Nelda's dress, gripping her ass cheeks and yanking them down onto his tilting hips, rocking her with his hands, pulling her into his rhythm, but it was a granite boulder he was humping away at, a woman of stone, unmovable.

'Let me up,' he said to her.

'I don't know if I should.' Nelda kept a warning grip on his wrists. 'If this is the only way we can talk to each other.'

Settling his back against the bed, Alex explained himself. 'I'm not doing any work. I can't think. I've got cotton candy stuffed into my head. It's a new thing, y'know, it scares me that I don't have one single idea. What does it feel like to be doing work, your own work? I can't remember, it's all a weird blur. Did I actually get a million-dollar business going? Did I know how to get that up?'

'Why should you worry about Heidi's opinion? She has hysterics all the time, *she's* the baby in the high-chair. And all that junk she's saying to you? It's all about her, Alex, all her fears coming out.'

'Oh, she's hell on stilts,' he agreed lightly, 'but she's got a *real* deep understanding of the problem. Even if I could stop things moving around me so I could concentrate on one clear idea, work up the sexiest business plan in commercial history, Nell, I swear I don't know how I'd get through any investment meeting. I can't say the words anymore. It's torturing me to death.'

'There's plenty of money.'

'No.'

'People help people.'

'No. Thanks very much. It's very Christian but it's not what I need.'

'You need to get back into your apartment.'

'It's not down to where I live, not *where*; it's how. I don't make anything, I'm not worth anything. You can't get much more basic than that! Forget the power to produce, I don't have the power to be a *consumer*. I'm somewhere way down below the poverty line, one of the trivial people. One of the spectators. I *don't* count and I didn't need to hear it from Heidi.' Alex glanced around his messy boyhood room. 'Did you do this: wonder how you'd end up when you were big? When you were *thirty*? Well, this is how I ended up.'

'You haven't "ended up",' Nelda's brewing impatience forced her to her feet, drove her across the room to work off some of the strain by picking up an armload of Alex's scattered dirty clothes. 'It's like the flu, you get better. If you're healthy underneath it.'

'This is terminal. It's bubonic plague. It's brain cancer.' Alex stretched out on the floor in a comforting box of sunlight. From there he said, 'Nelda? You can stop folding those, they're going into the washer.'

Her mind was not on his laundry. 'This isn't where I'm going,' she said half to herself, but for Alex's instruction. 'It's the opposite for me. Everybody at Wendywear's really excited about what I want to do with the company. Finally I know this is my real direction, definitely. Definitely.' As if being crushed under the mournful weight of it she said, 'It's with you. Alex, don't we love each other? I want us to be together, but you have to choose it too. So, there's some stuff I have to tell you.'

'You don't have any obligation to me,' he said, braced and noble.

'I owe you the truth, so you can make up your mind about things. I wasn't all-the-way truthful about something before. I was protecting myself, probably.'

He sat up to listen to the rest. 'From what? Who?'

'From your disappointment?' she still wondered. 'I wrote a letter to Jim one night, when you were all in Sacramento.'

'I want to know,' catching his breath, 'what good you thought you were doing. What good thing?'

'I didn't say anything *against* anybody. Will you let me talk?'

'Holy shit. In November? He knew about us *in November*?'

'Will you let me say what I said?'

'Worse and worse.'

'It didn't start out as any midnight confession, it wasn't even a letter to him when I started it. My brain was so tangled up. Maybe it was like, God wanted me to witness how much of a difference I made in Jim's life by showing how much grief it'd cause if I was unfaithful to him and he knew about it.' Nelda talked right through Alex's pained moaning. 'Writing the words down made it a million times clearer.'

'Where were you when Uncle Jesus, your imaginary friend, was laying out all the big decisions in your life? Just say it, Nelda, for your own mental health, stop this dishonest crap concerning Him Above! You wanted what you wanted, with me, with Jim, just say that. Start there. Am I talking to you now or am I addressing God?'

'Me, you're talking to me. You're fighting *with me*.'

'What could I possibly win?' Quietly he said, giving her a chance, 'Tell me what you put in the letter.'

'I wanted him to see if he could remember how easy we were with each other before we got married. If he could remember that, then he'd know what was going on with me and you. How I care about what happens to you. Other stuff, not about us.' He didn't have to ask, she fished out an example. 'Like somebody has to make up a new category for me. I think I'm a Completed Christian. Or I ratted out on that too. I was just trying to explain my feelings to myself. It all came gushing out of me, answers that turned into questions when I wrote them down. When I read it over I realized what it was, it was a letter to Jim. So I left it in his trailer.'

'And then what did he say to you?'

'Nothing,' Nelda said in icy disbelief. 'Nothing then. Didn't matter to him, no big deal.' She folded a dangling strap of hair back behind her ear. 'After a couple of days I went out to the trailer but Jim wouldn't let me in. He called me over to the back window and said he was sorry, he couldn't talk to me, he was working.'

'Sure, partnerships don't break themselves.'

'Then he said, "All the big changes are out in the open." Honey, y'know he didn't care if I stayed with him or went. Nothing, *nothing* . . .'

She let the tears run, too bravely, and that stiff courage snapped pretty quickly. What on earth could bring harm to Alex after this? He felt weirdly peaceful, thrown somewhere beyond harm. If he was totally unprotected now that was all right – what was left of his old life to protect? This bare intimacy Nelda held out to him found Alex unresisting. He snatched some tissues out of the carton on the floor and offered them to her, saying, 'Maybe he didn't read it.'

'There's one more thing.' Nelda brushed her cheeks dry and blew her nose first, then she said, 'I'm pregnant.'

'Ooh. Hey, what?' Alex folded up against the wall as though he'd been shoved into it. 'But the precautions! Every time! Every time we did it we used those rubbers. Didn't we make sure? I used a condom every damn time!'

'They must've leaked, one of them.'

'Oh, something's on its way.' Alex wagged his finger at it, whatever it was. 'Something. What is it? Because I *want to know*. If I can understand why this is happening I can deal with it.'

'Alex.' She said his name with infinite gentleness.

He twisted away from her. 'Let me deal with it.' Only he was sniffing more brokenly than she was. The finger he brought back from under his nose carried a smear of blood.

'Tilt your head back. Alex, here.' She knelt next to him, reached to support the back of his head.

'No.'

'If you keep sitting that way – '

'No!'

' – it won't stop bleeding.'

Blood drooled thickly from both of Alex's nostrils and each time he wiped at it he smeared his face with streaks of fresh red war paint. '*Good*,' rasping at her, fat drops of spit, mucus and blood sprinkling onto his shirt, his pyjamas, the carpet. 'I don't want it to stop!'

13   The Raven also the Dove

THE abysmal disappearance of the Reverend provided Munro with the chance to claim a higher rank in the order of JT's life. Crisscrossing the city, running between people and places he'd visited before with JT, picking up suggestions of where in his dark tribulation JT might have gone, this wasn't an errand Munro was sent on because he could drive a car. Before Ma even made her appeal to him he'd come to the decision to launch a one-man search party. If not Munro, then who? Every lesson in human behavior he'd received from JT, every Christian passion he'd absorbed through their years together determined that he'd do this, mandated it, fortified Munro for the task of finding JT and coming through with whatever help this great soul needed.

Who else was left in JT's shrunken circle of intimates who felt the same fierce attachment and ruthless loyalty? Munro's city-wide search shamed Nelda in her snug new coldhearted independence, his daily crawl from freeway to freeway, ten stops before lunchtime then ten more spread over a hundred miles of surface streets, showed up Ma's nightly doleful pestering for what it was, a selfish terror of being left alone. Who else survived the shocks, who else remained among the scattered, surrendered, demoralized, retreating family and friends of the Worldview community who quickened to understand the Reverend's ailing spirit as if it were his own? This inner connection between them became a vivid thing, bare and undeniable, when Munro finally lit on the suspicion that JT's most likely refuge was the high desert shelter of Sutter Grange, the settlement for the homeless that he had forced into being, a place whose history, practical value and moral triumph still bore the stamp of his identity. Also, Sutter Grange was an easy twenty-minute drive from radio station KOSO.

In Munro's mind JT was hanging on to see who, if anybody, emerged from the confusion to find him and if they had the courage to stay by his side. Munro was out of his depth. He didn't mistrust his perceptions enough to understand JT's ailment and if he couldn't understand the source of that deranging agony then Munro was not going to be much help to him. Flawed and powerless as he was, Munro could help me; he'd be my harbinger.

The sole surprise I got walking into Munro's house for the first time in a week was that it had not been burgled. The lights were on, the windows and doors thrown open behind their screens, the mailbox was choked with bills, junk mail, trade circulars and sixteen personal letters. All of these dainty pink envelopes had been delivered by hand, they were all from Ma Tickell and every one of them conveyed roughly the same puzzled and rankled message. 'Jimmy one time went to go stay in Downey over at Pastor Lopez. Did you go and talk to Pas. Lopez yet?' 'If you are back home tonite Tues. please call me up 1st thing. Why don't you tell me where you are looking?' 'Three days since you called me. Please give me some news to hook on to.' 'That woman's name is Julie or Louise. I'd like it if you corrected her manners when you get there. She said (in nasty voice) it was against r. station policy to give out personal information to the public. To his own mother? Yes!'

Just a quarter of the reel had cranked through the secondary video remote before the battery died. Whatever ended up on there, I could be pretty sure, wasn't going to add much useful detail to the shape of things since Munro had been spending less time in his workshop than he had in his bed. Only lately, goaded by Ma into recovery from the paralyzing blow of abandonment, was Munro up and active, combing Los Angeles for the friend who had meaninglessly disowned everything that was his.

The earliest pictures on the tape showed the clapboard walls vibrating in the first few seconds of the January aftershock. The most recent activity was an hour of actual time clicked off in stop motion frames, preserved slices of last week arriving like old light from a distant star. Munro scuttled through the recording, packing his taxidermy tools into a suitcase, loading the suitcase into the trunk of his car. The last frames caught Ma in that vacated room the next day. 'Munro? Jimmy?' As though saying their names out loud would make the boys stop pretending that they weren't there. 'Jimmy?' Ma must have had some idea that Munro was hiding her son out in his garage.

Any pursuit of JT had to stop short of knocking on his trailer door.

On the radio the emphatic words he used were *I do know you*, he said he sat with me in the same room when Bobby prayed for his financial ruin. Was this what he knew or only feared? I'd poison his reply if in the spirit of man-to-man honesty I asked him point blank whether he remembered seeing me in Sacramento or anywhere else. So, without a fanfare of trumpets I parked my van, camped where he could see me, another aging transient, and tried to be quietly conspicuous.

In the two and a half years since its founding, Sutter Grange had doubled in size and quadrupled its population. The twenty-four-month trial maintenance grant from the state was replaced (and increased) by a private endowment subscribed through the Academy of Motion Picture Arts and Sciences whose sentimental and effective strategists occasionally bussed actors and food parcels out to the site and bussed a few of the semi-homeless into Century City as guests of honor at charity premieres.

The compound rambled outward in every direction from its hub of homeless pods, those 'plastic shoeboxes' that gave Bobby such a sharp pain. Tents, shacks, the shantytown rooted itself in rougher acres of the scrubby desert, an overspill of gaggling children, forbearing parents and squabbling neighbors, all staking out liberties, prohibitions and property. Fittingly or wishfully, the place struck me as a Biblical settlement, the ideal locale for a fugitive patriarch.

JT had hauled his Airstream to a back corner of the camp where the sprawl thinned out and before Munro arrived JT was only seen outside of it once a week. After that no one saw him outside at all, the chores of filling the trailer's water tank, buying groceries and delivering to the back door of KOSO the tape of his daily broadcast now reliably carried out by his dedicated custodian. Munro also raised money when they needed it by driving to a dealer in Antelope Valley and selling off one or two rarities from JT's coin collection. While he was in town he scrounged work from veterinary clinics, picking up the odd toucan, pug or Siamese cat to immortalize for its heartbroken owner.

Without the help of any bug I heard JT welcome Munro back from shopping by hollering at him, 'What the damn hell are *you* doing here?' 'Where should I be?' Loaded down like a pack mule with groceries, Munro thought there was some other crucial errand he'd forgotten to run. As quickly as fire sears a struck match an enraging idea seized JT. 'Ratman! Ratman!' The crude force of the insult pushed Munro back and held him there while JT went on laying into him. 'Very convenient how we run out of food at the same time on the same day every week!' From there JT warned him that he knew all about the secret meetings Munro was having with the Governor and Oswald Pogenpohl. Two brown bags full of frozen TV dinners, toilet paper and candy bars were no protection against this. 'No, Reverend.' 'Then where else would you get the dose of Sodium Pentothal you injected into my Salisbury steak?' 'No, Reverend.' 'I'm not eating your food anymore. I won't eat your cooking. I can cook my own meat.'

And there it rested, or dissipated, until the next time the crosscurrents in him merged strangely and stirred JT into another fit of convoluted accusations. Stealing his clothes and soaking them in formaldehyde, that was what Munro was doing when he pretended to take them to the laundromat: 'It's working, Munro! It's working on me!' JT tore open his shirt to show Munro the claw marks across his chest and stomach and thighs. 'My skin itches all over! I'm scratching myself to ribbons! Happy, Munro? Why don't you look happy?' No more bizarre than the accusations that came before or after, I remember this one because it was the first time JT lashed out physically. He shoved Munro through the screen door, which sheared off its hinges, and he kicked him across the ground, pinned Munro against the rear wheel of the Jag and warned him, 'Shut up! Shut up! You're drowning out every voice I think with!' Neither of them mentioned or questioned these volcanic outbursts, Munro because they awed him, JT because he couldn't remember them.

One other strange new habit began around this time, more conscious and rational. While each broadcast went out on KOSO, JT stood in the open door of his trailer, grimly exhausted and shamelessly naked, arms lifted in a gesture both of benediction and surrender, and with the radio blaring out that week's message behind him he moved his mouth along with his recorded words. When I concentrated on what Jim Tickell wanted to say, and *said*, his display lost its profanity and circus act recklessness. To my mind it was a manifestation of something besides mental fragility, it obeyed his arrogant logic and described a buried sense and order which felt exactly like life to me.

The Reverend's full-frontal pastoral style whipped up less excitement around Sutter Grange than his inspirational agitating provoked at large. Many of the letters sent to him at the station came from Worldview holdouts arguing and pleading with JT to 'return in high vict'ry'. He answered them personally, on the air, elaborating obscure points of his disturbed and disturbing reinterpretation of God's Word. Disjointed howlings, traumatized insights, subversive revelations came spilling out of him, interlaced with gut-level insults and serpentine accusations against Oswald Pogenpohl, Bobby Dyson and Nelda, self-exoneration and glossolalia, at the same time every day and four times on the weekend:

March 18

Virginity *is not* a superior spiritual condition. It *does not* float you closer to God. Virginity is a disability that you can overcome and you ought to go out and overcome it as quick as you can. We shall overcome. Thirteen years old is a good age for it, a Biblical age. It's your inoculation against spiritual syphilis, because if you believe Jesus was the fruit of a virgin birth, well that's it, you're infected. Matthew doesn't agree with Luke. Mark and John don't bring up the dumb idea at all. It's the ones with sex phobias who want you to believe it. They see you believe, then they're all right . . . God's Word got physical, it became *flesh*, that's where God reaches in . . . He reaches inside my body, grabs a handful and *wrenches it* . . . Your body remembers what your mind forgets, Mrs Clodd. They trained rats to run a maze. They killed the rats and they fed the dead rats' brains to baby rats. When the rat babies grew up nobody had to teach them how to get around that maze, they already knew, they ate the memory in those dead brains.

March 23

The gift you got direct from God is the miracle of doubt. Without your doubt it's impossible to please God. Doubt is a tougher faith to hang on to, *doubt* overcometh the world. To think soberly according as God hath dealt to every man the measure of *doubt*. And fulfil all the good pleasure of His goodness and the work of *doubt* with power. It's the power behind the power of worldly change. Everything else is a rumor. Mr Barsumian, worldly change is God's faith in *us*.

April 7

Wake up, wake up. We're all copulating in a death camp. Accidents are part of the plan. Accidents are the whole *point* of the plan. Think of a flea on the face of a clock. Does he care what time it is? This economic recession is good for you, Ditmar Haggit! Ditmar wrote a note and asked me would I pray for him to get his job back. *Let it ruin you all the way*! Thank God for everything you've lost. You've been set free from the coagulation of consumer trash that's been standing between you and everlasting happiness . . . My life's stripped down to the bone, Ditmar, below the bone, and my troubles melt like lemon drops.

April 11

Expose your nerves! That's the commandment of the commandments . . . Take off all your clothes and eat tropical fruit! Feel the world on your skin! . . . Jesus walked in the garden with his disciples, he was there with James, Bartholomew . . . uh . . . Simon, Thomas, James . . . oh, uh, Sleepy, Sneezy, Dopey, Grumpy and Bashful. After the Last Supper. He told them, 'I would eat and be eaten.' Strip down to your bare flesh. Then strip your flesh away . . . before you're gathered and God does it for you.

Marshmallow soft consolation was never the service that JT's audience wanted him to provide and it wasn't what he expected from them, either. Consistently, with passionate insolence, he danced out of conflict and into collision, and when his daily prodding roughened into abuse he gave American Christians permission to turn vicious.

Munro salvaged all of the letters to JT that wound up trampled into the litter on the trailer floor. He dug around for their envelopes, folded the letters back inside and hoarded them in the car trunk, even the vilest ones. 'I would let the Lord deal with you as He knows how,' someone wrote anonymously from Canoga Park. 'I am praying every nite for a miracle hand grenade to explode up your anus.' Another, anonymously, 'It will delight Jesus to watch me sever your head off your neck. Because you drag my dear Lord's heavenly name down into the filthy mud of your opinions He will laugh and rejoice when I drag your limbs and torso in the streets by my car.' Another, 'I will personally hang your corpse upside-down on the KOSO neon sign. A good punishment for turning people against the true loving God.' Another, 'You are a truly amazing but nauseating excuse for a pastor. I would like to be there when you die so I can hear the pathetic account of your life you will have to give to Jesus Christ, your Creator and judge, who by the way happens to be a model Christian himself. You are a flea not a man. Are you prepared for the coming hour?'

14   The Talking Cure

THE men's shower block on the site occupied an unpainted concrete bunker, tiled and troughed inside without partitions, a humid barn that wore its functional, communal maleness unsubtly, inside and out. Women avoided the general area, sensibly cautious and, deliberately or not, as a recommendation to the men that they police themselves likewise around the women's showers. But it was there at the L-shaped wall that screened off the entrance that a woman ran up to me with a bouquet of advice.

'The girls and me don't mind your shows,' she said, a blush seeping under her waxy cheeks. 'But you better be careful of wild boyfriends on the rampage.'

She bounced at me as jumpy as a teenager, bounced from her ankles up, as if her feet were stuck in the hot asphalt. Small and thin, stunted, I thought, until I squeezed the glare of the sky out of my eyes and saw the hairline fissures stressed into the corners of her mouth and across her forehead. Three or four decades of wear, of over-use. 'Oh yes?' I said on the move. She stopped me with a daring smile, a brave assumption that I'd want to ask her who she was and who 'the girls' might be.

'Are you gonna be on TV again? You could do the same thing with no hassle on one of them late-night channels.'

She also assumed, probably because my hair and beard had grown out and I'd walked shirtless from the opposite end of the camp, that she was talking to Jim Tickell. 'Boyfriends don't have to worry about me. Or you girls, either.'

'We don't get worried by a naked man,' bouncing again as if the idea of seeing me without my clothes on jolted the springs in her legs. 'You ought to come outside next time instead of just standing there.'

'Not if I want to avoid those rampaging boyfriends of yours.'

'I'd protect you,' she said fearlessly. 'I'd shield you with my body.'

Leaning over her a little bit to make a joke of my height, I said, 'There'd have to be two of you for that.'

'I could bring a friend.'

'And who'd protect me from both of you?'

'Never know how things'll happen out, isn't that the fun of life?' I pried myself loose with a smile less daring than hers. She tugged on the corner of the towel I'd slung around my neck, she had something else to tell me. 'I think there's something wrong with your friend.'

'My friend?'

'Isn't he your friend? That funny little man who sleeps in his car?'

'The car. Not the blue van.'

'In the green Jag. You should go see what's wrong with him.'

I'd slipped into my impersonation of JT, his voice now, almost without being conscious of it as a deception. 'What should I look for? Where is he now?'

She sometimes saw Munro parked on the gravel brink that lay between Sutter's south fence and the boulevard of motels, gas stations and fast food franchises that ushered traffic past us into towns that weren't much more than outskirts themselves. I don't know when his hour-long, two-hour-long, crying bouts started. He'd sit behind the wheel and stare out over the dashboard and cry furiously, helplessly, suffocating under the thickening sediment of incomprehension that was separating him from JT. So it was a good thing, good for Munro, that he wasn't back from his round of errands when the crisis hit. He would have been another casualty.

It wasn't strange to see, far off in the trackless desert, the dust plumes of cars and pickup trucks rodeoing back and forth. At night pairs of headlight beams slashed through the chalky, gritty clouds of sand and dust kicked up by bullfighter skids and figure-eights. Beery rowdiness, local high schoolers showing off for each other, nothing more terrifying than semi-drunk Rebel yells from them as they looped down toward Sutter Grange on their way to the main road.

The Chevy cut its lights and its speed when it was close enough to be heard and seen, then pulled up, engine idling, just a car length away from JT's trailer. A man, not a teenage joy rider (his bald head coated in the shine of the mosquito lamp), politely called JT's name through the open door. He listened for a second, ducked his head inside and shouted as if over some noise, 'Got a present for you here, Reverend.'

The flash and flicker I saw, obscured by the door and the man's contorted posture, flew out of his hand before I knew what it was. The fuse burned long enough for him to walk back to his car and clear out of the way.

The space inside the Airstream ignited, glowed, huffed like a gas oven. Yellow light fought out of every window, roars and fists of heat cracked the glass panes. Smoke funneled out of holes torn in the trailer's metal sides, a gasp of orange-red flame broke through the middle of the roof. Aluminum strips bent from the blown-out window frames dangled, twisted and fell, flaming with rivulets of liquefied plastic, dripping lava down the trailer walls that pooled, still burning on the ground. From the floor under the kitchen, another explosion, a geyser of fire deflected by the rear axle wrapped itself around the outside wall, one of the propane tanks going up. The tires on the Jeep were burning, leaves of fire slapped at the chassis, feeling for a way into the gas tank. In the throat of the blaze coring the trailer room by room, wooden cabinets caved in, furniture toppled and burned, infant fires caught in the widening mouth of the furnace.

Against this berserk wreckage I stood unprotected, breathing the smoke-thickened, heat-thickened air; against the nauseating cruelty and perversion and fanaticism of this attack, against JT's murder, I was still alive. There was no time left at all for me to tell him who I'd been in his life and how he figured into mine, here was the next change to absorb. When the climate changes something is always prey to the weather, stupefied by the coldness of night, the dryness of the air, by new conditions that have slowly become precarious, changes of slow violence that land with sudden impact. These live, these are killed off. Any place belongs to the ones who can tolerate the deadly temperature, who move through the rift to find a margin to fill, the strong ones. Watching the others die makes the rest of us, gibbering in the background, greedier for life.

The shape standing against the bright doorway seemed to be a gust of smoke, smoke that hovered and blurred into human form. Headless, armless, it walked solidly out of the disaster in the direction of simple survival. JT's fingers were scorched and his legs below the knees were barnacled with blisters. The rest of him was hooded in his sopping wet bathrobe, its collar clutched over his head. The hem and sleeve edges smoldered, small flames guttered in dry patches on his back and I patted them out. He was naked except for the robe. He let it drop onto his shoulders. Smaller blisters flecked his face and neck like acne, his eyebrows were burned away, his beard was singed to ash-black stubble on half of his face, his hairline burnt back the same way, the border of a brush fire traced along his forehead. Supporting himself with a grip on my shoulder he said, 'I was in the shower,' then his legs twisted under him and he collapsed in the dirt.

When he revived only a few minutes later, he was still in my arms, both of us sheltered on the ground behind my van. 'Safe,' I said, 'you're safe,' propping up his shoulders, letting him settle against me.

'What music is that?'

'Jim, can you say where you are?'

'Right now?' JT looked but couldn't see around the front bumper. 'Music woke me up.' He stretched up again and saw the burning metal casings that used to be his Jeep and trailer. 'Did you do that?'

'I don't know who did it.'

'It didn't happen by accident, it wasn't somebody's *mistake*.'

'No. You're right about that.'

'I know people who'd jump for joy if I was out of the picture.' He let the statement weigh on me, watching my face closely, intimately. 'Here's a secret: You can push God too far. I guess He wants to gather me up to tell me to my face what a dumbass I am.'

JT's shivering calmed a little when I got my sleeping bag wrapped around him. 'Let me take you to a doctor.'

'Wait on it. Let me tell you, I know something. I know how they found me and who hired them,' he whispered at me. 'Governor Robert Patrick Dyson. He wants me to give a shit.'

Out of the physical shock rang the emotional shock but it wasn't Dyson at the core of JT's solitary pain. To keep himself battling he needed an enemy as large as a governor, but something bigger than that finally moved against him, God turned against him. At least I could try to relieve some part of that piercing heartbreak.

'Jim. Jim? Do you think you've seen me before? Not only around Sutter, I mean anywhere before.' He said nothing, too smart to be tricked into self-incrimination. 'The things that Bobby Dyson knew about you,' I said, 'he knew because I told him. I did. Do you understand what I'm saying to you?'

His expression slackened as he read my face. He knew me but he said he didn't. Then, 'What things do you think you know about?'

'Personal things.'

'Liar.'

'I've been inside your house. More than once. And Hummingbird Farm. Into Munro's house and your mother's. I monitored your phone calls and recorded your meetings. I filmed you and Nelda, you and your father, you and Alex Berry, I even have a reel of you and Marty Olansky. I was a guest at your wedding and at Oswald Pogenpohl's Hawaiian barbecue, remember it? Where you met Howard Porta. I have tapes of you driving around in your car.'

'Cockroaches get in everywhere, too.' JT took a breath and concentrated his strength in his voice, squaring up to me. 'You're just plain ubiquitous. Did you look at Nelda in the bathroom? Watch her on the potty, didja?' The thought tweaked a laugh out of him.

'I need to be honest with you. That's what time it is. Sincerity for sincerity,' I offered him. 'I heard you say that you knew I was there, at your meeting with Bobby in Sacramento. Did you see me in the room with you? Do you recognize me, Jimmy?'

A fresh spasm of shivers tensed his face but he didn't take his eyes off of me. He tried two times to speak, swallowing the few words he wanted to say. On the third try they came out in a slurred string. 'I noticed . . . when you weren't there.'

'They're only *men* who hate you. Little men. Not me. What do you think these pygmies understand? Bobby Dyson, Oswald Pogenpohl — they *imagine*, they don't *know*. To them it's the same thing. Out of all of them, here I am. I'm the one who knows why you did what you did. I watched you and listened and I understood.'

'Can't make . . . my . . . tongue work,' not only slurred but his voice slumped into a dying monotone. 'Are you . . . doing it . . . to me?'

I needed to ask two men at the front of the elbowing crowd to help me lift JT onto the army cot in the back of my van. As I spread the sleeping bag over him JT looked around at my receivers, tape reels, boxes of parts, rolls of cable, the silent and disconnected arrangement of electronics and he covered his face with his hands. 'You saw me . . . as low as a man can sink . . . Cold . . . Cold . . .'

15 My Better Angels

IN the unpitying brightness of the emergency room entrance, as the orderlies transfered JT from the army cot to a gurney, I saw that the injuries inflicted on him that night didn't end with victimization, shock, bruises and third-degree burns. The right side of his face drooped as if softened in the heat of the fire, his mouth tugged down on that side, beneath the smear of ash and dried blood where his eyebrow used to grow his eyelids sagged dully, laps of skin around a watery, inflamed wound.

I'm sure that the nurse at the admissions desk heard me the first time I gave her JT's name and our saying it back and forth to each other had less to do with correct admittance procedure than it did with certifying the strange luck that carried a celebrity into the hospital on her shift. I identified myself as the Reverend's close associate, more than plausible (and virtually true), since I was able to give her Gunter Thorsen's home phone number and in a matter of minutes Gunter provided her with the details of JT's medical insurance. Correct procedure seemed set to bar me from staying with JT in the examination room but his celebrity, combined with his obvious struggle to speak clearly, opened that door without a fight. In his croaking half-palsied voice he settled any question about being handed over like a pizza delivery. 'He . . . goes . . . *everywhere* . . . with me.'

On the walk down the main corridor, talkative with us now, Nurse Wade invited me to thank my own lucky stars for the mercy that brought us in while Dr Candler 'himself' was attending. Roger Candler's medical services corporation equipped and staffed emergency rooms in an archipelago of hospitals strung across Southern California and as a quality control check he'd work a half-shift in a different one of his ERs every few days. Since there were thirty-odd of these E-Med units, Candler was only out here for five hours every three months.

Very little in his appearance or general attitude seemed designed for comfort, his or anyone else's. It was a deliberate impression of sure-footed, battle-hardened experience, meant to rally his patient's emotional reserves. He stepped around me without a word and said nothing to the nurse until he'd finished examining JT's cleaned cuts, scrapes and burns. When he sat himself down on a low, wheeled stool behind the examination table where JT lay naked, Candler's round white shaved head made me think of the moon setting on a horizon of scarred desert ridges. 'You can finish dressing these burns, Dorie. Order an IV for him.' And half to her, half to JT he said, 'Let's give this man the Presidential Suite tonight.'

Straddling the stool, legs kicking, he scooted around for a closer look at JT's punished, paralyzed face. I saw a little of the under-appreciated performer in the flourish of care and attention, clinical detachment hustled out of the way by a showy frankness. 'We'd like to keep you with us for a week,' Candler put to JT. 'We can manage some of that pain for you and treat those burns on your legs.'

'Got . . . firebombed,' JT filed his complaint.

Candler stopped what he was doing, what he heard amazed him. 'Is that right?' He swiveled around to ask me, 'Is that right?'

I said, 'A propane tank blew up under his trailer.'

'If that rotten stuff is starting up again, well . . . ' Twice as concerned now he returned to JT, saying, 'Nobody wanted LA street people dumped in their backyard. Charity's a dead concept. They'll contribute their pennies or dollars, but nobody wants to bring it home.' He sympathized, 'You're always getting into the toughest causes, I think that's terrific. Have you been doing a sort of Mother Teresa thing out at Sutter?'

JT didn't answer him, I did. 'More like Robinson Crusoe.'

Medical treatment embarrassed JT, it reduced him, diminished him to an undeniable condition of animal need. Underneath the wreckage of torn and blistered skin, behind the face that was dripping from its bones, he was still intact, not sinking, not sunk, reluctant to stray into despair, desperate not to submit.

A soft click, the hum of an electric motor, the upper part of JT's bed elevated his back and now he was sitting up, in a kingly posture. Standing next to him, lord chamberlain as car mechanic, Dr Candler said, 'Let's see what we've got.'

Could JT touch his finger to his nose? With effort stiffened by the burns on the backs of his hands, yes he could. Could he follow Candler's finger with his eyes as he drew it along a short line, forward and back across JT's field of vision? With his left eye, yes he could. 'Do you get headaches very often?'

'Wrong question,' JT said. 'Ask me . . . when I don't.'

'And which side do you usually get them on? Can you remember?'

A transcendental gaze unfocused JT's eyes as he searched the ceiling, trying to get a grip on a wispy idea. 'Jim,' I said, 'tell him which side you get those headaches on.'

Candler touched JT's arm to call him back. 'Do you think you hear voices sometimes?' We waited long, empty seconds for an answer from him. 'What I mean is, are they ordinary headaches or do you get strange sounds or smells with them? Do you ever see or hear things that aren't really there?'

Wincing at the pain that strummed through him with his hacking laugh, wincing and laughing at the idiotic question, JT said, 'How do I know if they're . . . really there or not?'

In the corridor outside of the examination room Candler asked me whether I was in a position to give him 'a snapshot' of JT's medical history. His main concern was the partial paralysis, he said, and since I worked so closely with the Reverend I might have noticed if its onset had been gradual or sudden.

'He looked all right to me this time yesterday,' I said.

Carefully, ironically aware of what he assumed was my sensitivity in this area, he asked again about any aberrations or hallucinations that JT could be suffering, say, of a religious nature. The only honest reply to give him was that JT was a religious man. 'It's not an easy thing to tag a mental disorder as a symptom when nine-tenths of the normal, healthy population believes the same kinds of things,' Candler said. 'I'm not a psychiatrist or a philosopher, I know I'm wandering out of my territory, but if Mr Tickell talks to you about riding around the galaxy in a flying saucer or about his best friend who's a seven-foot-tall invisible rabbit then I'd get a sense of how things stand. But bring Jesus Christ, Jehovah or Allah into it and a patient might have some trouble accepting there's something wrong with them which requires treatment.'

'Hallucinations aren't part of the problem,' I said. 'Not as far as I can tell.'

'Exaggerated fears, any of that? Anything a reasonable person might possibly describe as paranoid fantasies?'

'Doctor, out of everyone I know, Reverend Tickell has got the best reasons to think the way he thinks. As a matter of fact, any fears that *would be* paranoid fantasies in anybody else, I'd say in Jim are inspired guesses.'

Reaching to open the door back into the room where we'd left JT, Dr Candler said, 'I'd like to schedule a CAT scan and MRI for him at Cedars-Sinai. We'll take some pictures of his brain and see where we go from there. Does he have family you'd like me to talk to?'

'What kind of shape is he in?'

Candler let go of the doorknob, considered my question. 'Walking is going to be a problem for three or four weeks. Half of that time he'll be in a wheelchair, then on crutches. If his house is full of stairs you might want to fix up whatever he needs in one room.'

'The house went to his ex-wife. He won't be going there. I thought I'd find a hotel suite for him.'

This plan triggered something in Candler's thinking. Helpful, gracious, he excused himself, signaling with spread fingers the five minutes he'd be gone. 'Let me make a call.'

The one-man struggle bowling toward me from the opposite end of the corridor was Munro, loudly failing to keep his emotions under control. Feverish worry made him look smaller, thinner, and with his mushroom-colored skin and sweat-darkened hair slicked in various directions against his scalp he looked even more the victim of hectic disorientation you see on the face of an adolescent boy.

'Is this the right room?' he asked me, breathing hard, pushing inside. The sight he had of his friend bandaged and sedated robbed Munro of his voice. He flicked at the tears in the corners of his eyes and finally said to JT, 'I got him to go up two hundred on that double eagle, Reverend. He was only gonna give me twenty-eight hundred but I got three thousand out of him, how about that.'

JT was out of reach, in a dead sleep. 'Munro?' I said. 'Did you call Ma?'

'What's that?'

'I know his mother's been waiting for a phone call from you. She ought to know about this, don't you think? You don't want to have to drag her all the way out here.' I told him, calmingly, that I was the one who took JT to the hospital and in the same tone I said, 'Tell her you'll bring Jim back in about a week, she doesn't have to call out the bloodhounds.'

Munro might have thought first of all that this sensitive personal information could have leaked to me in the shock and aftermath of the

285

attack, on the drive to the hospital in his pain and delirium JT might have babbled to me about Ma, but Munro came up with a less neighborly explanation for my presence there and at Sutter. With solemn contempt he said, 'Why don't you do it. Call her up on your hotline.'

'I think she should hear it from you, Munro.'

Mouth chewing air before the words came, he challenged me, 'Where were all you Worldview uppity-ups when the Reverend was hurting! You just ducked under your desks or something, you just hid in the middle of all our trouble! Crawling out now, though, when it's safe to come out, man. That's fine, that's real sick . . .'

If Dr Candler hadn't come in with the orderlies then I think Munro would have thrown a punch at me. 'You can pick up his prescription any time after nine tomorrow morning, Mr Ketchum. It's pain killers and antibiotics. He'll need them while he's convalescing.'

As the two attendants lifted JT onto a gurney, Munro presented himself to the doctor. 'Where are you taking him?'

I introduced Munro as another close associate. Candler shook his hand and then ignored him. On the second sheet of paper Candler handed to me he'd written down an address and telephone number. 'It's a two-bedroom house near the ocean, he'll be able to get around it with no problem and it's vacant until July 1st. All I have to do is tell my real estate guy to leave the keys out and you can get the place warmed up and ready. You'll have to bring your own sheets and towels, but the kitchen's got everything.' Still selling the idea, he said, 'You can settle Mr Tickell in after I schedule those tests for him at Cedars.'

One eye on JT as he was trundled away and one eye on me, Munro said to Candler, 'Talk to me about it. I'm taking care of the man. When he's out of here Reverend's going with me.'

'Where, Munro?' I said reasonably, 'His trailer's all burned to hell, he won't go back to Nelda's, Ma can't nurse him and he's not going to live in the back seat of your car, is he?'

16   The Invisible Hand Returns

JUST a few hours before he heard from Ma that his father was lying dead in the bathroom, JT said to Munro, 'Every time there's a disturbance, something shakes loose that uncovers what's been lying underneath there all the time.' Revelation unfolded in stages. This wasn't an abstract lesson to Munro – it described his entire history with JT – but the barrage of events lately over-stimulated him. To the veering changes that re-routed JT's life and upturned his own, Munro's reaction was vertigo and his response was prayer.

He prayed more often and grimmer with longing these days than he did when he was a little boy. In a voice that his mother would remember, Munro prayed for Jesus to guide his thoughts and feelings (not even these seemed to belong to him anymore), and to 'heal and beautify' every corruption of Christian health. He prayed for JT's relief and comeback, and through JT's recovery, his own.

The CAT scan revealed a half-dollar sized shadow, the MRI slices showed the brutal mass of the tumor colonizing its dark sphere of influence on the left underside of JT's brain. Dr Hoodbhoy, the Cedars-Sinai neurosurgeon whose consultation Roger Candler had arranged (giving me the guarantee that he was putting JT 'in the hands of a certified genius'), was a fine-boned Indian who reassured his patients with a quiet formality carried over from his term as a senior medical diplomat with the World Health Organization. As he described the shape and burden of the growth, poetically I thought, as a baby's fist pushing up past the brain stem, I could imagine him explaining the hazards of incest to some remote mountain clan with the same delicate directness and wryly humane objectivity.

It wasn't to JT or to me that the doctor had to repeat in detail the steps of the ten-hour surgical procedure he was proposing. Munro's knowledge of anatomy kept Hoodbhoy amiably answering questions that clarified the picture of JT's physical condition only for him. 'I think I get it,' JT said, nodding slowly when the two professionals stopped talking. 'I'm growing a crystal in my head.' That night Munro prayed for God to put everything back the way it was before – before the tumor, before the firebombing, before Hummingbird Farm, before Mister died, before JT married Nelda, ' . . . back when everything used to be a perfect paradise for us.'

In the new garage attached to their new house by the beach Munro reproduced his old taxidermy workshop. He built a long workbench against the back wall with his tool rack on the right and shelves and trays on the left. Small bundles of lumber, coils of wire, cartons of excelsior, sacks of plaster, tubs of latex, from scratch and from memory he remade the clutter of his North Hollywood nest. To an outsider the place had the atmosphere of a museum exhibit, a flawless mock-up – right down to the flaws – of some historic location, the room where a final night was spent or where a kidnapped heiress was once hidden. For Munro, sealed off there in his atelier most of the time, it was a private zone where the specialized objects derived their use and value from his skill, where he was as necessary and relevant to them as they were to him and, dog by dog, iguana by iguana, he had a tangible effect on things.

'Munro wants to poison me,' JT complained on the phone to his mother. 'He said he wanted to make dinner last night. And what he fixed for me was a scrambled egg, succotash and a square piece of cheese.' Ma told him that the menu was her suggestion, food that was easy for JT to chew. 'From now on,' he said, with Munro standing behind him, 'the kitchen's off-limits to him. Except to eat in.'

They ate dinner together at the rustic oak table, always some kind of red meat, grilled, fried, baked or barbecued, 'To build up my blood,' went JT's logic, but on the surface there were all the signs of a logicless craving. At every meal, busy with some other kitchen chore – grinding carrot stumps in the waste disposal, adding fresh charcoal to the barbecue – he asked Munro to cut his pork chop or steak into pieces for him. 'Not too small to where I can't taste it.'

'If I cut it up any bigger than that, you'll have to chew every bite for an hour.'

From the other end of the room JT directed, 'Use a sharp knife. You're not using the right knife.'

'It's the knife you told me.'

'That one's for the salad, it's the salad knife.' JT gave him a new knife that looked identical to the one Munro was holding in his hand. 'If you cut it too small it gets cold,' supervising over Munro's shoulder. 'And then I can't taste it.' The cranky squabbles erupting between them out of thin air were the noise of a married couple tied to each other by routines of incomprehension and neglect going back decades.

Before Dr Hoodbhoy came back to him with the results of the biopsy, JT's acceptance of his illness hinged on his intuition of it. It was an invasion that he and God were going to beat, even if it was also true that God Himself prescribed it as the next in the long line of personalized challenges. Jim's claim on a future was just as fierce as ever. Over a delicatessen lunch which Nelda repacked in a picnic basket and brought out to the beach, she added her own ringside cheer. 'You *have* to get back on TV, I mean it. Every other minister or whatnot who's on looks like they should be hosting Wheel of Fortune, and they talk like it's a game show, too.' Head up, jaw shoved out *à la* Benito Mussolini, he said, 'As soon as I get my old face back again.' Then he turned to show off his profile, the loose skin, the sagging eye, the collapsed mouth, 'My good side. You think they're ready for this?'

At the end of a tiring day spent with Munro reconnoitering convalescent homes, Ma seriously joked with her sixty-four-year-old son that they should move in together if they run across a place with connecting rooms. JT's view of his post-operative world remained set in the beach house with the addition of 'one or two pretty French nurses' who would make sure he did his exercises every day, 'chasing me around the furniture'.

None of these likely or unlikely possibilities, seriously or casually included Munro. 'Am I doing any good being here?' He said what was to him the unsayable before a spat about puny lamb chops blew into a brawl. 'Or do you want me to just leave you by yourself?' It wasn't a choice, it was a pang. Hard silence from JT. And more silence. 'Because if you want me to go on and get out of here, just say so.' Silence again. 'I want to stay, Reverend, I want to put myself second. You're not a hundred per cent like yourself right now, with being sick, so when you hop up and yell at me it doesn't count. I'm second to you and that's that, it's good, God said for it to be that way.' No reply. Munro's voice, breaking, 'You know me, right? I just care so much about how you are, I don't want you to worry. If you don't worry then I don't. They could come in and take everything of mine away right now. If you were still here and I was too, then I wouldn't let you down. I can lift a ton. I can love, you know, *so much*, that's how I feel about it. You lifted me up and now it's you're the one who's got to be in the hospital, it's all reversed around like it was planned out that way. Don't you think it was? I don't want to go anywhere else, Reverend, I want to stay with it.'

Silence wasn't only a shield put up against the claws of Munro's self-sacrifice, it was the space JT needed to clear around himself, the separation that allowed him to tackle the malignancy that was killing him. Munro was wrong about the tumor and its developing complications leaving JT less than one hundred per cent himself. In fact, I thought then, the opposite was true. The confirmation of the biopsy report freed him from having to waste any more of his own energy on the grind of physical survival. This cancer, like the earthquake that pulverized Hummingbird Farm, seemed to arrive with the clear intention of reminding him that the world he monogrammed was unsafe and shrinking, shrunken now to just inside the limits of his body and he was being squeezed out of there, too.

For a few weeks JT rode as a passenger on the therapies staged by Dr Hoodbhoy. These amounted to methods of slowing down some of the physical deterioration and deadening the pain that tunneled through him like a colony of fire ants. *Show Yourself, come on, come all the way in*, his invitation to God when the next piece of him stopped working – his right leg, his bladder, *and what now*? That was his real genius, locating God where God held Himself, just outside the far rim of what JT could imagine. He stopped bathing and wouldn't put on his clothes, countermoves to the robbery of his bodily functions. His leg was numb? He'd drag it around. His bladder leaked? He'd carry an empty milk carton. He answered back with any control he still had the strength to assert.

I watched him pace the rooms in thoughtful laps, bedroom to bathroom to kitchen to living-room and back again, Jim traipsed the route like a sightless man memorizing the floorplan. In his silence I could almost hear the crackle of circulating mental energy, his mind running hot in spite of the dampening effect of opiates and interferon. Then, as though he'd hacked it to the end of a cross-country trek, he sat himself on the bench at the kitchen table, winded, recovering, and he started to write. He wrote pages of notes, random fragments of six decades spread out for God to illuminate with connection and coherence; he began to set down his autobiography.

June 3, 1927. My new body. Welcomed. Their boy. Daddy takes a picture of me with his box camera. I am one or two months old, on a plaid blanket, naked in the backyard of the Iowa house. My fat legs and my little pecker. Perfect fingers, perfect toes, round little belly. My appetite (Ma testifies) so big she thinks I might have two stomachs or a hole in the one I've got. Stomach perfect.

After school, 1936 (?) I hide behind a whitewashed fence with my best friend John D. Sloan. We're stringing up a line of about thirty firecrackers, we want to see if we can make it sound like the fence was getting ripped up by machine-gun fire. While J. is hammering in the row of nails I light a match and set fire to the back of his hair. A few of the loose ones on top shrivel down to his scalp. 'I could've died!' he screams at me. 'My whole head could've lit on fire!' I tried to calm him down and deny my responsibility. 'Only it didn't,' I said.

The snow. Purple light in the square window of my bedroom. Lying on the floor with Patricia. 194–? She's got blue wool sailor's trousers on, thirteen buttons. She treats me like a fellow who knows what he's doing but she's the one who knows. I wiggle my way in. Fornication as sweet and wholesome as cornbread. The front door opens downstairs. My heart doesn't slow down, it's pounding while P. fumbles with those buttons. What scares me more is Ma finding out I've got my pet rat Ozbo in my dresser drawer (brought him in from his cage out back because of the freezing temperature). Fornication and obligation are on my mind that night. I think it's possible to do what I did with P.J. with every other woman alive.

On New Year's Day in 1932. I'm walking on the bright sidewalk with Ma. Skins of ice on puddles in the gutter. 'It's the day when the number of the year changes,' she teaches me. 'It changed from 1931 to 1932 last night.' I ask her, 'Is it going to be 1933 tomorrow?' She ties a dark red scarf around my neck and tucks it into my sweater. 'Snug as a bug.' I untie it and say the first words that pop into my head. 'God is the weather!' I don't know how I thought of that idea but as soon as I said it I felt the cold reaching in through my clothes.

*With Daddy in Cedar Rapids. Two hours before check-in at the airport. We
take a walk downtown, happen to pass a coin store. Liberty Coins. I said let's
go in, as long as we were there, as long as I still had my Lincoln head penny
collection. The owner showed me a rarity he had in his own collection for
twenty years and finally, today, he decided to sell it. In the case there was an
uncirc. 1909-S-VDB. It took all the cash money we had on us. Ma had to
Western Union the rest to me from Worldview. I walked out of the store with
the coin in my pocket and right with it I got the definite feeling of something
getting completed through me. Penny collections, I suppose.*

Against this came the preview of disintegration. No part of his health
could be restored and, as his time shortened, less and less could be
salvaged. 'Say the worst,' the relief JT argued out of Dr Hoodbhoy was
this unambiguous knowledge. Free of emotion the doctor described
the changes he expected – months, not years away – when JT lay
stagnant in a hospital bed, crushed almost as much by his treatment as
by his disease. He might lose his power to chew and the reflex to
swallow and the reply to this would be intubation. Liquid nourishment
will be seeped down a plastic pipe directly into his stomach; other
tubes will be plumbed into his mouth, bladder and bowel to siphon off
saliva, urine and feces. Bedsores will corrode his back, thighs and
buttocks. 'Say the worst.' Wounds will open that eat through the
flesh, dissolving it in a putrid mash of pus and decaying layers of skin,
and through the skin to the red muscle and tendons, exposing the
bone. His deathbed will be a messy progress of impotence, the life left
in him will seem to be there only as a cage for his dementia, his body
only fuel for his fever. Embraced by a coma at the end, his breathing
will be managed by a respirator; he won't be here anymore but he
won't be gone, simply overpowered. JT compared the picture of
himself sprouting wires, punctured by tubes and strapped to a hospital
bed, and the ugly futility of it to, 'Pumping electricity into a raw
steak.' So the seventh veil that God was ready to peel off would be the
humiliation of dependence and the dragged-out banality of dying.

And against *this* Munro slipped back into the garage, turned his TV
set on, kept it going day and night (his own little force field), and only
came indoors to eat and sleep.

The house was built at the foot of the beach canyon, or tucked into its
heel, a kind of landlocked cove at the base of a creased, humped slope.

Knee-high brush of biscuit-color wild grass covered the arches and hollows like a short haircut, parted sloppily down a shallow wrinkle in the ground where a creek trickled toward the backyard. Constant traffic on the Pacific Coast Highway blocked the sound of the ocean but salt foam was caught in the air, carried inland off stately slow breakers that were hidden by a bend in the canyon road where it merged with the coast.

In the week before JT and Munro moved in, while Jim was in Roger Candler's care receiving treatment for his burns, I fitted the beds with sheets and blankets, the bathroom with towels, toothbrushes, soap and toothpaste, I stocked the kitchen with food. Even without these signs of life the rooms were warm places, waiting to be joined and enlivened by a family they could call their own. The kitchen, most of all, smiled on the sentimental yen we have for the comfort of home, harking back to a nineteenth-century farmhouse with its wooden walls roughly painted slate blue and pale green, and its unfussy smattering of modern luxuries like the electric juicer and the indoor barbecue. A long, solid oak table, settled with benches, made an island in the middle of the room, it soaked up the morning light which filled the two large square windows that framed a view of the backyard. From there JT could glance up from his writing and see an old hulking oak tree homesteaded by a redwood treehouse, and re-enter his Iowa childhood.

That domestic dangers lurked in Munro's total incapacity to cope with JT's changing condition, I had no doubt, and the dangers weren't only to JT's physical wellbeing or mental balance. During the time that I had the run of the house I tailored in a small network of my audio-visual peep holes, absorbed as much by Munro's trouble as by JT's. At least twice a day he was reminded somehow – a scowl from Jim, an ignoring silence – that he was a distraction, unnecessary, shut out and that a will stronger than his pinned him without sympathy to these tough realities. But he stayed, Munro hung on.

He didn't torture himself with a choice, he quietly persisted with JT to the same end that JT fanatically persisted with the knowledge and pain of his cancer: allow everything to unfold, see what else is uncovered. For Munro that could only be the danger to his hope and faith in God's care. What would be left of him at the end of grueling months spent helplessly watching Rev. Jim Tickell slowly rubbed out of life? Broken, disgraced, obliterated, it was the 'justice' prayed for by JT's crazed enemies. Munro held me there as he emerged blindly into his own history. I went back to him and he continued to grip my attention, which was a strange surprise: then I knew I'd be hanging on after everybody he knew left him, one way or another, derelict and alone.

I parked my van in their driveway and checked into a beachfront motel just a fifteen-minute walk away. In the afternoons I transcribed any tapes that were worth replaying, and wrote up my notes. Every morning before either Munro or JT was awake I climbed into the van and spooled through the last day's recordings, editing and usually erasing all but a few minutes of the past twenty-four hours. In the clips that caught the two of them together, apart from recording the sullen weight they towed into the room with them, the tape might as well have been mute.

On the last reels recorded at the house there was nothing worth keeping – there was Munro finishing his work on a pedigree pug while JT slept, until seven o'clock at night. Around that time Munro shuffled into the kitchen for dinner and found JT firing up the grill to barbecue their pork chops. 'Reverend? What are you doing?' The sight of Jim walking around bareassed naked didn't startle him anymore, Munro's main worry was the sizzling fat that came spitting off the grill, which was at crotch-height. 'You should put on an apron to cook in,' advice that JT ignored with a vague did-somebody-say-something? expression on his face.

After two days of generally avoiding the kitchen, an area that JT staked out as his, Munro faced up to the heap of dirty dishes left over from a week of breakfasts and dinners. Coffee cups and glasses stood like bowling pins along the edge of the counter, waiting for the unconscious swipe that was going to send them flying. It came when his back was turned: JT made a reach for the meat fork and he knocked a water tumbler onto the floor, where it shattered. It might as well have fallen into another dimension, he didn't hear the crash, didn't see the sparkling mess on the slate tiles and, amazingly, didn't feel the broken glass on the soles of his feet as he crunched over it. His skin wasn't cut, there was no blood and when Munro turned around he saw JT sitting at the table again, lost in his writing.

From the chore of sweeping up the fragments and slivers Munro went over to check on their dinner. 'Turn those chops in ten minutes. Don't just forget you got them cooking, okay?' he said in the voice he'd use to talk JT down from a ledge, and then, responsibly, 'I want to go and get that doggy's eyeballs put in.'

Another man is party to this, he has a clear line of sight down to the back of the house from his post on the slope of the hill. Hazy summer light fills the whole yard, liquidly, so there is no glare on the kitchen windows and when JT comes to the sink for a glass of water he's outlined squarely by the window frame. From his waist up he looms in a soft circle, a giant in that porthole view, magnified into the foreground, arraigned in the crosshairs.

The man's arms are only a fulcrum under the rifle, it's Jesus who balances it there, Jesus Christ guiding and steadying his aim. As sure as he is alive, as sure as he knows that he is a good man, honest in thought and action, he knows what is in God's mind. *He* is in God's mind, locked in tandem with Rev. Jim Tickell, and God is in his mind: Look, I will show you the world that's coming after Jim Tickell starts to agitate people again – ashes in the street, cement dust in the air, sand and weeds blowing across broken sidewalks, mayhem. In the middle of all the destruction you'll see the Reverend blessing the dirt and calling it beautiful, calling loss gain, doubt faith, confusing you with questions, tricking you into questioning what has been given you to believe, dragging you down with him into the stink and slime. Mayhem. What are people who fail to worship God's glory and refuse to fear God's power? What are their lives, Tony? Judged. Show him my face, bring him this lasting judgment, picture this violent beauty. I love him with a bullet. Gather him to me.

The first shot tore up the flesh of JT's shoulder and twisted him sideways but he stayed on his feet, straining to see who was out there through the jagged hole punched in the window. He only saw the hazy yellow-gray light of that summer evening sinking into the hillside. The second shot hit the middle of his chest, it slammed him backward against the end of the table where he seemed to stop himself, holding his body up. Then I saw him do an even more remarkable thing. With upwelling strength, he forced himself along the table's edge, feeling his way like a blind man, until he made it all the way to the other end, and there he let go, slumped onto the bench. It looked, at first, that JT wanted to die (or be found) sprawled over his last writings, but he had his back to them and he flopped face down, intentionally, I'm very sure, onto the grill.

The boom of the shooting didn't bring Munro racing back to the kitchen. The loud crack of glass breaking might only have been another household accident he'd face, later. What brought him in, sniffing the air like a watchdog, was the smell of burning meat. A low ceiling of smoke clouded the kitchen and underneath it the upper half of JT's body was sprouting flames.

Only low choking sounds grunted out of Munro, socked by the berserk reality of the horror in front of him. Any thought was blotted out in a blur of physical effort, wrestling Jim's weight onto the floor, cradling him there in the slippery puddles of his blood, wet smears of it gritted with glass chips from the exploded window. Munro opened his eyes again, let himself look at the peeled shreds of JT's scorched skin, he moaned over the wounds and mutilation beyond healing, over the savage power of dumb hate that ripped his friend out of the world.

JT's shoulder and upper arm, his face, neck and half of his chest were burned black, his flesh roasted. Munro smoothed down the strands and clumps of hair that were still attached to JT's scalp and kissed him there with such tender agony that I thought he meant tenderness also to be his answer to the slaughter. Between soft barking cries he was saying words, or parts of words, his lips very close to JT's ear. Munro felt his way with his lips to JT's cheek, from there down his neck to his shoulder where his kisses sharpened into nibbling bites. He plucked at the crisp skin with his lips again, then with his front teeth, gnawing in one place, he didn't lift up his head for breath, he chewed a mouthful of dark pulp and swallowed it, agony into hunger, the taste of charred meat on his tongue, he bit deeper, into joint and gristle, not with the lust of an animal but flooded with emotion, human feeling, the unfillable hunger of agony that carried him, while he ate, outside of real time. Then, with a stabbing cry, Munro sat up, pushed himself away from JT's corpse, retched, vomited and blacked out.

So it was twelve hours after this when I sat at the kitchen table, alone in that desolate room with JT's shot-up, incinerated, maimed and dead body at my feet. With the other broken things — plates and jars knocked to the floor, handwritten scraps and blank sheets of paper, the smithereens of glass — it was another remnant of what had been there before, the house walled in the facts of disappearance, of permanent absence. A trail of Munro's handprints and kneeprints in soot and dried blood ended at JT's bedroom closet.

Behind the door, behind the suits hanging in their plastic bags, I found him squatting in the corner, arms folded around himself, his eyes dark as a bird's eyes, trapped and unblinking in the clammy whiteness of his small face. I touched his head and Munro whimpered, he let me stroke his hair and then, as though he remembered that he'd be punished for it, he ducked away from my hand, turned his face and shakily crawled to the other side of the closet.

The report I read in the *LA Times* said that Munro had been in the house with JT's corpse for thirteen days. Roger Candler's real estate agent discovered the gruesome tragedy when he came by to pick up the house keys. According to the article (but how could anyone know?), Munro was in the bedroom closet all of that time, like an abandoned pet, and if he had not been found he would have starved to death.

Tony Orr gave his occupation as 'Christian Soldier' when the police picked him up and he was charged with the Reverend's murder. 'It's a great day for Jesus Christ!' he said to the arresting officers as they bundled him into the back of the squad car. At the arraignment, shouting over his lawyer's advice and the judge's instruction to keep quiet, Tony defended his not guilty plea by declaring victoriously before the eyes of the world, 'The hand that hurts is the hand that heals.'

Consumers of news about the assassination read Tony's character into the photographs of him taken in his pre-criminal life which were printed and televised as soon as they surfaced. The fundamentalist crank. The religious purist. Devoted conformist. Over-eager misfit. Army reject. Gun club pro. As the biographical details came trickling out the notion of who he was expanded to fill the inevitability of what he did. It was all visible in his high school yearbook senior portrait: eighteen years old, lopsided hair *combed* that way, the plump unfinished face, the stiffly concocted, undirected smile, the varnish of lofty expectations. The exuberant missionary, the embryonic killer.

A significant piece of information about Tony Orr's background circulated early in the run-up to his trial. Three years before JT was killed Tony worked for him at Worldview Ministry. Jim Tickell accused him — unfairly, without any believable evidence or witness, claimed Tony — of theft and espionage, demanded a public apology and when he didn't get it, fired him in front of the headquarters' assembled staff. Exaggerated or not, such a clash held out a sane motive for retaliation, a spur to violence that a person didn't have to be a Christian to understand.

17   Closure

RABBI Isaacson would have to dig out a specific interpretation in the Talmud of ancient Hebrew social law before Alex's father felt relaxed with the idea of addressing him as Gerry. 'Especially at an occasion,' he debonairly assured Meyer, 'my first name isn't Rabbi.' Gerry's unbuttoned personability camouflaged the streak of conservatism in him which, at root, anchored him to the historical and religious terrain. More obviously to Alex, after a year of truncated chats with him in the classroom or parking lot when Nelda was the last student to leave, Isaacson wore his unpruned beard as a fusty Old World (if not Old Testament) emblem of his status as tutor and gatekeeper of the temple mysteries.

In his baggy black suit and thickly knitted dark blue sweater he projected the image of a home plate umpire, an impression of moral and practical authority that his scholarly opinions and broad build, both as solid as a backstop, would put across regardless of his credentials. The bundle of loose brown curls, only thinly brushed with gray as if a weak light from the floor caught the sides of his hair, gave the rabbi a Greek profile, sensual, botanically framed a face planted in the thick of human life.

Meyer's lazy absence from the synagogue, a tailing off which began right after his bar mitzvah over fifty years ago, seemed to make him more, not less, sensitive to the tribal etiquette. When Alex sauntered over with their ice tea, Meyer was probing Rabbi Isaacson for the official line on the morality of sending (or not sending) US ground troops into the abomination of Yugoslavia's ethnic civil war.

'Mud wrestling, Vietnam all over again,' was Gerry's rapid-fire judgment. 'If you're looking at it from the righteousness angle then a better comparison is Kuwait. Did you believe Bush when he told us we were storming in to liberate the freedom-loving people of Kuwait?'

'Saddam Hussein is no picnic,' Meyer said, starting at ground level. 'Another Hitler, no? Adolf of Arabia.'

'Granted. But George Bush couldn't tell the mothers and fathers of military kids that they were putting their lives on the line to protect our oil supply. He lied when he didn't have to,' his voice straining toward a conclusion, signposted by a wave of his finger in the air. 'Everybody can understand oil. You can fight a righteous fight over a national need. What can we actually accomplish in Yugoslavia? What righteous outcome, after we lose how much?'

'What can you do?' Meyer nodded sadly, dropping out of the debate without a direct answer to his original question.

'Want me to get you some food, Dad?' Alex picked up a clean plate from the stack on the buffet.

'I'm sticking with my drink right now,' Meyer said and inched out of the way to make room for Gerry. 'Let me clear the road.'

He sidestepped around the table, enslaved by a bad hip and hampered more than helped by a new aluminum cane. Alex remembered pictures of his father, snapped on the Atlantic City shore when he was younger than Alex was now, the scholarship linebacker, brash white sunlight reflecting off the sand and lacquering his bare shoulders, in the summer before he asked his steady girl, 'Do you love me enough to marry me?' In these last months he'd turned short-tempered with his wife, the pool of dimly graspable emotions darkening and deepening while he squeezed their froth to the surface — earnest spurts of family pride, light-hearted deference to his son's adult choices, a private pleasure in his pre-Colombian art collection, all slight shifts in Meyer's disposition which crept in, Alex noticed, since the hip-replacement operation. When he saw Nelda a smile flared across his face. 'Honey, the house looks like something out of a magazine, straight out of *House Beautiful*.'

'Which means you haven't seen upstairs,' she said, shivering at the work ahead. 'House Ugly. House Unfinished.' Eyeing the load of pastrami, potato salad, swiss cheese and bagels on the rabbi's plate, Nelda warned him strictly, 'You better be hungry for cheesecake, Gerry.'

Chewing faster, Gerry pointed to his mouthful of food, swallowed it, balanced his plate waiter-style on his fingertips and dug into his jacket pocket with his free hand. 'This is from me, not Beth-El,' he said, handing her a small white box. 'I think the temple gives you a datebook with a gold pen. Gold *plated*.'

'Alex, look.' Nelda lifted the small Star of David into the light, dangling it from its chain. Two intertwined triangles, descending and ascending, inside edges bevelled and polished against the brushed gold outer edges gave it a classical fineness which elevated it further, from a gift to an award.

'Here, I want to do it for you.' Meyer let go of his cane to fix the clasp behind her neck and then he held her hand, standing back to take in the full view of his fresh-minted Jewish daughter-in-law. 'You're a masterpiece.' Briskly changing down a gear he turned around to Ellen to say, 'What did you do with her present?'

'I'm going to get you a twenty-four-hour nurse,' she said, reaching behind him for the package he'd left on the mantel. 'Then I can run away to the south of France with the Sparkletts man.'

'To Van Nuys, you mean. That's where Sparkletts is.' Before Nelda had it unwrapped Meyer said, apologetically, 'It's second-hand but it's a first edition.'

The second Nelda saw the cover her cheeks heated and the blush spread to her ears. 'You'll never let me forget it, will you,' laughing and wincing at her old self, burying her face in the pages of this cherishable souvenir, a copy of Leo Rosten's *The Joys of Yiddish*. The real joy of the moment was that, apart from the rabbi, Nelda knew more about Judaism and Jewish history than anybody at the party, she had waded into her conversion with a scholar's appetite for broader and earlier factual knowledge and an actor's empathy for interpretation. She not only adopted the heritage, she ingested it.

'I won't forget it ever, either,' Meyer said to Gerry, a fresh audience. 'Nelda came over one time to pick Alex up and I saw her washing her shoe off with the garden hose. "What happened to you?" I asked her. "Oh my God," she says, "I stepped in a pile of dog schmuck." Can you picture it? A pile of dog schmuck!'

'Now I know,' Nelda came back at him with self-mocking complicity, 'I should have said dog schmucks, plural, right?'

Pained, laughing, Meyer told her that she was very disgusting, bestowed a bear-hug, and then said the clan elder, 'Just perfect for this family.'

'Somebody wants to talk to you, Lexie.' Coming up behind him here was Janice, walking her one-year-old niece in from the kitchen,

Sarah's miniature feet balanced on top of Janice's shoes. A grown-up stride away from the island of her daddy's black brogues she stepped off and tottered the rest of the distance, arriving with a soft jolt against the backs of Alex's legs.

She didn't hang around for long. From this beachhead she took new bearings and fluttered off again, upright then on all fours then back on her feet, a rugged explorer in her red flannel romper suit hand-decorated by Nelda with embroidered atoms and, on the back, a large black-on-yellow radiation hazard symbol. Their atomic baby. When she moved she left Alex with her aroma, it drifted upward in a warm column of air, a milky, thick scent, white cheese, buttercrust. 'What's over there, Pinky?' he asked her, watching her large head bounce with each clomping step, the licorice-dark wisps and coils of her unbrushed hair were Janice's careless comedy when she was an infant too, that was where Alex had seen it before.

Sarah propelled herself through the forest of lower limbs with the serious concentration and one-track intention that belonged to her father in his university days, headlong persistence that survived blasts of heat and cold out there in business for a while. Swinging along a chain of table leg and skirt hem handgrips and encouraging squeaks from her great-grandmother, she wobbled in with smaller steps like an ice skater stilted on her blades coming off the ice, to make a solid landing on the cement-gray sofa's far shore. 'Nn-ga!' she punctured the air (and her great-grandma's eardrum) with a shriek of success. Chubby legs bent and springy, Sarah pogoed her victory dance with a look over her shoulder at her daddy's whistling and applause.

So far, every dare she's faced she has won, sitting to standing, crawling to walking, at each turn stronger, surer of her skill, safer; in her gigantic benevolent world the idea of futility is as shapeless and foreign as death itself. Alex promenaded his daughter around the coffee table, holding Pinky's arms up puppetwise, steering her clear of corners and edges, then back to the home port of their sole surviving grandparent. Widowed this year, the shock of that icy amputation dulled steadily into lonely bewilderment, as though the manufacturer's lifetime warranty that was signed and witnessed in her childhood had been pettily revoked. 'So your Granddad didn't get to see her,' she said to Alex, opening her arms like cargo hold doors to receive Pinky on her lap. 'That's, well, Alex,' she didn't know how to condemn the rotten unfairness except to complain, with an injured shake of her head, 'that's a dirty trick somebody played on him.'

And on her, she didn't need to say. Alex had a taste of that same rawness scraped into the back of his throat, also from crying a powerless, useless complaint against the Manufacturer. The little girl squirming and huddling next to him now, this energetic personality in fizzy bustling health, was the child delivered to her parents unfinished, twelve weeks ahead of schedule. She could have sprawled in Alex's cupped hands, two pounds one ounce, her skin as thin as wet newspaper and the color of uncooked steak, an angry empress fighting her way into life. Nelda dubbed her Pinkenstein, thinking ahead to a time when her mummified start was safe enough in the past to be treasured as a sweetly gruesome joke.

The most nightmarish moment in the whole nightmarish drama came for Nelda in the frantic seconds after Pinky was born. Through her own electric fog of adrenaline, medication and blank rising terror she saw the nurses swoop in and wheel her (dying? dead?) baby away to a room somewhere behind a pair of double doors that splayed open on a shout of fluorescent whiteness, for an instant, and sealed it off from her again with her daughter inside it, out of reach.

For ten days Pinky lay on a sterile table under the dry shower of a heat lamp, a newborn marsupial torn out of her mama's pouch, with her eyelids held shut by thin strips of surgical tape, her indignant waxy lips clamped against what Nelda thought must be a cloud of pain. There they connected her to a bank of monitors that flashed digital and graphic read-outs of each breath and heartbeat, they plugged her into IV drips twenty-four hours a day, they transfused her (so it seemed to her parents) with more fluid than her toy balloon body could possibly hold. The greenish purple bruises on her arms, back and legs where needles had pricked her finally broke Alex in half and he crumpled into Nelda's lap, splashing tears, and didn't raise his face until he heard the nurse leave the area. Soon (and he was there to see this, too), the nurses had to hunt for fresh veins to tap in the side of Pinky's head and from such a pitiful sight Alex nauseously turned away. He locked his eyes onto the screen of the heart monitor as it counted each lub-dub of the brave giblet that went on tugging in her chest, *alive, she's alive, still alive.*

At the end of their first and last consultation with Dr Pine, chief of the neo-natal unit, the tough essence of his professional advice to

Nelda and Alex was that they should go home and try to rest. 'If you hear from me again,' he said starkly, in closing, 'things are not good.' So began two weeks of multiplying horrors, bleary strain. Away from the hospital they took turns acting as each other's consulting expert on premature babies, re-explaining the probabilities, signs and precedents, repeating what they knew, didn't know, couldn't know and guessed about the realities behind the daily fluctuations in Pinky's condition and the euphemisms ('negative outcome' was one of Dr Pine's) used to describe it. These conversations, which took on the tones and vocabulary that Alex and Nelda had picked up from the hospital staff, were meant to protect them from ambush by talking out their harshest fears. But hours of talk only carved the silent shape of a more fearsome question, said by remaining unsaid: the hovering mystery of the cause and, if their child died, of her obscure exit from their lives.

Into the vacuum went their suspicions about Nelda's diet or the effects of stress on her pregnancy, and after this line had been exhausted all that was left to ransack was Nelda's private hoard of superstitions. These came out at three in the morning, in the newly tiled kitchen, as Alex sat with her sipping Ovaltine and munching toast. At that deserted hour her baby's death sentence appeared to be a brutal preview of Nelda's own life from now on, the incarnation of her frailty and failure. Sarah's ghostly mission was to tease and deprive her mother, a glimmering lesson to drive home the remorselessness of the carnivorous Power Whom she had pit herself against . . . by betraying her husband with Alex . . . by wanting a family with him . . . by turning her back on Jesus . . .

Alex was so tattered by insomnia and guesswork that as wild as this hypothesis sounded (and implicated as he was in these anarchic crimes against God), Nelda's sense of doom spooked him. At that moment he felt himself falling through the floor, yoked to his wife by the supernatural persecution that their slackness obviously deserved. They didn't go back to bed and the hysteria loosened its grip as daylight filled the windows, letting Alex sink back into the saner pessimistic fantasy that they were waiting for Dr Pine to knock on the door — whereupon they'd be led out onto the front lawn to face a firing squad. At least in this swirling uncertainty the worst continued not to happen and they did what they had to do, which was to hold on to each other and will Pinky to pull through.

Now Alex knew how to read that self-satisfied look of mildly amazed accomplishment on his daughter's face. His grandmom patted Pinky's derrière and handed her over, saying, 'Doll, she's wet.'

Meyer grabbed the chance to hand down an article of family wisdom. 'I saw a nature show on PBS about birds. Alex, listen to this, it's my all-time favorite picture of fatherhood. The little chicks hatch out and Daddy Bird doesn't eat for, what was it, a couple of months *at least*. All he does is fly out to the ocean every day and bring fish back to the nest. He burps it all out, any fish he swallowed, burps it out into the open yaps of his kids. The mouths on these baby birds are as big as their whole body and they're screeching at him, shaking like crazy, "Feed me, Daddy! Feed me, feed me *more*!" '

Because he fed her (apple and pear juice at lunchtime), Alex is mopping up Pinky's tangy urine, swabbing baby lotion around the pillowy tops of her legs with a cotton ball, free of any Daddy Bird resignation to nagging duty and inhabited instead by this kicking, hungrily living human presence. *It's me she wants*, Alex thinks, folding the clean diaper up and over, safely packaging her, *she depends on me as if she chose me*, the direct claim she makes on him is repledged whenever she makes a noise: she cries out her next grievance or rise of pleasure and he is whisked up in a gust of instant necessity, doubling her comfort.

Alex is away on business tomorrow, to Japan. He's travelling there on a mission to sell an exclusive Wendywear licensing deal to a market-leading Tokyo department store, but the business of a major sale isn't a landmark in his professional progress, it isn't so much a scalp under his belt anymore. His relentless career ambitions have relented, collapsed inward, increased in another direction, continued into this unflinching care of his small Pinkenstein. Of that one thing he is sure, with her right now in this one unblighted tick of the clock.

She drowses, doesn't even feel Alex gently squeezing the pink ovals of her toetips, doesn't wake up when he lifts her into her crib. In the connecting bathroom he washes his hands and in the right-angled mirrors he catches sight of his profile, rounder under the chin, thicker under the jawline. Lately he has noticed surplus hairs weedily growing on his ear lobes, dark-colored, they make him think of insect legs. Now his morning routine includes patrolling for these little fiends and tweezing them out. Will his body just go on coarsening? He stopped trying to stay ahead of the crop of hairs invading his back between his shoulder blades and at the base of his spine, crinkly and black like migrated pubic hairs. Alex used to wear a T-shirt in bed to spare Nelda the ugly sight, but strangely for him, besides the new hairs, he's grown blasé about his sex appeal, or lack of it. His clock is running, the unconscious ride is over.

He is yanked out of this meditation by a panicky, shivering cry from the baby, suddenly awake in her empty room. Tweezers still pinched between his fingers, Alex bounds in again and finds Nelda already bending over the crib, testing Pinky's diapers, examining Alex's work.

There she is, the woman who emerged with him from the winding tunnel. Sallowness that had clung to her, slow to leave during the first months Pinky was at home, had gone, as though a wax casing had melted from her skin and let out the healthy dusting of freckles on Nelda's forehead, cheeks and neck. She reaches in to hoist Pinky over the crib's wooden rail, those long bare arms of hers italicising her tallness, two inches shorter than Alex but when he's standing next to her as he is now she seems taller, a sense that churns up a ridiculous pride. Since he's seen her so many times arguing the Talmudic toss with Gerry, he's come to adore her haircut – she started chopping at it little by little, compulsively, over the time Pinky was in the hospital – a lighter, honey-mahogany heckling of the rabbi's plumage. Nelda's broad face has been softened by near-disaster, spread out from her firm mouth, the unevadable focus of Alex's attention. She tells him which are the rising trends in children's wear and which minority styles are fast-dying fads; she spotted Drive-In and Space Era retrotrends that triggered giddy memories in parents of her age and she resold them the comfy wonders of their own childhood. The move that Nelda wants Wendywear to explore next is into children's furniture. Nelda has landed, she's made the company hers, turned it into her fate, and this settles Alex with a great stabilizing faith in his boss.

She nets him with a faintly imploring look and says, 'Didn't you come in here to change her dirty diaper?'

'She was dry five minutes ago. She's wet again?'

'Filled them up,' Nelda says, peeling the plastic corner tabs. 'The Grand Stinkeroo.'

'Comedian,' he accuses Pinky. 'Practical joke, you weasel,' and he gallantly accepts all responsibility. 'You go back to the party, Nell. I'll change that thing.'

'I'm on top of it.'

'Okay,' he says, and stays. 'I'll supervise.'

18   As We Fall into Flight

TO the prosecution, who aimed to use him as a key witness against Tony Orr, and to the psychiatrist whose interests lay in extracting a sequence of events and untangling the threads of likelihood and significance sealed inside his memory, Munro Fyke's life had crucial value. Could he testify? How responsive would he be, how reliable? What direct personal knowledge did he have of Tony's various activities at Worldview? How much did he see of JT's unnatural death, how much of that day and night could he recollect?

Dr John Gruen was the state's crafty choice of psychiatric expert, an unacademic professional whose performance in court was always confident and relaxed, jargon-free and pointedly insightful. He possessed a sense of vocation, a sympathetic curiosity that glimmered under his thoroughness, a quirkily poetic *feel* for people who have been forced out of the ordinary world by trauma, and this talent of his was inborn the same way that a responsive sensitivity to the emotion of color and the weight of form is there in an artistic prodigy. Shut out, knotted inside, disbelieved, skewed outside, demonized and demon-ridden, this is what we are at heart, Gruen's sanity (and not his training) told him, all of us. Every investigation he entered, every dossier he pieced together, every profile he wrote up was also a self-revealing act. It was just this human mutuality he used – not as a clinical tool but as a background assumption, an atmosphere – to connect with inmates whose shells hardened against the blunter techniques and rigid personalities of too many of Gruen's colleagues. Presented with Munro, who froze him out with lockjawed silence and whose fingers jumped to cover his ears as if any word spoken to him came as an assault, Dr Gruen sat silently in that room at the same time every day, mirroring back his patient's self-estrangement, wordlessly turning over the same two questions that were convulsing Munro's mind: *What is his condition now? What actually happened to make him that way?*

Nudging into his forties, Gruen was usually taken to be a decade younger, flatteringly in spite of early tall-forehead baldness which gave him the hyper-evolved cranial elevation (as he saw it) of a benign ambassador from the Crab Nebula. The horseshoe of hair that survived like a high-tide mark around the sides and back he mowed to a sandpapery stubble, which on a man built more sturdily would only have looked severe. On Dr Gruen the skinhead style hinted at harmonious asceticism, the in-the-world-but-not-of-it counterpoint of the temple devotee. He was not at peace, though, with the register of his voice, an octave too high, he thought, whenever he heard it played back on tapes of sessions with his patients; it made him sound breathless, excitable, a voice too thin to carry the accumulated weight of his knowledge and experience, as though the symphony thundering in his head only wheezed out of him through a squeaky accordion. His persuasiveness rested in his cedar-brown eyes, clear and inquisitive behind the functional, egghead, pre-war rims of his glasses, and accessible even from the other side of a room, they showed you as much of the raring student he'd been as the doctor he became.

Two or three times a day, in one-hour sessions, Gruen fished for a response with the bait of stray pieces of Munro's recent history: the day he chauffeured Ma Tickell around Ventura County, visiting convalescent homes . . . the day he moved into the beach house . . . his trips to the hospital with JT and Prof. Ketchum . . . Week after week the doctor piled up the tower of unjudged individual facts without Munro making any kind of claim on them at all. At least, by the third week Munro had stopped plugging his ears against Gruen's questions and, even if inertly, he was looking into Gruen's face.

Although he sat still for the drip feeding that kept him alive, Munro refused solid food. He only drank water and only water that he had seen pour out of the faucet directly into his plastic cup. This quirk (mixed in among cheek twitches, the sudden blinking of a boy about to be hit, a sullen kink knotting his personality), whatever its buried meaning, added to the impression that Munro had reverted to adolescence. Overwrought by garbled instructions jamming his brain, a sick chalkiness coating his skin, his uncut dark feathery hair sometimes dropping weak brackets around his starved cheeks, the sheltering curve of his spine, his caved-in chest, draped with his

307

hospital robe, hands clasped between his knees on the edge of his bed, stolidly distracted, he could have been sketched in an artist's notebook as a consumptive out-of-work Harlequin.

At one lunchtime session Gruen offered him a taste of the bacon, lettuce and tomato sandwich he'd brought from home and Munro reeled back from it as if it had shrieked out his name. Retching over the side of the bed, dry heaves scraping his throat, he said his first words to Dr Gruen, between moans and heaving belches he said, 'They can get in by a lunchbox. Under the white bread.'

'What can? Who can?'

He let Gruen comfort him. 'Things aren't okay where I am. The door ain't tight, so in they come.'

'Why do they want to come in here?'

'Somebody is. They have to. They want to try and eat me.'

'Who wants to do that?'

'Men from Canada.' Finally saying it was temporary relief.

'How do you know they're from Canada, Munro?'

'It's obvious,' he said, 'they want to make Canadian bacon out of me. Starting with my weenie. Going to have a weenie roast in Toronto and roast up my weenie in front of the president of Canada.'

Munro began to eat the food that was brought to him as long as it wasn't grilled, fried or baked, and it only took the smallest shred of ham rind or whiff of broiled fat for his meat horror to paralyze him. He was happiest with soft foods at the white/beige end of the range, mashed potatoes and applesauce, instant oatmeal, vanilla pudding. When Gruen asked him why he didn't like to eat anything meatier Munro huffily doubted the standard of Gruen's medical qualifications.

'Didn't any real doctor teach you about the human digesting track?' he inquired with a grim frown that said, This beats me all to hell. 'You can't eat hard food if you don't have a stomach. Are we all right on this now?'

'I just want to understand what you're saying. You weren't born with a stomach, is that what you want me to know?'

'Or not intestines, either.' Munro pushed his tray away. After a second or two he said, 'I know I had 'em before but God dissolved 'em out of me.'

'When did God take out your stomach, can you remember when that happened?'

'When I was asleep one time.'

'Did you feel a pain there? Was that how you knew things weren't a hundred per cent inside? Or did you throw up when you tried to eat?'

'I saw the effect of it in the morning. I got up,' Munro got up out of his chair and planted himself in front of the window, 'and when the light shined in it went through me. I could see my arteries and such, they were still there but not some of my vital organs.'

'It's pretty serious if you lose your stomach and intestines. Did you mention it to Dr Candler or did it happen later on?' Gruen tipped back in his chair and let his legs dangle casually under the table. 'Did you mention it to Dr Hoodbhoy?'

Munro said, the words trailing off, 'I don't know those doctors.'

'All right. Munro, I'd like to know where you were living when this thing happened with your stomach. Where was the window that the light came through?'

'Doctors couldn't fix it back, anyway,' Munro sidetracked. 'If Lord Jesus decides He has to dissolve out my vital organs one at a time for some reason, well, that's what's ordained, the end.'

Gently, Gruen suggested, 'I can't think of a good reason for God to want to injure you like that.'

'Well, sir,' Munro answered him rancidly, 'then you can't be a Christian, I guess.'

Three months along, Dr Gruen wrote in his preliminary report that there was progress in their mutual communication but that Munro *still lacked the clarity of mind which would imbue his testimony with any uncoded external meaning.* Munro persistently denied that he knew anything about, much less that he personally knew, either Rev. Jim Tickell or Tony Orr. Following the trail of depressive delusions (*his belief that he no longer possesses a stomach or intestines, that God or Lord Jesus has miraculously removed these organs and that he is able, even ordained, to continue living in this condition*), first of all back to the murder and cannibalism, Gruen heard the clear echoes of Windigo psychosis. Native tribes in the northern states and, yes, in Canada, the Cree and the Algonkians, fostered the belief that a person could be changed into a Windigo monster through dreams or spells and that once he'd tasted human flesh his appetite for it became ravenous, unstoppable. Someone afflicted with the sickness, who had in the face of starvation eaten a brother, sister, son or daughter, might beg to be killed. *In Fyke,* Dr Gruen went on, *acceptance of lifelong punishment for his sins against*

God expressed in his behavior toward Jim Tickell, might be viewed as a Christian translation of the syndrome.

Up to the time of this first assessment Munro avoided, in one way or another, references to the world outside. The view from his window, three storeys down, was of a tan brick courtyard, a place where staff from the hospital and students from the university would mingle for lunch or stroll through on their way to other campus buildings. Sitting at the table when his doctor came to talk, Munro made sure he kept his back to the wall 'with that painting on it'. Gruen pointed at the window and asked him if that was what he meant. 'Yeah,' Munro said, 'that ugly painting.' Why did he think it was ugly? 'It's supposed to show ice skaters but they don't even look like people.' What did they look like? 'Ice cubes.'

John Gruen's inspired shortcut was the gift of a radio. As soon as Munro was left alone with it he clamped the speaker to his ear and slowly tuned through the stations, stopping at the grainy hiss blowing like a sandstorm on the far edge of the waveband. He kept it playing all the time and the number of batteries he could get through came to be the running joke between doctor and patient, just as Munro's calmly obscure silence was his monotonous answer to the question, 'What are you listening to, Munro?'

Then abruptly, at the end of a three-day fast, Munro opened up.

'What are you listening to, Munro?'

'The Reverend.'

'I don't know who that is. What's the Reverend's name?'

'He's the only one I know of,' he told Gruen. 'He's the pastor who comes in and tickles my ears.'

'Tickles you with his voice, you mean? With what he's saying?'

'Jim's not saying what he says right now.' Munro twisted the volume higher, hunched against the speaker, the sandstorm shrouded his head. He spoke up over the noise, 'Have to keep it open. He comes and goes.'

After that, when Gruen could lead him into conversation about Jim Tickell, Munro spoke of him in the present tense. Not only was JT alive and healthy, but he was also just at the planning stage of his ministry. Everything lay ahead.

'I met the big guy last week,' Munro said. 'He hired me and you know what, Dr Gruen?'

'Tell me what.'

'It didn't matter to him how I've been in the hospital. He hired me anyway, so I'll be leaving here.'

'He sounds like he's a very understanding man.' Gruen dispensed a generous smile. 'You met him here?'

'Uh-huh. Down in the cafeteria. Reverend came in to visit his wife and his little boy, but they died.' Bizarrely, shockingly, Munro brightened up and elaborated, 'Lord Jesus ordained a car wreck for them so it could all work out.'

A white flare rocketed into the night. This was the real opening, the first time that Munro included an actual verifiable historical reality into his version of events. Dr Gruen learned during his interviews with JT's mother that the Reverend's wife and ten-year-old son had been killed when their car spun out of control on a quiet suburban street in the middle of a sunny July afternoon. Ruby Tickell died in the crash, Ma told Gruen, but James, Jr. drifted in and out of coma (as far as she could remember) for six or seven weeks. JT brought Munro home with him from the hospital along with the news that James, Jr. was dead. 'They just got talking one day outside my grandson's room. Jim said it got to him in a pure Christian way, maybe he was soft to it at that particular time, how much Munro cared about little children.'

Beyond the precise facts, Munro laid open his emotional stake in them, his appropriation of the force of circumstance. In the probation officer's notes, written over the eighteen months which ended the year that Munro started working for the Reverend, Gruen read: *Mr Fyke will not endanger any child's physical safety but his unusual attraction to children should continue to be treated*. Their weekly talks weren't limited to his rehabilitation, Officer Mears also noted down the dreams that seemed to intrude on Munro with more dramatic effect than episodes of his waking life.

One dream that he had often, before and after his arrest, stranded Munro outside the chainlink fence of a school playground. He is there always a few seconds before the lunch bell rings and he sees the empty playground fill up with children. They play four-square and dodge ball, they chase and tease each other, and all of them are little bodies full of light. He waves to them and the ones playing closest to the fence welcome him in, they tug the gate open and by now every face is turned his way like a field of sunflowers, welcoming, welcoming.

The first time he was chased off by a teacher when he followed his dream to Carpenter Ave Elementary School, Munro just didn't comprehend what offense he'd committed. 'The children all like me there,' he said to the patrolman who picked him up. He went back more than once, hid behind a bungalow and played handball unmolested four days in a row, until he was arrested again.

Carpenter Ave's teachers and parents were frightened and angry to find out from the police that Munro had constructed a 'fort' in the freshwater gully behind the school where he put on innocent 'show and tell' performances. He showed the children who visited him on their way home from school his latest piece of taxidermy, he told them stories that he made up about his invisible dog.

'What happened in these stories, Munro?'

'It'd be some kind of big adventure, but it'd always start out the same.' Gruen made a polite ushering gesture with his hand and Munro continued, 'I can't see Rudolph but I can see his pawprints on the ground, I can hear him panting. So I follow him out of my house and up into the hills usually and down the other side, which looks different for every story. It's a forest one time or it's a crystal city, whatever I think of. I follow him down because Rudolph always leads me to someplace where I don't have to guess about things, it's all there to see exactly like it is. Nothing is hiding, nobody tells any lies, any questions you ask you get the correct answer. The finale is always where things are really like they are. I made sure every Rudolph story had a good moral.'

On the day that Tony Orr's plea bargain was made public and his trial aborted, Dr Gruen visited Munro to explain the situation and supervise his discharge from the hospital. He found Munro sitting at his table, facing the window which outlined a bright square of vacated blue sky. His radio was in front of him, tuned to the familiar dry buzz of static noise, playing at a low, intimate volume. Racking sobs buckled his shoulders, Munro was crying his heart out.

He heard on the radio, he said, that the Reverend was dead. He asked Gruen if it was true. Gruen told Munro, 'Yes, it is. Did they say on the radio how he died?'

'Car accident,' Munro said. 'But I don't think that's right.'

'If you know something different, I'd like to hear what it is.'

'I believe they came in on him and I believe they cut off his head.'

'Was that something you saw? Who did you see come in?'

'Those illegal immigrants. From Toronto. They attacked Jim to make him shut up.' Brokenly, Munro said, 'All it takes is the sound of his voice. It hurts their ears like holy hell.'

'Are you sure they're from Toronto?'

'Yeah, I met them before.'

No procedural purpose remained for Dr Gruen to go on clawing through the cloud, it became a private necessity for him to complete Munro's psychological assessment and not just choke it off.

What is his condition now? Gruen answered, *Fyke's breakdown and consequent deviant behavior cannot be strictly summarized as a psychotic episode. His references to 'illegal immigrants' from Canada, responsible for his benefactor's murder, become plausible if we interpret 'Toronto' as Fyke's coded trope of the name 'Tony Orr'. To understand the cannibalism as a 'sane' (i.e., consistent, coherent) response to Jim Tickell's horrifying death, we need to refer back to an alleged theft noted in Orr's statement to Det. A. J. Polaire . . .*

In the totality of Munro's revelations to him, in his unfocused shifting memories and fractured biography, Gruen caught sight of a tendency which reflected his own hope for himself: the undiscouraged longing to see revealed in his choices a hint of elemental good. His true condition. He made choices, calculated or otherwise, as he reasoned Munro did, based on the confident suspicion that at his core, like the glowing fuel at the core of an atomic reactor, there was a primary, energetic particle of moral matter that charged and animated his life, and more than that, the animating force of this particle's existence was the single urge to express its presence. Assassin or agitator, vegetarian or cannibal, Gruen reflected, the essential belief was in something present and knowable, an indestructible good connected by the strings of our deeds to a sense of some nebulous original truth about ourselves. Who, after all, lives in the belief that his faults are unforgivable?

Tony Orr confessed that in 1989, while he was employed as a production manager at Wendywear Sports Casuals, a subsidiary of Worldview Ministry, he supplied sensitive and classified documents which detailed the church's income to a representative of then Assemblyman, now Governor Bobby Dyson. Tony's disillusionment with Jim Tickell's 'liberalism' was, he said, exploited by Dyson who at that time was conducting an independent investigation into the Reverend's financial dealings. (In a deposition Governor Dyson's chief aide, Marty Olansky, denied absolutely that he had ever received from Tony Orr or anyone else any information concerning Rev. Tickell that was not available in the public domain.) To authenticate the claim

Tony offered the inside knowledge that his source for the donor lists was Munro Fyke, who could corroborate the story.

In Tony's version of events Munro arranged to leave the d-list file 'accidentally' in the Xerox room, where it would be copied and immediately returned to him. The line that Tony fed Munro was as simple as this: he wanted the list of Worldview donors so that he could arrange a nationwide surprise party for the Reverend's sixtieth birthday.

The probing interest that John Gruen showed in this anecdote curled Munro back into a stymied defensive silence. It was that stifling, that muffled panic, which contained as much of the truth as Gruen would have heard in an outright admission. *What actually happened to make him that way?* According to Dr Gruen, this happened:

Munro was easily tricked by Orr into a theft which, discovered or not, burdened him with the heavy weight of disloyalty, and he carried the self-stigmatizing load of guilt and shame until those feelings were voided by the Reverend's killing. Guilt for the thievery and shame because God's foreknowledge of Munro's fault, his betrayal and its consequences had not been granted to him.

The moment before Orr's rifle shots crashed through the window, Munro and Jim were together in the beach house kitchen preparing dinner. Munro had just started to barbecue their meat on the grill, tending it while Jim went to the sink for two clean plates. The impact of the bullets striking his chest threw him backward into Munro, who was knocked to the floor. Above him, Jim fell dead across the scorching grill. When he held the burned body in his arms Munro knew that his own life ended there too, he had been hurled into a weightless zone of self-extinction.

He would have been conscious of nothing. Every border between his senses and the surrounding world would evaporate, time would collapse into this single stopped moment. His hunger is primitive, infantile, he breathes in the smell of meat, tastes salt on his lips, turns what is outside of him into part of him the way a baby does, by taking it into his mouth. As he tastes and chews, Munro opens his eyes; he is looking straight into his friend's dead face. In it he sees Jim's suffering and courage, wrongs he endured, love he had won, his grace in God, these qualities of his spirit infuse Jim's flesh. Munro chews and swallows, this is a religious urge: he wants to feel, and does feel Jim's spirit pass into him, it is a sacrament. Then time begins to pull him forward again, into a cage of concrete realities — he is alone in the house in the middle of the night, Jim Tickell is dead, there is his body, mutilated, defiled, no one is coming to help — this is when, probably, Munro is overwhelmed by the way things really are.

Ma Tickell decided before she considered the advice of the Worldwide trustees that no one would benefit, least of all Munro, if she took him in when the hospital and the courts released him. While JT was alive and in charge, her appreciation of Munro's familiar willingness was unsentimental, he was a fixture in her son's life. Now that her son was dead she accepted Munro as a keepsake, a remnant, a living memorial to Jim, an inheritance pointing to an emptier future for passing in the wrong direction, from son to mother.

The idea of resettling Munro in her home only came up in the discussion as an option to avoid, to stimulate suggestions around the table of low-cost low-profile alternatives. At the end of the breakfast meeting Ma seemed finally satisfied with the plan to move Munro into one of the unrented units in the Murryhill Building downtown, a neo-Gothic hotel that Worldwide had renovated and converted into bachelor apartments. Ma provided money herself for Munro's food and clothes in the shape of an allowance he'd receive in cash every two weeks, an arrangement that was explained to him by an assistant of one of the ministry's trustees. He was a peppy college boy with a scrubbed face and babyfine blond hair, somebody Munro had never met before, whose name, he said, opening the brownwashed door of the apartment, was Brent.

'Brent's going to come see you once in a while,' Ma advised Munro over the telephone while Brent was still there. 'Tell him if you want anything or if you get into a problem. Write it out on a list.'

'I won't need to. It's all right here for me. Thank you for it, that's all I want to say.'

'You know how it is, Munro,' she said, smiling thinly, 'we're the ones who're left.'

'I know that's right, that's a victory for Christ.'

'Everything's been a victory for Christ,' Ma echoed distantly.

Sunlight could only strain into Munro's two-room apartment, weakened by the effort of reaching down the long spine of the building over the thrusting ledges to his inhabited corner. The bedroom window overlooked a damp alley and faced the tall rear wall of a movie theater, the old Varsity. Sometimes late at night he'd hear voices drift up from the alley, rushed, Hispanic chattering after the crack and creak of the emergency exit door being secretly opened. For a few seconds, above the flutter of whispers and shuffling shoes, Munro could listen to the amplified, looming voices or the brassy throbs of music from the action on the screen.

Not much in his new home placed comfort ahead of function, its inspiration seemed to be the shelf. Every piece of furniture blocked cleanly into its ninety-degree nook was no more than a variation on the basic form, there was a shelf for sleeping, a shelf for sitting and in the kitchenette a few feet away there was a truncated shelf built like a counter in a diner where he could do his eating. The beginning and end of it, Munro thought, packed away in this twilight, this box, the cramped dimensions of his life, the only difference between this place and the hospital room was that he was free to leave it.

Saturday and Sunday were in themselves destinations. Munro took himself to morning, afternoon and evening services at the Baptist church in North Hollywood where he had worshiped before he defected to JT and Worldview. Every weekday, though, he'd make a sandwich for lunch and put it in a paper bag with a candy bar and a carton of juice or milk, dress up in his brown suit and ride around the city on buses until dark. Down Wilshire to the ocean, then back downtown on Sunset, hopping on and off wherever he wanted, strolling on to the next bus stop to ride the next bus that came, wherever it went. Up through Sepulveda into the San Fernando Valley, across and down into Hollywood, hopscotching invisibly around Los Angeles Munro always returned to his apartment with a lingering sense of natural freedom.

Sometimes at the evening end of one of these long hauls he'd run into a bus driver he'd met in the morning who'd ask Munro kiddingly if he was a disguised inspector from the RTD. 'No,' he'd say, deflating the joke, 'I'm just going on my errands.' Munro had an encounter like this on the day he wandered out to Burbank, past the airport, when something made him climb off at a stop across the street from the Worldview Life Ministry.

He avoided it. He walked around the corner and five minutes away his decision was rewarded by God. Munro found himself outside an elementary school at lunchtime where the children on the playground seemed to be splashing through the heat haze seeping up from the asphalt. With his lunch bag on his lap Munro sat on the curb to eat and enjoy the hand-ball dramas and jump rope comedies, the company of children. He rolled the cuffs of his slacks up to his knees to let some sun onto his almost hairless sickly white legs.

A knot of boys close to the fence called across to him and then, all at the same time, they gave him the finger. Munro waved back, half a sandwich in his hand. He must have been observed by a teacher on yard duty, or maybe a concerned neighbor, because when he started unwrapping his Hershey bar a squad car rolled up, its front tires narrowly missing his toes.

From the driver's seat the officer asked him, 'You local? You live here?' A broad, calm face, Aztec and serious.

'I'm eating my lunch,' Munro said, standing up, his trouser legs stuck, collared around his knees. He bent to unroll them, brushed them neatly and thought he was putting up a respectable show. 'I wasn't going to litter my trash, I'm careful about that.'

The radio in the car squawked, hissed, popped. 'I appreciate that. What's your name?' Munro gave it. 'You have any ID on you, Mr Fyke?'

'I never drop my litter, so it's okay. If I see any trash lying around I usually pick it up, even if it's not mine, which it never is,' he said and made the officer think he didn't understand the question.

'Your identification, that's what I want to see. Can you produce some for me?'

Munro felt a coil of air tightening behind his breastbone. Across the street another officer stood at the fence, talking to the four boys and glancing back over his shoulder. 'I'm a churchgoer,' Munro said, trying to ebb away along the sidewalk.

'Just stand there!' Officer Nuñez came out of the car to say it again, to make sure Munro understood him. His partner, also the size of a refrigerator, jogged over to back him up.

Officer Kobek shook his head, unbothered, a private understanding with Nuñez, and turned on Munro. 'It's going to get ugly if anybody sees you around this neighborhood again.'

Munro folded his lunch bag into a neat square, flattened it into his pocket, stared hard at the tips of Kobek's shoes. 'I'm sorry. What did I do?'

Slumping with a sigh of tortured patience Kobek said, 'You know what you did. You get your jollies by scaring little children. That's pathetic. By staring at them. Man, you're pathetic.'

'I waved hello at them.'

'Staring at them and waving, that's what they reported you did.' Kobek pointed his finger down the street and with the verbal swagger and imitation head honcho black twang of a man who means business he told Munro, 'Walk away, my man.'

It was an intentional lesson from heaven and it became clearer each time Munro replayed the scene in his mind, sitting in his favorite seat right behind the driver on the bus ride home. The message for him was, Don't leave your apartment. 'I won't,' Munro said, wagging his head from side to side, 'I promise I won't.'

The sorry spectacle of a man talking out loud to himself on a bus was a common enough hazard for regular commuters and when the bus was crowded it didn't lower the value of an empty seat. Munro glanced up to see how much further he needed to squeeze in to make room for the large man who was lowering himself into the vacancy next to him. Round haunches first then his massy side pressed against Munro, the man's chubby pink arm cocked in a V that rode Munro's thigh. In the afternoon heat this human planet pulled his own sweat heavy atmosphere down around him.

It was air too thick to breathe, Munro's face felt swaddled in it. His first pain was a hollow twinge deep in his throat, it shot out electric veins upward into his jaw and then crackling across his chest and down his arm. He sank sideways, folding onto the large man's lap. 'Sorry,' Munro meant it, he was contrite as he started to die, 'I'm sorry.'

With his heart panting in its own confused, stuttering panic he dragged air into his mouth, air that smelled of the rubber mats on the aisle floor, but each strangling breath stopped at the back of his throat as if he was trying to inhale fur. His gasps were made only out of fear now. His whole body was shrinking, receding from the interior of the bus, from the overhanging faces, strangers' faces bobbing in a ring around him like paper lanterns. He was falling away from them and rising away too, the curl of an undertow was prying him loose, lifting him out of the dissolving thicknesses of his body. Waves of fear and pain separated from him in the same instant, they were below him, part of the landscape.

Somehow Munro is in motion, aloft, sailing forward on a glory of yellow-white light, a luminous swell opening to him as he floats into it. A whorl in the middle of the light gathers into a face he knows, the clean shoulders underneath it almost solid, the muscular chest bare and unmarked. JT's mouth forms the syllables of Munro's name but it is the light that speaks, through him. He reaches out his arms, reaches down the way he would to a little boy who wants to be held, Munro is the little boy, held in the outpouring light.

He moves through the curtains of hazy ivory radiance to the morning he socked his baby sister on the arm on their walk to school, sending her home in gales of tears, terrified of him, from there to the fistfight with his father in the hallway between their bedrooms, from there to the long hitch-hike by himself in the Nevada desert, and the wordless thought with him there in the engulfing light is, *You'll finally know what you did.* His silent reply flies out of him, Munro asks to go back and try again.

A hurrying tide much stronger than this pulls him deeper into the light, which is not flaring now but shows its rim, a pearly circle shrinking slowly in empty space. Longing, unbroken longing propels Munro toward it and the light promises to tell him why he lived the way he lived, on the other side of the light is the way things really are. He glides closer and the disc begins to break up, specks of it shoot away from the disintegrating edges, Munro falls into the remnants of forgiving and then healing, of returning and then the hollow dark of the wall.

Acknowledgments

So through the eyes love attains the heart:
For the eyes are the scouts of the heart,
And the eyes go reconnoitering
For what it would please the heart to possess.
And when they are in full accord
And firm, all three, in the one resolve,
At that time, perfect love is born
From what the eyes have made welcome to the heart.
Not otherwise can love either be born or have commencement
Than by this birth and commencement moved by inclination.

By the grace and by command
Of these three, and from their pleasure,
Love is born, who its fair hope
Goes comforting her friends.
For as all true lovers
Know, love is perfect kindness,
Which is born – there is no doubt – from the heart and eyes.
The eyes make it blossom; the heart matures it:
Love, which is the fruit of their very seed.

Guirault de Borneilh, c. 1138–1200?

My thanks to the Authors' Foundation and to the Royal Literary Fund whose generous grants enabled me to continue working on this book. A loud hymn of praise also to Paul Clayton, Clare Dunkel, Rae & W. B. Fink, Guy Jenkin, Nick O'Hagan, Gary Olsen & Jane Anthony Grant.

In writing *Long Pig* I paraphrased the scholarship and leaned on the expertise of writers who command the subjects in which I can only claim an eager interest. I'm indebted to David Selbourne (*Death of the Dark Hero – Eastern Europe 1987–90*), Colleen McDannell and Bernard Lang (*Heaven, A History*), Stephen Jay Gould (*The Panda's Thumb, The Mismeasure of Man*, assorted articles), Philip Kitcher (*Abusing Science: The Case Against Creationism*, from which, additionally, I borrowed a line for the title of Chapter 9, Part Two), and finally, Judge William R. Overton's US District Court Judgment, *McLean v. Arkansas*, 1982.

For the Creationist approach to the Bible and to evolution I relied on the writings of Henry M. Morris (*The Long War Against God, Scientific Creationism, The Genesis Record* and *The Bible Has the Answer*, written in collaboration with Martin E. Clark) and various articles by Duane T. Gish, Robert E. Kofahl and R. L. Wysong.

JSF